PARACHUTE MINDS:

Leap of Fate

by

Jeremiah Sanchez

DORRANCE
PUBLISHING CO
EST. 1920
PITTSBURGH, PENNSYLVANIA 15238

Dorrance Publishing Co
585 Alpha Drive
Suite 103
Pittsburgh, PA 15238
Visit our website at www.dorrancebookstore.com

ISBN: 978-1-6480-4021-4
eISBN: 978-1-6480-4032-0

PARACHUTE MINDS:

Leap of Fate

Ancient Sanguine Prophecy

Facedown I wake, a morning scream
I share with you an impossible dream
As you know, we do not run
In the dark of night when the creatures come
My eyes were closed, I did not peek
As I was given answers I did not seek
We fear the dark as night, it hunts
Don't scream, don't breathe, squeeze both eyes shut
There is no protection in courage or love
They snatch us and take us into above
Reapers, evil, this much is true
Sleep faceup and they'll take you
The night is theirs and we can't see
If the stars still live or did they leave
But perk your ears, hear cautiously
For I foresaw a prophecy
Was it real or just a dream
We'll see what tomorrow brings
Seven shall come from "the other side"
Bringing with them death and life
What is life but once and done
What is death but then what comes
Riddles with power we can't control
Afraid to blend their different souls
What are souls but colors fleeting
Missing, smeared, just bodies bleeding

They run from "hell" and fight for "heaven"
These places have meaning to the coming seven
I do not know the beasts they are
But I see them flying on light from stars
Their desires and purpose remain unclear
But do not doubt, they are coming here
They'll walk upright, small ears and eyes
I cannot see clearly their shape and size
Pale faces that devour flesh
They fear not blend with food from death
They carry power we cannot imagine
I've but scraps for words to paint my vision
Be warned, within their company
A warrior, the like, we've never seen
Wielding death with reverent grace
They'll see at night as we do in day
The rules of life, to the warrior, bend
Those that hunt us may finally end
But be this warrior friend or foe
Until they arrive, we cannot know
Should they end the creatures of night
That we may gaze up and see starlight
We risk waking a forgotten hunger
Dormant ones from their ancient slumber
Fear their "hells" and seek their "heavens"
From "the other side" will soon come seven

1

Gideon smiled as he offered his hand through the car window. "Good morning. I'm Gideon. Thank you guys so much for stopping."

The couple tentatively looked at each other before shaking his hand. The woman gave a forced smile and nodded toward the van's sliding door. As Gideon opened it, the driver grunted.

"It's afternoon."

"What?" Gideon asked as he adjusted his backpack.

"You said morning. It's afternoon," the driver said, short and pursed. "Where you heading?"

"Eh, close enough. I like to think of every moment as morning, so I remember to treat it like a fresh start." Gideon thought for a second, trying to recall the second question. "Oh!" He shrugged off his backpack and groaned as he stepped into the van. "I need to get to LAX. So, anywhere you could get me in that direction would be greatly appreciated." He slid the door shut and rested his back against the worn seat.

The driver looked over his shoulder at him and then at the woman. "I'm sure we can work something out." He shifted and drove away.

Gideon threw a grateful fist into the air as he slumped on the grey middle row. "Thank you so much." It felt good to feel the motor carrying his sore feet. It was about time to buy new shoes. He always prolonged it due to the relationship he acquired with each pair. "So, what are your names?"

Without addressing his question, the woman cleared her throat, composing her nerves. "So, you hitchhike often?"

"More than the average Joe, I'm sure," Gideon chuckled the response. "It's cheap travel and a guaranteed way to meet new folks. The most trustworthy name for a group of people. Folks."

She gave an awkward laugh back. "Yeah, I'm sure. You've probably had some bad experiences with people doing it, though."

"Nope." Gideon leaned in to meet the people driving him. "Clean record."

The woman turned, clutching a gun, aimed at Gideon's stomach. Gideon's face went blank. He looked down at the small handgun while the driver kept his eyes on the road. There were random cars passing by them, but none were paying any attention. Traffic carried on as normal.

The woman's face was pale and beading. She blinked and swallowed. "Sorry to stain that record, but we're going to need you to give us your wallet."

Gideon puffed out his bottom lip and nodded. "Sure, you bet." His smile returned as he reached into his pocket. "Mind if I keep my passport, IDs, and plane ticket? You can have the money and everything else. I need to get a new wallet anyway."

The woman glanced at her boyfriend, who uncomfortably shrugged. "Yeah, whatever." She cleared her throat again. "Hurry up."

Gideon held up his wallet and started pulling out the specified items. As he did, he looked down at the gun. The woman's hand was shaking. Sweat wreathed her arms, and the barrel bounced back and forth across his torso.

"It gets easier over time," Gideon encouraged.

"What?"

"Guns. Robbing," Gideon said calmly. "I went through a klepto phase shortly after high school." He smiled as he reached out over the gun to hand her his wallet. She hesitantly took it as he continued. "I totally got shot once because of it, too." He laughed a little and reached down to pull up his right pant leg. He pointed at quarter-sized scar on his lower calf. "You know that term 'eating pavement'?" He grinned at her. "Well, I literally ate more than my share while running away with a purse. She was packing, and her aim was definitely not as slow as she was." He laughed and closed his eyes as he relaxed back against the seat.

The couple looked at each other, uncomfortable by his composure. The woman leafed through the wallet with one hand, keeping her gun somewhat aimed at Gideon with the other. She grunted.

"There's only forty bucks."

"Really?" the driver asked, his neck tensing.

"Yeah." Gideon sat forward. "I'm not much of a payday."

The woman motioned the gun toward Gideon's backpack. "What's in the bag?"

Gideon clicked his tongue. "I'm afraid unless you like random trinkets and sentimental souvenirs, you're not going to be too impressed with what you find in there either." He grabbed it and laid it across his lap. "I've got tons of small memories I've taken from travels. They mean a lot to me, but you're welcome to fish through and see if you think there's anything you could sell for a pretty penny—though that price is probably pretty accurate to what you'd get." He looked up at their frustrated faces, and the gun still aiming at him. "Or, if you'd like to roll the dice again, we can pick up another hitchhiker—see if they're worth more than me." He looked out the window, looking for another victim.

The driver shot him a confused glare. "We?" The van jolted back and forth, making them swerve as the engine sputtered. "What the hell?" The van stammered as they pulled to the shoulder. Once the engine was off, they looked out the windshield at steam rising from under the hood. The driver hit the steering wheel. "Great! This is just what we need right now."

The woman started panicking while keeping the gun aimed at Gideon. They had no getaway after they kicked him out. They hadn't had to actually use the gun yet, but this might require it.

Gideon squinted past them. "Happens all the time. Pop the hood."

He turned and slid the van door open without saying anything else. The couple watched as he walked around to the front of the steaming vehicle and waited. They looked at each other, unable to get a read on him.

The driver shrugged, reached down, and pulled the lever. As soon as it released, Gideon gave them a thumbs-up and lifted it. More steam rose as Gideon disappeared from sight, tinkering in the engine bay. Something clunked and then hissed.

"Ah, shit," they heard Gideon yell before he laughed. "Ow!" They listened as he kept rustling, and then he re-emerged at the driver's side window. He peered in at some bottles on the passenger side floor.

"Could I bother the nice couple for a couple?"

The man warily grabbed two water bottles and handed them over. The woman rested the gun on her lap, lazily keeping it pointed in Gideon's general direction.

Gideon took the waters and nodded. "Thanks." He walked back in front of the hood. After more fidgeting around and a yelp from what they assumed to be a burn, the steam dissipated.

"All right," Gideon yelled from in front of the van. "Give her a shot."

The driver inhaled and turned the key. Nothing. He tried again, and the engine coughed back on. The couple couldn't help giving each other relieved smiles before they heard Gideon from in front.

"Woo! That was a close one." Gideon shut the hood and walked back around. Before stepping in, he took the second bottle and poured it over his head. It spilled down his face and through his dark beard. He smiled and shook like a wet dog. "Man, I needed that. It's hot out here." He wiped his face and climbed back in. "All right, we're good, van's good, gun's good, let's go!"

The woman stared at him. "What's wrong with you?"

"What do you mean?" Gideon looked at her, caught off guard.

"What do I mean?" She looked at her boyfriend, who still hadn't started driving. "We're robbing you. I could shoot you, and you don't give a hot shit. You don't seem too concerned about dying. Are you high?"

"Not at all. Never really been my thing. Well, I mean, for a while there, yikes." Gideon winced and shook his head. "Mistakes were made, let me tell you. A cocktail of everything but the kitchen sink almost got me killed by some horses and—" He laughed and waved the memory away. "Story for another time, but no, I'm happier with the whole cliché of *getting high on life* thing now. When it comes to picking my poisons, I prefer adrenaline over substances anymore but to each their own. As Charles Bukowski said, 'Find what you love and let it kill you.'"

The driver and the woman looked at each other with a hesitant cocktail of confusion and intrigue. Gideon recognized it and smiled.

"For example." He lifted the same pant leg a little higher. "I went swimming with a great white once, and the sucker tried to eat me." He pointed at a couple scars gashed across his thigh and smiled. "Luckily, we sorted out our differences and had a good swim afterward, but chances are I'll get eaten one day. Or maybe fall to my death from a faulty parachute. Who knows?" He shrugged.

"You're insane," the woman blurted out as her focus shifted from the pistol to Gideon's stories.

The driver blinked a few times and then faced forward. He shifted into drive and started driving. He wasn't sure what else to do. It suddenly seemed rude to kick Gideon out.

Gideon didn't miss a beat. "So." He sat forward again, placing himself directly in front of the gun. "Still haven't gotten your names."

The driver's defenses were lowering. "Abraham." He paused. "And this is Tess."

"Nice to meet you two." Gideon's voice perked up at learning their names. "I've never actually met an Abraham before. Strong name." He reached forward and kindly patted Abraham on the shoulder before turning to Tess. "And Tess is a rare one. Exotic. It fits you." Tess cracked a slight smile, despite herself. Gideon nodded toward the gun. "So, Abraham and Tess, am I your first robbery or are you two seeing other people behind my back?" He winked.

Tess cleared her throat, suddenly questioning why she was still pointing the gun at him. "You're the third."

Abraham shot her a surprised glance and hissed, "Tess."

"What?" She raised her free hand defensively.

"Oh, wow." Gideon slapped his leg. "That's exciting. How'd the first two go?"

Abraham scoffed, "Perfectly." He shot another glare at Tess. "They got in, saw the gun, gave us their money, got out. You're the first not to be scared or mad."

"Oh, come on." Gideon waved a hand. "Please don't feel bad. You did a great job, Tess. The desired effect was achieved. Though I guess it would have been more helpful if I'd kept my hands in the air."

"So, what are you?" Tess asked as she slowly lowered the gun, relaxing it on the center console. "Some kind of homeless adrenaline junky or something?"

Gideon sighed and leaned forward, putting his head between their shoulders like a close friend. "Homeless adrenaline junky. Wandering thrill-seeker. Crazy person who gets bored easily. You know how they say that men are from Mars, and women are from Venus? I've been accused of proving it's true. I've been told I'm not from this planet by enough people." He chuckled. "Whatever." He looked out at the open road ahead of them, shivering at the thought of having to walk every mile they were passing.

"Now I'm curious," Tess said. "Where are you flying?"

Gideon's eyes lit up. "I'm heading to Venezuela. Have you ever heard of Angel Falls?" Both Abraham and Tess shook their heads, which fueled Gideon's desire to share. "It's the world's tallest uninterrupted waterfall. Height of thirty-two hundred feet. Elevation of forty-two hundred feet."

His hands helped animate the picture he was trying to paint. "It's absolutely stunning. Or at least it is in pictures. I want to climb it and then take a wingsuit and fly over the jungle." He grabbed their shoulders and squeezed. "Gah, I can't wait."

Tess brought her head back. "That sounds terrifying."

"Nah." Gideon waved away. "So, what about you two? Tell me the story of Abraham and Tess. What led you to this moment?"

Tess looked at Abraham and motioned for him to speak if he wanted. That way, he wouldn't be mad at her for gabbing. Abraham rubbed the bridge of his nose as he exhaled.

"I'm not sure what you're wanting to know. Do you want our life story or just why we're, you know, doing—this?"

"We've got a long drive still." Gideon's warm voice helped soothe the uneasiness. "So, I'll choose C: all of the above. You two seem like you must have an interesting story." He smiled. "I love stories."

After a few hours of driving the seemingly endless stretches of Californian interstate, the van pulled into LAX's parking structure. It was a busy day at the airport. People hurriedly walked to cars, terminals, and luggage centers. Conversations buzzed with anticipation or frustration from time constraints, and nearly every parking spot was taken.

Finally, on the third floor, the van found a vacant spot. Abraham pulled in and stopped, leaving the motor running.

Gideon wiped his eyes and stretched his mouth, sore from laughing. "That sounds fundamentally ill-advised, wild, and like an overall good time, my dear Tess. And you never found your bra?"

Tess shook her head, hilarious tears streaming down her cheeks as Abraham managed to answer. "Probably better after all that mustard."

They all burst into laughter again. "One of the best nights I ever had," Abraham said with a twinge of sadness. "I miss those days. Mistakes don't hurt as bad when you're young."

"For sure." Gideon tried to get himself under control. "Reminds me of some time I spent with some aborigines at the base of one of my cliff-diving trips in Australia. Those crazy bastards are some seriously crazy bastards."

Abraham turned and looked at him with an impressed head shake. "You've spent time with aborigines, too?"

"Oh, yeah, they're crazy. Dry humored asses." Gideon chuckled. "Over the course of my stay there, they invited me to partake in a coming of age ceremony for the young boys. They said I was young in spirit, so I fit in with the children pretty well." He shook his head. "Or at least that's what my translator boiled it down to."

"That's amazing." Tess had her chin resting on her hands as she listened intently. The low hum of the engine, along with Gideon's soothing speaking voice, all but lulled her to sleep.

"Who the hell all have you hung out with?" Abraham blurted out. "Have you been knighted?" His sarcasm barely hid the sincerity of the question.

"I wish." Gideon playfully jabbed Abraham's shoulder. "I haven't been knighted yet but maybe one day. It's added to the bucket list. Sir Gideon. Kind of has a nice ring to it." He looked down at his watch and nodded. "Oh, man. Well, I've gotta go get felt up by TSA. Thank God for you two. I'm a few hours early."

Tess smiled through a frown. "I'm kinda sad to see you go."

"Likewise." Gideon reached up and rubbed her shoulder before lifting a finger. "Oh!" He grabbed his backpack and pulled it onto the floor in front of himself. He opened it and reached inside, rummaging around. It took a moment before he stopped. "There you are." He pulled out an old wooden compass with cloudy glass. As they looked at it, he took his pant leg and rubbed it a little, trying to clean it up as best he could. "I got this gem from an old Somalian ship captain. Now, that man had one of the longest beards I've ever seen."

Abraham squinted. "Like a Somalian pirate?"

"Yup," Gideon said with a smile. "He had some crazy stories, but my favorite was this epic tale of being lost at sea in the middle of a hurricane. He told me about how the weather—the water, rather—snatched his crew members out of the boat, as if by unseen creatures in the waves tossing around them. The way he told it, it was kinda haunting and scary. He said the only thing he was able to cling to for hope was this compass. He had tied his leg to the ship's wheel so that he'd either be kept safe from the storm, or he'd be guaranteed to go down with his ship. Real old school guy."

"Wow," Tess said. "That's intense."

Abraham stared at the compass. "And that old thing managed to guide him to shore?"

"Yep. Alone, injured, starving, and beaten half to death by a hurricane—this little navigator saved him." Gideon looked at the broken trinket. "He said a good compass should be in the hands of the lost, not wasted in the pockets of those who know where they are." Gideon's expression grew sincere as he looked up at Abraham and Tess. "I hope it helps you two find what you're looking for." He placed it in Abraham's hand. As Abraham and Tess silently looked at it, digesting, Gideon's full smile returned. He nodded. "May death not find you sleeping."

Abraham and Tess stared at him with mystified interest.

"What?" Tess asked. "What does that mean?"

Gideon grinned understandingly. "Means live your life with purpose. Put simply: die living. Don't live dying." With that, Gideon opened the van door and stepped out with his backpack. After a deep breath, he closed the door and walked away. Each step filled him with more excitement for what was to come.

Gideon paused. Standing off in a shadowy corner of the parking garage was a man. Something felt off. The man stood with perfect posture, hands in his pockets, well-kept hair, and a rather unassuming face, but he was staring directly at Gideon. There was something familiar about his expression—something that reminded Gideon of the Mona Lisa's signature smirk, as if the man knew something that Gideon didn't.

He jumped as he heard Tess yell.

"Gideon! Come back real quick."

Gideon double took, jerking back into the moment. He smiled back at Tess and then turned to look at the man, but he was gone. Gideon studied his surroundings. He laughed at himself. The man was just another traveler.

"Focus," he told himself. His eyes disobeyed, again scanning the garage for the cryptic stranger.

Gideon shook his head. He turned and rushed back to the van.

"Coming," he yelled as the energetic bounce returned to his legs. A few hours of rest in the van had been needed. It was a relieving luxury, but he was happy to be back on his feet. "What can I do for ya, Tess?" He smiled into the passenger window, leaning in on his elbows.

Tess held out his wallet. "This is yours."

Gideon's smile fell as he saw tears welling in Tess' eyes. He reached out and held her hands over the wallet, taking a moment to recognize the sacrifice she was surrendering to.

"You'll find yourselves. I believe that with all my heart." He took the wallet and nodded to them warmly.

Abraham cleared his throat. "I'm really sorry for being the first black marks on your hitchhiking record."

Gideon waved him away. "Oh, please. It's better now after getting to know you two. This is how they usually go."

"At least—" Tess reached down and grabbed the gun off the passenger side floor. "At least take the gun. It's the only souvenir I can think of to give you from this, uh, experience." She felt foolish saying it out loud.

Gideon gave a deep belly laugh. "I'm not sure bringing a gun through an airport would be very helpful in reaching Angel Falls. You know, between a firearm and a beard, TSA might, you know—" Tess shook her head, embarrassed for not thinking it through. She put it back on the ground and nodded. Gideon kept chuckling. "I appreciate the gesture though. If you want to give me a keepsake, I think I could get away with a bullet. I mean, so long as it's an empty shell."

Abraham smiled back, fighting through his guilt. "I think we can do that." He opened the glovebox and fished around until he found an empty casing. "Perhaps this will be one of your stories one day."

Gideon nodded while smiling at the bullet. "Oh, it will be. I get the privilege of carrying part of your story—your soul. I'm all the richer for it."

Abraham smiled back, unsure what else to say. "Safe travels, Gideon."

Gideon dropped the bullet into his backpack and scoffed. "Where's the fun in that?"

He heard the van drive off as he walked away. It had been a good day filled with the adventure of meeting new people. It was almost as fulfilling as an adrenaline rush.

He waited until he reached the sliding doors before he looked at his wallet. Minus the items he'd removed, everything was back in place, but something felt off. It felt thicker. He opened the fold and leafed through the bills. There were seven hundred-dollar bills along with the money he'd had prior. He smiled and shook his head. He could only assume they were from the previous hitchhikers. Gideon turned and stared at the parking structure.

It was time to begin his next chapter.

2

The sound of his heart pounding in his ears was the drum beat that pushed Gideon forward. The possibility of falling four thousand feet didn't scare him. Rather, it inspired him. He loved being face-to-face with death and challenging its claim over his soul.

The low-floating clouds around Auyantepui Mountain were otherworldly. They wrapped around the vast landscape of green trees like a breathy halo, greeting the earth from the heavens. The plateaued summit wasn't far away, so Gideon fought through his raw lungs and climbed harder, forcing himself past fatigue and weariness. His breath was heavy, but his determination pushed his fingers to the next hold. He knew he should be planting anchors as he reached certain heights, but he wasn't slowing down for anything, so on he climbed.

For a moment, his vision pulsed to black and his lungs fatigued. It wasn't the climbing or the altitude, it was something else. He paused, clinging to his handholds as his back weakened and sweat poured harder down his face. As his pupils dilated, he reached into a pocket with his free hand and withdrew a yellow vial. The top of the rock-face was only a few feet away. He knew he was capable of pushing through and reaching it before taking the medication but if he was going to overcome the throes of death, it would be from where he could fall the farthest—where salvation and adrenaline overlapped. He popped the lid open with his thumb and tapped the tube until two pills fell into his mouth. He swallowed and focused on breathing, wishing the effects were instant.

His hand reached up and grabbed the solid rock that formed the top of Auyantepui. He winced and grunted as he pulled himself up and over, flopping onto his side and sucked oxygen. He lay next to the edge of the forty-two-hundred-foot cliff he'd just climbed and smiled. He'd made it. Sweat streamed through his beard and extremities as his pulse maintained its losing race.

He shrugged off the backpack and set it on the ground before stepping to the cliff's edge. With outstretched arms, he stared proudly over the distant jungle and roared into the sky. His Tarzan yell echoed for miles, bathing the trees in his energy. After his voice faded, he laughed, listening to wind carrying it away. He could hear startled birds taking flight around him, and roaring water crashing below. It was a moment frozen in time, and it helped put his life in perspective—something he constantly sought.

"You seem unafraid of death."

A calm, buttery voice spun Gideon around in surprise. He saw a tall man leaning against a tree about thirty feet behind him.

"You scared the crap out of me," Gideon chuckled. "I thought I was alone."

"We're rarely alone." The man's voice possessed an immediate confidence that lured Gideon in, not that that was a difficult task. Gideon smiled and grabbed his backpack off the ground. As he went to walk over, he paused, goose bumps seizing his arms.

"Wait, you're the—the guy from the airport. The parking garage. How the hell did—"

"You don't fear death atop a mountain or from a gun aimed at you," the stranger said as if he was reviewing Gideon's résumé.

"You followed me all the way to Venezuela from Cali?"

"Yes. Airports are great for, as you would say, people watching. You caught my eye."

"Flattered but your stalker status is boss level," Gideon said with a hesitant grin. "You here to kill me?"

"Something tells me it wouldn't scare you if I was."

Gideon considered the answer and then studied the man's quaint clothing. "You don't look to have any gear on ya. You climb up a different route?"

"I'm not much of a climber. I took a lighter way."

Gideon walked half the distance between them and then turned to gaze out over the view again. "It's stunning. I've always wanted to come here and see Angel Falls from the top." He nodded a couple times, soaking it in. He turned. He took a few steps and walked up to the man with an outstretched hand. "I'm Gideon."

The man tentatively stared at Gideon's offered hand, as if he didn't feel safe shaking it. After a strange moment, he reached forward and awkwardly shook it. Gideon took a quick first impression. The man was lean and neatly presented. His skin looked radiantly smooth; enough so that it momentarily perplexed Gideon since they were in such a rough environment. The man's light hair was orderly and simple, and his green eyes were treasure chests teeming with secrets. He was clad in a casual pair of jeans, white shirt, and a basic pair of white sneakers. His entire outfit was spotless. It looked as if the man had simply appeared there without journeying through the unavoidable jungle. He didn't even have sweat stains on his white shirt.

"Gideon." The man mulled the name over for a moment. "What's your last name, Gideon? Where are you from?" It almost looked like his mouth blurred as he spoke. Gideon shook his head, sure he'd seen it wrong. Likely his medicine hadn't fully kicked in, or the altitude was getting to him.

"Green. And the States." Gideon oscillated as he pointed, realizing that he had no idea which direction the United States was. He turned back. "You look as clean as a soldier's bunk. It's like you didn't go through any of the jungle to get here. What's your name, stranger?"

The man smiled and avoided the question. "Gideon Green. I can imagine that name comes with a certain level of ridicule."

Gideon shrugged. "I like the way it rolls off the tongue. Color psychology says green is representative of balance, harmony, and growth." He smiled. "How about you? Name and place you call home?"

"I'm not from around here, and I go by many names."

Gideon squinted as a slow nod expressed his piqued curiosity. "You, sir, are cryptically mysterious." He waved his finger playfully.

"I'm a traveler, an observer, a recruiter, and I prefer title over birth name."

"All right." Gideon nodded with interest. "Well then, Mr. Traveler, I'm unable to phone a friend or ask the audience, so how did you manage to get here without a single stain or scuff? Is there a washing machine around here I can't see?"

"Let me ask *you* a question." The traveler stepped forward with unspoken authority. "You give off an unusually positive charisma which, in my experience, suggests you've overcome difficult obstacles and risen anew, rather than be defeated by the challenges of life that tend to cripple most."

"Wow." Gideon's eyes widened as he smiled with even more interest. "That got deeper than the Mariana."

Traveler slowly nodded. "Was it lost love, lost life, failure, or rock bottom, as you all would say, that gave you your demeanor?"

"All right." Gideon sat his backpack back down. "We're diving right in, are we?" He took a deep breath and maintained eye contact with Traveler. "I've experienced failure through lost love, and I've experienced rock bottom through lost life. I guess you could say both were necessary. Death can be a catalyst for freedom. Does that answer satisfy?"

Traveler smiled. "While most fear death, more fear the vulnerability of their true selves—an issue you do not appear to suffer from."

"Nah." Gideon shrugged. "I'm a pretty open book. You, on the other hand, though intriguing, seem to be written in a language I don't speak."

"Ah, language barriers." Traveler clicked his tongue. "There are billions of languages and yet we all function on the same fundamentals."

"Billions?" Gideon shook his head and raised his eyebrows. "Where all have you traveled, captain philosopher?"

Traveler stared at him like a man trying to figure out a puzzle before he had all the pieces. "Why was your love lost, and do you miss her?"

Gideon's face immediately lit up as the question triggered memories. "How do you know she wasn't a he?" He gave a challenging stare that seemed to have no effect on Traveler's patient expression. "There was no tragic ending or epic finale. We separated amicably. Thought she was my soulmate, but she knew I wasn't hers. The fiery passion of youthful romance. It leaves an annoyingly permanent impression."

"If you're an open book, you're sure a short one," Traveler said, looking disappointed.

Gideon responded with a laugh. "Ah, I see how this is going to be." His eyes briefly landed on the ground as he stared through it. He took a deep breath and looked up. "Do I miss her? Yes and no. I miss her in the sense you're talking about, but I remember the way she made me feel every day." He turned and looked over the vast ocean of trees spanning around them. "I see her in everything, in everyone. She may have forgotten me by now, but I'll never forget her. Love—well, true love, isn't a season that changes with time; it is the sun through which all seasons change." He smiled and closed his eyes as he recalled her face. "If feelings of love come and go, they were merely seasons, and I thought she was more than that. One day I'll find the right sun for my world. One day I'll find my home."

Traveler took a step closer, a satisfied look on his face. "I believe I've found the peak of a massive iceberg." He nodded approvingly as he stared deep into Gideon's eyes. "Gideon, my new friend, it is love like that that poets bleed."

Gideon nodded. "This world has no pain deeper than missing someone you can never have back."

"There is infinitely more love to explore beyond this world."

"Ah, you're a spiritual man," Gideon said with an understanding nod. "Starting to figure you out." He took a deep breath and looked up. "Oh well, right? It's better to have loved and lost…"

"Right. One of the quotes you all cling to after heartbreak as a methodical means of accepting that which is out of your control. But it's true."

Something about the cadence of Traveler's voice captivated Gideon. It was as if he knew something that Gideon didn't.

"I couldn't agree more." He studied Traveler's fixated face. "I feel like I'm staring at a Picasso painting for the first time. I'm fascinated, but I don't fully understand what I'm looking at yet. What's *your* story?"

Without acknowledging Gideon's question, Traveler continued, "I can understand unbreakable charisma, but you're here, unafraid of the repercussions from jumping off of Angel Falls." He motioned to Gideon's bag, obviously containing a parachute. "What arouses my interest is that you're doing it alone. No friends, no group, just you. That's either the most foolish and dangerous endeavor, or you're a passionately liberated spirit. I pride myself in seeking out individuals with those traits. Do you face your fears, or are you without fear entirely?"

Gideon scoffed happily. "Oh, come on now. Most people have more purpose than just wandering around with a boner for near-death experiences. I think I'm pretty alone as that sort of addict, flirting with my own violent demise and all. If we're all destined to end, I'd rather it be exciting than slow and decaying."

"I respect that perspective. Very few will ever feel that alive. It's a freedom I've always wished I had the courage to surrender to. Maybe you could help teach me."

Gideon slowly nodded. "Which brings us back to that unanswered question: Why did you follow me to Venezuela, on a big ol' mountain all by *your*self, with clean clothes, and no gear? I'm still banking on murder."

Traveler looked around and gave a small smile. "Coincidentally, Angel Falls is one of the beauties I've had yet to visit while passing through." He turned back to Gideon. "Tell me about the lost life and rock bottom that freed you to be who you are."

Gideon exhaled through his nose as his smile left for a brief moment. He looked down at the ground, delicately running his fingers along a linear scar on his left shoulder. His tank top framed it like a tortured piece of art. They both could feel the silence. Gideon gently patted Traveler's arm as his smile returned.

"That's the only chapter of my book that's not available to read on the first date."

"Now you have my attention, Gideon." Traveler's tone grew low, as did his eyebrows. "What keeps that one locked away? Too personal? Scarring?"

"You prod about as much as I do, but your tools are a little blunter," Gideon chuckled as he tried not to think too much about the yellow vial in his pocket. "Honestly, I believe that even the most personal story should be shared if it serves a purpose," he stated confidently. "However, that story doesn't fit in this conversation. Perhaps, if our paths meet again, the circumstances will provide the right stage." He smiled, slightly pleased to have the mysterious Traveler begging for something he couldn't have. "But—" He lifted his finger. "—if you want to discuss scars, that's a road I can go down all day long." He smiled as he squatted down to lift his pant. As he did, Traveler noticed all the cuts, wounds, and various healed scars that Gideon already had visible.

"Gideon, as a man with no physical scars myself, I've learned enough about you to be intrigued. It's not something easily done, and even harder to maintain. I'm going to offer you something that I offer very few but want to offer to those who are worthy."

Gideon let go of his pant leg and stood up with some peculiar curiosity. He stared at Traveler through squinted eyes and a half smile. "Worthy? Hmm." He stroked his beard. "Sounds to me like one of the most interesting job propositions I've ever heard, or a really good line for hooking weirdos like me. Or maybe a bad Craigslist ad." He shrugged with a smile. "But I'll bite. Here, in Venezuela, randomly on top of a waterfall, what's the offer? I'm not giving you a kidney. I've been down that road before."

"Before I explain, I must ask what will possibly be the first of many 'what-if' questions that will continue, depending on how you answer."

"I like this game already." Gideon beamed with excitement at the mysteriousness. He rubbed his hands together. "Ask away."

Traveler stepped closer with his head tilted to the side. "What if you could go on an adventure that offered thrills and adrenaline-fueled, near-death experiences that only a handful of people will ever even *hear* about, let alone attempt — but it would require losing all of your scars?" He waited as his question sunk in. "Every single scar you have that reminds you of a shaping experience in your life would be gone. You'd have no physical mementos of your past, only the memories. But you would be free to go on an adventure beyond your wildest hallucinations."

"You mean wildest dreams?"

"Is that how the saying goes?" Traveler asked, surprised by his mistake. "Yes. Dreams."

Gideon mulled over the bizarre question. "So, just to double-check if I'm understanding correctly: Hypothetically, what would I choose between the reminders of my past, or a future so crazy that I may as well be helping the Fellowship return the one ring?"

"Think more out of this world than returning possessed jewelry to a ghost furnace."

Gideon smiled at Traveler's joke and then looked down at some scars on his arms, reminiscing over the stories that gave them to him. He caressed the scar on his left shoulder again. "Well, as long as we're asking hypothetically, I would be willing to let go of the lessons learned in blood — if I was promised the impossible. I've still got the stories up here." He tapped his head. "It's not the things we do in life that we regret. It's the things we don't do."

"Very true." Traveler peered deep into Gideon's eyes with sincerity. "Now, take away the hypothetical."

Gideon smiled. "All right. I'm ready to see behind the curtain. What's this mysterious offer?"

"Before I present the offer, it requires a second what-if question to cement your curiosity in fact rather than fiction." Traveler's eyes were storming with anticipation. It was easy to see. Gideon motioned for him to continue. Traveler leaned forward. "What if I could beat you to the base of Angel Falls without any climbing gear or parachute?"

Gideon chuckled. "I have full faith in you becoming a human pancake with an overabundance of syrup. But then I'd never get to hear the offer." He laughed as he eagerly awaited Traveler's response.

Traveler smiled. "All right. Well, if you're interested in adventures, only a handful of others have been offered, if you're curious about opportunities beyond anything you've ever heard of, my offer awaits you down there." He motioned over Angel Falls.

3

Gideon stood at the edge of the waterfall. He stared down over the raging river shooting over the drop. It was staggering. It was so steep that he couldn't see where the water landed, making the leap all the more tempting, all the more seductive in its call to his soul. The cold rush of perpetual mist, along with the loud roaring, heightened his pulsing senses. It was time.

Traveler joined Gideon near the cliff, studying the red wingsuit he'd changed into. "So, in essence, you'll coast down?"

Gideon nodded excitedly. "I like to think of it as flying." He flapped his arms a couple of times, looking at the strong coasting material. "You've never seen one of these?"

"No, I've only been here a few times. There's a lot I have yet to see." Traveler's comment rendered a quizzical glance from Gideon. Traveler ignored it. "How long did it take you to master this?"

"Well, to be honest," Gideon grinned, "I got ahold of this wingsuit via trade for some steel-toed boots. I feel like I got the better deal, but the dude was super happy." He shrugged. "Anyways, I just decided to just baby bird it. You know, throw myself out of the nest and see if I'll figure it out before I hit the ground." He smiled without hesitation. "Can't be too much harder than normal parachuting."

Traveler stepped forward and grabbed Gideon's arm. "This is your first jump?" His collected tone sounded surprised at itself for the concern. "You'll be near terminal velocity. What if you crash?"

"Well," Gideon shrugged, "I guess I wouldn't get to hear your proposition. So, you'd better hurry up and beat me down there so you can catch me." He winked. "It was nice to meet you, Mr. Traveler." He reached into his pocket. "Normally, I like to give a parting gift when I have a unique encounter, but unfortunately I left my goody bag down there. So, all I have right now—" He pulled his hand out of his pocket and extended it toward Traveler. "—is a friendship bracelet I got from a Ugandan kid after he beat me in a game of soccer. He totally cheated but there was no ref." Gideon smiled. "So, this is for you." He opened his hand to show a bracelet made of hand-woven leather and earthy beads. It had a couple red stains on it. "Sorry about the blood. I scraped my elbow on the climb up." Traveler took it and held it as he stared at Gideon.

"First impressions are typically presented with the best foot forward. They only leave subtle clues to character flaws." Traveler's eyes narrowed as he studied Gideon. "I have yet to see any obvious ones from you. I'll have to look closer."

Gideon smiled. "Well, I hope that curiosity doesn't haunt you, because, as we discussed, I may not survive. So, maybe my flaw is stupidity and recklessness." He laughed. "Besides, even if I do survive, unless you run down there like The Flash to present me this opportunity, our paths may never cross again."

Traveler gave a subtle, but confident smile. "Our minds, just like that parachute attached to your back, work best when they're open."

"Hey, you got that quote correct. It's a good one." Gideon fawned skyward. "I think it was Plato who said—no, Aristotle. It was Aristotle who said that it is the mark of an educated mind to be able to entertain an idea without accepting it as truth."

"I like that quote. Would your quote of breaking a leg be appropriate to say now?"

"Funny you say that. I've actually broken my leg skydiving before. But you know what they say, third time's the charm."

"Which is now?"

"Nah, this is the second." Gideon pulled his goggles down over his eyes and smiled. "Well, Barry Allen, see you down there." He saluted Traveler. "May death not find you sleeping!" With that, he turned around and leapt off the edge, immediately disappearing from sight as he dove toward the earth.

Traveler stepped forward and peered over. Gideon had already become a dot, aiming straight down alongside the waterfall. Traveler smiled at the fearlessness.

"You scare me," he said as he stared into the distance below. "You're perfect."

Wind and water tore at Gideon's face. He reveled in the beauty of its natural power and unparalleled intensity. With his arms and legs tucked tightly together, his body formed a perfect arrow shooting straight down. He could feel the material of the wings flapping violently against his sides. Though he was almost mile high, the ground was closing in quickly, the sheer mountainside passing by him like a blur. He assumed it was probably the right time. His heart raced as he opened his arms and spread his legs until the suit went taut. Wind instantly hit the wings, catching the tight canopies and sending him soaring forward. The dynamic of the wind rushing against him immediately shifted as he gained a sense of control over his direction.

Gideon yelled against the rushing air, tilting side to side and rocketing at a steep angle. He smiled, his cheeks flapping nonstop. The rush felt like a cocktail of speed and ecstasy. He'd tried both individually, never simultaneously, but he bet the combination would be similar. The lush jungle below him was a giant earth-colored haze as he flew over it. The roaring wind clogged his ears.

Being his first time, he had no idea when he was supposed to rip the chord. *Baby bird. Baby bird. Baby bird.* The ground was getting dangerously close, so he figured it was as good a time as any. He gave a little shrug in the air and pulled the chord. The parachute shot out and opened, immediately yanking him backward. The violent jolt made him yelp as he continued careening toward the ground with perilous velocity.

The tree line covering the jungle was mere seconds away, and Gideon laughed as probable injury closed in. He quickly realized he'd pulled the shoot too late. Fear would do nothing to help, so he surrendered, yelling as he spread his arms and legs. There was nothing else he could do to slow down or brace for impact at full speed.

Before he knew it, the trees swallowed him, and he crashed into an onslaught of branches and leaves. It happened so fast, and his adrenaline was so high that he didn't feel anything. Just the rush in a blur of green. His parachute caught in the trees and he came to a violently abrupt stop.

Gideon's legs swung back and forth, dangling in the air as the trees shook from the crashing entrance. His heartbeat rang like a deafening drum in his ears. He started laughing. Broken branches and leaves fell around him like rain, and everything finally came to a stop.

"That was incredible!" Gideon's voice echoed through the empty jungle, startling the remainder of birds that hadn't already taken flight from his clatter. "Holy crap, Batman."

As his heart began slowing, a new sensation registered. He winced in pain and looked to see a surprising amount of blood streaming down his left leg. There were tears and gashes all over his wingsuit, with cuts and scrapes visible. He scoffed and groaned as he realized his left leg was broken. Nonchalant dismissal was his instinctive coping mechanism as pain flooded his brain. His teeth ground together. Sweat immediately poured down his face. He reached down to touch it to see how bad it was. He grimaced. His thigh shifted in two different directions as he wiggled it. It was easy to tell that his femur was broken in two. The more he dwelled on it, the more excruciating it became. Shock helped dull the full force of it.

"Well, golly." He chuckled and groaned in pain and rolled his eyes. "Gideon, ol' boy, if you're going to break your leg every time we skydive, we're not going anymore." He grunted. "Let's see how you get yourself out of this one."

"What if I told you I could assist?" A voice came from beneath Gideon.

Gideon twisted in the air and looked down to see Traveler walking into his line of sight. Same as on the top of the mountain, Traveler's clothes were perfect with no sign of sweat or wear.

He smiled up at Gideon's awestruck expression. "I'm not sure which seems to be hurting you more: your broken leg or your broken grip on what you believe is real. How can I possibly be down here, Gideon?"

"You—" Gideon forgot about the pain for a moment. "I suppose, uh, logic could explain it by suggesting you're one in a pair of identical twins. Though I don't understand why you'd go to the trouble."

"Oh, sure, that could explain it away perfectly. We even have matching friendship bracelets with matching blood stains." Traveler smiled with bold confidence and tossed the bracelet up to Gideon. Gideon caught it and slowly took his eyes from Traveler to the familiar item. It was the exact same bracelet he'd given him. "Also, I feel bad for telling you to break a leg, now."

"But how—how did you, uh, how—" For the first time in a long time, Gideon wasn't sure what to say, or more importantly, what to believe.

Traveler smiled. "Do I have your attention now, Gideon Green?"

4

Suddenly, being stuck in a tree didn't matter. The fading adrenaline was forgotten. The pain was forgotten. He had no idea how Traveler had managed to beat him to the base of the mountain range. Between the drop and the distance, he knew he must have gone at least a mile or two. His focus completely switched to the peculiar stranger as his mind overflowed with questions.

"You have one hundred and twelve percent of my attention, Mr. Traveler." He shifted his dangling body around as he stared down. "How did you do that?" He smiled through the pain, unable to contain his curiosity.

Traveler smiled back and walked toward the base of one of the trees that Gideon was stuck in. "Well, what if—" He grunted as he leapt up and grabbed the lowest branch he could reach. "What if I told you—" Branch after branch he climbed up toward Gideon. "—that I'm not from around here?"

"No, really?" Gideon sardonically remarked. He shifted to curiously watch Traveler despite his leg's increasing discomfort. "Where are you from?"

Traveler quickly ascended the tree until he reached the height Gideon was dangling at. "That's a lengthy explanation."

"Well, I don't think I'm going anywhere soon." Gideon motioned down at his bleeding leg as if it was no big deal. "By all means."

Traveler balanced on some branches. He contemplated where to begin his explanation. He gave a small smile as he reached his hand out into a sunray breaking through the trees.

"What if I told you that you've barely scratched the surface of the scientific possibilities held within the properties of light?"

"Of light?" Gideon glanced quizzically at Traveler, who was obviously beating around a rather large bush.

"Yes, the properties of light are incredibly intricate and expansive." He waved his hand around in the sunray as he spoke. "And while you've scratched the surface with say, lasers, you're barely seeing a snowflake on the iceberg's tip."

Gideon raised an eyebrow. "You sure do love your icebergs." He smiled. "What do you mean?"

"If you hold a magnifying glass, for example, and focus your sun's light, you can make a fire or burn ants, as so many children relish in." He continued moving his hand through the sunrays shining through the trees. "If you focus light even more, you create a laser, and as far as you know at this point, lasers can be focused enough to cut through metal, aid in vision repair, perform other medical tasks, remove tattoos, and many more impressive uses."

Gideon winced through a nod. "All obviously comparable to a snowflake."

Traveler smirked as he kept looking at the sunbeam. "What if I told you, for example, that light has elasticity properties?"

"Elasticity?"

"Yes."

"Like, elastic in, say, underwear lining?"

Traveler laughed and nodded. "Yes, like underwear lining." He looked at Gideon. "Do you know how fast the speed of light is?"

"Um." Gideon rubbed his chin. "I'll take a stab in the dark. Pun intended. One hundred thousand miles an hour?"

Traveler smiled. "One hundred and eighty-six thousand, two hundred and eighty-two, point three, nine, seven miles per *second*."

Gideon's eyebrows rose. "You've done your homework."

"Twenty-eight of my years of it. Additionally, you've learned that—"

"Your years? Why do you keep saying '*I've* learned?' Who's I, or we? Or *your* years? Who's we?"

Traveler grinned, knowing Gideon didn't understand what he was hinting at. "A broader sense of the word. Not you specifically." He smiled. "You, as a people, have additionally learned that light can be bent, its speed slowed and manipulated by the gravitational pull from celestial bodies, planets, stars, black holes, etcetera."

"Us as a people? Americans? Where are you from?"

Traveler dismissed Gideon's naivety with a patronizing smile before continuing. "The speed of light is light's speed if it's untampered with. As far as your top minds know, it is the unbreakable speed limit of the universe. But, once you break down light's electromagnetic photons beyond what you are currently capable, they can be manipulated and harnessed in such a way that it reacts elastically, and its speed can be exponentially increased, just like pulling a rubber band back and shooting it forward. The farther you stretch it, the faster it becomes."

Gideon smiled like a little kid. "Okay, I'll humor you. The sun is the most powerful rubber band gun in the world...er...space, rather." He chuckled. "What should I do with that information? Egg Pluto?"

"Well." Traveler thought about how he wanted to approach the next step of the conversation. He looked up at the distant mountain Gideon had just dived off. It was a perfect colloquial transition. He smiled. "You just dove off a cliff less than one mile high." Gideon turned and looked at Angel Falls as he listened, the distant waterfall playing a hypnotic backdrop. "What if I told you that I know of a cliff six miles high that you can jump off of without any parachute, and it's possible to land relatively safely at the base?"

Gideon squinted at him. "Relatively. Ha!" He cleared his throat. "Instinctively, I want to giggle about how possible that's *not*, but you've made me question reality a bit today. Or maybe it's the blood loss." He winced as his leg throbbed. "So, let's humor you. If that *was* possible, I'd say that once my leg heals, you'll need to show me this impossible cliff-diving experience. Where is it, oh, traveled traveler?"

"I'd be interested in showing you firsthand, but before I do, you should have a drink. You're losing a substantial amount of blood from that leg." He reached into his pocket and pulled out a small water bottle. "This is called a light shot." He stared at its contents then handed it over to Gideon.

Without any hesitation, Gideon grabbed the bottle and spun the cap off. "Thanks!" He brought it to his lips so fast that he spilled some onto his face. Dehydrated was an understatement. The bottle crumpled as he chugged all of its contents without taking a breath. Once it was empty, he closed his eyes, exhaled deeply, and inhaled even deeper. "I needed that."

As he caught his breath, a strange tingling sensation began in his stomach. He raised an eyebrow as the peculiar rush spread around his torso and coursed through his arms and legs. He dropped the bottle. It almost felt as if his body parts had fallen asleep and gone numb. Then sudden, needle-like tingles appeared as feeling returned with a vengeance. As soon as his body adjusted to the cold prickling, his arms and legs felt hot. He turned and glared at Traveler with a violated expression as he groaned and gasped.

Traveler gave an understanding nod. "We need to set your leg before we go." He adjusted on a thicker branch. Once he had a maintainable grip with his thighs, he reached out and placed both hands around Gideon's broken leg. He felt around a little, figuring out exactly where and how bad the break was. Gideon's eyes fluttered and rolled back, overwhelmed by the pain and the drink's sensations.

"What did I——" His mind itself felt odd. Suspicion of being drugged disappeared as he actually felt heightened cognitive function.

His eyes widened and his breathing slowed a little as the colors of the jungle around him radiantly glowed. He felt Traveler's fingers moving across his thigh like a piano, trying to find the exact spot. Gideon couldn't tell if he felt enlivened or betrayed. Either way, he barely felt anything as Traveler grabbed hold of the top and bottom of his leg and twisted. *Snap!*

Traveler looked Gideon up and down, examining his condition. "You're almost there." He reached one hand up and held it open toward the sun. "Are your toes tingling yet?" He closed his fist as if he was grabbing something. His question made Gideon look down toward his feet. As a matter of fact, he noticed that his toes were tingling, but not in a normal way. They felt like they were being electrically shocked. He nodded vigorously as it intensified.

Traveler nodded and smiled. "Good. You're ready. It's time to go." With that, he firmly grabbed the back of Gideon's neck.

Gideon watched with a puzzled expression as Traveler looked up toward the sun without squinting. "Go where?" he mumbled as his pupils throbbed. "Where on Earth are we —"

Traveler opened his hand.

Gideon's vision was illuminated by bright light. He felt weightless and painless as a cold wind filled his lungs. Everything went white.

5

Gideon smacked his lips without opening his eyes. It felt like he was coming out of a deep sleep at one hundred miles an hour. His eyes shot open as deep breath poured out of his reinvigorated lungs. White light faded from his vision, revealing foreign surroundings. His eyes were as wide open as they could be, and he had no idea where he was, and no memory of getting wherever it was. Catching his breath wasn't necessary since he immediately felt back to normal. In fact, he felt better. Where was he?

As he took in his surroundings, it all looked relatively similar to where he'd just been. There were large trees and thick foliage, but he was definitely not in Venezuela anymore. Everything was different. The air felt a bit thicker and his body, oddly refreshed. He saw Traveler standing next to him with an excited grin plastered to his face.

Gideon blinked rapidly. "Did you drug me?" He was quickly regaining feeling in his extremities.

"I wouldn't word it that way. I told you it was a light shot. I'll explain everything in due time."

Gideon's eyes darted around, instinctively making sure he wasn't in any danger and that Traveler hadn't done anything to him. "Okay. How long was I out?"

Traveler leaned forward, looking into Gideon's eyes like a doctor performing a checkup. "You weren't sleeping, but you were comatose. It's a little harder to explain, but I'll work on it in small steps. We were lit for a little over fourteen of your hours."

"We were lit?" Gideon squinted as feeling returned to his torso. "Is that a new drug or something?"

"No. As I said, you were not drugged. I gave you a highly complex solution that makes your cells compatible with light's properties, as I was previously explaining." Traveler continued checking Gideon's pulse and looking him over as he spoke. "Your body underwent such intense pressure that you went into a heightened sense of comatose shock. All you should remember at this point is a white light and a sensation similar to wind."

Gideon nodded as he struggled to recall anything more than what Traveler had just described. "That's pretty accurate. Where are we?"

"We're at the top of what we call the Roaring Valley. It's the six-mile-high drop I was telling you about."

Gideon's mind raced. "There's no cliff that high anywhere on Earth." He looked around, seeing no snow or ice. "And if there were, we'd be covered in snow. Well, maybe underwater. There could be some abysses there, I guess. No." He shook his head. "I don't know. Where are we?"

"I haven't lied to you. We are where I said we are."

"We are where you *haven't* said we are," Gideon clarified with a perplexed shrug. He looked around and studied his surroundings again. It just looked like lush jungle. "But you claim we were only high for fourteen hours. That's not enough time to get anywhere even remotely close to what you're describing."

"Gideon," Traveler chuckled. "First of all, we weren't drugged. I didn't drug you. Secondly, as you said, there's no place on Earth that matches the description I've given you. So—" He waited for Gideon to start piecing the puzzle together. "What if I told you we aren't on Earth?"

Gideon's wandering eyes stopped as he stared directly at Traveler, looking for the slightest hint of sarcasm. There was none. He cleared his throat. "You're suggesting we're on another planet?"

"Precisely."

"Another inhabitable planet?"

"Habitable. And yes."

"Potato, tomato." Gideon thought for a moment. "Is that even possible? Wouldn't I have seen space? Stars? Light-speed warp and stuff?"

Traveler smiled. "Your sci-fi films have great imagination, but no, it doesn't work quite like that. You were transported at exponential speeds of light *as* light, so light was all you would have seen if you'd been conscious."

"Wait," Gideon puzzled. "So, you were serious about light being elastic or whatever." His eyes darted around aimlessly. "Nah, that doesn't make sense." He chuckled in shock. "How does that work? How does light have elastici—? Can you seriously explain that?"

"Sure." Traveler shrugged. "I can do that. It only took twenty-eight of my years to study, understand, and master as little as I have. If you'd prefer me to teach you about the intricacies of elastic light rather than explain why I've brought you here, just have a seat and lend me a few decades of your life. It'll be much like you sitting with Aristotle, as you quoted, and explaining how cell phones work."

"Okay, that's fair. Uh, then—" Gideon tried to wrap his mind around it all. "I, uh, how do you explain —" He wasn't sure how much of any of it he believed.

Traveler nodded understandingly. "You're so confused and focused on what I'm saying that you haven't even taken the time to check on your leg."

Gideon brought his head back. Traveler was right. He'd completely forgotten about his broken femur. The instant his focus was back on it, he realized he was standing. That was impossible. The pain alone should have him on his back. He looked down. He was in his regular clothes, leaving his body visible. There was some dried blood on his leg, but no injury. After a few quick breaths, he reached down and grabbed his thigh, hesitantly squeezing it. There was no pain. There was no break. It was as if it never happened.

"What the hell?" His curiosity trailed off as he stared at the impossibility. "It was broken. I remember. I saw it myself. Wha—what did you do?" His normal happiness and confidence were both scrambled.

"I'll explain, but it requires you to keep your mind open. I know it's a lot to take in right now. Parachute that mind, Gideon."

Gideon slowly nodded as he stared at his perfectly functioning leg. "I'm listening." The distant sounds of the jungle faded into the back of his mind.

Traveler started gently, "Okay, I know everything I'm about to say is going to sound impossible to you, but you're going to have to accept it as fact." Gideon gave Traveler a slow thumbs-up as he continued. "When light travel was discovered, it was also inadvertently discovered that light is so powerful, pure, and unadulterated that it, in turn, *corrects* impurities and imperfections during transit. It's the only way biological matter can be carried by light's power." He chuckled, still amazed by the truth of it. "The man who first stumbled upon light travel, also stumbled upon the most perfect and complete healing power."

Gideon's wide eyes turned up toward Traveler. "*Light* healed me?"

"Yes."

"Light? Just light?"

"Yes. This is going to sound absurd to you, but what if I told you that light has the power to cure diseases, heal injuries, remove scar tissue, and in turn, slow the aging process?"

"Wait. What?" Gideon's heart raced. "Scars? Diseases? How much of me did it heal?"

"I just told you. Everything. It healed all of you. It does during every jump."

Gideon immediately shifted his attention to his hands at the mentioning of scars. He stared at his skin, now smooth and radiant as if newly born. It almost appeared as if it was glowing, it was so perfect. An odd expression of yearning came across his face as he looked up his arms, seeing no familiar scars. For the first time in a long time, Gideon wasn't his positive and chipper self. He sighed, distracted from the awe of it all as he started looking around the ground, searching for something.

Traveler watched him curiously. "Are you all right, Gideon?"

Gideon didn't look up. "All diseases?"

Traveler slowly nodded, taking in Gideon's peculiar reaction. "Yes. Completely and fully. New sickness and disease can still be acquired, of course, but any that you had previous to jumping are erased as if they never were."

Gideon froze in place. All expression vanished as he digested the answer. For a moment, it looked like his mind left his body entirely. He cleared his throat and continued looking around the ground. "You said that light slows the aging process?"

"Yes," Traveler said under his breath as he watched Gideon continue scouring the ground. "In fact, it reverses it at first. At least that's how it appears. It washes away years by purifying a lifetime of physical decline, slowing aging down to a crawl if jumps are consistently made." He was explaining wonders beyond Gideon's knowledge and Gideon was distracted. It puzzled him.

Gideon nonchalantly nodded. "That's cool. So, how old are you then?" He finally squatted down and grabbed a jagged rock from the dirt.

Traveler narrowed his eyes. "How old do you think I am?"

"You look about mid-thirties."

Traveler chuckled, "I'm one hundred thirty-one in my world's years."

"Your world's years?"

Traveler nodded. "Orbital paths and whatnot. I assume I don't need to explain the differences therein to you."

Gideon stared at him in amazement as he stood up with the rock in hand. "So, you're not immortal or anything magical like that? Just, uh, so healthy that your body's basically dying at an incredibly slow pace?"

Traveler nodded. "Exactly. I know it's hard to fathom, but to me it's similar to you explaining cell phones to someone from the fourteen-hundreds. It's just common knowledge."

"Huh." Gideon puffed out his bottom lip and looked around at the untouched landscape. "So, is this the planet you're from?"

Traveler stared at him, more and more interested in why he wasn't enthusiastic about what was being explained. Something was off. "No, this planet is actually farther away from my home than Earth. A few thousand years less advanced, as well."

Gideon nodded as he pulled up the sleeve covering his left shoulder. "I have about a thousand questions." Then, without warning, he brought the rock up and swiftly sliced down his shoulder, cutting a thin line down to his bicep.

"What are you doing?" Traveler shrieked a fast step backward. "Why did you do that?"

Gideon stared unwaveringly at the bleeding cut. He dropped the rock and pulled his sleeve back over the slice. As his shirt absorbed the streaming crimson, his shoulders slumped as if the dead weight of a corpse had just been lifted from them. He immediately smiled and nodded to Traveler, returning to his regular, energetic self. He pulled his posture upright. His eyes glowed as his lips upturned.

"That's crazy! So, where's this cliff?"

"I think I've made a terrible mistake," Traveler murmured to himself, stumbling a little as he backed away.

6

After unanswered silence, Gideon asked again, "You said we're near the cliff?" He looked around, eager to explore.

Traveler slowly nodded. "Yes. It's, um—" He cleared his throat, hoping it would help his mind focus again. "It's over there." He pointed off in a general direction without taking his eyes off of Gideon shoulder.

"Well, let's go." Gideon's excitement seemed authentic. It was as if he hadn't just gone dark and sliced his flesh open.

"I'm sorry," Traveler remarked, unable to switch mindsets. "Are you all right? Why'd you mutilate yourself?"

Gideon chuckled, "It's barely a mutilation. Just a small cut." He glanced at his shoulder. "Looks like the bleeding's already slowed, too."

"Why did you do it?"

"It's just a reminder," Gideon said, dismissing it as nothing while shaking his left arm out. "All right, let's go check out this crazy-ass cliff."

Traveler exhaled hesitantly and started walking, keeping a concerned eye on his companion. He worried that maybe Gideon wasn't sane or that he had unresolved issues that would surface after being exposed to the wonders even more mind-bending than light travel.

Gideon, on the other hand, was fully energized and ready to go. He strode confidently, taking in his surroundings as he happily stepped next to Traveler. All the foliage was richer and thicker than he was used to. Trees that reminded him of prehistoric slideshows loomed over their heads, dwarfing the Venezuelan jungle they'd left. The air felt thicker and cleaner. It was difficult to explain, even to himself, but it was as if he could taste the lack of pollutants he was accustomed to on Earth.

"It smells so clean here. I love it." He smiled up at the bright sun that looked the same as Earth's. For a moment, he questioned the reality of them having traveled through space at all but walking on two completely healed and healthy legs was an irrefutable reminder that there was much he didn't understand.

Traveler nodded, still trying to shake off Gideon's behavior. "There's not much human life here, and those who exist haven't polluted the planet yet."

"That's fascinating." Gideon's smile grew as they began pushing through some hanging vines and branches. The scents from all the foreign plant life around them were intoxicating. He couldn't get enough. Deep breath after deep breath, he drew in as much as he could. "There are a lot of variables and possibilities I haven't even begun to consider. That's fun."

They entered a clearing. Gideon looked at the barren stretch of land, void of any plant life. The jungle just abruptly ended at the tree line, leading to a flat, dirt-covered bit of land at the edge of a cliff. Gideon stared at it curiously. Beyond the edge there was nothing visible but clouds. He didn't have to peer over to see that the drop was immense. He couldn't see any distant land from his viewpoint. It was like they were at the edge of the world.

"What?" He was beyond intrigued. Without waiting for any instruction or explanation from Traveler, he walked over to see what was below. "Why is there no life near the edge?"

"Because this world is much younger than Earth, and what lies at the base of the cliff is a unique landscape that is much more barbaric and harsh."

"And *this* is the part where you elaborate."

As Traveler responded, they both walked to the cliff's edge. "Hundreds of thousands of years ago, still millions of years into this planet's infancy, the valley below was primarily comprised of sand. Due to the fact that the valley is so deep in the planet, the temperature varies drastically. It's much nearer the core. Heat from the planet's sun during the day absorbs into the sand at such a high temperature that it cooks it. It spans out for eleven of your miles—a measurement I'll primarily use to explain things to you—and slopes up on the other end, leading back into jungle." They peered over. There was nothing to see but clouds, they were so high above the base. Gideon thrived on the dizzying power of heights, and the view below him triggered the strongest dizziness he'd ever felt. The cloud cover looked to be about a mile below them, and what lay below the clouds was a complete visual mystery.

"So, we're jumping into lava down there?"

"Come on, Gideon," Traveler smirked. "You strike me as an educated thrill-seeker, not a naïve adrenaline junky." He squinted, challenging Gideon's intelligence. "What happens to sand when it's cooked?"

Gideon smiled. "There's a big, ol' dance floor made of glass down there?"

"That's better." Traveler grinned. "An open mind isn't anything special if it's not sharp." The comment made Gideon smile. "The glassy ground gets so hot during each forty-nine-hour day that it's impossible to survive down there."

"And we're supposed to jump down ther—"

"It gets so hot that all the heat and steam billows up to create thick cloud cover, which in turn, traps the heat and makes it even *more* of a scorching valley. We would be cooked alive if we jumped down there right now." Gideon grinned as Traveler took the dramatically scenic route to explain. "Each evening when it cools, the transition is so quick and so drastic that the heat rises like a wind." He pointed down. "In a few minutes here, those clouds will quickly rise up this cliff face and shoot into the sky above. The instant they do, a cold wind will rush in after it, as it does every night. The wind comes at hundreds of miles an hour, roaring through the valley from the other side, and finally crashes into this cliff. In summation, it tempers the valley."

Gideon's smile grew. "So, we're going to wait for clouds that are all but on fire to pass over us, we will then leap off a six-mile-high cliff without any gear, hurl helplessly to our deaths, and then be saved by a tempering, cold wind rushing up at us faster than an F5 tornado?"

"And—" Traveler raised an eyebrow along with his index finger. "— the wind rushes through the valley so quickly that our window only lasts between three and five seconds. If we mistime it over or under, we'll either get rushed up too early and then fall to our deaths, or we'll miss it all together and—splat." He smiled slyly, ready for Gideon's courage to falter.

"You've got to be kidding me."

"Too much for you?" Traveler's tone was half-triumphant and half-disappointed.

"Not too much! It's the right amount of something I now know I can't live without." Gideon laughed. "This is so awesome." As his excitement reassured Traveler, they both saw the clouds begin to rise.

"Wait for my instruction." Traveler's stern tone did nothing to mask his own fear.

They watched the clouds steadily climb. Gideon anxiously shifted his weight back and forth, humming as he stared at the ballooning cumulus, flaring warm flashes and swells of red, orange, and yellow hues. It was surreal to see clouds rising with nothing else standing above them. They were so thick and massive, heaving and rolling, and so full of steam and gas that it almost appeared as if the cliff was sinking into the ocean of heated clouds.

Traveler took several deep breaths and glanced at Gideon. "You ready for this?"

Gideon smiled back at him. "Are you?"

"I hope so," Traveler nauseously admitted. The clouds were rising faster.

"You jump between planets, but *this* scares you?"

"It's very different."

"Then why are you doing this?" Gideon asked. "I could go it alone."

"I need to know if you possess the courage for whatever lies beyond the unknown." Traveler's answer drew Gideon's attention away from the cliff. "And I'm hoping I'll be the first of my kind to, as well."

"What do you m—" Gideon's words were swallowed by the roar of rushing clouds exploding up over the cliff, instantly shrouding them in furious whiteness. The thick wind burned their eyes, shooting up their nostrils, their hair whipping around as Traveler grabbed Gideon's arm. He pulled him close and yelled directly into his ear.

"My calculations were off! We need to jump *now*!" His words barely made it through the roaring wind, but the message was received. Gideon grabbed Traveler's shirt collar and yanked without a second thought.

"You got it!"

They couldn't see what was happening, but Gideon pulled them over the edge, nonetheless. Massive gusts of stifling heat blasted against their bodies as they free fell into the thrashing wind.

They struggled to gain control of their flailing bodies in the tempestuous squalls. It took some breathing adjustments and physical maneuvering, but they both slowly managed to aim their faces downward with their arms and legs tucked together.

Traveler's nerves were on edge, and his adrenaline was almost as high as his fear. He was petrified in the burning wind. Gideon, on the other hand, was howling and screaming in the literal heat of the moment. A shaking smile plastered to his face, and his hands couldn't help coming out to form finger guns. He laughed wildly and pantomimed shooting into the clouds he was bulleting through.

Their difficulty seeing through tears got harder with every wave of heat blasting into them. Then, after a few stinging blinks, the white clouds faded and rushed overhead, leaving them behind.

"Oh, wow!" Gideon's words disappeared in the violent wind as he stared down at the remaining four-or-so miles to the ground. He'd been skydiving many times, but those memories were instantly dwarfed in comparison to the alien chasm. Rather than seeing squared off farmlands or cities a couple miles below, the foreign planet's surface shone brightly, reflecting sunlight breaking through the exploding clouds above them. Just like Traveler had explained, the cooked sand spanned out for miles ahead of them, glowing like an abyss of jewels. They were so high above the ground that Gideon could see more of the planet's curvature than he ever could back home.

In the distance, the valley was vast and wide, but it funneled together, narrowing near the cliff's base. All the wind was going to crash up at them full force. Gideon glanced backward at the sheer cliff wall they were falling next to. It, too, was worn smooth from millennia of relentless wind shaping it into a flat wall of hardened rock.

"This is out of this world!" Gideon laughed at his own joke, knowing that Traveler couldn't hear anything he was saying. As he took in the majesty of the view, he turned for a moment to look over. He wanted to see if Traveler was enjoying the adrenaline rush as much as he was. He chuckled in the wind as he saw Traveler frozen in his falling position. Traveler was terrified, and he couldn't hide it. His skin, which Gideon had previously marveled at, was turning pale. Gideon wondered why he'd brought him there, let alone partaken in the jump. He suspected a hidden agenda, but that only added fuel to his intrigue.

As they continued to fall the last couple miles, their eyes widened at what they saw. From the far end of the Roaring Valley, a massive blast of cold wind was shooting across the ground like a shock wave from an atomic bomb. Even with the roar of the wind around them, they could hear rumbling from the shock wave tearing across the valley. Being so high above the ground, they could see their impending fates closing in on them at hundreds of miles per hour. Without any gear, they were left at the mercy of nature's grandeur. The importance of their jump's precision became a more inescapable reality. Either way, it was too late to change anything.

Traveler's stomach churned. He all but threw up trying to keep his composure, as the ground began to visibly close in. He had calculated their jump down to the very second, but he couldn't help second-guessing the likelihood of death. There were so many variables, and he hoped that his math had been perfect. They were falling the last mile. The valley was no longer a distant thing. It was coming up fast.

Gideon's tear-filled eyes were peeled, his smile was as big as it could be, his cheeks filled with wind. He stared at the shock wave rolling in. He couldn't tell if their timing would work, but he was exactly where he wanted to be, regardless. As the ground seemingly flew up at them, he thought the wave still looked too far out. They were going to crash against the glassy bottom. Traveler closed his eyes and flexed his jaw, as Gideon laughed in the face of their fate.

The roaring shock wave blasted into the curved base of the cliff and exploded up with a thunderous boom. Just as they expected to *splat*, the murderous cold collided, flipping them upward, hurling them against the smooth cliff face. Deafening roars from the shockwave shooting up into the sky jumbled their brains as chaos blurred.

Then, just as quickly as the cold wind had flung them back up, it passed and ascended into the sky above. Gideon and Traveler resumed falling at a slower pace. The smoothed base still had some grooves and bumps, and they felt all of them, but to their relieved surprise, they slid down the sloped base and came to a stop. Everything went silent.

7

From his back, Gideon stared up, marveling at the heat clouds dissipating in the distant sky above them. All that remained was vibrant blue and the planet's bright sun. The solid ground was tolerably warm after the freezing wave tempered it. The rush was over, and everything was calm, but Gideon's pulse was nowhere near slowing.

"Woo!" He shot his fist into the air, unable to catch his breath. "That was incredible! Thank you! Thank you. Thank you." He turned and looked at Traveler, who had his hands over his face. It looked like he was having a panic attack. Gideon smiled. "You all right there, Spaceman?"

Before Traveler could respond, he rolled onto his side and vomited. He groaned and heaved as his face slowly regained some of its color. After another heavy spew, he wiped his mouth and coughed.

"The fourth phase isn't worth it."

Gideon shook his head as he sat up with a smile. "You've never done that before?"

"No."

"How many people have?"

"None. The concept was all theoretical, based on observation of the valley's unique phenomena and makeup."

"So, we're the first? That just puts me over the moon."

"Literally," Traveler chuckled, still shaking his nerves. "I had to see if you could handle uncharted territory."

"I love it. Why on earth did *you* jump?"

Traveler feigned a laugh. "Your choice of words, Earthling." He groaned again as he shakily sat up. "You're not the only one being tested."

"Ooh." Gideon's eyes widened. "Tested?" He looked around the glass valley shining with earthy tones. "And what, pray tell, am I being tested for?"

Traveler spilled a strained exhale. "That's harder to explain. And much harder to believe." He looked around. "We need to leave this planet before it gets dark."

The response intrigued Gideon. "Why is that?"

"The indigenous."

"The indigenous?" Gideon's eyes twinkled. "Are they, like, some sort of dangerous aliens?"

Traveler rolled his eyes. "Before we go any further, you need to understand the difference between aliens and monsters. Aliens exist, but not in the sense you're thinking." He smiled. "There aren't any green-headed beings or bizarre creatures with magical powers, like healing index fingers. We've found thousands of planets that support life, but contrary to your imaginative films, there aren't any 'aliens.' Only people."

"Humans?" Gideon asked, both impressed and disappointed. "Homo sapiens everywhere?"

Traveler tilted his head back and forth as he considered how much to divulge. "One way to speak it. Do you understand why humanity evolved to the dominant species on your world?"

Gideon shrugged, wanting to hear Traveler's words more than his own educated guesses. "En*light*en me."

Traveler shook his head with a grin. "As your people would say, underwolves are the most challenged, so they must evolve to survive."

"Underwolves? Oh." Gideon chuckled. "Underdogs."

"Is that the saying?" Traveler squinted and then continued. "Humans don't naturally possess any evolutionary advantages. We can't fly. We can't run, swim, or jump with any competitive edge on what you call the food chain. We don't have protective feathers, scales, or fur. We're relatively weak, barely able to carry the equivalent of our own bodyweight. No claws or fangs, limited eyesight, hearing, and sense of smell. The list goes on." He laughed to ease any potential insignificance the truth could make Gideon feel. He'd seen it before. Most people, in his experience, didn't handle being insulted well, not even on an evolutionary level against the entire species—especially not from an alien.

Gideon smiled at him. "We're the weakest kids on the playground."

"Yes. Yes, we are. Embarrassingly so," Traveler said. "On Earth, your ancestors had to find a way to survive in a world occupied by millions of species, all of which were more qualified to survive than you. So, your brains developed, and as selection would have it, that advancement proved to be more advantageous than any claws or wings ever could be." He paused. "Well, that and our thumbs, but most worlds' versions of primates have those." He held one of his thumbs up and stared at it. "And look how far you've come: the third phase."

"That's gnarly," Gideon said, his steps bouncing as he thought about it. "And that's the same on every world? Biologically, we suck the most everywhere in space?"

Traveler nodded. "If not for our brains, we're the most useless stacks of meat."

"I'm going to find a way to turn that into a pick-up line," Gideon said with a devious smile. "So, just to make sure I understand this correctly," he bunched his lips and considered his options, "you're saying there aren't any alligator-people *anywhere* in the universe?"

"Alligator-people?" Traveler was taken aback by the question's absurdity. "Why would there be alligator-people?" He understood what Gideon was trying to ask but the wording was ignorantly childish, wishful even in its silliness. "The reptilian species you're referring to on your world alone hasn't evolved in, I'd guess, hundreds of thousands, if not millions, of your years. They don't need to. They're not being challenged in any way that demands development. They're masterfully effective predators without enough competition to need any improvement. Intelligence is spurred by the evolutionary need to overcome obstacles threatening a species' survival."

"Ah, I guess that makes science-y sense. So, no bird-people, tiger-people, or any other animal hybrids we fantasize about."

"Why would they be hybrids?" Traveler asked. "What evolutionary advantage would animals acquire by gaining our inferior bodies?"

Gideon clicked his fingers with a wink. "Just further proving your point. Making me feel stupider than Jupiter." He dropped his shoulders in feigned disappointment and then laughed the idea of humanoid animals away. "You're going to do that a lot, aren't you—ruin my imagination with logic?"

Traveler nodded. "And challenge your comprehension of the very fabric of reality and possibility with facts that your imagination hasn't even begun to consider. It'll balance itself out."

Gideon grinned. "And just like that, I forgive you. So, us human-people all the same everywhere?"

"Oh, no. We are as diverse as the stars themselves, but we're all humans. On larger planets with stronger gravity, people are shorter and denser, built a bit more like your great apes."

"What?" Gideon laughed his question out. "That's crazy."

"On smaller planets with weaker gravity, people are much taller and thinner, more fragile in structure."

"I guess that all makes sense. Because, well, more science." Gideon beamed. "I want to meet them."

"I'll introduce you to some, but it's ill-advised to expose ourselves to the people of this planet."

"Yeah, no planet likes perverts." Gideon smirked.

"No. No. No. Not like that. I mean their exposure to us." Traveler obliviously looked around, hoping he wouldn't see anyone. "The humans here aren't as developed. They're about as advanced as your Neanderthals."

"Cavemen? How are there cavemen?"

"Each planet is a different age and therefore, each has differing degrees of development, advancements in technologies and, of course, ages of humanity."

"Really?" Gideon smiled. "So, not every planet is as advanced as Earth?"

"On the scale of the least advanced planets to the most advanced that my people know of, Earth is on the higher end of the middle."

Gideon laughed. "So, I must come off mind-numbingly uneducated to you."

"I mean——" Traveler shrugged. "You have much to learn, but you're open-minded and that's a more important trait than smarts."

"Well, that's a relief. Can't have you traveling with a dummy." Gideon winked. "Are you the most advanced?"

"To our knowledge, we were the second."

"Were?"

"It's a long story that you might hear another time, but as far as we know, we're now the most advanced. There could be an older planet, but if so, we have yet to discover it. Or for them to expose themselves to us."

"You must tell the best bedtime stories," Gideon said with a smile before looking around. "So, why can't we meet the Neanderthals? It's not like we can't get away if they try to hurt us."

"It's not for our sake," Traveler responded as he looked up toward the sky, calculating their next jump. "They've barely discovered fire. If they see us, it'll overload their minds with too much that their underdeveloped brains can't comprehend. They'll either go insane or deify us."

"Yeah, I could see that." Gideon kept scoping the horizon, hoping to at least see one. "So, just to appease my inner child, are there planets with knights? Pirates? Futuristic places with flying cars? Horse and buggy, Sherlock Holmes kinds of times?"

Traveler nodded. "They all have their own variations of similar timelines with unique differences."

Gideon jumped to his feet. "That's incredible. I want to see all of them."

"That's a large part of your test." Traveler sluggishly forced himself to his feet with less motivation.

Gideon was vibrating. "What is this test you keep hinting at?"

"It's the adventure I was telling you about."

"This isn't it?" Gideon motioned around them.

"This isn't even the beginning." Traveler wasn't intending to make Gideon smile with his cryptic tone, but it couldn't be helped. Gideon thought for a moment as he looked around the glass valley. He took in the sights of cooked sand, surrounded by distant walls of the surrounding jungle. He maintained his smile as he nodded in response and started walking away.

"Well, I can't fail a test I haven't even started yet."

Traveler cocked his head. "Where are you going?"

"I'm gonna go meet some cavemen." Gideon's tone may as well have been smiling itself.

"No!" Traveler immediately started after him. "They're not ready for someone as advanced as you."

"Come on," Gideon chuckled. "I'm not going to teach them calculus or show them fireworks. I just want to meet them."

"No, Gideon." Traveler was walking fast, but Gideon's motivation made him difficult to keep up with. "They're underdeveloped beings. They're not intelligent enough for you."

"Pff," Gideon scoffed playfully. "Sonder."

"Sonder?"

"Everyone has a story." The concept filled Gideon's lungs with more vigor. He walked faster. "Sonder is the realization that every person we come in contact with has their own story as vivid and complex as our own. It's being aware of the fact that we're surrounded by hundreds, thousands, millions of lives, each intricately elaborate, each filled with hopes, dreams, disappointments, failures, unique personalities, and differing life experiences." He sighed dreamily. "It's realizing we'll appear in more lives than we'll ever know. In some, we'll merely be a stranger sipping coffee in the background. In some, we'll play a pivotal role in their decisions, beliefs, fates."

As Traveler finally caught up, Gideon smiled at him. "Part of the creed I live by is to try to improve every life I come across, or to at least make a new friend everywhere I go." He winked at Traveler. "And aside from a group of Russian mobsters, my friend list is currently lacking in Neanderthals."

Traveler grunted with frustrated intrigue. "A true philosopher's soul. So, your brain must be buzzing now that your concept of 'sonder' has just expanded beyond just Earthlings."

"Oh, you have no idea," Gideon's words burst out. "Now, not only is every person unique in their story, but every *world* is." He looked at Traveler with challenging sincerity. "So, if you want to take me planet-hopping as an audition—or test for whatever this mysterious adventure is—you need to understand one thing."

"What's that?" Traveler asked hesitantly as he looked at Gideon's blood-soaked shoulder.

"I'm on board. Like, fully on board. But—" He raised his finger. "I refuse to visit a planet without meeting the people who live there."

Traveler shook his head as they kept walking. "You could be the most promising mistake I've ever made."

As they climbed out of the Roaring Valley, Gideon stared out over the lush jungle covering the young planet. Beautifully uninhibited foliage stretched to the horizon. The only obstruction to the view was the cliff they had dived from. It astounded him that he could no longer see the top, as clouds had regathered a few miles up its face.

"What's the youngest habitable planet that's been discovered?"

Traveler stepped up next to him and looked around. "This one's nowhere near the youngest habitable planet. But, as far as planets habited with human life, it's in its earliest phase. As I said, there are countless planets that possess the ability to sustain life that are void of humanity—for now."

They started walking directionless into the jungle, immediately surrounded by primitively monstrous trees and vibrant plant life.

"How many phases are there?" Gideon was eating up every word.

"There are three major phases of human development, each breaking down into smaller, more detailed phases within. Each one is fueled by exploration, for as each human of every developmental stage of every world knows, we are inherently curious creatures. We want to know all that is and push every boundary and rule we're told exists."

"Oh, that I do." Gideon smiled. "So, what's the first major phase?"

"Exploring one's planet."

Gideon reached out and grabbed a hanging fruit that looked to him like a softball-sized orange pear. "That makes sense." He took a bite, spilling juice down his chin. After chewing, he gave an approving nod and motioned for Traveler to continue.

"Every world with human life starts the same way." They climbed over a large, fallen log. "It's the longest and slowest of the three. Once survival needs are met, humans explore. Each in their own way, they always document their surroundings and create maps until they can't go any farther."

"Stopped only by oceans, I'm assuming?"

"Very good. Once their body of land is fully explored, they fight for dominance until a hierarchy of control is established." Traveler brushed a branch out of his face.

"King of the hill is such a fun game," Gideon chuckled.

"The game never changes. The hill just gets larger." Traveler cleared his throat. "Sooner or later, humans gain enough courage to match their curiosity and explore beyond their shores. They take to the water to see what mysteries exist beyond the known horizon."

"Ah, that's so exciting." Gideon shook his fists. "Sometimes I wish I didn't know what was beyond, so I could see if I had the courage to experience that. Stupid maps and stuff."

"In time, we'll find out if you do." Traveler glanced at him with much unspoken. "Eventually, humans explore every corner of their planet until they discover, document, and name it all to illuminate the unknown."

"And then king of the hill resumes."

"Indeed."

"That all makes sense. And the second phase is?"

"The second phase is exploring the possibilities held within the physical properties of their world."

"Science!"

"Yes, science and tools. Manipulating the environment around us; typically evolving from agriculture into industrialization. From there, most worlds learn to wield electricity, and it's only a short journey from there into technology. Earth is well into its second phase. It's even in the infancy of flirting with its third."

"Our third phase? Which would be what? Exploring beyond one's planet?"

"Correct. See, you're not so painfully ignorant after all." Traveler gave a playfully condescending smile. "The third phase is exploring the universe."

"Do your people have space shuttles? Or, um, spaceships? Or have you always traveled by light?"

"Oh, we created shuttles similar to yours. All who reach the third phase typically do. Though we barely expanded on them, as we were shown—or I guess I should say, we discovered light travel early on in our third phase."

Gideon sighed, disappointed. "We squabble so much amongst ourselves—king of the mountain and all—that I feel like we've shied away from our third phase. Like, we send drones and stuff out, but we don't really focus much on sending people out into 'the final frontier.'"

"Space is not the final frontier," Traveler eerily commented. He paused, staring through the ground. "For most worlds, it's not too far into their exploration of space that they inevitably stumble upon light travel." He shrugged. "Shuttles immediately become obsolete, and light becomes the future."

"That's crazy to think about," Gideon said while pondering it. "All of our efforts and movies lean toward mechanical engineering to explore the heavens. Wouldn't have guessed the most efficient means to be biological."

Traveler nodded. "If you think about it, we are made of the same elements, the same ingredients, as the stars themselves, so it makes sense that our bodies would be connected to the heavens more so than our lifeless creations."

"Poetry," Gideon said, unable to stop smiling at the wonder of it all.

Traveler recognized the awe. He always loved sharing the miracles of light travel with lesser developed minds. "We've merged them a little, but we haven't fully explored carrying inanimate objects by light yet. We're still experimenting with that. I'm just glad we've at least managed to send clothes. We used to lose our clothing when we were lit and end up on other worlds completely nude, sometimes without hair. Even our eyebrows didn't make it in the beginning." He shook his head at the memories. "We're always workshopping the light shot, trying to improve it. We've only managed to develop it to bring small items by hand. Anything large is impossible at this point. That's why spaceships and shuttles are obsolete. We can't bring them with us. The journey is too far for their speeds." He shook his head. "So long ago."

"I love that discovering light travel is part of your history books," Gideon said. "And yet, it's not even a distant glimmer in our future."

"I'm sure the people of Earth will start seeing that glimmer sometime within the next century or so."

"That's a fun thought. So, you're still in the third phase then?" Gideon's tone sharpened as Traveler nodded. Gideon all but clapped his hands. "I heard you say something about a fourth phase after we survived that awesome jump." He pointed his thumb over his shoulder toward the Roaring Valley. "Have you flirted with the fourth yet? What is the fourth?"

"You could say we have come close to the fourth."

"What is it?" Gideon stopped; he was so curious. There was a phase that even Traveler's people hadn't reached.

"The fourth phase is the exploration that you're being tested for." Traveler's response turned Gideon's smile expressionless. They stopped walking, standing still with eye contact maintained in silence.

Gideon cocked his head. "Do you have any idea what's—beyond the horizon?"

"No."

"Hm. Have you at least dipped your toe in the water?"

"Only enough to make ripples," Traveler said with a haunted tone. "It will be your job to go beyond."

Gideon raised an eyebrow. "Earth sent monkeys into space before humans because they were expendable."

Traveler nodded. "Wise."

Gideon cleared his throat. "I'm your monkey?"

"So to speak."

"What is it?"

"It's—" Traveler's eyes fluttered as he struggled to find the right words. "We don't know exactly what it is." He sounded scared, spooked. "We haven't yet mustered enough courage to venture beyond the known horizon, though our curiosity is begging us to."

Gideon's smile slowly returned. "And now it's begging me to. What *do* you know about it?"

"Your mind will need to open a bit more before we cross that threshold."

Gideon huffed. "Mr. Traveler, curiosity is killing this cat." He pointed at himself. "And I'm pretty sure I've already used up my other eight lives. That's not very ni—"

A distant grunt interrupted him. They both turned and looked in the direction it had come from.

As they scoped their surroundings, they saw a couple slumped-over beings behind some bushes a few hundred feet away. Gideon took a small step forward as his eyes widened. They were difficult to make out from behind the thick shrubbery, but their grunting continued. One stood up just enough to expose long brown hair and a heavily protruding forehead. It ducked back down and continued grunting with the other. Gideon's mouth hung open with pure, enamored excitement.

"That's—them," he sharply whispered. "It's them. Those are cavemen." He all but jumped up and down. "I'm staring straight at real-life cavemen."

"Shh." Traveler held a finger up. "Okay, we've seen them. Time to go."

"Psh. Fat chance, scaredy pants." Gideon started walking toward the bushes, but Traveler immediately grabbed his arm.

"They don't even have loincloths, they're so primitive," Traveler murmured back. "If you go over there, they won't be able to process what they're seeing."

"You think they'd be uncomfortable because of my clothes?" Gideon snorted. "To be fair, I'd rather be comfortable, too." With that, he retracted his arm and quickly stripped his clothes off.

"Gideon," Traveler's whisper shot out. "Get back here."

Buck naked, Gideon tried to mimic the primal posture he saw as he meandered toward the Neanderthals. He slumped and walked with a hunch, grunting as he hobbled. Traveler couldn't help but chuckle amid his concerns as he watched Gideon's naked body lunging toward the Neanderthals.

Gideon stumbled a little as his bare foot stepped on something pokey, but he regained composure and continued grunting. As he drew closer, his presence became known. The two Neanderthals peeked up over the bushes at him. Their wild brown eyes were wide open and their breathing, agitated.

Traveler watched in tense anticipation as Gideon stopped. He expected the primitives to turn and run at the sight of Gideon, but to his surprise, they crept forward from behind the bushes. They weren't far from Gideon, and even with their cautiousness, they studied his scent.

Gideon was blissfully vulnerable, overflowing with childlike wonder as he looked at them. They were thicker, with shorter legs and longer arms, both mostly covered in matted black hair. Their anatomy was definitely human, but there was a strong simian element. It was easy to discern a male and a female. He assumed they were a couple. He giggled to himself silently as he realized how preposterous he was being to think of them romantically. "Mates" was probably more appropriate than "couple." Their faces possessed such clear expression, full of intelligent potential.

The two indigenous people waited to ensure there was no threat, and then slowly approached Gideon. He'd half expected them to walk like gorillas, using their fists or trotting on all fours, but they moved perfectly fine on their short legs and large feet while their arms dangled.

Traveler held his breath and lifted a hand toward the planet's sun. He wanted to be ready to go if need be, but he was enjoying the show. The Neanderthals were naturally strong beings, and they had an animalistic temperament. There was plenty of capacity for entertaining mishap.

The scene grew quiet as they stopped a few feet shy of Gideon. The female waited, staring him up and down and breathing heavily through her large nose, obviously curious about the unfamiliar male. After a moment, she tentatively stepped forward and sniffed Gideon's face. Her breath was rancid, but it was a dismissible detail. She pulled back before returning and sniffing his chest and shoulders. It wasn't hard to see how much she was enjoying his unfamiliar aroma.

Gideon sniggered, "Hey, that tickl—um, I mean—" He resumed grunting and then sniffed her back, mirroring her behavior, reveling in their animalistic formalities.

The female's mouth opened, and her excitement rose as she jumped up and down once, hooting at Gideon's response. Gideon was a little hesitant, wondering, if like chimpanzees, they possessed surprising strength. He didn't want to get hurt, but if by any chance he did, the experience would be worth the risk.

The male started howling and grunting aggressively at their interaction. Gideon looked over just in time to see him grab handfuls of dirt and leaves. The cantankerous male threw them in the air and loudly yapped. Gideon smiled and watched him snatch whatever he could off the ground and throw it into the air.

Gideon nodded and squatted down to do the same. He grabbed handfuls of twigs and dirt, and threw them upward as he, too, howled and barked. They both continued repeating the display as the female enthusiastically spun around. The air around them thickened with dust, dirt, and an array of small, jungled items raining over their heads.

Traveler stifled a laugh as he watched. He partially hoped that Gideon was unaware that he was competing for the right to mate. He knew that whichever male emerged dominant would earn the attention of the female, and he also knew that there was no possible outcome that he wouldn't be entertained by. He hated admitting it to himself, but he was fascinated by Gideon's intrepid need to interact.

The male abruptly stopped. Gideon followed in suit and ceased his movements. He could feel his speeding pulse trying to catch up with the playful behavior that still had dirt raining down onto them. He followed the male's gaze as they both turned to look at the female.

She looked back and forth between them, sizing them up one at a time. Her energy was visibly raised, as well. Gideon was so caught up in the moment of meeting real cave people that it took him a minute to realize what was happening. His eyes widened and he couldn't help the goofy grin as it dawned on him, but before he could do anything, the female grunted and motioned her hand in his direction. She dropped down to her fists at the end of her long arms and turned herself around. Without hesitation, she aggressively started backing up toward him.

Gideon lurched backward just before she reached him. "Oh, no. No. No. No." He began laughing hysterically. "I'm sorry to lead you on." He laughed harder as the predicament escalated. The female backed up faster, obviously frustrated by him denying her advances. "Stop. Stop it." He giggled. "Listen, it's not you. It's me."

Then, as he turned around to run away, he was surprised by the male swinging a rock into his face. *Crunch!* The blow knocked him back a few strides.

Traveler watched from a distance, afraid to yell out. He brought his hands up to his mouth, unsure of what else to do. Gideon had bitten off more than he could chew, and Traveler was worried he was going to choke on it.

Gideon stumbled but maintained his footing as he brought his hand to his bleeding jaw. The male had hit him hard enough to rattle him. Gideon looked over to see him barking at the female in a way that he could only translate as betrayal. He still couldn't remove the smile from his bleeding face. The situation was too funny to allow a sucker punch to dampen his mood. He looked around. A tree next to them immediately caught his eye. A bulbous, blue fruit was growing out of its branches about ten feet in the air. An idea hit him almost as hard as the rock had.

As the Neanderthals began shoving each other, Gideon jumped down next to them with arms full of blue fruit. They scooted back, startled. Gideon wasn't sure if they were good climbers or not, but either way, he figured some free food would probably help calm them down.

His simple peace offering silenced their bickering. It slowly drew them nearer. They reached out and quickly took all of the fruit, immediately shoving as much as they could into their mouths.

After the male devoured two with what seemed like an inhale, he looked at Gideon and reached out to touch his jaw where he'd whacked him. He whimpered sympathetically in a way that Gideon could only translate as an apology. Gideon smiled back. The male sighed and reached out, offering Gideon the small, bloodied rock he'd hit him with. The caveman's expression begged Gideon to take it. Gideon's smile grew as he accepted the gift and looked at the blood smear. In his mind it was the perfect souvenir. He turned from one to the other and gently patted them both on the bushy backs.

"May death not find you love birds sleeping." He added a couple grunts and huffed breaths to blend his words with their way of speaking, and then turned toward Traveler.

As Gideon made his way back, he glanced over his shoulder at the Neanderthals, who'd clearly settled their differences and hobbled away together. Traveler looked at Gideon, who was still naked and bloody. He shook his head at the red rock in his hand.

"You really enjoy collecting bloody mementos, don't you?" His tone was full of amused judgment. Gideon smiled back as he put his clothes on. Traveler continued shaking his head. "Are you happy? Did that go how you wanted?"

"I got to hang out with cavemen. It's been a good day."

Traveler raised an eyebrow. "You got beat up by one caveman and almost molested by another." They laughed as Gideon shrugged dismissively.

Once Gideon had all his clothes on and the bloody rock was securely in his pocket, he looked up at Traveler with a satisfied grin. "So, what's next?"

"You're going to be a handful," Traveler sighed. "I still haven't recovered from, uh, whatever that just was." He laughed a little.

Gideon nodded. "Yeah, I wish I had my backpack. This rock would feel right at home there."

Traveler looked back up toward the sky. "I think I know where I want to take you next."

"You think?" Gideon smirked. "You haven't planned out how this test is going to go?"

"This test," Traveler remarked snidely, "requires an open mind— from all parties involved." He stared into somewhere unseen, peering beyond the alien sky. "And not just in hypothetical, philosophizing theories, but in very real, unpredictable circumstances. So, no, I'm, er…how would Earthlings say? Playing it by nose. Such an odd saying."

"By ear." Gideon chuckled. "But, okay. Fair enough," he said with his regular smile. "So, how does this light travel work? Like, what is the step-by-step process for a jump?"

"Well." Traveler brought his head back and took a deep breath. "That's a very lengthy explanation. It took all twenty-eight years of my education to master all there was to learn, and my people are still discovering more about it every day."

"Wow. Okay, just give me the Hallmark card version then."

"The what?" Traveler looked at him, confused.

"Right. Um, just give me the condensed version."

"Okay, I'll see how well I can explain this." Traveler looked up at the planet's sun. "First, I have to calculate how far away the selected destination is. I have optical implants—" He pointed at his eyes. "—with a fully interactive map of everything we've explored and documented. It refreshes and updates every second as each of us observers continue exploring the farther reaches of space and mapping it. We're constantly looking for more habitable planets. We're constantly seeking more to learn."

"That's so cool," Gideon said. "And will I have to drink a light shot before every single jump?"

"No," Traveler said. "That's a onetime consumption. It has converted your cells to be permanently harmonious with light. They'll forever reproduce with the genetic mutation of light compatibility."

"Thank God." Gideon chuckled. "Would've done it, but glad I don't gotta."

"Anyway." Traveler focused. "So, I calculate the distance to the destination, which takes into consideration the gravitational pull of every single planet, star, and other celestial body between. It factors in the combined weight of everyone jumping. I then have to time my jump so precisely that I am propelled with proper planning for millions, if not billions, of lightyears of distance and every single moving body in between. I ensure that our space forecast provides clear passage, without any meteors, asteroids, or anything that can get in the way. I ha—"

"What happens if you come in contact with an asteroid?"

Traveler scoffed, "Our cells—our matter is, in essence, transformed into energy that's the equivalent of light when we jump. Wherever the light that's carrying us hits, we reassemble." He nodded up into the sky. "So, if we hit an asteroid or meteor, we reassemble in space and suffocate."

"Seriously?" Gideon's eyebrows rose.

"Yes. Your blood vessels burst, whatever parts of you are facing the nearest sun will likely sunburn without any atmosphere—all depending on your proximity—and any and all exposed fluids boil. Spit, sweat, blood, urine—which, chances are, you will empty your bladder and bowels, so boiling urine and bowel movements." Traveler looked down, grossed-out by his own explanation.

Gideon chuckled. "Sounds like taco Tuesday. How would it boil? Is it hot?"

"No, it's quite cold, actually. But due to pressure, it—think of it more like violent evaporation."

"That's bizarre."

"Indeed. It's called shadowing."

"Huh?"

"When your light comes in contact with an obstruction and you die in space, the only part of you that reaches your intended destination is your shadow. Or at least, that's the poetic way of looking at it. Anyway, it's the assigned term. 'So-and-so's been shadowed.'"

"That's actually really cool," Gideon said and smiled. "How often does that happen?"

"Well, as our technology increases, and so does our understanding of light, our ability to accurately forecast every detail between millions and billions of lightyears of space also improves." He took a breath. "And the more all of that increases, the more the number of shadows decreases." As he thought about it, he looked in the direction of the Roaring Valley. "Though, as you saw, sometimes we make mistakes with timing. No one's perfect. That much is still true everywhere."

"Well, good. That's a reassuring expectation." Gideon thought about it all. "So, you say light has elasticity."

"Right."

"So, along those lines, if you figuratively stretch it too far, does it shoot you too fast? Like a bug on a windshield?" He slapped his hands together.

Traveler nodded. "Good question, and yes. That's another calculation prerequisite to each jump. Not enough tension and the light beam slows you enough to become more susceptible to other bodies of gravity. Can't linger too long in space without all the moving parts coming into play and pulling you in unintended directions."

"Makes sense, I guess."

"Too much, on the other hand, and you're guaranteed to hit your target, but in overly focused light, well, you essentially become a laser. You'll burn a hole into the planet and reassemble at the deepest part of said hole. You literally dig your own grave."

"Wow. How large is the margin for error?"

"Let's just say that it's been the number one cause of death for our people for the last century."

Gideon blinked rapidly and smiled as he shook his head. "I'm being thrown into the most dangerous situation that exists for the most advanced people in the universe?"

"That's one way to look at it."

"Oh, man." Gideon grinned. "That's exciting. So, what's the second highest leading cause of death for your people? Cancer?"

"Oh, no, that's eradicated. We removed disease from our people with light purification a long time ago."

Gideon's smile faded a little as he rubbed his shoulder where he'd cut himself. "That's rather amazing."

Traveler nodded. "Yes, it is. The second leading cause of death is murder, and even that's almost nonexistent."

"If your people represent anything along the lines of where mine are heading, the future sounds pretty promising." Gideon's smile returned. "So, if there's no disease, minimal murder, and only some lethal mistakes made randomly through space, do your people have a population problem?"

"Yes and no." Traveler looked up as he saw the planet's sun heading toward the horizon. "Yes, we have too many people for our planet, but no, because of the uninhabited planets capable of supporting life. They're basically vacant homes."

"Well, that works out well." Gideon looked up to the sky, imagining all the worlds that existed. "So, do all your people just jump from planet to planet at will?"

"No. Light jumps are limited to those with proper training and policed by our government. The simplest way I can think to explain it is picture the pilots of your fighter jets. The training is extensive, and it's limited to government-sanctioned activity. Although there have been cases of trained individuals going rogue and disappearing amid the many worlds in the universe just so they can explore at will without any supervision. We say they've 'gone dark.'"

"Legit. I'm digging all the shadowy names. So, if light jumps are limited to government-sanctioned agents—" Gideon slugged Traveler's arm. "—you're a pretty big deal on your world."

Traveler couldn't help taking some pride as he allowed a responding smile. "You could say you're riding first class."

"Well, aren't I just a lucky lady?" Gideon laughed.

"Don't speak too soon," Traveler said as he pulled a slender grey device out of his pocket.

"What do you mean?" Gideon looked down. "What's that? Wait," he stuttered with what might've been actual nerves. "Is that a probe, mister alien?"

Traveler stared at Gideon blankly. "Do you——do you really think I would——" He shook his head. "No." He shivered at the idea. "What is wrong with your people?"

Gideon grinned. "Couldn't help myself. Okay. What is it?"

"You don't speak the language of the indigenous where we're going. Like I said at the top of Angel Falls, there are billions of languages and you don't speak them. That's going to be an issue."

"Do *you* speak billions of languages?" Gideon asked a little apprehensively as Traveler lifted the device up.

"No, but this helps bridge that gap." Traveler placed the end of the metallic rod up to Gideon's ear, pressing it uncomfortably far inside. Gideon winced, but held still as it kept sliding in. Traveler looked him in the eyes. "Take a deep breath." Gideon inhaled and held it. As soon as he exhaled, Traveler pressed a button on the other end. A sharp pain flooded Gideon's inner ear. Traveler retracted the rod, allowing Gideon to stumble back and clutch his head. "The ringing will stop momentarily."

"Wow, that sucks!" Gideon laughed to stifle a whimper. "What is that?"

"It's a state-of-the art translator that contains every language we know of."

"That's pretty cool, I'm not gonna lie." Gideon tried not to tear up.

"It's set to English, so everything you hear will be translated to English." Traveler reached out and delicately reached into Gideon's mouth before he could react and snapped a second item into Gideon's inner cheek. Gideon yelped as Traveler explained, "Everything *you* say will be translated to emit the language of any person you're speaking to. And don't be confused if when the first time you speak to each person of a different tongue, they look at you peculiarly. The translator blurs your mouth muscles until it establishes a convincingly deceptive control of the foreign language. In essence, it makes it *look* like you're speaking their tongue as well," he smirked. "Though the less intelligent someone is, the poorer of a job it does translating their words. I've met some people that sound absolutely ridiculous being translated." He chuckled.

Gideon smirked as he kept rubbing his ear. "That's incredible. I wish I could've had this during all my travels. Really would have helped some misunderstandings." He cocked his head to the side. "So, that means you don't actually speak English?"

"Correct. My language sounds a bit closer to your Chinese than any other Earthly language."

"You're kidding." Gideon grinned in amusement.

"I'm quite serious. If it wasn't for the translator in my ear, you wouldn't understand a single word I say."

"Huh," Gideon marveled. "Then I'm glad I have one, too, now. Anything else before we go?"

"That should suffice for now. Are you ready?"

Gideon nodded as the throbbing began subsiding. "Where are we going?"

"Well, you spoke of wanting to see pirates or knights, right?"

Gideon took a step forward. "Dude, shut up. Don't toy with me. Are you serious?" He started bouncing in place. "Which are we going to see?"

Traveler smiled. "I don't care to ruin that surprise."

Gideon eagerly shifted back and forth with childlike impatience as Traveler reached toward the setting sun. Watching him prepare for their jump was like witnessing a master magician. Gideon stared upward, imagining the mysteries of wherever they were heading. They were about to travel to the third planet he'd ever been to: an impossible reality that he'd never pictured would be his life.

Traveler smiled at the sky, closing his hand as he grabbed something that Gideon could only assume was a beam of light. It was something to behold. Traveler slowly placed his free hand on Gideon's shoulder. Just the touch made Gideon giggle in anticipation. He was much more alert and aware for his second jump. He wanted to make sure that he was completely immersed in the moment so he could experience every ounce of the phenomenon.

"All right, Gideon," Traveler peered deep into the changing orange and purple colors of the evening sky. "Are you ready?"

"Oh, I'm ready, Spaceman!" Gideon's excitement burst out of him. He felt tingles course through his entire body as Traveler opened his fist. Then, in an instant, everything went blinding white as he felt a cold wind swirl around his body.

8

The illuminating light faded, leaving Gideon feeling like he was being roused from a restoring nap. His eyes shot open, but he rushed to take in his new surroundings. He caught his breath and tried to focus so he could explore wherever Traveler had taken them. This time around, he was prepared to be unprepared. He was impatiently expecting the unexpected.

Before his other senses kicked in, his nose and lungs absorbed their new location. The air was thinner than the jungled, Neanderthal planet they'd just left. He squinted, trying to find any familiarity. He was reminded of spending time hiking in the Rocky Mountains, or at least the altitude felt similar.

His eyes caught up, dilating and looking around to see forestation. Pine trees, or some kind of trees with longer needles than he was familiar with, surrounded him on one side, and on the other was a mountainous slope leading down to a beach about a quarter mile away. Beyond the beach was an ocean with waters reaching the horizon.

"What's the name of this planet? I totally forgot to ask about the last one." A cool breeze kissed his skin, and he could smell the saltwater halfway up the mountain. His question went unanswered, aside from unfamiliar birds chirping around him. "Traveler?" He looked around, not seeing Traveler anywhere. "Traveler?" His voice echoed down the mountain. No response. Just more birds taking flight at his yell.

As Gideon looked to see what kind of birds they were, his peripherals caught movement. There was a distant figure walking into sight down on the beach. His cry for Traveler had drawn attention.

Gideon smiled. "Traveler?" His question was, again, unreturned, as the distant person motioned to someone else. Gideon stared, managing to make out more detail. The man moved a little, causing bright light to reflect and flash away. Gideon smiled. "Armor."

He immediately started trotting down the mountain. It was impossible to predict if the knight would be friendly or hostile, so he kept his hands visible. As he all but jogged to the beach, a few more men stepped into sight from behind the tree line at the ocean's edge. Gideon's smile grew. There were a bunch of them, a least ten, and he couldn't wait to meet them.

He glanced down as he realized he was still wearing the clothes he'd put on that morning in Venezuela. He wasn't sure if the knights would respond well to his foreign attire. Then, as he thought about it, it dawned on him that he'd been awake for what was probably the equivalent of a day and a half and he wasn't at all tired. He didn't feel hyper beyond his excitement for where he was, but his body wasn't fatiguing. It was obvious to assume that the two light jumps had rejuvenated his body. At that rate, would he ever feel the need to sleep? The thought trailed into the realization that his shoulder must have been healed again. He reached up and grabbed it. Sure enough, the cut was gone, and there was no scar. Before he could process it, he'd made it to the beach.

The instant his feet hit sand, he stopped to see at least fifteen men surrounding him with hungry expressions, all buried beneath thick beards. They had on random assortments of armor, but not polished and clean the way he'd envisioned. A few of them had helmets, foreign and alien in design. Each was grungy and worn, but evidently sturdy. They were definitely from a different culture, and Gideon was inundated with curiosity.

Some knights had breastplates, and some didn't. All of them had swords or other melee weapons on their hips. One continuity Gideon noticed were scarred lines on both sides of their necks. Something ceremonious, he assumed. Additionally, some of them had scale male coating their arms or legs. Most of the armor had holes and dents from combat and wear.

What puzzled Gideon was that the men without helmets had rags wrapped around their heads like bandanas. All the clothing they were wearing beneath their armor reminded him of pirate lore. Loosely fitting pants and baggy shirts, once vibrant, now faded, hung around them like old flags. Gideon's emotions flickered between excitement and something dark, as he rubbed his shoulder.

"Pirate-knights," he growled with a ravenous grin.

A heavy-set man tilted his equally thick helmet back and studied him up and down. "What insanity are you speaking?"

Gideon looked around. "You look like two of my favorite things blended together."

The men turned and looked at each other, puzzled by the strange wording.

A gruff voice scratched out of the tallest of them. "Where do you hail from?"

"Hail," Gideon scoffed, trying to force himself to smile sincerely. "I'm from —" He considered the best answer. He was about to point toward the sky but didn't want to be killed on the spot for witchcraft. "I'm from America," he stated, wondering how they'd react.

"America? Where is America? I've never heard of this place," the same voice barked back.

"It's, uh——" Gideon looked around and pointed unsurely. "I don't know exactly which direction it is from here, but it's very far away."

"It surely must be. Do all men in America wear such curious clothing?"

Gideon nodded, "We do. Men and women alike."

One of the other men scoffed, "That's far too fine a linen for a woman."

Gideon puffed out his bottom lip and muttered beneath his breath, "Oh, right. Of course you're misogynistic pirate-knights." He couldn't help the visible wave of judgment seething out of him.

"Speak up!" one of the men growled. "What words did you speak to yourself? Are you conjuring something?"

"No, Lancelot," Gideon sardonically spat. "Merlin and I just look a lot alike."

The man glared and drew his sword. "He mocks us." He scowled at Gideon with a devilish smile. "Perhaps his insolence will diminish when he dangles before the faihrgrreys."

The others chuckled and drew their swords as they walked toward Gideon. He knew he needed to change his mood if he was going to survive. He looked around for something to cut his shoulder with, but he was surrounded by sand, and it was all finely sifted. Before he could find anything, the men seized him by his arms.

Gideon glared at them. "Would you be so kind as to do me a simple favor?"

The same man got close to Gideon's face. "What favor do you ask, bait?" he sneered.

Gideon cleared his throat as he stared back. "Before you take me wherever you're taking me, would you please take that blade of yours and cut me from the top of my left shoulder—to the bottom?"

Some silence passed as the man studied Gideon and then slowly smiled. "The bait wishes the faihrgrreys to smell his blood in the water, that we may have a swifter voyage." He brought the top of his sword up and placed the sharp tip against Gideon's shoulder. "I will oblige your insanity." He slowly dragged the blade down, taking his time as blood trailed, cutting a deep gash into Gideon's shoulder. Gideon didn't even wince as he held eye contact with the brutish knight. As soon as the slice was complete, the man stopped and leaned in closer. "To here, you say?"

Gideon glanced at the laceration. He took a deep breath at the familiar sight and then exhaled, closing his eyes and dropping his head.

After some composing breaths, he looked up and nodded as a fresh smile graced his face.

"That's perfect. Thank you." His positivity returned. "I'm Gideon." He looked around at the armored pirates. "What are your names?"

The man leaning in observed Gideon's shift in energy. "A man who feels no fear when he bleeds." His smile disappeared and then came back as he nodded. "An admirable trait. Aside from two women in my bed, bleeding is Grimleck's best reminder to smile." He took a deep breath. "Gideon is your name?" Gideon nodded, finally taking the time to relish the fact that he was surrounded by medieval warriors. The man pulled back, retracting his blade as he stood tall. "Sir Tereth, first mate of the *Crimson Shadow*."

Gideon's eyes widened. "*Sir* Tereth, *first mate* of the *Crimson Shadow*?" He shook his head. "That's the most badass name ever! And such a perfect mashup of knights and pirates."

Sir Tereth cocked his head to the side and squinted. "What are these knights and pirates you speak of, Bait Gideon?"

Gideon, still held by the other men, thought about it. "Two different kinds of warriors. Knights look kind of like you, armor and all, but pirates sail the sea and dress in rags." He motioned at some of the other men's clothing. "They're very different, but both so cool. Basically, I want to be one of you."

The men laughed.

"Your insanity is richly entertaining," Tereth bellowed above his thick beard. "Dangling you before the faihrgrreys will nearly be regretted." With that, he nodded to the others.

Before Gideon could say anything, a sword hilt cracked the back of his head, and everything went dark.

❄

Gideon's vision blurred as he slipped back into consciousness. The not-so-gentle bouncing of being carried roused him from the tongue-numbing slumber. He wasn't a small man, but whoever was carrying him had him flung over their shoulder, walking as though he weighed no more than a towel. His hands were tied behind his back and his ankles were bound. The feeling of rough ropes chafing his skin was an irritating reality to wake to. He tried to look around, but a thick sack, reminiscent of burlap, covered his face. He could hear an array of movement and voices, and he smelled an interesting combination of water and sweat. A painful throbbing pulsated from a lump that he was immediately aware of on the back of his head. The sting of his left shoulder against his shirt was the only pain that brought a wave of relief.

After a few more heaving strides, he was stood up, and the sack ripped from his head. Gideon blinked in the daylight. He was surrounded by armored pirates, many more than were on the beach. They were all going about their business, randomly glancing at him.

A giant smile appeared on Gideon's face as he looked beyond them. They were on a pirate ship, a real pirate ship. He could feel the ocean swaying beneath. He looked out and saw the beach disappearing in the distance, the mountains behind it looking no larger than anthills as the horizon stole them away.

As he took it all in, a confused expression joined his smile. The ship wasn't the regular shape of any boat he'd seen. It was circular. He looked around, and sure enough, the flat deck of the ship was a perfect circle. It had to be at least forty feet in diameter. Thick, black, steel rails lined the border, and every few feet around the edge were short, mounted cannons, aiming out toward the sea. The solid perimeter of fire power left no blind spot, though Gideon was curious how they managed to steer a round vessel.

His question was partially answered as he looked up to see a black mast mounted to a massive, swiveling gear in the center of the deck. He took a moment to marvel at the mechanical ingenuity, noticing more steel gears at the base, connecting the swivel to a robust steering wheel made of hefty wood. On one side of the ship was a visible staircase leading below deck, and Gideon desperately wanted to go explore. Staring at the ship's grandeur had him all but drooling. There were paintings thematically covering most of the ship that looked similar to Viking-style dragons, with the exception of wings. They looked like giant serpents, each with one large, fish-like tail fin. They artistically complemented many facets of the ship. Gideon was in heaven.

"Bait Gideon," Sir Tereth's stout voice beckoned his attention. Gideon turned around to see Sir Tereth standing with the burlap sack in one hand and his sword in the other. "Welcome to the *Crimson Shadow*."

Gideon smiled. "This ship is amazing!" He wanted to throw his fists in the air, but the ropes kept them immobilized.

Tereth held his stare before nodding. "That she is. You show a peculiar admiration for a ship that possesses your demise."

Gideon looked from Tereth to everything going on around them. "Is it called the Crimson *Shadow* because of the sexy black on black design?"

Sir Tereth stood taller, obviously taking pride in what he was about to say. "All who challenge this ship meet their end sinking to the depths, drowning in their own blood. The last sight their dying eyes glimpse is the fading silhouette of this ship. The *Crimson Shadow* is their final moment before the abyss claims their souls—or the faihrgrreys claim their bodies."

"Holy badass." Gideon smiled. "What are faihr—" He rolled his tongue, trying to match Tereth's annunciation. "Faihrgrreys?"

Tereth's smile turned to sinister anticipation. "You'll see soon enough, Bait Gideon." He motioned to a couple of the men. Before Gideon could look to see what was being communicated, some of the knight-pirates grabbed him again and hoisted him into the air.

"*And* we're crowd surfing." He looked around as they carried him toward the edge of the ship. "I'm not a strong swimmer without my arms and legs, just so you know."

"You won't be swimming," one of the knights retorted. "It should feel more like flying."

"Release the feeding stick, men!" Sir Tereth delegated.

A knight untied a rope leading up to two massive spars that made up the primary structure of the mast. The larger of the two was made of a crude metal and had many horizontal poles with the sails attached. The smaller of the two spars was a long wooden rod with steel rings lining it every few feet. Gideon watched as the wooden one was lowered by ropes, hinging at the swiveling base. As it descended, its length became apparent, extending a good distance beyond the ship's railing.

Gideon was intrigued. "So, context clues suggest you're hanging me in front of some kind of fish that helps pull the *Crimson Shadow*, like a hot dog on a fishing pole in front of a fat guy on a treadmill?"

Sir Tereth raised an eyebrow at him. "I know not of the last part which you spoke, but you seem to have a basic understanding of what is to come."

"So, how does it normally work?"

"You wish to know about the functionality? Not to plead for your life?"

Gideon shrugged and smiled. "It's fascinating."

Sir Tereth looked tentatively from him, out toward the fully extended pole. "On a normal voyage, wild game is dangled at the end of the feeding stick." He pointed with his armored hand. "The faihrgrreys are chained to the ship and pull it in pursuit of the bait."

"And then, once you reach your destination, you give them the wild game, I'm assuming?"

"Yes. The island where we captured you, we sought the face of a man with three eyes, and new bait for the *Crimson Shadow*."

"A three-eyed man?" Gideon's eyebrows rose.

"A rock that resembles a man's face with three eyes. It had buried a clue beneath it."

"Wait. You're on a——a real life treasure hunt?" Gideon wiggled with excitement.

"We seek the legendary treasure of Yagūl."

"Oh, tell me the legend." Gideon leaned forward with twinkling eyes.

"You haven't heard of the—" Sir Tereth brought his head back and looked at Gideon through narrow eyes. "I ought not share details of our voyage with the bait. The captain would not approve."

"That makes sense." Gideon smiled. "Well, being as we're no longer on the island, it's safe to assume that you found the next clue to this treasure of Yagūl, right?"

Sir Tereth refrained from telling Gideon more, though he felt compelled to. He motioned to some men who were waiting for his command. They grabbed Gideon and walked him over to the base of the extended pole. As they wrapped more ropes around him and lifted him up, he glanced overboard at the waters to see these faihrgrrey creatures. There was nothing.

"Well boys, I hope this is a long voyage. I gotta get *one* of you to tell me this legend at some point before I become fifty shades of faihr*grrey*." He chuckled. "Let's get on with it."

Sir Tereth shook his head at Gideon's madness. "Pull!" At the command, the others slid Gideon's bound body out along the extended spar. It took a few heaves until they got him to the pole's end, dangling over the ocean.

Gideon looked down to see choppy waters a good ten feet beneath him. Though the spar was about as thick as a full grown aspen tree, it flexed and bowed, dipping him closer and farther from the temperamental waters. He was about twenty feet from the ship's edge, and powerless.

As he admired the cool blues and greens of the ocean, he saw something move beneath the surface—something large. It appeared and then vanished, but the glimpse looked like an enormous, grey snake, twisting and writhing in the depths. Gideon recognized what he'd seen painted on the ship. He looked around. There was no land in sight. He couldn't help wondering if Traveler had been shadowed during their jump. If so, there would be no leaving this new planet.

As if provoked by his thoughts, his yellow vial began slipping from his pocket, flirting with gravity. The ship's dipping and bowing shook it farther out, and Gideon's restraints prevented him from grabbing it. His fingers stretched, reaching for the rattling tube but they were too far away. He panicked. One rocking wave pushed the vial out and it fell, white pills vanishing into the choppy ocean.

Gideon froze, his eyes glued to the abyss, his medication swallowed by dark blue waves. They were the last he had and there was nowhere on this medieval new world to refill his prescription. If what Traveler had explained was true, then he didn't even need them anymore. He was healed. That didn't matter, though. Tears welled as Gideon said goodbye to part of himself sinking out of sight.

9

Gideon saw something as he stared into the waves. It swam near the surface again before disappearing. He leaned as far forward as the ropes would allow. He was anxious to see these faihrgrreys. The small, choppy waves were thick and dark, making it nearly impossible to see anything beneath. The ocean's secrets were its to keep.

Something red caught Gideon's eye, drawing his attention to his shoulder. His cut was bleeding through his shirt and dripping down the ropes. Blood was pooling at a dangling point, forming a droplet. Gideon stared at it, impatiently waiting for it to fall. The ship dipped and rose in the ocean, causing a few drops of red to break away. Gideon watched them fall to the ocean's surface in what looked like slow motion. They hit the water and disappeared. Gideon's eyes narrowed as he waited. He heard the groaning ship and smelled the array of salty mist and wood but didn't see anything.

Then the ocean's surface exploded as four monstrously large heads burst out of it. Gideon craned his neck as far back as he could. It was difficult to make out the details of the thrashing beasts. Their unrelenting aggression and violent screeches carried across the vast ocean, longing to feed on the bait's soft flesh. There was no clarity, just a frenzy of grey serpentine bodies and fangs. They were twice as long as any crocodile Gideon had ever seen and as thick as a horse's mid-section.

Gideon's pulse was racing, and his mouth hung open in awe of the terrifying denizens of the deep. As soon as all four of them caught Gideon in their sights, they unified in their efforts to rip him down, biting, chomping, screeching, and howling as they swam toward him, tugging against their chains. The ship began pulling forward as the faihrgrreys swarmed after him, straining to break free of their restraints.

As their frantic behavior became more uniform, eight more faihrgrreys burst out of the water and joined the struggle to get Gideon. All twelve pulled the *Crimson Shadow*, gaining speed as they hungrily roared.

Once he had the faihrgrreys' full attention, their tailfins working with all their strength to get to him, Gideon studied them. Their long, snake-like bodies were completely grey and smooth, making movement effortless. They twisted and squirmed beneath the water. Only their heads and last curve of their necks extended above the surface, arched up like cobras. Their faces reminded Gideon of orcas, simple and crude with rows of small, dagger-like teeth. The only variances in their snakelike bodies were powerful tailfins, propelling them forward and pulling the ship. Gideon stared into their black, soulless eyes and grinned.

"You must smell divine!" Sir Tereth shouted from the ship's railing. "You wouldn't even find time to pray to Grimleck if they had you. They'd tear your limbs away like bread in water." The ship's speed kept gaining, and a few of the men cheered at the long-awaited movement.

Gideon looked back with eyebrows raised. "They're huge!" He chuckled in amazement. "How often do they eat?"

"Oh," Tereth thought, "they feed on whatever swims by. But they only feed on their favorite delicacy, human flesh, on rare occasions. So, they're *very* excited for you!" He heartily laughed, trying to strike fear into Gideon.

84

Gideon skipped over Tereth's comment. "So, do you just catch them wild? Or do you raise them from baby sea monsters? How does it work?" It was difficult to yell above the roaring beasts.

"Do you—" Tereth stammered, unable to figure out why Gideon wasn't fazed. "Do you not have faihrgrreys in your America?"

"Heck no." Gideon looked back and forth between Tereth and the sea monsters. "I've seen some large anacondas in the Amazon, but these suckers are mammoth."

"They are quite daunting." Sir Tereth's voice trailed off. "You're truly unfamiliar with faihrgrrey raisings?"

Gideon shrugged to the best of his ability. "I've never even heard of them."

Sir Tereth stared at Gideon, mulling over the option to have an actual conversation. "When they're born, they're no larger than my arm." He held his arm out as a visual aid. "We have a lake we raise them in in the land we hail from." He stared at Gideon's eager eyes eating up every word. "We train them with food as they grow, slowly introducing them to chains around their bodies."

"They must grow fast." Gideon looked from Tereth's arm to the full-grown faihrgrreys in the water. "How often do trainers get eaten?"

"Ha!" Sir Tereth's outburst roused some confused glances from the others. "You could say they're always hiring! Though there aren't many applicants," he bellowed, laughing at his own joke.

"Yeah, I bet. So, do you just train them to pull ships, or do they do anything else? Any tricks?"

"We ride them for speed duels."

"Speed duels? What's a speed duel?"

"You haven't even heard of speed duels? America must be a boring land!"

Gideon chuckled, "Compared to this, for sure." He wiggled in the unyielding ropes, trying to get a little more comfortable dangling in front of twelve hungry mouths.

"Are you mad?" Sir Tereth asked.

"Huh?" Gideon turned his attention back to him.

"Are you mad? You do not fear death, even when it is inescapable."

Gideon grinned, "We're all going to die. If I end up dying here, being devoured by sea monsters on a pirate ship during a treasure hunt, well, that's a hell of a way to go!" He stared at Tereth with conviction. "Those who fear death are the mad ones. They fear something promised to us all. Doesn't make sense to fear the only truth."

"You give sound reason for man to live a warrior's life—bathed in blood with a smile on his face," Tereth retorted as Gideon's words resonated within him. "I like you, Bait Gideon. I will be sad to see you eaten."

Gideon puffed his bottom lip out and nodded. "Yeah, I'm sad I'll never get to see the treasure of Yagūl. You'd better at least tell me the legend before I go to Chomp City!"

Sir Tereth leaned over the ship's railing and looked at the hungry faihrgrreys as he contemplated sharing the story he'd been raised on. As he watched the storm of fangs, he shrugged and looked up.

"I suppose I don't find any harm in sharing the old story with a man who's going to die." He cleared his raspy throat. "Legend says that Yagūl was a—" His voice trailed off as he squinted into the distance. A sly smile appeared on his face. Gideon turned to follow his gaze. It took him a second to see what Tereth was looking at. A couple miles out was another ship. It didn't look like it was moving fast, but even just sitting there, it caused hysteria on the *Crimson Shadow*.

Sir Tereth stood tall and yelled, "Battle stations, vaquilemen! We've got an intruder in our waters!" As soon as his words left his lips, all the pirate-knights cheered at the action and ran around the ship, getting prepared. Some manned cannons, making sure they had enough cannon balls and torches. Others ran below deck to get armor, swords, and shields. A few men began climbing the mast like monkeys to drop more sails. All the while, Sir Tereth walked to the steering wheel and slowly turned it, aiming the mast and the feeding stick holding Gideon toward the new ship.

As Gideon felt the movement of being swung, he stared out at the other ship, vibrating with anticipation. He wasn't wanting a fight, but it was a fairy tale coming true for two pirate ships to encounter at sea. The faihrgrreys turned toward where Gideon hung, tilting the entire ship as they changed direction. Gideon listened to the susurrating sounds of the knight-pirates yelling and cursing threats across the waters at their enemy.

"You will sink by this day's end!"

"None survive the *Crimson Shadow*!"

"Prepare to be devoured by our faihrgrreys and forgotten by Grim-leck!"

"Our cannons will take off your heads!"

"We are *Crimson Shadow*! The depths hunger for your souls, and we will feed them!"

"Grimleck will not save you!"

One of the men waved his hands at the others. "Hold! They send an emissary."

Everyone looked closer and saw what the man was yelling about. A small boat was halfway between both ships, slowly rowing toward them.

Sir Tereth motioned to the men. "Bring the bait in. We wait for them here. Make them tire their arms a little more."

They smiled at his instruction and went to the post that Gideon's rope was secured to. They unbound it and began pulling him in with one strong heave after another. Gideon's body slowly slid with each jerk. The faihrgrreys frantically swarmed and chomped up out of the water, trying to get a bite as he passed over them. Their teeth missed by a few feet, but it did nothing to deter their efforts. Gideon squinted at the splashing water hitting his face.

Once they'd pulled him all the way back, the men left him bound to the base of the feeding stick and went back to their duties. The circular ship immediately began slowing, coming to a bobbing stop in the tumultuous ocean.

"Captain on deck!" Sir Tereth's booming voice grabbed the attention of all the working hands. Everyone turned and faced the stairwell. Gideon was eager to see what the captain would look like. Fast footsteps suddenly tore up the stairs as an old man with a long white beard burst on deck with the energy of an adolescent.

"Where are they?" The old man's raspy voice undersold his visible zeal. Gideon was surprised, and pleasantly so. The old captain was wrinkled and thin behind his fluffy beard, but his eyes and smile were vibrant. Clad in leather armor, baggy clothes pouring out from underneath, and a simple helmet, he ran to the edge of the ship and leaned over the rails. "Aha! There they are!"

Sir Tereth stepped up next to him, a head taller than the old man. "Captain, we brought the bait in, that they may tire reaching us."

"Brilliant." The energetic captain slid back and forth on the railing, impatiently wanting the action to begin. "Bring in the faihrgrreys. I don't want the beasts to end the fun before it begins." He playfully elbowed Tereth's hip.

Tereth nodded. "Yes, captain." He turned to the other men. "Bring in the faihrgrreys' chains!"

A couple men ran below deck. Gideon could still see the creatures swimming around at chain's length as he peered over the edge. He heard some wheels and gears turning below deck and, in turn, the faihrgrreys began disappearing beneath the water. He was fascinated by the technological ingenuity of the underdeveloped world. Just one of the countless variables in progress, he figured.

The ocean's surface returned to being simply choppy without the splashing of monsters. The men stood by their stations, many manning cannons, others preparing melee weapons, all waiting for their captain's orders. Gideon watched with a big smile on his face.

The captain leaned in toward Sir Tereth. "They clearly don't wish for a fight, or they would have brought their full ship to us." His old voice was worn, but it had prepubescent verve. Gideon was perfectly close for eavesdropping, and he was taking full advantage.

Tereth shook his head. "No. They want something. Sending an emissary suggests their ship is too slow to gamble on challenge."

"Agreed. They must be without a depth feeder."

"Or they have one with an empty box." They both laughed, quickly joined by the men in earshot. Gideon had no idea what was so funny or why, but he was enjoying their foreign banter.

"We seek no blood!" a loud voice shouted from the approaching boat. Everyone's attention turned to see them a few hundred feet away.

The *Crimson Shadow's* old captain leaned over the edge and yelled, "Who are you?"

"I am Sir Pin, first mate of the Ithálic. We saw your sails. You are *the* Captain Pyboo of the *Crimson Shadow*, yes?" As the boat drew closer, Gideon got a better look. There were three men, all dressed similarly to those on the *Crimson Shadow*. Two were rowing, while the one speaking stood tall.

The white bearded captain nodded vigorously. "Captain Pyboo I am. The *Crimson Shadow* we are. Do you come to admire our beauty?" He gave a large, fake smile, showing his crooked, yellow teeth as he sensuously posed.

"We do wish to gaze upon its magnificence," the man yelled.

"You should paint a picture. It would surely last longer," Captain Pyboo snorted back as he slapped the rail.

Gideon couldn't help laughing. "You've gotta be kidding me."

The man in the boat ignored the ridicule and continued, "We also hear Sir Bazik is a champion depth feeder."

"Oh, that he is. He's undefeated!"

"So we've heard tale." The man motioned toward the *Crimson Shadow*. "We assume you have more than enough faihrgrreys to pull your ship. *Our* depth feeder, Sir Pettesh, wishes to take one off your hands." The man's flattering tone changed to threatening.

Captain Pyboo brought his head back and blinked in surprise at the man's audacity. He smiled and looked up at Sir Tereth.

Tereth leaned over. "Do you wish to see Sir Bazik's box, buffoon?"

"No need," the man yelled back. "Rumor has it it's already full."

Captain Pyboo started laughing. "It won't close!" He kept his eyes on the little boat while motioning back to his men. "Sir Bazik!" One of the pirate-knights walked up next to Captain Pyboo and Sir Tereth. Gideon took a first impression. It was obvious that this pirate-knight cared about his armor, as it was more polished than the others. Captain Pyboo raised an eyebrow at him. "Bazik." He nodded down toward the little boat. "Sir Pin here thinks their depth feeder, Sir Pettesh—" he shrugged, spitting the name, "—can take one of our faihrgrreys."

Sir Bazik scoffed. "But your ship is so far away!" He all but laughed his words out. "By sending that child's bath toy of a boat, I assume that means your faihrgrreys have you at a syrup pace in the water. Sir Pettesh's box must be vacant. Might it be put to better use if you used it as an oar?"

The man in the boat nodded, undeterred. "*Two* faihrgrreys then. Or does our empty-boxed champion scare you?"

Sir Bazik glared at Sir Pin's brazen insolence. "How many faihrgrreys does your ship possess?"

"Two," Pin sneered. "We wager all we have. You don't possess even the confidence to wager a small portion of what you have. The rumors of your courage and skill must be false. Or perhaps you hide behind your slithering pets while you sleep at night, praying to Grimleck that they will save you from Yagūl!"

Sir Bazik scowled down at him. "Your challenge is accepted, fecal crust! But I demand the prize be larger." He squeezed his sword, wishing he could cut Pin down then and there. "The victor not only claims two faihrgrreys, but they also claim the loser as *bait* for their ship!"

Both Captain Pyboo and Sir Pin brought their heads back, shocked, even offended, by Bazik's demand.

Pin stammered, "You wish death upon the loser?"

"We are depth feeders, are we not? Let us not dance around the title. Not this time. Not now that your disrespectful words have wrought my wrath upon you *and* Sir Pettesh. Unless *your* courage is a façade, and it is *you* who fears *me*!"

10

The crew of the *Crimson Shadow* watched as Sir Tereth helped Sir Bazik into his speed-dueling armor. Every pirate-knight was humming an ominous tune that seemed to fill Sir Bazik with reverent purpose. The ceremonious armor was dark grey, unlike the regular chrome colored steel of the other breastplates and helmets. Additionally, they had brought up a box about ten feet long, and three feet wide. It looked to Gideon like a coffin.

The box was red, with a black faihrgrrey painted around it. It stood on end next to Sir Bazik as he prepared himself. Gideon watched with intense curiosity. He wished he wasn't tied up so he could help somehow. Instead, he turned and watched the emissary return to the *Ithálic*. Once Sir Bazik was fully armored, the humming stopped, leaving only the melody of choppy waters.

"Oh, it's about to go down," Gideon said to himself.

"What is going down, Bait Gideon?" Sir Tereth asked as he approached.

Gideon gave an acknowledging smile and used his head to motion overboard. "It's an American phrase meaning something exciting is about to happen."

Tereth stepped up next to him and slowly nodded as he followed Gideon's gaze to the *Ithálic*. "Then it certainly is about to go down—to the depths," he said in a gruff tone. "I'm interested in your bearing witness to speed dueling for the first time. And with this unprecedented wager, you are to witness a battle hitherto unheard of."

"Yeah, I'm hoping I've got a good view from here," Gideon said, getting amped up.

"I have never met a person who had not even heard of speed duels, let alone faihrgrreys. So, alas, it should be entertaining to simply witness your reaction."

"Oh, I'm excited," Gideon smiled. "So, how does a speed duel work?"

"Well," Tereth explained with animated hands. "Both depth feeders ride faihrgrreys at each other, and—"

"They *ride* those things?"

Tereth chuckled. "Oh, Bait Gideon, you are in for a vicious spectacle of combat. They cannot ride just any faihrgrrey. Only select faihrgrreys are trained for speed duels. If they rode an untrained beast, they'd be devoured before the taunting." He cleared his throat and pointed toward the waters. "Three times the depth feeders will ride at one another. Upon their first passing, the challenging depth feeder—Pettesh—will taunt their foe. Upon their second passing, the responding depth feeder—Bazik, who we know will emerge victorious—" he nodded at Gideon assuredly, "will then return a good taunting."

"They pass each other twice just to talk shit?" Gideon laughed.

"Shit? Speaking of fecal matter?"

"Uh, they just insult each other on the first two passes?"

"Yes." Sir Tereth looked at Gideon, surprised by his surprise. "You are not familiar with this tactic?"

"Oh, I'm familiar with it." Gideon smiled. "I just love that it's protocol for you scallywags." He shook his head as his smile grew. "Definitely not politically correct, and lemme tell ya, that's more refreshing than a cup of coffee."

Sir Tereth lowered his brow and blinked Gideon's ramblings away. "You have an odd way of speaking, Bait Gideon." He focused and motioned back out at the ocean. "On their *third* passing, ooh!" He shivered with anticipation. "That is when we behold glory. That is when it—goes down. They ride at each other with long poles beneath their underarms and aim to unfaihrgrrey the other!" He raised a fist, his blood pumping.

Gideon stared at him with his mouth halfway open. "Jousting? You're *jousting* at sea?" He jumped up and down as much as his binds allowed.

"Jousting?" Tereth tasted the unfamiliar word.

"It's, uh, it's what we call speed duels. Two knights ride on horses and try to knock each other off with lances."

"Interesting custom." Tereth thought about it. "What are lances?"

"They're what we call the long poles."

"Hmm, lances. Lances," Tereth tested the way it rolled off his tongue. "I like the word. Perhaps we should adopt that portion of your 'jousting,' as we have no official name for the poles."

Gideon smiled at him, "Ah, that would be so cool. This is all too cool."

"It is a little chilly this day, but I would not venture to say it is cool. Unimportant. Anyways, whoever arises victorious claims the faihrgrrey of the fallen, along with their lance." He winked at Gideon after using his word.

Gideon nodded back approvingly. "Is that what their boxes are filled with? The lances of those they've unhorsed? Er...unfaihrgrreyed?"

"Yes. And Bazik's box is full already," Tereth boasted. "We'll have to find somewhere to put Pettesh's." He stared out, a little more grimly. "And you may be in luck, being as Bazik is demanding Pettesh as bait in the end."

Gideon loved the pirate side of the knights. "If that ends up being the case, am I relieved from being your master baiter?"

Tereth shrugged. "I do not know if that will get you off so easy."

Gideon laughed at the joke he knew Tereth was unaware of making. "Doesn't matter. Should be interesting either way. I can't wait." He looked out at the water, urging the event to get a move on as he squirmed his nose. "I've got an itch on my nose. I don't suppose you'd be willing to scratch it for meager bait like myself?"

Tereth chuckled at Gideon's way of talking and raised his sleeved arm to Gideon's face. "It causes no harm." Gideon leaned forward and pressed his nose into Tereth's arm, wiggling it around until he was satisfied.

"So much better. Thank you, sir."

"Sir *Tereth*," Tereth clarified before pointing. "Bazik is ready." They both turned to watch.

Sir Bazik was riled up and huffing heavy breaths as he stepped to the railing. He grabbed a rope ladder and tossed it over, watching it unravel until the end splashed into the ocean. All of the *Crimson Shadow* watched with eager anticipation. Sir Bazik stood taller, regal, reveling in the event to come, motioning nonchalantly to the other pirate-knights.

"Loose N'reeuh!"

One man nodded with an aggressive laugh and ran below deck to do Sir Bazik's bidding.

Gideon looked out to the water and saw that the *Itbálic* had gotten closer, only a few hundred feet away. "Oh, there they are."

"They shall only come a little closer," Tereth explained. He leaned in and bounced his eyebrows. "Gotta make sure everyone can hear them— talking shit."

Gideon nodded with playful approval. "You said it perfectly."

"Ah, there's my beauty," Sir Bazik beamed with pride.

Everyone looked down to see a faihrgrrey bursting from the water. The giant serpent's head was all that stayed above the surface as its thick body slithered like a sidewinder through the ocean, circling the ship. It roared and screeched, shaking its wet face and chomping at nothing. Gideon marveled at the size of its mouth. It could easily fit a man's head inside with room to spare. Its nostrils flared as it smelled the air, sniffing for what it was trained to seek out. After a few laps around the ship, the carnivorous beast slowed by the ladder. It rolled and writhed through the water, displaying its sheen skin as it splashed and screamed. Finally, it came to a stop at the base of the rope ladder, growling as it waited, waving in the water.

Gideon raised his eyebrows. "I can't believe he's going to ride that sea monster."

"Oh, of course," Tereth said nonchalantly. "That is N'reeuh, Bazik's personal pet. He's trained her from a mere serpent, ridden her countless times through smooth waters and storms alike, and unfaihrgrreyed dozens of challengers from her back. He's undefeated on her, and all on the *Itbálic* know it to be true."

They watched as Bazik descended the ladder as coolly as he could amid the awkwardness of his heavy armor. It was obvious how prestigious of an event it was, as all his shipmates stared in awe. He stopped just above the surface and squatted down on the lowest dry rung. With one yell and an experienced leap, he landed on N'reeuh's back, a few feet behind her massive head. He situated himself, getting a good grip on the small fins running along her spine. Once he was positioned, he looked up.

"Ready!" he shouted with an outstretched hand. A pirate-knight dropped his lance. Everyone watched in awed silence as it twirled through the air. Bazik swung his arm around with dramatic flair and caught the lance's handle. The men cheered with demands for bloodshed. Bazik twirled the lance around his head and nodded to all aboard the *Crimson Shadow*.

Gideon was completely entranced by the spectacle of knights jousting on serpents in between pirate ships. He could barely contain himself, but the ropes were doing a great job of it. He leaned toward Tereth while staring at Bazik, parading back and forth in front of the ship.

"How often does this happen?"

Tereth glanced at Gideon and then back out. "Uh, it depends on the success of the depth feeder, Bait Gideon. The more successful the champion, the more sought after they are by ships of other lands." He pointed at the *Itbálic*. "That tattered ship treads in dangerous waters by challenging the *Crimson Shadow*. It has but two faihrgrreys, meaning they've traveled slowly to find us." He spat overboard. "Even should Sir Pettesh emerge victorious, their return voyage with four faihrgrreys would be a treacherous journey, and the original two faihrgrreys they exhausted on their hunt for us would likely perish before reaching their home shores."

"Then why do it at all?"

"Pride, Bait Gideon. Honor. As you know, blood is a reminder of life." His tone was serious. "The prestige of victory, be it in combat or speed duels, means more than air to our lungs, or food to our bellies." Loud cheering erupted in the distance from what sounded like an army. Tereth slapped the railing and yelled, "We begin!"

They both stared out, seeing Sir Pettesh riding a faihrgrrey toward them from the *Itbálic*. All the rival pirate-knights gathered around its railing, shouting for their champion.

At the sight, Sir Bazik aimed his lance upward and kicked his heel into N'reeuh's side. The faihrgrrey immediately focused and turned her snout toward the approaching challenger. With eerie movement, she slithered forward through the water like a tree-sized anaconda. Gideon was mesmerized by the way the depth feeders rode them, their bodies carried left, then right in the serpentine motion. He imagined it had to be much more difficult than riding a horse in a straight line.

Once both depth feeders were maybe one-hundred-or-so feet away from each other, they pulled back on their beast's fins, bringing them to a stop in the water. The jerky waves danced around the stillness of everyone's anticipation.

Gideon leaned toward Tereth and whispered, "What happens now?"

Tereth leaned in and whispered back, "The display of boxes. It's a ceremonious moment allowing each depth feeder to gaze upon each other's previous victories." Right on cue, they watched as one of the knights aboard the *Crimson Shadow* stepped up next to Bazik's box.

"Behold!" He unlocked and opened it. As the wooden flaps parted, a display of lances bound together gathered everyone's attention. There was a wide array of different colored lances from many unfaihrgrreyed champions. Bazik didn't acknowledge it, but rather stared directly at Pettesh.

Captain Pyboo pointed at Bazik's box as he leaned overboard, glaring with crazy eyes. "If it would please you, we will bring out his second box." Pettesh didn't flinch at Pyboo's taunt. He just sat on his faihrgrrey, maintaining his unwavering stare down with Bazik through their visors.

Everyone turned and watched a man aboard the *Ithálic* unlock Sir Pettesh's box. Gideon squinted, trying to see. As soon as the wooden flaps opened, all the men on the *Crimson Shadow* burst into laughter. It was empty.

Pyboo slapped the rail and waved his hand out. "Ha! Hahaha! You clearly wish to be put out of your misery. Get on with the duel! I am sad this will likely be over faster than my heart desires. I was praying to Grimleck for a worthy challenger—not target practice!"

At his instruction, a loud drum rang out from aboard the *Ithálic*. The deep, resonating echo signaled for Sir Bazik and Sir Pettesh to kick hard into their faihrgrreys. The massive beasts' tails propelled them forward with powerful, slithering motions. Waves trailed behind them, both depth feeders holding tight and aiming their lances ahead. The churning ocean bowed and sank as the two enormous creatures swam faster.

As the two serpents passed each other like rocketing sidewinders, their bodies all but slid against one another in perfect harmony. It looked like two S's fitting together as tightly as puzzle pieces, narrowly avoiding collision.

Sir Pettesh yelled, "I shall claim the great Bazik's dueling stick, and all shall see him sink!"

Heckling and booing rang out from the *Crimson Shadow*, while the *Ithálic* erupted with cheers and threatening cries.

Gideon shook within his ropes. "Oh my god, this is awesome!" Sir Tereth smiled. It reminded him of the first time he'd seen a speed duel. Gideon tried to point, shoving his nose outward like a finger. "Ooh! Here we go!"

They watched as the depth feeders charged each other again, their faihrgrreys roaring at the palpable tension. The waters flexed and bowed as they slithered faster, both men kicking their heels and yelling. With a ferocious rush, they glided at each other, almost crashing a second time.

Sir Bazik roared, "You will dangle as my bait before the day's end!"

Pettesh was unfazed, imperceptibly tossing a handful of something into Bazik's face as they passed. Powder rushed through Bazik's eye slots and into his eyes, flying up his nose and down his throat. He groaned and clawed at his helmet with his free hand as the serpentine motion jerked him side-to-side through the choppy waves. The faihrgrreys quickly reached their trained distance before turning around to charge a third time.

Gideon's eyes shot open. "Pettesh cheated! Did you see that? He threw something."

Sir Tereth stopped mid-cheer. "He did what?"

"He threw something! There's something in Bazik's eyes."

They watched Bazik struggling to aim his lance as they turned. Pettesh tucked his tightly under his arm, aiming it at Bazik as he launched forward. Bazik grunted, unable to see through tears and struggling to wedge his lance. With his vision damaged, he nearly fell off N'reeuh's side.

"See? He can't see," Gideon blurted out, wanting to physically point at the injustice.

Tereth squinted and looked closer, trying to focus amid the deafening cheers from both ships. He jerked up, standing tall and pointing to the speed duel.

"Pettesh is a cheat! Bazik has been blinded!"

It was too late. Before Tereth's words could reach anyone, the depth feeders sped past each other. *Crunch!* Pettesh's lance hit Bazik's breastplate dead center. Tears flowing, eyes stinging, Bazik flipped backward, tossing his lance as he fell headfirst into the waters. His body disappeared as choppy waves swallowed him.

Loud boos and cries of foul play erupted from the *Crimson Shadow*, while rejoicing could be heard from the *Ithálic*. Sir Pettesh took a victory lap, yelling as he held his lance high in the air. He rode around in front of the *Crimson Shadow* and pulled back, stopping close enough for them to hear him.

"Your champion sinks! I claim his dueling stick!"

Tereth all but jumped overboard as he roared back, "You filthy cheat! You lack honor! You lack honor!"

"Shall I fetch his body before the depths claim him?" Pettesh sourly spat.

"Do it now, you worthless worm," Captain Pyboo yelled, furious about needing him to.

Pettesh laughed before turning his faihrgrrey around. He rode to where Bazik sank and ushered his beast to go after him. His faihrgrrey obeyed, shooting its head underwater and diving down below. Pettesh took a deep breath and held tight as they submerged. All conversations and cursing went silent as they disappeared, leaving only swirling, dark water where they'd been.

Everybody tensely waited, praying for them to resurface. Finally, Pettesh's faihrgrrey burst up through the water, carrying Bazik in its jaws. Bazik gasped, gagging for air as water spilled from his armor. Pettesh took a deep breath and yelled victoriously as he snatched Bazik's floating lance from the ocean. He held both lances high, boasting his victory against the famed depth feeder.

"Loose one more faihrgrrey of your choosing that I may claim my prizes," Pettesh spat out. "And take your last look at your champion, for he dangles before the *Ithálic* this night!"

As everyone's blood boiled on the *Crimson Shadow*, Gideon couldn't help an outburst, "*I* challenge you, Sir Pettesh! I challenge you!"

11

Sir Pettesh turned in the water, looking up to the deck of the *Crimson Shadow*. "Who challenges me?"

"I do!" Gideon brazenly belted.

Everyone looked over at him and started laughing. It did nothing to dampen Gideon's glare at Sir Pettesh, who, when he saw who challenged him, also burst into sarcastic hilarity.

"Do not be absurd, bait," Pettesh yelled back. "I challenge only champions. You have nothing to offer my box." He turned to ride back to the *Ithálic*.

Sir Tereth backhanded Gideon's chest over the ropes. "What were you think—"

"I spit on your lack of honor," Gideon roared down at Pettesh. "Accept my challenge or be forever cursed, known for being afraid of *bait*! Pussy!"

Pettesh spun around in the water and stabbed Bazik's lance through the air at Captain Pyboo. "Silence your bait! He stains your ship by challenging me."

Pyboo stood still for a moment, stroking his long, ratty beard. After some deliberation, he looked from Pettesh to Gideon and back. He cleared his throat and walked over to Gideon.

"What experience have you with speed dueling before being captured? Many victories?"

"Today was his first day of even *hearing* of speed duels," Tereth's rough voice responded faster than Gideon could.

"What?" Pyboo leaned in. "Never have you seen a duel before this day, and you wish to participate against a depth feeder that unfaihrgrreyed *Sir Bazik*?"

"He cheated." Gideon ushered Pyboo to see the truth. "I'm pretty sure I can take him."

"Take him where?" Pyboo asked.

Gideon smirked. "To the depths," he said with a twinge of dramatic darkness.

The edges of Pyboo's mouth curved up, exposing multicolored teeth. "And what is your name, bait?"

"He is Bait Gideon," Tereth answered.

Pyboo got up close to Gideon's face to study him. "There is fire in his eyes." He leaned in closer. "Are you brave or merely crazy?"

Gideon thought about his answer for a moment. "A sane man can talk himself out of a courageous act. That's easy. And common. But a man *must* be crazy to answer bravery's call."

A grin crept onto Pyboo's wrinkled face. "Bait Gideon," he mulled the name over. "Bait no longer. Untie him."

Tereth blinked rapidly, unsure of what he'd just heard. "You're allowing this?"

"Yes, I'm intrigued, and I wish for more entertainment. Provide me with it." With that, Captain Pyboo stood as tall as his bowed back allowed and looked out to the ocean where Pettesh was impatiently waiting. "Do you accept the challenge, Sir Pettesh?"

Pettesh brought his head back and scoffed. "What? You—you can't—you're not truly considering an offer from bait?"

"Do. You. Accept?" Pyboo yelled in a patronizing tone. "The simplest of questions eludes you." The *Crimson Shadow* laughed.

Pettesh's smirk turned to an insulted glare. "You do not honestly dishonor *me* with a man who is not even a vaquilemun—let alone, a depth feeder."

Sir Bazik grunted from Pettesh's faihrgrrey's jaws. "You dishonored *me*, cheating—whore," he growled as he struggled to see or breathe, dipping in and out of the water.

Sir Pettesh glared up at the deck. "He has no training. He will likely fall from the beast's movement before I land even a blow."

Gideon shrugged as Tereth untied him. "I mean, if you can't handle it."

Pettesh grimaced. "What are the wages of this challenge?"

Pyboo motioned for Gideon to answer. "This is your doing. Make your offer."

Gideon nodded as he finally slipped his arms free of the ropes and rubbed them. "Well, if I win, we take all four faihrgrreys, we get Sir Bazik back, and you replace me as bait for the *Crimson Shadow*. Basically, same wager as before. But if you win, you get the faihrgrreys and two baits for the *Ithálic*." He pointed a thumb at himself as he tried to summon his inner pirate.

Pettesh shook his head and scoffed. "I accept your challenge, bait." With that, he kicked his heels and rode his faihrgrrey forward, bringing Sir Bazik's body to the base of the rope ladder. The sea monster splashed Bazik into the ocean. He grabbed the lowest rung, groaning as he pulled himself up.

Pettesh relished his pain for a moment and then turned around to prepare to kill Gideon.

Gideon stepped out of the last of the ropes and straightened his clothes. "All right. Let's do this." He walked toward the ladder. Sir Tereth put a hand on his chest.

"You must first put armor on."

"Nah." Gideon shook his head. "No armor for me. Let's just rock and roll. I get the gist of the joust. Give me a lance, I'll talk shit, he'll talk some

Old English shit, and then bam." He slapped his hands together. "We duel. Boom." He nodded. "Armor would just slow me down." Gideon turned to Pyboo, who was grinning at his energy. "What lance do I use?"

Pyboo pointed at Bazik's box. "Choose any dueling stick you wish, madman."

Gideon all but trotted over to the open box. "All right, all right, all right." His fingers danced through the air as he mulled over the options. A black lance with swirling blue and yellow paint caught his eye. "That'll work." He pulled it from the box.

Tereth stared at him wearily. "I advise you to dress yourself in armor. Should Pettesh land a blow, it will surely impale you without it."

"I'd better not let him hit me then, huh?" Gideon winked. He took a moment just in case he didn't survive. "Sir Tereth, I have truly enjoyed meeting you." His smile shrunk a little. "Should the last thing I see be the *Crimson Shadow*, I have a personal farewell: May death not find you sleeping." Before Sir Tereth could respond, Gideon carried the black lance over to the rope ladder and climbed down.

Pyboo stepped over beside Tereth. "I believe him to be mad."

"There is no question. He is without any doubt a madman."

"I like him." Pyboo smiled and walked to the ship's railing, where Bazik was recovering.

Tereth followed. "Never before have I beheld bait unafraid of death."

As Gideon descended the ladder, all the men aboard the *Itbálic* snickered and laughed at the unarmored man. Pettesh rocked back and forth on his faihrgrrey, exaggerating his guffaws. He tilted his helmet back and wiped some tears.

"What—what kind of joke is this?" He laughed and pointed at Gideon, who was waiting on the lowest rung. Gideon waved at him like an old friend.

Bazik coughed from on board and motioned down. "Who—is this man?"

Tereth shrugged. "He is—I do not know. Captain says he's a madman."

"Truly," Pyboo piped in. "In the experience of my years, madmen are most dangerous." He leaned forward. "And most entertaining!" He laughed maniacally and watched with dwindling patience.

Bazik stared. "How can he expect victory with no armor?"

Pyboo shrugged. "Perhaps he'll be impaled."

N'reeuh swam toward the rope ladder as she'd been trained to do. The enormous faihrgrrey stopped in front of Gideon, waving around in the waters, staring at him. She was visibly uneasy with the unfamiliar person waiting for her. Bazik was the only man she was trained by and comfortable with. She snapped at Gideon, chomping in the air as a warning for him not to come any closer. The loud smacking of her bites made Gideon lean back.

"Whoa, girl," he ushered, calmly waving his hands. It wasn't working. N'reeuh kept biting and groaning as her large body gently slithered back and forth like a sidewinder.

Pettesh shook his head. "The faihrgrrey will likely send him to the depths before I have the chance." The men aboard the *Ithálic* laughed.

Bazik leaned over the railing. "N'reeuh!" His voice immediately caught the beast's attention. She looked up and hissed. Bazik extended an open palm toward her. "N'reeuh, obey or die," he barked. The large faihrgrrey's tongue vibrated as its head lowered, still growling at Gideon. Bazik pointed to Gideon with his other hand. "Get on before she changes her mind."

Gideon gave a quick salute. "Yessir." He pushed off the *Crimson Shadow*, leaping from the ladder's rung. He landed with both legs on either side of N'reeuh's thick back. He grunted, trying not to show the pain from crushing his groin. Faihrgrreys were definitely firmer than horses. "Oh boy," he beamed under his breath. He could feel the raw power of the animal breathing beneath him as his feet dipped into the cool ocean. "I've got this. You're just a slimy horse." He prayed he was right. After all, horseback riding wasn't too difficult. He sighed. "All right, N'reeuh, let's be friends." He grabbed onto one her spinal fins. "I'm really tough meat. You wouldn't like me anyway." He chuckled some nerves away as his pants absorbed water up to his hips. "All right, here goes nothing."

He kicked his hiking boots into her sides. The trained faihrgrrey launched forward with a single whip from her powerful tailfins. Gideon held on tight, tilting backward as they lurched through the ocean. Pettesh laughed at his struggle.

Gideon did his best to stay atop the serpent as N'reeuh swam forward, her body slithering left and right. It was more difficult than he'd anticipated, and very different from horseback riding. Trying to keep the lance steady seemed like an impossible task. He couldn't help waving it through the air like a loose tooth.

"Less horse, more inner tubing." It clicked in his brain and he began shifting his weight to compensate for N'reeuh's abrupt side-to-side motions. As he began understanding the movement, N'reeuh swam into position, facing Sir Pettesh from a good distance away.

Gideon looked at his adversary and then from one ship to the other. "Well, I have no box. And I know this fool—" He pointed at Pettesh. "— only has one lance he doesn't deserve. So, let's skip the foreplay."

Pettesh shook his head and sighed before motioning up to Captain Pyboo. "Get on with it. I will make it as quick and free of pain as possible for your bait," he sneered.

Pyboo scratched his scraggly beard. "What an exciting afternoon."

Tereth nodded. "That it surely is."

"All right, you vagabonds—begin!" Pyboo yelled out to the *Ithálic*. *Boom!* The drum echoed over the ocean.

At the sound, both Pettesh and Gideon kicked their faihrgrreys. Water splashed, and the ships cheered. Both beasts instantly tucked their heads and rocketed toward one another. Gideon struggled to maintain his grip as the unfamiliar jolting demanded expertise. It was immediately harder than the gentle slither before. He knew N'reeuh could easily whip him off if she wanted to, but she stuck to her training. As both faihrgrreys swam toward each other, Pettesh aimed his lance upward as was custom.

Gideon followed in suit, struggling to keep his from shaking as he just tried to stay on N'reeuh's slippery back. They were about to pass each other, and it was Gideon's move. He was ready.

He leaned toward Pettesh and yelled, "You're nothing but a Bazik bitch!"

They whipped past each other, splashing up water in their wakes.

Puzzled, Pettesh glanced over his shoulder as Gideon rode away. "What?" He squinted amid the loud cheers from both ships. Pettesh barely paid attention to his faihrgrrey turning. Gideon's taunt didn't make any sense.

N'reeuh spun around in the water, preparing for the second charge, all but throwing Gideon with her powerfully nimble body. He held on tight with his legs and left hand, trying to simultaneously keep the lance up. It was proving to be quite the task, and he loved it. He was in the moment: his favorite place to be.

Gideon studied Pettesh in the few brief seconds he had. There was no powder in his hand this time, only a confidence in his eyes knowing he could easily defeat Gideon.

They charged each other a second time. It was a little dizzying to Gideon, trying to focus on where Pettesh was as they were both careened side-to-side, while at the same time racing toward each other. There were so many moving parts, so many variables. It only made it all the more exciting.

Whoosh! They almost collided, and Pettesh barely had time to throw out what was supposed to be his taunt.

"What is a 'bitch'?"

"You are!" Gideon yelled back as they stormed past each other and prepared for the final charge. Gideon knew he had no chance of out-jousting Sir Pettesh, so he had to add some Earthling flare. A risky idea flirted with him, and he only had a little faith in it. The worst that could happen would be dying while jousting on sea monsters, surrounding by knight-pirates. He shrugged as N'reeuh spun around and aimed them at Pettesh.

Both faihrgrreys sped toward each other. Gideon's pulse quickened as he loosely held his lance by his side rather than tuck it under his armpit. He smiled, barely prepared and yet overly ready.

Pettesh, on the other hand, expertly tucked his lance in his armpit, steadily aiming the long pole at Gideon's defenseless chest. He knew it could kill him, even impale him, and he was okay with either option.

The beasts swam toward each other with splashing ferocity to the chants from all hungry onlookers. Most of the men leaned over their rails to see what would happen to Gideon without armor. A few shielded their eyes, squeamish at the idea of impalement.

It was time. Mere seconds before they were about to collide, Gideon coiled back and hurled the lance forward, under-handing it at Pettesh's face like a javelin. Pettesh's eyes shot open. He jerked to the side, losing sight of Gideon as he narrowly avoided getting hit. As soon as it flew past him, he turned back to reengage, only to see Gideon airborne from N'reeuh's back. There was no time to react. Gideon poised himself mid-air, and with one swift motion, drop kicked Pettesh's chest with both feet. Pettesh dropped his lance as he flew backward, flipping into the ocean.

Gideon landed unevenly on Pettesh's faihrgrrey and quickly scrambled to grab on as he was whiplashed the other direction. His hands managed to catch a couple of its fins as his lower body flung off and splashed into the water. The violent side-to-side momentum threatened to throw him completely in. He grunted and pulled with slipping fingers, hoisting himself onto the faihrgrrey's back. It wasn't until he was securely straddling the beast that the roar of the *Crimson Shadow* reached his ears.

Pyboo's contemptuous laughter echoed as he pointed shamelessly at the other ship. "Grimleck pisses upon the Ithálic! Our madman bests your champion!"

12

The planet's sun kissed the horizon, promising rich golds and purples across the waters. The *Crimson Shadow* had left the *Ithálic* stranded without any faihrgrreys in the middle of the ocean. It was a harsh reality that Gideon had to adjust to, but to the pirate-knights, it was life. They hadn't, however, left all the men of the *Ithálic* to their fates. Pettesh was dangling as the new bait of the *Crimson Shadow*. He'd moaned and screamed, begging to be released from his binds. Once he'd started crying, he'd been gagged, and after hours of being ignored, he finally tired, staring hopelessly at the fangs hungering for him.

In the fading light, Pyboo stood on deck in the middle of his crew. He raised his arms. "Behold, our new champion!" He motioned to Gideon.

The men cheered and clapped, reliving the unparalleled speed duel.

Pyboo ushered for silence. "He began this day wandering an island alone. He became bait, surely doomed to be swallowed by teeth and waves." The men chuckled at the lighthearted fact. "And *then*!" Pyboo held a finger up, pausing for dramatic effect. "He saved Sir Bazik from the same fate, defeating the sinister cheat, Sir Pettesh—without any armor, no less!" He leaned forward, gasping as if he was hearing the story for the first time. The animated captain joined the men in boisterous cries.

Tereth and Bazik stood on either side of Gideon, lifting his hands into the air, victorious.

Tereth dropped Gideon's fist and slapped his back. "Bait no longer!" There was more cheering for Gideon, while others spat insults at Pettesh, hanging over the darkening ocean.

Pyboo motioned for silence again. "Let us take a vote!" He waited for them to quiet down. "What say you all, shall I cut him as a vaquilemun?"

Uproarious yells of support erupted at the idea. Gideon squinted as a few more stern pats to his back shoved him forward.

"Vaquilemun?"

Tereth stared in disbelief. "You have not even any *vaquilemen* in your city of America?" He heartily laughed. "We are all vaquilemen." He motioned around at the men. "Warriors of our city of Dragūm." The men shouted, sloshing mugs of what Gideon assumed to be their version of beer as they cheered with patriotic pride at the mention of their homeland.

"Oh, gotcha." Gideon smiled. "In America, we call you knights. Or, I mean, our warriors are called marines. Either way." He laughed and then abruptly stopped. "Wait. You wanna *knight* me?" His eyes widened as his smile grew.

Pyboo laughed at Gideon's odd manner of speaking. "You displayed courage." The men cheered. "Skill!" More cheering. "Unfaihrgrreyed your enemy!" Screams on the verge of frenzy. "And did it all without armor or training! Madman! Madman Gideon! *Sir* Gideon!" The ship exploded in yelling and screaming as more beer sloshed and the men chanted "Sir Gideon" into the evening air. Gideon, incredibly worked up, lifted a mug of beer that he was handed and yelled along with them.

"Sir Gideon! Sir Gideon! I love this!" he hollered into the sky, his voice drowned out by everyone else's. He wished he could go find Abraham and Tess on Earth to tell them that he *was* getting knighted after all.

The chanting went on until Captain Pyboo approached Gideon with a sword in either hand. He raised them into the air, closing his eyes as if waiting for the heavens to descend and join them. A hush fell over the ship.

Tereth leaned in next to Gideon's ear and whispered, "On your knees."

"Thanks," Gideon whispered back before dropping down. The *Crimson Shadow* was silent as Gideon waited, kneeling before Pyboo. After maintaining the dramatic pause, Pyboo opened his eyes and brought the swords down, placing their edges on either side of Gideon's neck.

"Grimleck, witness! Grimleck and all men here, bare witness! Gideon, this day, on behalf of our savage king in Dragūm, I ascend thee from bait to warrior, and from warrior to vaquilemun!" With that, he pulled both swords, drawing a thin line of blood on both sides of Gideon's neck. Gideon winced a little at the sting, flexing his jaw, but he maintained eye contact with Pyboo. Pyboo retracted the swords, and the loudest roar yet burst out from the crew.

Bazik yanked Gideon up by his arm and grabbed the back of his neck, roughly shaking him. "*Sir* Gideon, the mad speed dueling vaquilemun of the *Crimson Shadow*!" He cracked their foreheads together, holding them in place as he laughed wildly into Gideon's face. Gideon grabbed the back of Bazik's head and laughed back, enjoying the ridiculous ceremony as blood trickled down his collarbones. The other men swarmed him, punching his shoulders in congratulations and sharing more beers than he knew what to do with.

Sir Tereth looked Gideon up and down. "Now that you belong to the *Crimson Shadow*, we must remove your clothes of America and give you more suitable attire."

Gideon joined the crew below deck, finishing a feast in honor of his ascension. He was wearing baggy pants and a long-sleeved shirt that reminded him of a pirate costume. It was awkwardly sewn together in comparison to the clothes he was used to, and it was coarse and scratchy. Additionally, he'd been given a full suit of armor that had been stacked next to his sleeping quarters. He could select whatever he felt like donning in the morning. All his regular clothes had been tossed into a large iron fireplace below deck, where the vaquilemen were relaxing and sitting on pillows, boxes, and hammocks. The ship's rustic bowels reminded Gideon of cheap bachelor pads he'd rented back on Earth. The warm yellow glow of the fire shone brightly on their faces as they stared into its hypnotic flickers.

Gideon looked at Pyboo, who sat a few men down from him, smoking a pipe exactly how Gideon envisioned an old pirate captain should. He studied the old man, watching the way his crazed, old eyes gazed unblinkingly into the flames.

"Captain Pyboo." He broke the quiet of crackling embers. "Now that I am a vaquilemun, would you share Yagūl's legend with me?" he asked as politely as he could without begging cross-legged in front of him. The question roused excited murmurs about treasure and fears from the other men as they eagerly waited to hear the tale they'd been raised on.

Pyboo took a deep hit from his pipe and held it as he turned to meet eyes with Gideon. A sly smile graced his old face as he gently blew the smoke through his nose. Ever-so-subtly, he shifted and faced him, allowing the crackling fire to set the scene before he spoke.

"Once, before time began ebbing life away, legend says a powerful conjurer named Yagūl lived alone, shrouded in dark magic and mystery." Pyboo's normally energetic voice was hushed and haunted. "Somewhere in the vast oceans, he marinated in solitude on an island he'd conjured from the ocean's belly itself. He lived in a massive castle without any servants or friends. The castle's tallest tower was so high, that it was twice that of the tallest oak." Pyboo slowly waved his hand about, illustrating the grandeur. Gideon and the other vaquilemen listened, hanging on Pyboo's every word. "Though he was powerful—powerful enough to consume invading ships with flames from his eyes—he grew lonely. With no lover to share his powers with, his life became but for not." Pyboo adjusted in his seat. "So, Yagūl ventured across the waters in search of a woman to keep him warm for the rest of time. Some say he built a boat for his hunt, while others say he walked the waters on foot."

"A Jesus imposter." Gideon nodded.

"He found a kingdom on a distant isle and desired its princess the moment his eyes fell upon her. He transformed himself into a handsome gentleman and wooed her until her heart was his and her father agreed to their matrimony. The king sent a ship full of gold and jewels with his daughter when they ventured back to Yagūl's home."

"So far, it sounds like a fairytale," Gideon remarked.

"It darkens." Pyboo's eyes lowered. "Upon arrival, Yagūl's princely façade disappeared, and the princess saw him for who he truly was: a conjuring deceiver. She feared him, cursing his ugliness and deceit, refusing to be his bride." Pyboo cleared his throat and drew upon his pipe. As smoke poured from between his lips, he continued, "Yagūl was furious with the princess' betrayal, so he locked her away and horded her treasure."

Gideon nodded. "Princesses always be getting locked away."

"Yagūl's loneliness grew, knowing that the one woman that had grown to love him hated his true face. He ventured out again, taking to the waters until he found another distant land. Again, he wooed the land's princess under a disguise, and again he won her heart." Pyboo cleared his throat. "Again, he returned her to his home with riches from her land, and again, the princess cursed his appearance when the veil was lifted. Yagūl locked the second princess with the first, and his gathering treasure grew—along with his loneliness. His façade always vanished on his isle, so none could love him." Pyboo leaned forward. "For years and years, this repeated. Yagūl gathered countless princesses and countless ships full of treasure. Those who say he can walk on water, say that some nights he wanders across the ocean, standing outside of sleeping ships, cursing them with insanity and luring men to their deaths, drowning them with the songs of captive princesses."

One of the men shivered. "Keeps me up at night, thinking he could be standing in the blackness outside the *Crimson Shadow*." Some of the other men laughed at him.

"Yikes," Gideon remarked.

"As legend grew, ships began hunting for Yagūl, either to claim his amassed treasure or his amassed collection of princesses." A few of the men nodded at the thought of a harem, but Pyboo maintained stern eye contact with Gideon. "But every ship that has ventured out to find Yagūl's isle has never again been heard from."

Gideon smiled, growing restless. "That's exciting," he said in a low voice, as if not to allow the legendary Yagūl to hear him. "What makes you so confident to think you can survive going after him? I mean, if the stories are true."

"Oh, they're true," one of the men piped up.

Pyboo finally smiled. "I fear no man, vaquilemun or conjurer. I am Captain Pyboo, and we are *Crimson Shadow*," he threatened the words.

"We are *Crimson Shadow*," some of the men echoed with whispers, corralling their moral.

Gideon puffed out his bottom lip and nodded. "We are *Crimson Shadow*. So, what is the plan of attack if we find Yagūl's isle?"

Pyboo raised an eyebrow and nodded at the deck above. "Fire every cannon, put Yagūl out of his lonely misery, claim a princess for every man, and live lavishly on more riches than any of us can imagine!"

Gideon thought for a moment. Without Traveler, he was stuck on the barbaric planet and was going to have to adjust to the lifestyle. He patted some ash off his new clothes and nodded. "I like. So, what's our next move?"

Pyboo looked to his first mate. "Tereth?"

Tereth cleared his throat and exhaled some smoke from his own pipe. "The clue found beneath the three-eyed man foretells a map of the stars on the Isle of Beasts that will guide us to Yagūl."

"Ha," Pyboo spat his laugh out. "The clue is in the hands of monkeys."

"Monkeys?" Gideon asked, intrigued.

Tereth nodded. "The Isle of Beasts is a no-man's land, ruled by monkeys."

Gideon smiled. "Seriously? Like 'ooh ooh, aah aah' monkeys?"

"Yes. However, the monkeys on the Isle of Beasts love men due to the gifts men can provide, such as food and shiny trinkets. They love gifts from man to such great extent that they stockpile items to trade in preparation for any voyage that stops at their shores. They will bring sticks, rocks, and jewels if they find any, or anything they believe might be worthy of trade."

Gideon snickered, "That's absolutely bananas. So, the last clue might just be handed to us if we give them some meat?"

Pyboo nodded. "Good thing we have leftovers." Some of the men laughed.

Gideon smiled. "That's so cool." He chewed another bite. "What kind of meat was that, by the way?"

Tereth leaned toward him while staring into the dying fire. "Pettesh."

Gideon's eyes shot open. "What?!" He instantly had an odd feeling in his stomach.

Pyboo nodded. "Figured we'd beat the faihrgrreys to him. Besides, we can get new bait on the Isle of Beasts tomorrow."

"We ate Sir Pettesh?" Gideon gasped the words out, nauseated after stuffing his face so full.

"Oh, of course," one of the men blurted out. "We were considering eating you. Thank Grimleck he became bait and you became vaquilemun."

Gideon looked around with wide eyes. He could see some of the men trying to stifle laughter, their tight lips quivering. They were holding perfectly still, as to maintain their self-control. No one would look at him. His heart started slowing down as he smiled.

"Holy crap, I believed you!" They all erupted in laughter. Gideon slumped and started laughing himself. "Dear God."

Tereth wiped some tears from his eyes. "Oh, Sir Gideon, that was so good it was without price." They kept laughing, some doubling over. Tereth slapped Gideon's back. "We were just talking shit."

Gideon chuckled at Tereth's misuse of the term. "You got me good." He shook his head, unable to stop smiling. "So, what was it actually?"

"Oh, just a king boar we hunted earlier this day."

Gideon nodded. "That makes more sense." The men kept laughing at him.

Pyboo smiled a big, toothy grin before standing up and spitting on the dying fire. "All right men, rest your eyes, for on the morrow, we voyage to the Isle of Beasts."

13

The next morning, Gideon woke to the hustle of the crew yawing and grumbling through their pre-dawn tasks. Pettesh resumed groaning and wiggling, begging to be let down, and the men took turns waving at him as they passed by. He was their entertainment during the tedious sunrise chores.

Gideon had quickly gotten dressed, tossed on a random assortment of armor, and then joined in on the work. Before the planet's sun had even risen, he'd learned how to let the faihrgrreys' chains out so they could begin their heading, how to set the sails of the mast, prep cannon balls, clean the deck, and a few other remedial tasks, and they hadn't even had breakfast yet. He'd even managed a short sword-fighting lesson with Tereth before Pyboo sent them back to work. All in all, Sir Gideon was thoroughly enjoying his first official day as a vaquilemun.

Once all the morning preparations were in place and the sun was up, Gideon and Tereth stood at the ship's railing and stared out at the horizon ahead of them. Gideon closed his eyes and took a deep breath, inhaling as much of the sea air as his lungs could hold. He was a vaquilemun sailing an alien ocean, looking for treasure. He even had a sword, foreign and heavy as it may be. Life was going well. He didn't waste time wondering what would come next or stressing over the what-ifs of where he'd been. His journey had taken one very unexpected turn after another, and he was embracing it. More than anything else in that moment, he was just grateful for the translator. Being stuck on an alien world wouldn't be as magical with language barriers. He exhaled and looked out.

"Where is the Isle of Beasts?"

Tereth nodded out. "That is the Isle of Beasts." Gideon followed his gaze and stared out past the faihrgrreys and Pettesh. He saw it, far out in the ocean. On the edge of the horizon lay a series of islands. Gideon bit his lip and smiled.

"Arrrgghh, matey!" He lifted his fist toward the Isle of Beasts and elbowed Tereth excitedly.

Tereth chuckled. "Another American saying?"

Gideon nodded. "Something like that."

"Captain!" Tereth yelled. "She is on the horizon."

"Yes!" Pyboo's elated cry below deck may as well have been right next to them. His scurrying feet came scampering up the stairs until he was pressed against Tereth's side. "Oh, men." He leaned between them, placing his hands on their shoulders. "We close in on Yagūl this day."

The *Crimson Shadow* lowered its anchor a ways from the island's shoreline. Only a handful of vaquilemen stayed back with the ship, while the rest had taken smaller boats ashore. As they rowed with meat prepared for trade toward the Isle of Beasts, they could already hear the squawking and howling of monkeys among the cornucopia of trees. The humans been spotted, and that helped usher things along. They stared at the island makeup. It was dense and towering, looming, even, as they grew closer, spanning more than a mile, with high, forested mountains adding to the mystery of it all.

Gideon looked at Tereth. "What does this map of the stars look like?"

Tereth shrugged. "At this moment, your conjecture is as good as mine. We will scour the isle until it is found. Just pray that the monkeys have not already offered it for trade to any prior ship."

"Good point. I hadn't thought of that." Gideon stared at the island as they closed in on it, thinking over any kind of game plan. "It's too bad treasure maps and clues are never specific. It could be stones organized to resemble astronomical designs. It could be a piece of paper. Perhaps there's a crazy, old wizard who lives among the monkeys who will give us some poetic clue. I feel like it only ever gets more complicated."

Tereth and some of the other men chuckled at him. "Your mind is truly a wild place I wish never to visit." Tereth playfully elbowed him.

Gideon smiled. "Sometimes even I get lost in it."

"However, do not joke about wizards, Sir Gideon," Tereth said with a solemn tone. "They are not to be trifled with."

Their conversation was cut short as their boat came to a stop in the sand a few feet from the beach. At the scraping of the wood, the forest's squawking and howling grew louder. The other boats stopped next to them, and all the vaquilemen stepped out, splashing as they pulled their crafts ashore.

As they left the boats behind, monkeys ran out from behind the tree line with shrieks and grunts, leaping hysterically, waving their arms, random items shaking in their hands. Gideon was the only one smiling at them as they came running up, some on two short legs, others galloping on all fours. There were hundreds of them swarming from seemingly everywhere. It was impossible to communicate with the raucous clatter flocking the beach.

Gideon studied them, trying to see if there were any physiological differences between them and the monkeys of Earth. Sure enough, he recognized that, though they were pretty similar, they looked like the lesser developed monkeys he'd seen in museums and paintings. Their foreheads and eyebrow ridges protruded more than those of chimpanzees or any of the great apes he was familiar with. They were less humanistic and more animal. He smiled.

The wild simians surrounded them, hooting and yelling with aggressive excitement as they held out their trinkets like beggars bouncing up and down. Some began throwing their offerings at the men's feet as they yelled for food. Shiny rocks, uniquely shaped branches, shrubbery, roots, and even a few items from previous ships, such as gold and coins, landed on the ground in front of them. As more and more monkeys swarmed the beach and threw their gewgaws, the pile grew.

Some of the men laughed, enjoying the ease of receiving offerings from wild creatures, while others tentatively kept hands on their swords in case the monkeys attacked. They'd heard tales of men being killed and eaten after providing no food in return for the gifts.

The deafening sounds of wild shrieking only made Gideon's smile grow. He laughed at the absurdity of it all. He squatted down to get a better look at them as they continued adding gifts to the pile.

Tereth finally motioned to a couple of the men behind him. They tossed a few large bundles out toward the desperate animals. The monkeys moved out of the way, allowing the bags to hit the beach and spill open, pouring out loaves of bread and random chunks of meat and bone. An uproarious frenzy broke out as they began fighting for scraps; pulling, pushing, biting, and throwing each other for portions. The men laughed at the chaos. The monkeys that managed to grab a piece of bread or meat scurried away with their prize clutched tightly in their hairy hands, disappearing into the forest to eat.

Gideon slowly shook his head. "This is nuts."

"No, Sir Gideon, we brought only bread and crab," Tereth yelled over the screeching and yelling.

Gideon chuckled. "Well? Oh. Shall we pilfer through it all?"

Tereth nodded and motioned to the others to start going through the offerings. As the monkeys continued fighting over food, the vaquilemen began by tossing all the sticks and stones away, scaring some of the monkeys in the process. Gideon dropped down and helped, throwing most everything to the wayside. They sorted through it all swiftly, as it wasn't hard to discern bits of nature from actual items of worth. They collected all the familiar-looking offerings into a bag, finding coins, cups, a couple knives, hats, and a few more miscellaneous things the monkeys had taken from previous ships.

Tereth looked around and grunted. "No maps?" he asked as the sounds of monkeys slowly died down. The men shook their heads, double checking the sand around to make sure they weren't missing anything. Tereth sighed. "Then we must search the island ourselves. And now we've lost most of our bread," he grumbled.

Gideon popped his neck and looked around at the remaining monkeys scurrying away. "Is there anything dangerous here? Or just monkeys?"

"Oh, there exist beasts of danger on this isle. Keep your sword at the ready. Don't want you getting eaten on your first day as a vaquilemun."

Gideon fervently nodded. "That'd be such a waste of my awesome skills."

As they got ready to go exploring, a voice from the tree line caught their attention. "Is this the item you came here seeking?"

The vaquilemen all drew their swords at the surprise, looking to see who had yelled. They stared, poised and ready on the sunlit beach as a cloaked man with a hood, tall in stature, stepped out from behind the trees, walking past the remaining monkeys. Gideon and the vaquilemen waited without speaking, studying the approaching man. To their knowledge, there wasn't anyone inhabiting the island aside from the wildlife.

The man walked up, standing a safe distance away. With one motion, he lifted his hand and brushed his hood off his head. Gideon's eyebrows rose.

"Traveler?"

Tereth sheathed his sword and smiled with outstretched his arms. "Diviner!"

Gideon looked from Traveler to Tereth, perplexed. "Diviner?"

"A wizard. You were right." Tereth said as the other vaquilemen sheathed their swords. "The kindest diviner I've met."

Gideon squinted at Traveler as he approached them. "You don't say."

Tereth nodded. "I haven't knowledge of what he's doing *here*, but you will like him. I am sure of it." He stepped forward and clasped hands and forearms with Traveler. "Diviner, old friend, how are you?"

Traveler squeezed and smiled. "Sir Tereth, it has been too long." He stepped back and patted his shoulders. Gideon stayed behind, confused but curious. Traveler released Tereth and stepped toward Gideon with an outstretched hand. "Gideon."

Gideon slowly extended his hand back and shook Traveler's. "Hey, man. How ya been?" His tone trailed off. "And it's *Sir* Gideon now."

Tereth looked back and forth between them, dumbfounded. "You two have met?"

Traveler nodded. "Indeed. We've met." Without explaining further, he reached into his robe and pulled out a small beige cloth with markings on it. "I believe this is what you came here for." At the comment, Tereth and the other men crowded in, trying to see what it was. On the jagged cloth was a drawing of stars with arrows pointing toward a familiar constellation.

Tereth took it, studying it as he brought it close to his face. "Yes. How did you know we sought this item?"

Traveler raised an eyebrow. "Diviner, remember?"

Tereth nodded, humbled and mortified. "Of course. Of course. I apologize."

Gideon stared in amazement. Traveler had them eating out of his hand, and he had to know why. Tereth gave a self-assured smile to the men. "It is good fortune to have Diviner's *divine* powers working for our cause without even our knowledge. Grimleck must have guided him here."

Gideon's questions compounded as they continued going unanswered. Tereth stepped away, obsessively studying each marking on the cloth. His men followed and then leaned in, trying to see over his shoulder as he walked. They were perfectly distracted.

Traveler took the opportunity and leaned in next Gideon's ear. "I'm impressed. You're alive."

Gideon whispered quickly. "You—where did you—hmm." He brainstormed as the words stuck in his throat. "You sent me here, expecting me to get killed?"

"No." Traveler scoffed. "Expecting nothing. Prepared for anything. The second part of your being tested was seeing how you would fare in a dangerous and unknown land, unprepared."

Gideon cocked his head to the side. "That was a *test*? I thought you'd been shadowed on the jump here."

Traveler nodded. "That was the intended impression: for you to feel alone and have to fight for survival."

Gideon slowly shook his head, trying to wrap his mind around it all. "What the hell is it that I am being tested for?" There was a twinge of frustration in his voice, but still not the anger Traveler expected and even wanted to draw out. It just further intrigued him.

"I can't tell you that. Not yet. For now, you are simply required to trust me. There is more you must first understand before the bigger picture is revealed."

Gideon glanced over at Sir Tereth and the other vaquilemen. They were still studying the map, completely oblivious to their conversation. He cleared his throat and turned back.

"All right, well, assuming I agree to resume this adventure with you, what happens next?"

Traveler met his irritated tone with a confident smile. "Well, my original plan was to come aboard the *Crimson Shadow* and save you, should you even still be alive. Then we would leave this planet in search of the next recruit for our expedition."

Gideon gave a small smile back. "You really thought I'd be in trouble here, huh? That they'd kill me?"

Traveler nodded as he noticed the healing cuts on both sides of Gideon's neck, "Indeed. Though it appears that you've not only survived but have been initiated as a vaquilemun. That's impressive for a single day surrounded by—them." He looked to the vaquilemen. "Even by my standards. Especially after being sexually assaulted by a Neanderthal. How did you manage that?" He pointed at the scabbing cuts.

Gideon raised an eyebrow. "I started off as bait, then challenged one of their enemies to a speed duel and won."

Traveler brought his head back. "What? You speed dueled? On a faihrgrrey? And *won*? How were you not eaten?" His baffled whispers were sharp. Gideon nodded and shrugged, more interested in where Traveler had been. Traveler smiled. "I think you may be the best candidate for this expedition I've found in a long time."

Gideon chuckled under his breath. "Oh, how I've missed your shadowy ways of wording *everything*." He checked again to make sure the vaquilemen were still obsessing over the map. He turned back. "So, this next recruit. What person or kind of person are you looking for?"

"*We* are looking for a person with a mind as equally open as yours, but next we seek a spiritual leader."

Gideon smirked. "You're looking for an open-minded, religious person? That's a challenge in and of itself."

"I expect it will be. I have heard of one such man that we will go see." He reached his hand up and wrapped his fingers around an unseen beam of light. "Are you ready?"

"Hold up." Gideon reached forward and grabbed Traveler's wrist, pulling it down. "Hold on now." He almost glared. "You stranded me here, thinking I would get killed as a bizarre excuse for a test. I passed. With flying colors, I believe." Traveler nodded in agreement but was confused as to why Gideon was stopping him. Gideon leaned in. "If you want me to go any further with you, we finish what we started here. I want to conclude this hunt for Yagūl's treasure. Then and only then will I agree to jump to another planet. Otherwise, I'm perfectly content staying here as a vaquilemun of the *Crimson Shadow*."

Traveler flexed his jaw, a little perturbed by Gideon's stubbornness. "You are aware that I could simply take you with me, whether or not you consent?"

Gideon smiled, ready to play and challenge Traveler's reserve. "I think we're both smart enough to know that you're not going to do that. You need me, not only willing to go, but excited to be your guinea pig."

Traveler stared deep into Gideon's eyes, frustrated, but compelled to know more about him. "That is the unfortunate truth." He exhaled. "I agree to your terms. We join them until the treasure is found, and then we seek the next recruit. Yagūl's treasure may be your goal but the fourth phase is mine." They both slowly nodded in understanding of each other's position.

"Oh, it's mine, too," Gideon said before shaking his head. "Man, I really thought you were dead." He chuckled. "So, what's this planet called?"

Traveler looked around. "We call each planet the name its inhabitants give it. This one has been named Cul." His annunciation was quick and sharp.

"Cul. Cool name, I suppose."

Traveler smiled. "It's a fascinating planet. Have you figured out why their ships are round?"

"Nuh-uh."

"Look at the night sky tonight." Traveler pointed up. "They have nine moons. As I'm sure you can imagine, the simultaneous gravitational pulling on their tides from the multitude of moons causes all sorts of uneven and choppy waves. Early on in their civilizations, they built ships with similar shape to those of Earth's, but the waters toppled and sunk them all. This resulted in the design like the one you've been on."

"Hmm." Gideon thought. "That makes sense. That's pretty nuts actually. Science is a truly beautiful woman when you get to know her."

Traveler looked up and then back down at him. "Oh. And I put good use to my time while waiting to see how you would do here." He reached under his robe and grabbed something. "I went back to Earth and secured this for you in case you survived." He pulled out Gideon's backpack.

Gideon's eyes widened. "What? No way!" He smiled and took it, immediately opening it to look at all the trinkets inside he thought he'd lost. While Traveler looked up at the sky, Gideon slipped the Neanderthal rock and a random item from the beach into his bag.

Traveler looked down nodded. "All right, let's go get the vaquilemen moving."

As they turned to the men still gawking at the map, another monkey came running out of the forest, desperately screaming and flinging its arms. Everyone looked to see a large black predator bounding after it. The beast pounced on the monkey, snapping its neck with one swift bite. Gideon leaned forward and stared at the creature as it dragged the monkey's body back toward the forest. The carnivore was black and smooth, with a long head and small mouth, and humanoid arms and legs.

Gideon froze. "Wait. What the—" The predator looked eerily like the alien from the movie *Alien* that he'd been raised on. The longer he stared at it, the more it looked reminiscent. He looked closer. Even the way it fed was uncanny in its similarity. Something small kept shooting out from its mouth, protruding beyond its fangs, taking little bites from the monkey's carcass.

Gideon slowly turned and pointed at it while looking back and forth between the beast and Traveler. "Is that a, umm—"

Traveler watched the spectacle of nature as if it was nothing special before finally acknowledging Gideon's confusion. "Oh, right." He smiled. "I forgot the people of Earth made a movie about a distorted version of them."

"But—" Gideon stared at the creature. "—how did they know what it looked like?"

Traveler inhaled and looked at him. "Not everyone can handle this adventure, Gideon. Most don't even survive it. On one of my recruiting attempts, I recruited an artist from Earth—a visionary, I thought. You may have heard of him."

Gideon looked from Traveler to the vaquilemen, who were enjoying watching the carnivore drag the monkey away.

Traveler chuckled at a long-lost memory. "He passed the first test, and even survived the second here on Cul. But, by the time I got here, he'd lost much of his sanity." Traveler sighed at the memory. "It was all too much for him. I brought him back to Earth and returned him where I found him."

"What...?"

"Upon my next visit to Earth, the same visit when I ended up finding you, I do recall seeing that he'd ended up painting many of the things he'd witnessed during our short expedition together, and that your film industry had made these animals—" He pointed at the black creature disappearing into the forest. "—into horror movie monsters." He scoffed. "They're really quite nonviolent, actually. Well, when they're not hunting. They're just animals like your lions or bears."

"That's crazy." Gideon stared at the spot in the forest where it had dragged the monkey away.

"Indeed. It's phenomenal how a disturbed and misunderstood mind can create beauty through art."

Gideon smiled as the philosopher in Traveler emerged. "Often times the misunderstood are the way they are—quiet, mysterious, off-putting, crazy, or whatever—because they know something others don't. It's like the universe has given them a beautiful gift that no one can see, and the only way to share the impossible is through art, be it song, dance, painting."

Traveler's eyes lit up. "The misunderstood are the true pioneers, and the purest form of humanity."

Gideon raised an eyebrow. "To ever be fully understood would be a tragedy, as it would mean that there is nothing more to learn about you."

Traveler matched Gideon's smile, once again seeing the man he'd met atop Angel Falls. "One of the fundamental reasons I selected you as a candidate is that I don't understand you. I can relate to you in one way or another, but I don't understand why you are the way you are. I'm excited to see what kind of art you'll create during all of this."

Gideon maintained his smile. Though Traveler was unpredictable and dangerous, he knew he was, as well. There was a mutual understanding growing between them. Gideon chuckled and redirected the conversation back toward the beast that had disappeared.

"So, do they have acid spit?"

Traveler laughed. "No. No. No. That's nonsense."

"Of course. *That's* nonsense?" He scoffed. "What are they called?"

"Um, I forget. I believe they're called weavers or something like that."

Gideon nodded as he thought about everything. "So, I'm not the first you've recruited for this mystery job?"

"No, you are not. However, since most die, and those who don't typically lose their minds, you're currently the front-runner."

"You have other candidates right now?"

"I don't, but other colleagues of mine are recruiting throughout the universe. We are all working toward the same goal, and we need as many potential candidates as possible to ensure we have the best crew. Or at least *a* crew for the mission into the fourth phase."

Gideon marinated in all the information as he looked over to the vaquilemen. They appeared to be getting ready to head back to the *Crimson Shadow*, while respectively letting the two of them talk, uninterrupted.

"Well, Mr. Traveler, as seems to be consistent with our little talks, you have my full attention again."

Traveler smiled, finally having Gideon's interest back. "Good. I would be concerned if I didn't." He started walking, Gideon following close behind, slinging his backpack over his shoulder. "Now, let's go find some treasure," Traveler said, admitting to himself that he was looking forward to it.

14

That night all hands were on deck, staring at the stars. Captain Pyboo had the map in hand and hadn't stopped looking back and forth between it and the twinkling sky. Sir Tereth was standing directly behind him, ready to help and relay instructions. All other crewmembers stood around, quietly hosting their own conversations about excitement, treasure, and princesses. They kept their voices to themselves as to not disrupt Pyboo's navigation.

Gideon and Traveler leaned against the back railing as a chilly breeze whispered past them. Gideon was staring up with his mouth agape as he marveled at the four moons he could see. They lit up the night sky in a way he'd never seen back on Earth.

"It's almost as beautiful as the northern lights," he yearned.

Traveler smiled at Gideon and then looked up at what was old news to him. "Indeed. It's quite the spectacle. My planet has two moons. And it's a bit smaller, so we can usually see both."

"Really?" Gideon looked at him. "What's it called?"

"Whewliss." He pronounced the name with a little whistle at the beginning.

"Whewliss. That's pretty." Gideon mulled the name over. "Rolls off the tongue."

Traveler nodded. "It does in any language."

"So, is that part of how it works?" Gideon thought out loud. "Smaller planets go through phases a little quicker? Like exploring their globe goes faster, so they advance more rapidly?"

Traveler nodded. "Indeed. Large planets take a long time to reach the second phase. Their people spend lifetime after lifetime after lifetime exploring everything there is to explore. In turn, development advances at a slower pace."

"Hmm, the smaller the planet, the smarter the people."

Traveler chuckled. "Not always true, but more often than not, the smaller the planet, the more *advanced* the people." A couple of the faihrgrreys groaned as they continued swimming forward, desperately pulling the ship toward Pettesh. The sound reminded Gideon of a question he'd wanted to ask Traveler but forgot about since thinking he'd been shadowed.

"You said there were no aliens on other planets. So, explain faihrgrreys. And that monster on the Isle of Beasts."

Traveler stared at the stars. "Every planet begins with similar millions of species at the microscopic level at the infancy of habitability. Each species adapts uniquely on different planets based on a long list of variables, such as gravity, distance from their sun, ever changing ecosystems, developmental shifts, extinctions, you understand." Gideon nodded as Traveler spoke. "So, based on the necessity for survival, they grow and evolve in unique ways, different on every planet with diverse environments. As you will see with many of the human beings on planets we'll visit, the animal life is even more diverse and complex, with trillions of variations across the universe." The moonlight on his face added another layer of wonder to his explanation.

"Oh, man." Gideon stared up into the darkness, yearning to see every inhabited world in existence. "I want to visit other planets' zoos."

Traveler grinned. "There is an uninhabited world that was turned into a sanctuary for endangered species through a multi-planetary effort. It has since been named Animars."

"That's—amazing." Gideon buzzed. "Do we get to go there?"

"No," Traveler said. "It is strictly prohibited for humans to visit Animars. The only Animartian life is that of the ever-evolving animal kingdom."

"Animartians?" Gideon smiled in awe. "That's the coolest name for anything that's ever been. Why can't people go there?" he pleaded.

"You have enough common sense and experience to answer that on your own. The greatest threat to animals and ecosystems is humanity." He could see Gideon's agreeable expression of guilt. "We tranquilize the animals, send them to Animars the same way I sent you here, and that's the last of our role in preserving threatened species. Anything that happens to them there is for nature to dictate."

Gideon grinned warmly. "Your people sound super cool—like genuinely good-intentioned folks."

"We try to be. We even tried to repair some of our own wrongdoings by cloning salvaged DNA from extinct species whose extinction we had any hand in. Those clones were also sent to Animars."

"I can't wait to see your world." Gideon sighed disappointedly, knowing that begging wouldn't get him a one-way Animars ticket. "There's gotta be some crazy fantastic stuff out there."

Traveler smiled. "Probably the most accurate understatement." He shrugged. "And a good tagline for our adventure." They both smiled.

"Oh!" Gideon leaned closer as a question almost exploded out of his head. "If there are that many differences throughout all the galaxies, are there worlds where dinosaurs didn't die off and are still alive?" His whisper may as well have been a shout.

"Indeed. Many planets still have versions of what you consider prehistoric life, in fact."

"What?" Gideon's childlike eyes gleamed. "Where? Can we go to *that* one?" He was struggling to keep his voice down.

Traveler stared back with eyebrows raised. "Most of the planets where dinosaurs still live have them as their dominant species." He tilted his head forward. "I'll let you take as much time as you need to figure that one out."

Gideon smiled. "You're afraid to go there."

"Yes." Traveler nodded unashamedly. "Yes, I'm afraid of being eaten on a planet comprised of carnivorous wildlife the size of buildings." He laughed at Gideon's desperate expression. "I draw the line at dinosaur-run planets. They literally ate the platform for humanity to thrive."

Gideon squinted, unable to shake the desire. "New goal: Talk you into growing a pair so we can visit *Jurassic World* in 4D." He smiled at Traveler, who was sternly shaking his head. "Ah, come on, Spaceman. Don't you have fancy, futurey tech to keep us safe from places like that? Protective force field bubbles or something?"

Traveler smirked back. "Don't you Americans possess enough nuclear weapons to wipe the Middle East off the face of the Earth?" Gideon smiled at Traveler's choice of response. "Controversy always circles the ease of resolving conflict with absolute power. I could keep us safe on a planet with dinosaurs, but not without putting them and their natural order at risk." He paused, knowing what he was about to say would really light Gideon's imagination on fire. "Besides, any planet where dinosaurs have survived—if you think about it—has allowed them millions of years of evolutionary development. They're much smarter and more advanced than how you're picturing them."

Gideon's eyebrows lowered. "Get out of here. How smart?"

"Who knows?" Traveler nonchalantly dismissed. "My people have left well enough alone. We have bigger issues to deal with than wondering if dinosaurs have discovered fire or invented a massive wheel."

Gideon rolled his head around. "*Dude.* You're killing me," he groaned. "That's my favorite 'what if' you've thrown at me so far."

"I'm not even getting warmed up."

Before Traveler could continue teasing Gideon's fascination, they heard footsteps. Captain Pyboo and Sir Tereth approached. Pyboo gave a toothy nod toward Traveler.

"Diviner. Sir Gideon." They both nodded back. Pyboo sighed, obviously too excited to sleep. "How do you two know one another? We have been taking wagers. Some of the men believe you conjured Gideon into existence in order to create the maddest man alive." He scratched his scraggly beard. "I have placed bets on him being your descendant, though I cannot imagine you spending enough time with a maiden to create one." He laughed a raspy hoot. Gideon and Traveler looked at each other, waiting to see if the other would answer.

"He is my apprentice," Traveler said.

Pyboo and Tereth shot each other relieved glances before turning back. "Well," Pyboo smirked, "good thing we didn't feed him to the faihrgrreys."

Tereth fervently nodded. "I swear we did not harm him." Gideon smiled slyly, curious as to what their previous experiences with Traveler were that left them so afraid of disappointing him. Tereth cleared his throat. "Sir Gideon requested I do it." He begged Traveler to believe him. "Part of becoming a diviner, I imagine."

Traveler looked at Gideon. "You what? He what?"

"His shoulder." Tereth pointed. "He had me cut it—to make the darkness leave his eyes."

Pyboo shot Tereth a sharp glance. "You did not inform me of this." His normally friendly tone was sharp and fearful. He looked at Traveler. "I beg you, please do not put a curse on our voyage."

Traveler looked at Gideon's clothed shoulder, once again disturbed by the mutilation. "There will be no cursing." He looked at Gideon, remembering how uneasily cautious he was of him. "As you guessed, Sir Tereth, it assisted with Sir Gideon's—temperament."

Gideon's eyebrows rose. "Yes, and thank you for your assistance. Damn near surgical, my good sir." He winked, his tone unveiling no answers to Traveler's dark curiosity.

"Thank Grimleck." Pyboo exhaled in relief and backhanded Tereth. "We almost fed a wizard's apprentice to faihrgrreys." He shook his head and began laughing to ease his own fear.

Tereth shrugged defensively. "How was I to know?"

Traveler turned his head to them, his eyes lingering behind to stare at Gideon a moment longer. "Do not concern yourself over the matter."

"Oh, but of course." Pyboo raised his hands and eyebrows respectively. "We wish not to trifle in the matters of magic, especially not opposing *masters* of the craft." He motioned to Traveler. "I feel safer with you by our side as we hunt Yagūl."

Tereth nodded in full agreement. "Yes. Yes. Sir Gideon is quite the warrior, as well. You would have been proud of his dueling without armor. Though, as a diviner in training, I'm sure he did not even need its protection." His desperate flattery was more than apparent.

"Oh, please." Gideon waved the oversaturated compliment away. "Oh!" He perked up, suddenly sitting forward and grabbing his beloved backpack sitting next to his feet. Traveler, Pyboo, and Tereth all watched as Gideon opened it and rummaged around inside.

"Come on. Come on. I know you're in here somewhere," he muttered as random objects and items shifted and shuffled. Though the moonlight was bright, the inside of his backpack was pure blackness, so he was relying solely on his fingertips. "Aha." He removed his hand triumphantly. The other three leaned in a little, trying to see what he'd grabbed. Gideon smiled up at them with an outstretched hand. "I know we're going after a treasure much greater than this, but just in case we come up empty-handed, I want you to have something."

Pyboo reached over and grabbed a large round coin from Gideon's palm. "The markings are strange to me," he exclaimed as he admired it.

"It's an old gold coin from the Spanish Armada," Gideon said, reciting what he'd been told. "I think it's from the eighteen-hundreds, er... seventeen-hundreds. I don't know. I've never been good with history." He leaned forward and stared at the familiar item like an old friend. "I was in a place called Spain, running with the bulls." They all shot him a quick, unfamiliar look before turning back to the coin. "I befriended a local at the start. Her name was Abrienda. She said her name meant 'opening,' which turned out to be funny—but not funny—but funny. She went by Abby."

They intently listened to his weirdly worded story while evaluating the unfamiliar coin.

"So, it starts and we're running from the bulls. It's hard to explain how liberating and terrifying it is." He chuckled. "Have any of you ever seen bulls?" They all nodded. Gideon smiled, relieved that they at least had somewhat similar animals. It made the story easier to tell. "It's this bizarre event where tons of people run through narrow streets with angry bulls—like lots of bulls—all trying to mow the people down. It's crazy. I swear the hairs on the back of my neck were standing so tall that they all but jumped off my skin and ran for their own safety." He chuckled. "Anyway, at the end of the race, I'd luckily made it unscathed, without any horns up my ass. However, I turned back to see how Abby had fared. Turns out, she'd been gored. Big ol' hole, or *opening*, right in the middle of her stomach. One of the bulls had got her good." His expression turned sincere. "So, I'm first to her side, and I'm holding her hand while she starts talking about how she's sure she's a goner. It was pretty intense." Gideon cleared his throat. "As she's expecting to take her last breath, she grabs that coin and hands it to me. Says it was her good luck charm throughout her entire life—that she got it from her dad as a little girl. She said that even though the luck had obviously worn off, she wanted me to have it since she was going to die. Then ambulances came and took her away."

He sat for a moment, reliving the memory.

"Anyway, a couple weeks later, I received a postcard from her. Apparently she had survived, so the whole thing was a bit dramatic. Her luck charm had worked after all." His smile returned. "Figure you guys might have better luck during this whole venture if you have Abby's coin."

Pyboo and Tereth glanced at him with confused expressions and then returned to looking at the gold coin. Tereth gawked at it as if it was priceless.

"I have no idea what a postcard or an, um, amba lamps is. But to be able to survive an impalement to the stomach due to a coin—*that* magic we certainly welcome. The markings are so strange and detailed."

Traveler studied the interaction, quickly assessing that Gideon probably handed out items from his bag frequently. He was beyond curious about Gideon's background, between his reckless bravery, his mysterious need to mutilate himself, and how well he managed to fit in with new peoples.

"Captain!" one of the men nervously yelled out.

Pyboo pocketed the Spanish coin and turned to his post. "What?" he snapped, a little annoyed to be taken away from the conversation. The crew lined the ship's front railing, blocking the view of whatever had their attention.

Tereth, being the tallest, managed to see over them. "What sorcery is this?"

"What?" Gideon stood up, his attention piqued. As the *Crimson Shadow* continued forward, the mystery grew closer. They were approaching a thick fog covering the ocean. It looked like a dense cloud was sitting on the water's surface, spanning for miles. They were still a ways from it, but it shrouded anything within it. The fog wasn't moving or blowing in any direction. It was sitting still, as if it belonged there. A hush fell over the men as they all stared, a few of them trembling. Gideon could feel the uneasiness in the air as lifetimes of legends and superstitions swept through the crew. Ghost stories of lost ships, sea monsters, and dark magic played at the front of the vaquilemen's imaginations.

One of the men stepped back and glanced helplessly at Pyboo. "Captain, shall we steer around? Find another route to Yagūl's Isle?"

Pyboo squinted, slowly lifting the cloth map up. He studied it and then stared up at the stars. He did it one last time to verify his own fears. After a lengthy inhale, he let his breath out through tight lips and stared ahead.

"We brave the fog. According to the map, Yagūl's Isle resides within it." The men's shoulders tensed, their hearts sinking and palms sweating.

The night immediately felt colder as death's promise crept up their spines. Pyboo and Tereth walked to the front of the ship, once again leaving Traveler and Gideon to themselves.

Gideon immediately leaned in next to Traveler. "All right, science master, explain."

Traveler tried not to grin. "Did they tell you the legend of Yagūl?"

"Yup."

"Do you want me to ruin the magic with science?"

"Hmm." Gideon hadn't thought about it. "I guess not. Let me enjoy it a bit longer before you take away the fear of the unknown." He smiled back. "Is there a scientific explanation for the fog, though? Or is this just straight up pirate spookiness?"

Traveler tried to keep his chuckle under his breath as to not frighten the vaquilemen any more than they already were. "There could be a somewhat dormant volcano somewhere within that emits gas and steam, there could be geysers, or we could just have the dumb luck of a descended cloud gracing us for *spooky* effect."

"Gotcha." Gideon looked up at the fog as they approached. "So, do you know what we're going to find in there?"

"You mean aside from Yagūl walking on water, luring us out to our deaths, using the eclectic songs of kidnapped princesses?"

"Sounds like Greek mythology," Gideon observed. "But, yes, aside from a Jesus Christ impersonator, what else *lives* in the fog?" he asked with scary eyes, as if telling a campfire story.

Traveler shrugged. "I'm not sure. I've never traveled there before. It never served any of our purposes."

"How exciting." Gideon's eyes lit up. "Somewhere *you've* never been. Wait. So, how'd you get the map?"

"Get it?" Traveler looked down at him disappointedly. "I drew it. I travel between *planets* and have technology beyond these people's comprehension. You don't think I have the capability of checking the geography, finding out where this legendary island is located, and drawing a map?"

"Oh." Gideon finally took the time to notice that the inside of Traveler's robe was the same material and color as the cloth the map was drawn on. He looked at the bottom of the tunic and saw that a piece had been torn off. "Does it ever get exhausting being the smartest man in the room?"

Traveler smiled. "Just wait until you see Whewliss. Then I won't seem like the smartest man in the room anymore."

"Huh," Gideon thought, once again fascinated. "So, is there anything dangerous in the fog? Or just another deserted island?"

Traveler's face straightened, his tone turning sincere. "Prepare yourself for anything on this primal planet. I have no information as to what potential dangers exist within the fog." As his words left his mouth, the *Crimson Shadow* soundlessly crept into the outskirts of the dense white mist, thick wisps engulfing the ship.

"Hold the course, men." Pyboo's jittery command was met with silence as the *Crimson Shadow* was swallowed by the soupy fog, light tufts of white swirling behind where it entered.

15

The voyage into the fog went by with tension so palpable that Gideon could all but chew it. He had no idea how much time had passed. There were no phones, watches, clocks, or any familiar tools; only medieval mysticism. The vaquilemen were eerily silent, keeping their ears alert for the faintest of sounds. Their eyes were practically useless, as the fog only gave them starving glances of anything. Claustrophobia rattled their sanities. At several points, the white was so thick that they couldn't even see each other standing a couple feet away. Deep groans and echoing creeks quietly snuck out from the ship's wood and mast, escaping over the unseen waters.

Blind minutes crawled by like hours as the only movement was the slow breeze breathing through the deck. Sir Pettesh had gone quiet, feeling even more alone at the end of the feeding stick than normal. He was afraid to beg for his life, terrified that Yagūl would hear him and devour his flesh right off his bones before the vaquilemen even knew what had happened. Even the faihrgrreys swam forward in silence. It was as if the normally noisy beasts could sense horrors around them that no one could see.

Gideon, still leaning against the back while the crew huddled together, whispered in Traveler's ear. "I don't suppose your cool eye-doohickey can see through all this fog?"

Traveler scoffed. "My optical implants are capable of seeing across the entire universe, technologically efficient at forecasting billions of lightyears of distance filled with incalculable moving parts, and precise enough to help coordinate bodies moving at amplified light speed safely from one planet to another. But, no, I can't see through the fog. I can look up and get a map of the galaxies projected into my eye, but if I look out into the waters, I see white. Same as you." They chuckled at the silly handicap. "Most of Whewliss' implants are powered by light. In the darkness, my optical barely helps, and thick clouds scramble the light."

"You sound like my last iPhone. It was so smart, with the coolest apps and capabilities, but I remember a time when I had full battery and no service." Gideon shook his head. "Got me in trouble with some cartel fellas. Oh, Miguel." He smiled at the memory. "At least you can get us out of here if we get in too big of a pickle, right?"

Traveler nodded even though Gideon couldn't see him. "Indeed. As long as I have enough time to prepare and a break in the cloud."

"Well." Gideon gently patted Traveler's back. "Here's to the gamble." He sighed. "And hey, I forgot to mention when I could see it, but that robe is very becoming on you, *Mr. Diviner*."

"Thank you," Traveler said, enjoying the light conversation among the otherwise petrified shipmates.

"Do you go by different names everywhere you go?"

"Eh." Traveler shrugged. "I let people call me by whatever they know me as."

"You classy broad, you," Gideon tittered.

"So." Traveler's tone shifted. "When are you going to explain your shoulder to me?"

Gideon paused before answering. "You know—I—I still don't know if any of this is real. I could have crashed into the Venezuelan jungle, and this is the crazy coma dream that my mind concocted." He chuckled but Traveler didn't. It was easy to feel how uncomfortable the unaddressed elephant in the room was making him. "I don't want to wake up if this is a dream. Telling you the story behind my scar would jar me awake in a cold sweat, screaming." Gideon sighed. "Listen, I get that my need for it comes off as psychotic—maybe even threatening. It's something I never thought I'd have to endure twice but I need it. I *need* it." He cleared his throat as some unwanted emotions tried to venture through his veins. "I assure you it's not a danger. It will never hinder our adventure. It's just a scar that—I need."

Traveler considered how to respond. "I don't wish to pry so hard that it backfires, and you ultimately shut me out altogether, but may I instead ask one of my favorite questions?"

"A what if question?"

"Yes, a what if question."

"I think I know this one," Gideon ventured. "Lemme guess. What if we go to a new planet where I arrive without the scar, and I don't cut myself?"

Traveler nodded. "With psychic powers like that, I might make a diviner out of you after all."

Gideon feigned a smile as he contemplated one of the few topics he didn't enjoy. "Well...I...I..." The discomfort was more than apparent in his whisper. "I get angry. It's like, hmm." His hands tried to express what his words couldn't, pantomiming squeezing through his skull. "It's like there's this darkness that—I—I don't care about anyone or what happens to anyone. I feel...manipulative, and I want to—to free the darkness and let it control me. I want to hurt people." He almost growled the last part out. He grabbed his left shoulder, feeling a twinge of pain from the cut. It immediately made him slump as a deep exhale poured from his lips.

"Hmm." Traveler was inexplicably concerned. "Well, I may not be allowed to know what happened to you, but I greatly admire the man it's helped shape you into." He stared at Gideon, though he could barely see him. "In fact—and don't tell anyone—but I'm jealous of the freedom it's given you."

Gideon forced a smile and nodded back. "Sorry. I don't mean to dampen the mood with the skeletons in my closet—especially since these bastards believe in reanimated skeletons. But, like I said, it'll never be a problem that affects you. It's just something that I need to do for myself."

"Unless it puts me or our mission in jeopardy, I will not push the issue, nor send you back to Earth." Traveler squinted, wanting to see whatever expression was on Gideon's face. "But, if you ever want to talk about it, I'd be *very* interested in just listening. I wouldn't even respond if you wouldn't want me to," he assured. "Your backstory has become one of the two things I'm dying to know more about."

"Well, I'm flattered." Gideon returned to his normal self. "I'm guessing the other is this mysterious fourth phase?"

"Indeed." Traveler's tone was backed by a maelstrom of concerns.

Gideon pined for some sort of light-shedding hint. "It's not venturing into death, is it? Like what's on the other side?"

"I honestly don't know. It could be."

Gideon leaned close enough to see Traveler's face in the dense white wisps. "Hold the phone, Mr." He studied Traveler's evocatively unsure expression. "Is the fourth phase the afterlife? It'd make sense."

"No. No. No." Traveler stumbled through his response. "It's not that. It's, uh, it's not death, but it could be. I don't know." He couldn't formulate a coherent sentence to accurately depict what it was that he didn't know.

"Wow," Gideon remarked as he brought his head back, his eyes set on Traveler's ghostly silhouette. "You know more about everything than anyone I've ever heard of. Like, Einstein could take a class from you. In fact, I'm sure he would have loved to. Did you ever meet him?"

"Actually, yes, I—"

"Sorry. I'm rabbit trailing right off topic. You really know nothing about something you're training me for? How does that work? How can you effectively prepare me for something you don't even know how to prepare me for?"

Traveler held perfectly still, as if he had been anticipating the question. "Why did I send you to this planet, Gideon?"

Gideon situated himself, aware that the question was a test. "You said you sent me here to see how I would fare in a dangerous and unknown land, unprepared." He recalled Traveler's exact words, slinking back a little as it made a smidgen more sense. "You wanted me to adapt, improvise, and survive. You're Miyagi-ing me."

"I'm what?"

"Training me while I'm oblivious to the training taking place."

Traveler nodded. "I'm preparing and training you as best as I can guess will be most helpful."

"You're a man who has spent his entire life as a student of light," Gideon said. "But what you've been training for—training every potential recruit for—the greatest adventure you have ever heard of, is all just a stab in the *dark*?" He was amused by his play on words, but curiously hesitant about what it implied. His breathing quickened, his heart beginning to race as a realization dawned on him. "Your people found something, didn't they?" Through the whiteness, he could see Traveler's eyes twinge with fear at the question. "Something they weren't supposed to find." Gideon was unaware of the haunting tone his own voice was taking on. He waited, mulling his questions over. He could see sweat beading on Traveler's forehead, and then he was gone in the fog again. "And you don't even know what it is." He clasped his fingers together. "Oh my, my, my, Traveler. You, sir, have me till death do us part now."

Traveler quickly composed himself, clearing his throat and adjusting his collar to allow his skin to breathe. "Indeed. Now we just need to find more minds as eager and open as yours."

"Right. Right. Right." Gideon leaned in, shifting back and forth as his brain raced with questions and theories. "You say we need a holy man or something next, right?"

"Yes."

"Who else? How many are you supposed to collect?"

"Three. An open-minded, athletic individual without fear: you. I know it's specific, but it's required. You will spearhead the expedition. We need an open-minded individual who is also a leader in spirituality, so they can pray to whatever entity or entities might exist, should that prove to be necessary. And lastly, we need an open-minded individual well versed in all aspects of scientific study and practice. Together, the recruits will explore, study until they understand, and ultimately, document all of their findings to return to Whewliss."

"Why not you?" Gideon scoffed at the obvious answer. "You're king philosopher, after all. You're better versed in science than probably most everyone else in the universe." He smirked. "That's fun to say."

"No," Traveler said deadpan. "I will find another. Or another of my people will assemble a team before me."

Gideon tilted his head. "All right, so *what if* you train three of us beyond your expectations, ready for damn near anything, and then once we go to wherever this mystery is, we discover we've been trained the wrong way and we're completely unprepared for what's in store?"

"I don't have much of an educated response for that," Traveler admitted. "You could be fine. You could die. You're going of your own free will. You can back out at any point. All who are recruited and survive their testing are free to quit if the fourth phase scares them away."

"Mmm." Gideon shook his head. "I suppose I'd better just focus on Yagūl for now, because this is going to consume me."

Right on cue, one of the vaquilemen's voices interrupted their conversation. "Captain Pyboo!"

Gideon and Traveler jumped to their feet and joined the other men blindly walking forward and feeling around as they made their way to the front of the ship. Pyboo's signature scampering bound across the deck without concern for his lack of sight.

"What do you see?" his raspy voice begged.

"Captain," Tereth's normally booming voice whispered. "Directly ahead of us."

Gideon and Traveler reached the others, who were crowding the rail. The fog lightly parted as they crept forth through the still waters. Only then did it become barely visible. They squinted, straining their eyes. They were slowly floating past an island, not fifty feet away. Barely discernable amidst the soupy fog was a massive silhouette: a castle. They all looked around for the most obvious clue. The tallest turret they could make out was at least twice as tall as the surrounding trees.

Pyboo's eyes peeled open as his breath escaped him. "Yagūl."

A chilling breeze moaned through the treetops, seeming to come from the castle. They meticulously studied their limited view of it, scanning for signs of life. If a squirrel had scurried through a tree, they would have responded with cannon fire. As they stared, ominous silhouettes of sunken ships extended their burnt remnants above the water's surface. The men's already quivering spines grew weaker at the sight, passing by sunken ship after sunken ship. All their predecessors were dead.

Tereth, visibly trembling, stared wide-eyed at the burnt wreckages. "Captain, what is our course of action?" The other men shot glances toward Pyboo, waiting to see what he'd say. They would have been perfectly fine turning around and fleeing with their tails tucked, but they knew Pyboo too well for that.

Pyboo took a deep breath and let it out as he began nodding. "I am *the* Captain Pyboo. You are the crew of the *Crimson Shadow*, vaquilemen of Dragūm," he sneered, getting himself amped up. "We are not a measly ship of women." His speech demanded that his men find their courage. They all squirmed and adjusted, trying not to be the scared one of the bunch. Pyboo turned his glare from his crew to the daunting castle.

"Prepare every cannon ball we have. We rain steel upon Yagūl this day and claim his gold and princesses for ourselves."

16

After quietly reeling in the faihrgrreys and rolling up the mast, the vaquilemen stood behind the cannons, aimed at the castle. The morning sun crested, giving the smothering fog an eerie glow. The *Crimson Shadow* sat dead in the water, blending in with the graveyard of ships around them. The fog wasn't letting up, with thick gusts of white playing peekaboo with the castle. All the men nervously waited, anxiously dreading Pyboo's command. There weren't any visible enemies, but they could feel a presence watching them. The castle could have very well been empty, or perhaps filled with every sinister horror they'd feared since childhood.

As Pyboo stared at the castle, preparing to give the order, Gideon saw something. A light orange glow from one of the shorter turrets flared up, barely noticeable in the fog. Then it was gone. Gideon pointed.

"Did you guys see that?" His question made everyone scour the visible parts of the castle, trying to see whatever he did.

"What do you see?" Tereth sharply whispered. They all stared where they saw Gideon pointing. Gideon strained his eyes, wondering if he'd seen anything at all.

"I thought I saw—" An orange glow appeared on the same turret. It got larger. Or closer. They couldn't tell. But then, before they could make sense of it, the glow tore through the fog, suddenly becoming two flames flying at them.

"Arrows!" Tereth yelled, shattering the quiet and causing everyone to duck. Both arrows flew high over their heads and stuck deep into the mast's main spar. They looked up to see flames begin devouring up the wood.

Pyboo boiled up with a violent cocktail of fear and rage. "Fire the cannons! Fire all the cannons!" The men reacted like an explosion, scrambling to their feet and scurrying to the cannons as more orange glows appeared and caught flame to the ship. They grabbed torches and set cannon after cannon off. *Boom! Boom! Boom!*

Smoke filled the air, already thick with yelling, and yellow and orange fog. In the panic-ridden madness, the cannons fired without being aimed, randomly hitting the castle's outer walls or missing altogether in the water. Three more flaming arrows flew in from the sky. One ignited the deck, another deflected off some armor, and the third sunk deep in a vaquilemun's neck. The man's shirt caught fire as he gurgled.

Pyboo's indiscernible shouts were muted by cannon fire as two more men dropped from raining arrows.

"Abandon ship!" Gideon screamed. "The *Crimson Shadow* burns! Abandon ship!" Without waiting for anyone else, he grabbed Sir Tereth and dove overboard. Traveler was the only one to heed his advice. He dove after them while the rest of the vaquilemen stayed aboard, manning their stations, firing back. *Boom! Boom!* Gideon, Tereth, and Traveler couldn't hear themselves hit the water amidst the deafening blasts, which muffled beneath the surface.

Cold. Wet. Dark.

They emerged, bursting out of the water for fresh breaths.

Tereth immediately turned and roared at Gideon. "What are you doing?"

"The ship is on fire," Gideon said quietly, hoping not to draw attention to them as they swam ashore. "If you want to win this fight, it won't be from the ship. They need to storm the castle with their swords or they're going to burn."

Tereth looked around and realized he was right. They reached the mossy shore and crawled, as to hopefully stay out of sight.

"Look." Traveler pointed up toward the same turret. Gideon and Tereth followed his gaze to see a barely visible silhouette ducking and peaking up, continuing to fire flaming arrows down at the *Crimson Shadow*.

Gideon's eyes darted around. "Do you see anyone else?" Traveler and Tereth shook their heads as they, too, searched for any more warriors guarding the island. They only saw the silhouetted archer.

"Fire all cannons at the turret!" Pyboo's echoing voice could be heard mere seconds before two of the cannons aimed up and fired. Fog swirled and smoke bellowed behind the blasts. Just as they exploded into the turret, shattering rock and dust through the air, the archer leapt off. The shadowy silhouette sprouted wings midair and coasted down. As the archer disappeared into the fog-shrouded castle, it howled an animalistic cry, echoing through the mist. Gideon's eyes widened even more as he shot a finger forward.

"What the hell? Did you see that?" He turned and looked at Traveler, whose jaw was hanging open. Gideon nudged him, demanding he respond. "He grew wings! *Wings!* Did you see that?"

Tereth was in shock. "It's—it's—" The words clogged in his trembling throat. "It's Yagūl! It's him. He-he can *fly*. He's even more powerful than the legends say." His normally booming voice was shrill and high, his genitals in the grip of the myth. He cowered, struggling to stand, let alone storm the castle.

Traveler searched for any more movement. "That doesn't make sense."

All the cannon fire and screaming died down as everyone stood still. They'd all seen it. The archer had flown down, literally sprouting wings mid-air.

Tereth yelled, "Captain Pyboo!" His foolish outcry made Gideon roll his eyes at giving their position away. Pyboo and the remaining vaquilemen slowly peered overboard and stared down through the fog. Tereth waved, trying to make himself visible. "We must storm the castle!" Pyboo and the men looked around at the burning ship.

"Untie Pettesh." Pyboo pointed at the only man close enough to see clearly. "We need every sword we have if we are to survive this day." The man ran off to obey as Pyboo motioned around the heated fog. "Overboard, men. We charge the castle to drive our swords through Yagūl's heart."

"Captain." The Vaquilemun's voice shook as he returned. "An arrow burned through Pettesh's ropes. He fell to the faihrgrreys."

Pyboo narrowed his eyes. "Yagūl's fire found its marks. Our ship burns and our bait is eaten. Yagūl wishes we never leave this place— that it become our grave." He snorted through his thick mustache. "Will we surrender to such a fate?"

"No!" the men shouted in unison.

Pyboo nodded. "Fire the last of the cannon balls! Then we charge!" Some of the men used their briefly inspired goose bumps to obey, screaming with the explosions. Loud cracks and blasts rang out as the cannon balls smashed into the stone walls, tearing out chunks and breaking bricks apart.

Gideon, Tereth, and Traveler shielded themselves from falling debris. The stronghold was withstanding the assault surprisingly well, but holes were beginning to compromise a couple turrets. Traveler pulled Gideon close and yelled into his ear.

"I may be able to get us out of here! But we need to get farther away from the castle!"

Gideon nodded. "Okay! Let's do—" His eyes widened. Traveler followed his gaze and jumped back. The archer was flying down from another turret much closer to them, firing arrows at the men still aboard the *Crimson Shadow*. Again, they watched as the cloaked warrior was carried by actual wings. The same eerie howl echoed through the fog as it coasted down. The warrior was heading straight for them, its silhouette growing darker as it closed in from the murky sky. Gideon grabbed Tereth and Traveler and yanked them up to run.

"Come on! Let's—"

Ting! An arrow glanced off his breastplate.

"Holy—!"

Another arrow whizzed by him, finding its mark in Traveler's calf. Traveler grunted, crumpling to a knee. Gideon lurched after him. "Traveler!"

"Come to me, dark conjurer!" Tereth yelled as he unsheathed his swords to face the archer.

Two arrows glanced off his armor. Tereth squinted through the thick fog as the warrior emerged, swooping down and kicking him in the head. Tereth stumbled, dropping a sword and falling to his back. He roared and scrambled to his feet, only to find the warrior had already vanished in the whiteness.

"Sir Tereth!" Pyboo's familiar voice spun him around to see a handful of remaining vaquilemen gathered. Tereth wiped some sweat from his eyes and pointed toward the castle.

"He flew down! He *flew*! He got away before I could cut him the dirt."

Pyboo nodded. "Let us give chase. Yagūl dies this day!" At the captain's command, two men hoisted Gideon up and shoved him forward. They all yelled with drawn weapons and charged. Gideon struggled against their shoving to get back to Traveler, but it was no use.

"Gideon!" Traveler yelled more out of frustration than pain. "Gideon!" He ground his teeth, acting fast as he grabbed the arrow sticking out of his calf. After a quick breath, he flexed his jaw and pulled. It slid out smoothly, followed by a red stream. Traveler winced but wasted no time as he reached into his pocket and pulled out the same small, metallic rod he'd used to implant Gideon's translator. He firmly pressed one end against the wound and pushed a different button. A bright fizzle made him yelp as the tool instantly cauterized the bleeding hole. He exhaled sharply before pocketing the rod and trying to stand. He fell to the ground and groaned. After a few deep breaths, he tried again.

Gideon and the vaquilemen ran through the fog until they reached tall, front double doors. The fog was thinner nearer the fortress, and the large wooden doors were open. They could see inside, but they stopped, hesitantly scoping out as much as their limited sight would allow. A hollow-sounding howl screeched along the chill wind as they saw nothing within the entry way. There were no decorations, no statues, no paintings, no people—nothing but an empty, dirt courtyard. The ghost of a room had the remaining vaquilemen huddled together with swords drawn. They knew Yagūl was somewhere within, waiting for them, taunting them, hunting them as they hunted him.

Gideon was overcoming his own fears by focusing on the fascinating individual holding off an entire ship. He was concerned about Traveler but had to weigh priorities. He was sure the advanced Spaceman could probably fend for himself while they faced the daunting warrior. At least he hoped.

Pyboo took a couple steps forward, trembling as he held his sword toward the entryway. "Do not fear, mighty vaquilemen. This is our destiny. He is but one man, wizard or not, demon or not—he is only one."

The men exchanged nervous glances, trying to muster the nerve to follow Pyboo's obsessive determination farther into death's domain.

Then, as if summoned by Pyboo's words, the demon warrior appeared at the far end of the courtyard; the fog dissipated enough to reveal him waiting for them. They all froze. The warrior was facing them with four swords drawn.

Gideon jerked his head back. "What?" No one heard his rhetorical question.

The cryptic fog gave them brief glimpses at the demon. The warrior was clad in a brown hooded cloak with a black cloth draped around his face, and there was some kind of winged creature wrapped around him.

The men's fear-ridden eyes quickly studied the warrior and the animal holding onto his back, realizing the beast had six long arms.

Gideon saw it being about the size of a chimpanzee, and it was piggybacking the archer. He thought its face and limbs resembled that of a massive sloth, and attached to its longer front two arms, were wing-like flaps of skin similar to those of flying squirrels. Its arms, belly, and face were fuzzy, but its back was covered in armored scales that reminded Gideon of an armadillo.

Its top and bottom limbs were wreathed around the archer like belts, but its middle arms wielded the second pair of swords. The creature held them about sternum high on the warrior, mirroring his motions.

The warrior spoke.

"Leave or be buried here."

The woman's smoky voice was low and fierce.

The men all perked up, standing a little taller with puzzled expressions. They slowly turned and looked at each other as their trembling stopped. Pyboo scoffed and then chuckled amid the otherwise haunting silence of the courtyard.

"Ha! Ha-ha!" He sneered. "A woman?" He laughed harder, stabbing his sword into the ground and leaning against it as he keeled over. "We feared a *woman*! What fools were we! Ha-ha!"

The vaquilemen slowly began chuckling, still a little wary of their newfound foe. It snowballed into laughter as the warrior stood statuesque, unwavering, unintimidated, unafraid. The animal wrapped around her back growled at the invaders, baring its baboon-like fangs.

Gideon was the only one who took a couple steps backward, waiting to see how it was going to play out. He wasn't smiling, laughing, mocking, or saying anything at all. He kept creeping backward. He could sense the trouble they were bringing upon themselves, like rabbits oblivious to a fox.

Pyboo tried to get control of his laughter as it hurt his sides. "Oh, Grimleck! Ha-ha! There is no Yagūl here." He motioned to his men. "Slay the woman, and then we shall scour for treasure."

Three of the remaining vaquilemen gripped their swords and charged forward. There was no more fear or hesitance. They were ready for the easy kill, roaring and swinging their blades overhead.

The warrior waited, her pet roaring, deep vibrational growls seething from its mouth as the men swung their swords. With quick reflexes, the woman lifted her blades, glancing two away as the creature blocked the third. The warrior tilted, brushing the swords away, ducking, and pivoting before the men could re-engage so the creature could stab deep into one of their thighs. The warrior spun with the grace of a dancer, slicing both blades across another's stomach. The creature barked as both men fell, screaming. The third man's eyes shot open. He hoisted his sword and chopped down. The women squatted, crossing both of her swords above her, catching his as the creature plunged its second blade into his chest.

Pyboo gasped as his men collapsed before him.

Sir Bazik stepped forward, drawing his sword as all mockery melted away. "I will slay you this day, witch." He was the only vaquilemun covered head-to-toe in armor.

The woman put her swords away, followed by the creature sheathing its. She grabbed the bow from her back and reached up, pulling an arrow from the quiver strapped between her and her pet. All in the same swift motion, she loaded and drew the arrow, aiming it directly at Bazik's chest.

"Leave my isle," her unyielding tone growled.

Bazik smiled. "May you find great entertainment in her death, captain."

Pyboo patted his shoulder pads. "Do not make it too quick. I wish for something amusing."

Bazik nodded. "Yes, captain."

As he took one step forward, the warrior loosed her arrow. *Ting!* It bounced off Bazik's breastplate, making the men laugh.

"You shan't kill me so easy." He took another step forward, savoring the anticipation. He opened his arms, making himself a broader target for her to humiliate herself.

The warrior reached back and leafed through her quiver until she found a heavier, metal arrow. With another swift motion, she loaded and drew it back as far as her arms would pull. The men laughed at her having learned nothing. She pulled back farther and farther until her arms shook. Bazik took another step forward, scowling through his visor.

"Take your best shot, *woman*."

"Cooby," the warrior said. At her command, the creature resituated around her. It quickly placed one of its paws over her hand on the bow, while another of its clawed hands helped her pull the draw string. With their combined strength, they got an extra few inches, pulling the bow near a breaking point.

"Now," she said with cool confidence.

Whoosh! Crack! Everyone turned to see Bazik pinned against stone wall behind them with the arrow feather-deep in his chest. He grunted as his head dropped.

Gideon gasped, "Oh, shit."

The creature drew its swords as the warrior held both of hers toward the vaquilemen. "Surrender your desire for our holy treasure, or shall I bury you."

Pyboo trembled as he looked around to see who was left. His heart sunk as he counted Gideon, Tereth, one other vaquilemun, and himself. He gulped his crippling fear down and turned back to face the warrior.

"A blade for each of your throats," she threatened. "Run."

Her words were received.

Pyboo shakily held his sword at her. "Retreat to—to the—the *Crimson Shadow*." His crumbling words fell out of his mouth like dry crumbs. They turned and ran without hesitation, but Gideon didn't budge. He stood, staring at the woman, still holding blades at them.

Tereth glanced over his shoulder as he fled. "Sir Gideon, run!" His words didn't even reach Gideon's ears. He looked at Pyboo. "Why doesn't he flea? He will surely die!"

Pyboo looked at Tereth with all the confidence he could muster as his old legs scrambled. "He is either bewitched, or he stays behind to face her. Diviner versus witch."

"Truly the most fearless man I have ever encountered."

"That he is. We will sing songs of his madness till his return to us, hero or ghost."

The three of them ran back through the fog, the bright yellow glow in the sky guiding them to their burning ship.

Traveler hobbled through the whiteness, finally reaching the entryway where Gideon stood. He quickly assessed the situation, seeing that the woman had every intention of killing them.

Gideon dropped his swords and lifted his hands. "I surrender," he said, enthralled. "We mean you no harm, but I totally get it if you wanna kill us." He couldn't help grinning. "But I must know: What is your name?"

The warrior stood silent, obviously trying to decide whether to kill Gideon. She didn't move. All four swords remained pointed at him. After prolonged tension, she responded without lowering her blades.

"I am Dumakleiza Yagūl, last of the Yagūlamites."

Gideon rolled the name around in his mouth, "Dumb-uh-clay—"

"*Doom*-uh-clay-zuh," she said with stern stiffness.

Traveler whispered, "Gideon, we should go."

Gideon ushered him to be quiet. "That's a beautiful name. What's that thing on your back? Your pet?"

Dumakleiza held her swords a little tighter as she studied Gideon through the black wraps around her face. "You should run while I still allow it."

Traveler nodded from behind the doorway. "She's right. Let's go."

Gideon took a slow step toward her with hands lifted higher, slowly spinning to show that he had no hidden weapons. "I'm not here to hurt you. I swear it on my life. Kill me if you must, but I just gotta meet you."

Dumakleiza held her position, confused. "Provide me any reason why I should not skewer you where you stand and leave you as a sacrifice to Grim."

As they held their standoff, Dumakleiza's creature cooed and dropped its swords. It scurried down her body like a monkey descending a tree. Dumakleiza furled her brows as it leapt away and scampered toward Gideon.

"Cooby." Dumakleiza barked. "Cooby!"

Cooby ignored her and edged closer to Gideon, sniffing the air curiously as it strolled on all six feet. It didn't appear threatened by his scent, unlike with the vaquilemen. Gideon's eyebrows rose as he watched the peculiar creature approach him on a multitude of monkey paws. It moved like a giant, adorable spider, all six legs moving simultaneously.

"Hi there, Cooby," he said warmly, a little worried that Dumakleiza would lunge at him. He slowly squatted down and extended his hand like he would toward a new dog.

Traveler clenched fistfuls of his cloak. "Gideon, what are you doing?" He wanted to grab him and leave the planet, but in the fog, that was going to be a difficult task.

Cooby stopped a few inches shy of Gideon's hand, tentatively sniffing. It took a small scooch forward and licked Gideon's fingers. It cooed again, seemingly pleased and ready to play.

Dumakleiza slowly lowered her swords. "Who are you?"

17

Gideon and Traveler stared out of a window in the castle's main hall. Dumakleiza stood a couple windows down, peering through her black cloth at the two intruders. They watched as the yellow glow of the *Crimson Shadow* disappeared through the fog. Pyboo's eccentric voice echoed across the waters.

"Hurry, before that witch burns down the rest of the ship. And grab a bucket. Put out that fire!"

"Captain," Tereth could be heard hushing him in the fog. "Keep quiet, for she may be listening."

"Oh, please," Pyboo snorted back. "That mad witch cannot hear our words out here." His voice turned to a mocking tone. "I dare ye to fly out here, you feeble woman." Even with the boasting threat, he timidly kept his voice down.

Gideon chuckled, picturing Pyboo shaking his hips like a sassy six-year-old, taunting Dumakleiza. He turned toward her. "You could literally hear everything we were saying before we even got here, couldn't you?" She slowly nodded while keeping a wary eye on him. Gideon smiled. "The acoustics just send voices right to you. Great tactical advantage over intruding ships." He stared out, seeing the *Crimson Shadow*'s glow completely gone, leaving only whiteness. "I wonder what they're using as bait to get away."

"One of their fallen," Dumakleiza unsympathetically said. "I can see the body on the feeding stick."

Gideon clicked his tongue. "Oh." He knew there was no way she could see in the fog but assumed she was right.

Her glare remained unwavering. "Who are you two, and why have you come to my family's isle?"

Gideon and Traveler looked at each other. There wasn't an obvious answer. They took a moment to look around while they mulled over responses. The great hall had a few tables without any decoration or food. The walls were barren, just grey stone with limited light shining through the arched window wells. Amidst the depressing emptiness of the high-ceilinged hall, Gideon and Traveler were glowing, reflecting yellow hues of shimmering gold stacked neatly on a table next to them. Gideon glanced at the two, small piles of gold, gems, and jewelry as Dumakleiza glared at them, still holding a sword with Cooby on her back. Killing them was still the most probable outcome.

"Is that not why you are here?" She pointed her blade at the gold.

They both shook their heads.

"No. No. No," Gideon said. He was reckless, but he wasn't that stupid. And Traveler just wasn't stupid. Gideon smiled and held one hand up as if swearing into court.

"I promise we're not here for your treasure." He looked at it. "Though I'm a little surprised that *that's* what everyone comes here for. I thought there'd be more."

Dumakleiza scoffed and sheathed her sword. "Where do you come from? What are your names?"

Before Traveler could say anything, Gideon spoke up. "I'm Sir Gideon of Earth, and this is Traveler, the diviner from Whewliss."

"What?"

Traveler returned a cockeyed expression. "Whoa, yes, what?"

"I have heard of neither of these lands," Dumakleiza remarked as she reached up and removed the black cloth from her head. As it undraped her face, Gideon's jaw dropped a little. Her eyes pierced like lightning, a mysterious intensity seething through them. Her right eye was blue ice with hints of mint speckled around it. Her left, however, dazzled an effervescent purple iris. Her exotic allure was unlike anyone Gideon had ever seen. The beauty of her dark skin glowed with rich, ethnic color, chocolatey and olive, white freckles speckling her cheeks and neck. Her cheekbones were carved out of angelic marble, with thick, curly black hair dangling in front of her face like bouncing, spiral staircases. A caged ferocity was held within her flexed jaw, but Gideon couldn't take his eyes off her purple iris.

Traveler interrupted the infatuated silence as he feared Dumakleiza's holstered aggression. "We're very gracious for your mercy and hospitality. As soon as this fog dissipates, we'll be on our way."

Dumakleiza sighed, "Grim, grant me patience."

"Grim?" Gideon asked as he gazed upon her. "Like Grimleck? I heard the vaquilemen speak the name many times. Is that your deity?"

"Grimleck is god." Dumakleiza postured herself rigidly. "And those heathens know nothing of him. They do not love him as I do—as a true servant of Grim should."

Gideon prodded deeper. "That's why you call him Grim. Grimleck is formal, and you feel more of an intimate relationship."

"He is the only father left for me."

Gideon nodded understandingly. "Which is why you prefer more of a personal connection. Friendship, rather than regurgitating religious doctrine." There was a tense silence as both Traveler and Dumakleiza stared at Gideon's fearless approach to her faith. Traveler hoped that Gideon hadn't crossed a line. Dumakleiza slowly reached up and scratched the underside of Cooby's fuzzy chin next to her face.

"What manner of man are you?" Her posture felt comfortable relaxing a little as she digested his response.

"What do you mean?"

"The only people ever deemed trustworthy by Cooby—aside from myself—were my parents and my brothers. Even with them, it took years before he would approach them with comfort. He's lived on my back for most of my life. Carrying him has made my body strong. He attacks anyone if they draw near me. My protector and only friend." She took a deep breath and studied Gideon through her unyielding eyebrows. "Why did he approach you as if you were me?"

Gideon shrugged. "Haven't you heard? I'm training to become a diviner."

"Drop the charade, Sir Gideon of Earth. I share no likeness with the superstitious simpletons you arrived with. And I recognize more intelligence than the average man within you. Do not insult me. Either of you." Her fierce eyes looked back and forth between them.

Traveler smiled. He found himself enjoying Dumakleiza denying Gideon's sarcasm any leeway.

Gideon cleared his throat as his eyes met hers. "I've always liked animals. Cooby kinda reminds me of a Rottweiler, er...dog, or pet, I used to have. I mean, he never rode on my back or helped me fly." Gideon chuckled. "But he was there for me after I lost *my* best friend. Saved me from some bad situations—that I got us into. Miss that dog."

At the brief mentioning of his name, Cooby climbed down Dumakleiza's back. He whined a fang-filled yawn and scampered over to Gideon's boots, panting expectantly. Gideon smiled and squatted down, eagerly scratching the underside of Cooby's jaw, trying to mimic Dumakleiza's technique.

"Hey buddy." Gideon smiled as Cooby's front four arms playfully kick at the affection. It looked like a strange combination of a dog and a centipede the way it moved. Gideon chuckled and kept scratching.

Dumakleiza stood her ground, studying them. Without Cooby on her back, it looked to Gideon like she was wearing a medieval version of sweatpants and a hoodie. The only protective armor she'd had on were the thick plates scaling Cooby's back. He admired the inventive teamwork, turning back to Cooby. The curious creature cooed louder and pawed its front hands at Gideon's beard.

"So, Dumakleiza," Gideon said while Cooby nibbled on his finger. "You said you're the last of the Yagūlamites." He looked up at her. "What happened to the rest of them?"

Dumakleiza bored holes through him with her steady glare. "We are the descendants of Yagūl," she said, hesitant to express any emotion or share too much.

"How much of the legends are true? I'm sure I can rule out walking on water, but what about princess hostages, dabbling in black magic, etcetera?"

Dumakleiza scoffed, "I am fifth generation Yagūl. We are a family of holy purpose, devout in our worship of Grim, absolute in our protective constitution. My great-great-grandfather, the first Yagūl, built this castle with his wife, who was a princess. But she was not kidnapped nor held hostage as legend has falsely claimed," she hissed. "They lived a long life in each other's arms, dedicated this castle to Grimleck, and had a son, raising him on Grim's holy teachings. As they grew old, their son, the second Yagūl, my great-grandfather, set out and found *him*self a wife in a foreign land. She also was born into royalty and was happy to find faith and live a life dedicated to worship. We committed ourselves to solitude, only venturing out to expand our family name."

"Medieval warrior missionaries," Gideon said.

Dumakleiza shot him a glare before continuing. "No Yagūl has lived forever in this life—only in the next, in Grim's castle of light—but my ancestor's name has been passed down, shrouding my family in the accursed legend. The outside world has conjured up false tales. It was not our doing nor desire." She cleared her throat as her pulse quickened. "Greed has infected men like a plague, poisoning their minds, tempting them to hunt us, to *kill* us—all to steal our gold, which we possess only as holy sacrifice to Grim."

Traveler nodded as the mystery began to make more historical sense. "How many invading ships has your family sank—before they were killed?" He immediately regretted his insensitivity. "I'm sorry. You don't have to answer that."

"The number of evil ships we have burned into the depths are as many as there are drops of water in the seas." Dumakleiza's jaw flexed. "I have been raised in holy combat since I was a girl. I have been fighting the greed of men my entire life. This last winter, my brother, Gakālis, was slain by cannon fire." She blinked rapidly, regaining control of her emotions. "He was the last. I have been defending my home alone with only my Cooby."

"That's rough," Gideon said sincerely as Cooby curiously pulled at his arm. Gideon tilted a little at Cooby's demanding attention. "It is tragic to see any heart broken, but it's devastating to mourn a last surviving relative." He slowly nodded, his eyes going vacant. "If an angel is condemned to eternity alone, even heaven feels like hell." He looked down, staring through the floor as something unseen tormented him.

Traveler wanted to dismiss Gideon's comment as desperate flirtation. However, the sincerity in his shaking voice suggested a scar that light couldn't heal. He brainstormed, determined to unravel Gideon's mystery.

Dumakleiza took a deep breath and exhaled, trying not to let Gideon past her defenses. She watched as Cooby cooed and crawled behind Gideon, cocking his head to the side and looking up at the strange man. Then Cooby leapt up and landed on Gideon's back. Gideon snapped out of his emotional moment as the surprise made him stumble backward. Cooby quickly situated himself until he was comfortable. With his two winged arms wrapped around Gideon's shoulders, his middle two holding his chest beneath his armpits, and his bottom legs wrapped around his waist, Cooby chirped. He nuzzled into Gideon's neck with the fuzzy sides of his face.

Dumakleiza allowed a sliver of a smile. "I request you address me by the name my father called me: Duma."

Gideon giggled as Cooby tongued his ear. "I'd be happy to."

Duma cleared her throat and corralled her emotions before looking at Traveler. "The fog should lift over the next few days." She sheathed her sword. "Until then, you are welcome to take refuge in the chambers which belonged to my brothers. If you damage anything, I will kill you."

"Thank you," Traveler meekly responded. He hadn't moved since they'd entered the room. He pulled a wooden chair away from the closest table and sat down before looking back up to her. "So..." He wanted to direct the conversation to more philosophical waters. "What's Grimleck's story?"

Duma perked up at the topic. "Grimleck's story is a long one, his legacy vast. The iconic moment that changed all life eternal. He was executed by the very people he loved. All while walking among them like a mortal man of Cul."

Traveler and Gideon looked at each other with the same strange expression before turning back to her. Traveler lifted his head.

"Was his execution quick or was it ceremonious?" He was obviously getting at something, and Duma wasn't sure how she felt about his tone.

"Ceremonious. Have you heard his story?"

"No," Traveler said truthfully.

"Grim was publicly put through the excruciation of table bending, for all of his followers to bear witness and fear the same demise should they sacrifice their prayers to him," Duma said with pained conviction.

Traveler shook his head, nausea creeping in.

Gideon cocked his head to the side as Cooby stuck a curious finger in his ear. "What's table bending?"

Traveler's throat tightened. "A horrid, barbaric form of execution. It's nothing short of torture."

"What is it?"

"It's, uh —" Traveler was having trouble stomaching the description.

Duma, on the other hand, bled the story. "They laid him on his back on a stone table and tied him down so he could not move, regardless of how valiant his struggle. His arms were placed outward, beyond the table," she explained quickly. "Ropes were tied to his wrists with stones slowly added to the trays below, until the pressure became too great and his elbows snapped backward. Table bending wraps the condemned around the table like a tablecloth made of blood and splintered bone. He lay in destitute agony, bleeding out through protruding bones—straining and cracking with additional stones being added—flesh, muscle, and tendons ripping away." Her severe detail had Traveler's face twisted.

Gideon slowly nodded with raised eyebrows. "*Okay*." Cooby buried his face in Gideon's neck and purred as Gideon shook the visual away. "I admit that's not how I'd want to go." He swallowed his distaste and looked at Traveler. "Sounds a lot like Christianity."

Duma cocked her head a little. "What?"

Traveler took a deep breath and let it out, trying to calm his stomach. "Indeed. There are many religions paralleling Christianity." As they spoke, Duma listened intently. "God walking among men as a man, being betrayed and hated by those he loved, executed publicly, raised from the dead, and ascending into the heavens, where he waits for his followers. It's a religion with details mirroring others found on many places."

"Really? How many planets have one like it?"

Traveler closed his eyes, immediately flush at Gideon's slip of the word "planets." "All similar stories take place near the middle of each *place's* first phase."

Gideon realized what he'd done as he felt Duma's confused energy trying to figure out what they were talking about. "Huh. That leaves a few big philosophical questions just hanging out there, waiting to be plucked."

Traveler nodded, eager to play his favorite game. "Okay. Okay. Okay. *What if* there is one and only one God? What if he travels to different places at similar phases of development?"

Gideon smiled and nodded. "Exactly. What if you were to travel to the exact right place at the exact right time, and find him before his execution?" He squinted, pondering his own question. "What would you say to him? What would you ask him? Would you try to stop the execution? Or allow it, knowing it's his intended purpose there?"

"Or," Traveler interjected, "what if each religion is imagined by the people of each place? What if each requires a similar story, a similar hero, savior, deity to worship in order to function? In order to create some natural order—or hope—demanded by their DNA? We are all innately designed to worship something or someone. What if we all so desperately crave the same story that our similarities outshine our differences by exposing paralleling dreams of an unprovable savior? What if it's something we all desperately need in order to provide a sense of existence postmortem? And undeserved love. Impossible hope. So, every place imagines the same fantasy and writes similar fiction to direct their morals. Sure, a few details vary, but the fundamental basics are constant."

"Or what if—" Gideon racked his brain, trying to think of a fun third alternative. "Someone from the one, er...*place* more advanced than where you're from—which I still want you to tell me the story of—but what if one of *them* has been traveling and recruiting acolytes?"

Traveler smiled condescendingly at him. "That's impossible. Well, there's one man that could be doing—" He shook his head. "Even if that was the case, explain each of their executions."

"Oh, right." Gideon pondered. "Hmm." He tapped his index and middle fingers together. "Hashtag: advanced science? Explains all things I don't understand." He chuckled. "Though it *would* explain ascending into the heavens after their resurrections, light and all. But yeah, I guess their deaths wouldn't make sense. Especially the super violent ones."

"Or—" Dumakleiza stepped forward. "*What if*," she spat derisively, "they are not *places* you are referring to, but other worlds?" She stared at their immediate bewilderment. "I believe I insisted that you both cease your patronizing, as I am no close-minded simpleton. I recognized your intelligence because my mind is not void of it." They both looked at her, trying to hide all expression. She wasn't having it. "I am no fool. And I do not fear that you are not from Cul. So, as I previously stated, cease the insulting charade." The demand from the lethal warrior struck fear into Traveler. He took a deep breath, carefully calculating his response.

"It's not what you think. We're both actually from——"

"The stars," Dumakleiza said with unruffled understanding. "I pray to the heavens every morning and every night. You do not believe I possess the ability to conceive that among those very stars, others may live? Confirming this truth only strengthens my faith." She took a couple confident steps forward. "In fact, that truth reveals the answers I have been struggling to find concerning you two men of foreign accent and ways of speaking." Dumakleiza was sharper than her appearance gave off, and she had no interest in wasting her time hiding it.

Traveler took another deep breath as he struggled to think. "Yes." He gulped. "We are from the stars."

Gideon smiled slyly, admiring Duma for more than just her beauty. "Never judge a book by its cover."

Dumakleiza glared impatiently through her multicolored eyes. "Now, answer my first questions honestly or I shall again withdraw my swords. Who are you? And why are you here?"

18

Traveler tried to maintain eye contact with Dumakleiza's unwavering stare as she bored holes through him.

"We are who Gideon said we are. That was the truth. And we're here to, uh—"

"We're here for me." Gideon smiled and took over. He knew Duma was onto them, but that didn't mean he had to divulge everything. "Traveler is training me, and part of my training was surviving the vaquilemen's barbaric ways."

Duma turned from Gideon to Traveler. "Training him for what?"

"An adventure," Traveler quickly said, hoping it would be enough.

"A mission," Duma translated.

"Yes, a mission involving great adventure."

Duma slowly nodded, accepting their answer as truth. "On your world?" She pointed to Traveler.

"No." His answer made her point to Gideon for the same question. Traveler shook his head. "Not on his, either."

Duma looked at Gideon. "Then why did you not flee with the cowards when they ran for their ship? There is nothing for you to gain on my isle."

Gideon shrugged. "I don't know. I felt like staying here would be more exciting. I always follow my gut over my head."

"That was a dangerous gamble."

Traveler nodded. "That's the only way Gideon gambles." He secretly loved that someone else was feeling the same judgment for Gideon's reck-lessness, even if it was someone willing to kill them both.

"You do not fear death?"

"Ha!" Traveler blurted out unintentionally. "That he definitely does not. I wouldn't be surprised if he impaled his stomach on your sword just to scratch an itch on his lower back."

The comment made Duma grin a little.

Gideon smiled at the lighthearted transition. "So." He closed his eyes and mouth as Cooby's long tongue licked up his face. "So—" He giggled in the saliva coat. "What kind of animal is Cooby? Now that the cat's out of the bag, I gotta tell you, I've never seen anything like him on Earth: my planet."

Dumakleiza genuinely smiled at his interest in her pet. "Cooby is a tanion. The first to be domesticated by my knowledge." She walked over, standing in front of Gideon, but her eyes were on Cooby. She reached out and scratched under his chin, making his beady eyes roll back, and coos pour from his lips. "They are normally a peaceful animal, murders of them living in trees. They typically avoid danger." She leaned forward and wiggled her nose against Cooby's. "But I trained my Coobs to love killing alongside me." Her playful tone straightened. "There is more war-rior in this little tanion than in any of the men who died here today." She patted his armored head. "When he is fully grown, all will fear him."

Gideon watched the dynamic of owner and pet. "How big is he going to get?"

"About—" Duma tilted her head back and forth, her tone relaxing. "By my best prediction, perhaps two times the size of his body now."

"Really?"

"I must train myself to be able to carry his weight when that day comes."

"Oh, I can imagine it already gets tiring to carry him around."

"No." Duma's simple but stern response made Traveler smile.

Gideon grinned. "Just kidding then." He looked around the cold, barren castle. "So, other than pray and fight off ships, what do you two do for fun?"

Duma beamed, showing the first sign of vulnerability. "Come with me."

Dumakleiza opened a hatch above, shedding light and cold air down into the dark tower. Gideon and Traveler climbed up a ladder below her. They crawled out into the white fog, squinting as they found themselves on a turret. There wasn't much room to move around, and the view was nothing but cloud all around. Gideon walked to the stone rail walling them in and peered over. He looked around, struggling to see anything.

"Which tower are we on?"

"The highest," Duma said as she helped Cooby down from her back.

"Wow." Gideon waved his hand around through white wisps, recalling it being the same spot he'd first seen Dumakleiza's orange glow. "I bet the view is gorgeous when there isn't any fog."

"It is. The whole of my isle is visible from this place. The ocean is like a painting, made only the more beautiful by the corpses of ships."

Traveler stood on the opposite side, still wary of her. "Is the fog a frequent occurrence?"

"Every week it comes. Every week it leaves. The view from up here makes the solitude worthwhile." Duma sighed. "But the next day, it always returns. I know not why. Perhaps that is the reason my great-great-grandfather chose this place to build my family's castle." As she spoke, Cooby crawled up onto the wall and perched. He pawed at Duma, yapping, moving his front arms around, readily stretching the skin flaps. Duma smiled and pulled a palm-sized fish from her pocket. She held it up, teasing him. "Are you ready, my Coobs?" Her voice grew playful. "You ready? You ready?" Cooby was getting wild, yapping and barking, grabbing for the treat right out reach. Dumakleiza wound, grabbing her bow and an arrow. She fluidly stabbed the arrows tip through the fish, simultaneously loading it onto her bow and drawing. With a controlled release, the arrow and treat flew off into the fog. "Go get it!" Cooby screeched and leapt after it, spreading his winged arms and disappearing into the whiteness, squalling. Duma laughed for the first time since they'd arrived. She stowed her bow and watched where Cooby had flown.

Gideon leaned over the stone railing and strained his eyes. "I wish I could see him coast all the way." He stared in the general direction, still able to hear Cooby echoing down.

Duma pointed down into the whiteness. "He is on the ground, sniffing for the fish." Her finger moved, appearing to be following Cooby's movement.

Gideon looked at her before glancing back down through the fog. "Can you see him?" Dumakleiza nodded nonchalantly. Even Traveler squinted, confused. Gideon wasn't sure if he believed her. "How can you see through this soup?" He smiled. "It's your purple eye, isn't it? Some kind of genetic mutation? X-ray vision or something?" Traveler shot him a disappointed look, condemning him for referencing more scientific development that Duma couldn't understand. Gideon shrugged back. "What? It's your fault I'm so open to new ideas, Spaceman."

Dumakleiza ran her index finger down her face next to her purple eye. "My father believed it a gift from Grimleck. It doesn't fare well in the light of day. I wear a patch in the brightness. But in darkness —" She pointed vaguely around them. " — or fog, it thrives. I can see better with it than my right eye in times like this."

"That's an incredible gift," Traveler quickly said before Gideon could. He knew it was a rare genetic mutation, nearly unheard of, but he wanted to leave well enough alone. He leaned forward to take a better look at it. He'd never actually seen one in person before. He'd studied the way purple irises, or "Dragon Eyes," as they had been scientifically named by his people, mimicked nocturnal eyes, glimmering in darkness. When he'd read about them, he'd marveled at how they were almost superhuman in night, fog, smoke, or rain. There was still much unknown, and he was fascinated getting to actually see one in person.

"Hold up." Gideon's intrigued smile grew. "So, lemme summarize really quickly here: You are a highly skilled warrior, whose life has been dedicated to prayer, you're incredibly intelligent and perceptive, you can all but fly with your pet, and you have a magic eye?" He grinned from ear-to-ear and looked at Traveler with a begging expression.

Traveler shook his head. "No." He found Dumakleiza fascinating, as well, but he didn't feel safe with her. Gideon's smile kept getting bigger. Traveler kept shaking his head. "No."

"She's very open-minded. Just saying."

"Do not debate in secrecy in my presence," Duma insisted while pointing at Gideon. "What are you going on about?"

Traveler spoke up for them both. "He wants you to leave Castle Yagūl and go to other planets with us, but I know you have sworn an oath to your family to stay here. I won't ask you to break a sacred oath." Thinking on his feet wasn't his strong suit, but he was confident with that one.

Dumakleiza mulled the idea over as she held her signature glare. "I swore an oath to dedicate my life to Grimleck and to protect my family's holy treasure. We believe that one day, he shall return and accept our offering." Her eyes narrowed as she slowly nodded. "But Cooby and I grow lonely here. We grow tired living in constant fear of attack, always needing be on our guard. And—" She perked up. "—I would honor my family more if I were to carry a portion of our treasure into the stars." She smiled boldly. "Should we happen upon Grim in the vastness of the heavens, I shall hand our gold to him, that he may recognize the Yagūls' holy dedication to his name." She nodded. "I accept. I will go with you, but Cooby comes, as well."

Traveler shook his head. "No. This is a very bad idea. You're not ready for what is out there."

"Come on," Gideon argued, "think about it." He pointed at his fingers to make another list. "She's open-minded, *bleeds* her faith, is a badass warrior—so there goes your concern of a recruit easily dying. Plus, she can help protect *us*. And she has night vision. Plus, think about it: Do you really think this other holy guy you wanna go interview will be as open-minded and self-sustaining? Duma, here, can probably handle unexpected situations better than me."

"If by handle, you mean kill, then you're probably right." Traveler sighed. "Listen, no offense—" He motioned to Dumakleiza. "—but at your level of development, there is just too much that you wouldn't understand, and I cannot risk someone as primitively dangerous as yourself in advanced, civilized societies. Much of it would be sensory overload and you would likely lose your sanity in the ever-expanding ocean of technological innovations."

Duma gave a puzzled expression. "I do not understand what that means."

"Exactly." Traveler threw his hand out, demonstrating his point.

Gideon grinned a clever smirk. "Does the fourth phase have anything to do with a civilized society?"

Traveler flexed his jaw. "No."

"Do you want someone prepared for a dangerous adventure, who can handle themselves in unexpected situations, where others would likely die? Or do you want a civilized priest that's up-to-date on his dinner party etiquette?"

Traveler glared at him. "You think a medieval mind can handle a world like yours? Or an even worse idea: like mine?"

Gideon shrugged. "If you're so scared, just give her the test. I know you had one planned for the guy we were going to go see next. If she fails, I'll shut up and we can leave the beautiful, strong, open-minded, spiritual, flying, superwoman behind so we can find someone better." He winked.

Traveler's tense mouth hung open as he glowered. "You are unbelievable." He turned to Dumakleiza, who was impatiently glaring. "All right Duma, *what if* Grimleck is not the real god? What if Grimleck never even existed?"

Duma rolled her tongue around mouth as she studied Traveler's question and tone. "Should it be revealed to me that Grimleck is not god, and that my entire life up until that moment has been a wasted lie, then I shall dedicate the rest of my years to searching for the real god."

"Okay," Traveler said to the expected answer. "And what if there is no god? Nowhere in 'the heavens,' anywhere among the stars, nowhere on Cul or any other planet, and nowhere 'within us.' It's just us. What if we live by no divine creator, no holy purpose, and there is no afterlife? What if this life is all we have, and we were created by random chance, chaos, by fluke science, or magic as you would call it? What if everything you've ever believed is a lie, and you've been praying to nothing and to no one?" His voice bit at her like a rabid wolf.

Dumakleiza clicked her tongue with a blank expression. "*If* there is no god—no gods, no heaven, no hell—then this *is* heaven, and this *is* hell. This life would be everything." She breathed lowly. "And if that were my truth, it would render all morality of my nonexistent soul moot and pointless." She lowered her brow as she truly considered the question's ramifications. "And if that were true, why would I care for anything other than myself and the amount of pleasure I found in this life?" She shrugged. "I would dedicate my existence to the pleasures of my flesh, tasting the finest wines, devouring unmoderated feasts, lying with any man or woman of my choosing, killing without reason or regret." She challenged Traveler with a confident stare. "And I would venture to the farthest corners of creation, exploring all existence there is to explore until death came for me."

Gideon puffed his bottom lip out. "Oh my."

"I see," Traveler said deadpan. He wasn't sure how he felt about her response.

"That is my answer to your question," Dumakleiza said as she took a step toward Traveler. "But I see more than a thinker in your eyes, Diviner." Her voice grew suspicious. "I see fear. It does not require my purple eye to see the dread that follows you." She leaned forward, looking deep into Traveler's nervous face. "I believe you to be a man of high intelligence. I believe there is no shadow of knowledge that makes you truly afraid. At least nothing known, nothing that cannot be explained with your magic." She leaned in closer, making him uncomfortably lean away. "And yet I see terror in you. It is not of me, or of anything normal, such as heights or spiders and their webs. No, there is something beyond explanation, beyond reason—beyond your science that terrifies you." She stared deeper. "And it *haunts* you." It was making sense to her. "It is the adventure that you prepare Sir Gideon to face, is it not?"

Traveler flinched so subtly that Gideon barely noticed it.

Gideon was enthralled. "Damn, girl." He leaned his elbows against the stone wall.

Dumakleiza brought her head back. "I believe that *you* believe in a higher power, a god, though you do not know which one. And while you enjoy testing my conviction, that is all your last question truly was: a test of my mind—while yours has been made up for much of your life. You believe in more than you let on, and yet, whatever it may be that you fear, it makes you question all that you know to be true."

Gideon slowly clapped. "Wow. And you don't think she's a good choice."

Dumakleiza fixated her hungry eyes on Traveler. "I have honored your question. Now, it is your turn to consider mine." She allowed a moment of silence first. "What if Grim *is* god?"

Traveler snorted through his nose with a surprised and impressed smile. "Perhaps we will find out." He reached under his robe and pulled out his plastic water bottle. Gideon smiled as he realized what Traveler was doing. Traveler stared at Dumakleiza. "If you truly believe you possess the courage to walk among the stars, drink three quarters of this."

Duma took the bottle and studied its foreign look and feel. "What about the rest?"

Traveler kept his eyes on hers as he pointed over the edge of the turret. They could hear Cooby yapping as he climbed up toward them, crunching and chewing. Gideon smiled. They were going to bring a pirate with them through space. They were going to bring a pirate to other worlds. He couldn't wait.

"I sure hope whatever scientist we find can handle all this awesome." He looked at their eclectic trio.

Traveler looked to Dumakleiza. "Get him to drink the last quarter." He pointed at Cooby as the playful creature reached the top of the turret and perched on the edge, waiting for a second fish.

Duma smiled at her animal companion. "Coobs, we are off to the stars!"

19

Once Dumakleiza and Cooby recovered from their violent reactions to the light shot, she'd asked them to follow her below the castle so she could show them "something of great importance." Cooby happily rode on Gideon's back as he and Traveler followed Dumakleiza down a dark stairwell into the bowels of Castle Yagūl. The only light they had was the ominous yellow glow of her torch. As they descended into darkness, even the air breathing through the castle disappeared. They felt completely alone in the silence. It was off-putting and intriguing at the same time. Cooby squabbled as he groomed Gideon's hair. He calmly enjoyed himself, while Gideon and Traveler stayed tense in anticipation for whatever Duma was leading them toward in the benighted crypt.

They reached a short hallway at the bottom of the spiraling stone stairs. Duma held the torch forward; dancing flames casting a yellow glow that exposed a wooden door at the end of a hallway. She reached her free hand into a pocket and pulled out a single key. She offered it to Gideon and nodded toward the door.

Gideon smirked. "There better not be a dragon."

"A dragon?" Dumakleiza asked.

"You know, a giant flying lizard that breathes fire and eats princesses."

Duma's eyes widened. "Such horrors exist?"

"No, I—never mind," Gideon chuckled and took the key from her. "Come on, Spaceman, let's unlock the door at the end of the dark hallway in the dungeon of a scary, legendary castle. What's the worst that can happen? Maybe hot oil? The rack?"

Traveler rolled his eyes and followed after him. "I worry about you like a parent worries over a toddler."

"So, you *do* love me." Gideon practically skipped over to the wooden door, his shadow darkening as Duma stayed behind with the torch. He squinted, trying to see as he slid the key into the lock and turned it. A heavy sound echoed out somewhere inside the stone walls. He pulled. It creaked as it slowly slid out. The bottom of the wood scraped along the stone floor as if the door hadn't been used in years. Once it was completely opened, Gideon and Traveler stared into the pitch-black room, straining their eyes to see anything.

Duma walked toward them, illuminating each step with fire. "In my absence, this is what the enemies of my family will find of our holy treasure." She stepped up next to them and shined the torch through the doorway. The room lit up, exposing all that was within it.

"There's nothing here." Gideon stared at the barren room made of stone bricks.

Duma smiled. "This is true. They will search the castle and their hunt will yield no booty."

Gideon snickered, "Booty..."

Traveler turned. "So, the gold on the tables upstairs *is* all the amassed treasure your family has collected?" His tone was obviously dissatisfied.

"I did not say that," Duma remarked as she turned and started walking back through the hallway. She stopped halfway to the stairs and put her hand on one of the stones in the wall. It looked no different than any of the others, flush and flat alongside the others around it. Duma pushed on it with her full bodyweight, struggling and straining. It scraped and slid deep into the wall until she'd forced it all the way in. *Clank!* Some dust spilled out from between the cracks as the wall shifted. Gideon and Traveler stepped back. The sound made Cooby chirp. Duma stood perfectly still with her torch lighting the secret stone door opening. Deep groans and aches echoed through the dungeon's hallway until the secret passageway was open.

"Holy cow, Batman." Gideon stared with wide eyes as the light from Duma's torch reflected like beautiful stars in the hidden chamber. Piles of gold and jewels filled the room which, at first glance, looked to be at least fifteen feet in length and width. Duma extended the torch deeper inside, illuminating bright yellows, blues, reds, and greens reflected from the gems, rare stones, and golden artifacts. There were crowns, jewelry, and copious amounts of coins and trinkets made of gold, silver, and alien gemstones.

"That's more impressive," Traveler admitted.

"Question," Gideon said as an observation struck him. "Do people of every world horde similar treasures? This is all the same stuff we covet back on Earth."

Traveler nodded. "Scientific answer is pretty simple: Our eyes are drawn to anything that sparkles or twinkles because biologically we're wired to seek out water in the distance."

"Makes sense." Gideon nodded, too distracted by the jewels to dissect the topic further.

Duma stared fondly at the riches tucked away in secret. "The treasure above is simply a decoy, that if anyone overtakes us and finds it, they will be disappointed but convinced that it is all we possess." She pulled a couple brown sacks from her pocket. "But it is *this* treasure I shall bring a handful of into the stars. It shall be meek, but at least a token of my reverent sacrifice I wish to bestow at Grim's divine feet." Dumakleiza's eyes twinkled as she stared at her family's legacy. "Only ever will this treasure be used to safeguard my soul."

"You put Scrooge McDuck to shame. Dear god." Gideon continued looking over the shimmering mountains of gold.

Traveler smiled at Gideon's comment as he also stared. "Aren't you taking *your* planet's god's name in vain, Gideon?"

"By saying Scrooge McDuck or dear god?" He winked and then returned to watching Dumakleiza dig around and handpick specific treasures to add to her bags.

"The latter." Traveler's eyes remained fixated on Castle Yagūl's wealth. "One thing I've been curious about regarding Earth's Christianity is taking the Lord's name in vain. I have many questions about it— but one that stands out above the rest."

"What's that?"

"The trinity."

"A confusing topic for anyone."

"Yes, I could see that. But, between the Father, the Son, and the Holy Spirit, two of the three have been turned into exclamations that are considered offensive. If someone utters 'God damn it,' or 'Jesus Christ' in a derogatory tone, they are taking the Lord's name in vain. However—" He held his hand up. "No one uses the Holy Spirit as an exclamation."

"Huh." Gideon scoffed a smile. "I've never considered that. I wonder if the Holy Spirit has been grateful to be left out of the name calling."

Traveler lifted a finger. "Or if after thousands of years, it's getting jealous and wants to be included—even if it is blasphemous in nature."

Gideon grinned mischievously. "Strange that we're wanting to curse in a castle. We must have turrets." Traveler stared at the ground, knowing there was a bad joke he was missing. Then he got it, and then shook his head, unwilling to give Gideon the satisfaction. Gideon smiled. "Poor Holy Spirit. I'll hook him up. Or her. It? Who knows?"

Traveler chuckled. "What are you talking about?"

"*Holy Spirit*, look at all that treasure!" Gideon pointed into the stocked room with an over-exaggerated smile.

"Oh, no." Traveler pinched the bridge of his nose, unable to conceal his grin. "You're going to make a habit of that, aren't you?"

"Oh, I'm contacting the copyright people first thing if I make it back to Earth. Make a dollar every time someone says it." Gideon let out a giggle under his breath. "Holy Spirit, *I'm* going to be Scrooge McDuck."

Duma shook her head with a confused smile as she walked away from the treasure room and closed the door behind her. The false wall slid shut, once again blending into the other stones as if it didn't exist. Duma cinched her sacks shut and tied them off before looking up at Gideon and Traveler.

"I'm not sure of what you two speak regarding spirits, but I am ready to depart for the stars."

Traveler shook his head. "Not yet you're not. Come upstairs. I have something for all of you."

"Ooh" Gideon raised an eyebrow. "Presents?"

"Something like that."

Once they returned to Castle Yagūl's main hall, Traveler pulled off the robe he'd been wearing since the Isle of Beasts. He laid it over one of the tables and opened the flaps. Gideon and Dumakleiza watched as he pulled out a black plastic bag. It was one-by-two feet and about one inch thick.

"What's that?" Gideon asked.

"It's a vacuum-sealed bag; as you say, cutting edge technology from my planet. It contains outfits that are customary on a handful of planets I packed for." He unzipped the end of it and pulled out what looked like three, multi-patterned pieces of printed paper. After he laid them out side-by-side, they began to expand. Gideon watched in curious awe as Dumakleiza backed away with her eyes peeled.

"What sorcery is this?"

Traveler looked at her. "You need to prepare your mind to handle many things you won't understand if you really want to go on this journey. There's no such thing as sorcery or magic of any sort on any world. Everything can be explained by scientific principles."

They watched as the three expanding pieces of paper began to take shape into full articles of clothing.

Gideon turned to Traveler. "Wait. You're giving us the right clothes for the next planet? You're not going to test Duma like you did me?"

Traveler slowly blinked. "She has lived her entire life bathed in violence, constantly prepared to defend herself against invading forces. The only categories that she needs to improve on are preparedness in scenarios involving civilized societies, and scientific understanding, and that's where we're going. All will be tested." He nodded toward Dumakleiza, who had four swords and a bow strapped around her waist.

"Touché," Gideon said.

"My translator doesn't recognize whatever you just said but I'm sure you get the idea," Traveler said as the outfits fully expanded into shirts and pants. They looked to Gideon like black formal attire with silver linings and collars. They appeared to be made of some kind of flexible, elastic material, presumably due to whatever unexpected sizes their wearers would be. Traveler pulled out three more items. They looked like wide, black belts as they, too, expanded.

Dumakleiza pointed at them. "What are those?"

"Those are neck, back, and knee braces."

"Braces? What are braces?"

Gideon gave an unusually intrigued squint. "Where exactly are we going?"

"We're going to a planet called Thamiosh. Its development is a little further along than Earth's but not by much. It's about the size of your Saturn, and the gravity is close to twice that of Earth or Cul. The back and knee braces are to protect us while we are there. It'll be an exhausting journey but hopefully worthwhile. We can't stay there long, or we'll die from the gravity alone." Traveler looked at Duma. "You will probably not be able to carry Cooby there. He'll have to walk on his own."

Duma pulled her head back. "You shan't find it an easy task to keep us apart."

Traveler scoffed, "Feel free to try."

Duma cautiously narrowed her eyes. "Is the world safe?"

Gideon chuckled. "Nothing about this adventure has been safe. That's half the fun."

"From what I've heard of Thamiosh, it is both safe and unsafe. It is ruled by a high society that oversees everything. However, there are rampant gangs that populate the majority of the planet beyond what's governed. We shouldn't have to deal with the slums, but from what I hear, the high society isn't much better. Who we seek shouldn't take us anywhere away from the main city."

"Who do we seek on this world of Thamiosh?" Dumakleiza asked.

Traveler reached forward and felt the clothes, making sure they were fully expanded. "I've heard about a scientific mind well beyond Thamiosh's technological advancements. In fact, if the rumors are true, he might even rival the brightest minds of Whewliss."

Gideon perked up. "Someone that might be smarter than you?"

"Indeed. He knows less than I do. However, with a mind as bright as his is rumored to be, he has the potential to pioneer us into a new age once educated." Traveler's tone grew solemner. "That is, if our venture doesn't kill us all. Not only will he hopefully be smarter than my people, but braver. That is the primary prerequisite." He cleared his throat and perked back up. "Now we just have to wait until this fog clears and we can go test our wills against the planet's unrelenting law of gravity."

20

After two days inundated with smothering cloud, the fog began to dissipate. Traveler was the first to notice as the sun crested into view. The hard part was going to be getting Gideon and Dumakleiza focused—maybe just Gideon. There was no more time to waste in a medieval castle when they needed to continue recruiting and working toward the final goal: the fourth phase. As Traveler predicted, Gideon had happily lost himself in the study of Cul's history, Duma's religion, and anything else the Earthling could get his meddlesome hands on. The cut on Gideon's shoulder was only one of his many new healing injuries after insisting on learning sword-fighting techniques from Dumakleiza. That lesson, Traveler had thoroughly enjoyed watching.

After some ushering, they gathered out in front of Castle Yagūl, clad in the outfits Traveler provided. With braces covering his back and knees, Gideon stood in a black shirt with a silver collar, sleek white pants, clean black shoes, and his backpack slung over his shoulder. Traveler wore a similar outfit, but with a taller collar and longer sleeves. It wasn't difficult to tell that it was more distinguished attire for where they were heading. He needed to visibly be the highest-ranking of their party. Gideon knew it was a wise move, but he couldn't help a smidgen of jealousy. Duma stood in a black and white formal button-up blouse that reflected dancing light like the water's surface. She wore business-casual pants with lightweight black shoes. Cooby was simply Cooby, except that they had a back brace on him as well. Even the tanion had to be kept safe, so Traveler had cut a human brace apart, improvising it around Cooby's frame.

"This clothing is so light and flexible," Duma remarked as she moved around and waved her arms. "It feels as though I am wearing nothing other than these, uh, braces, they're called? It is like comfortable armor. Never before have I desired to sleep in armor."

Traveler looked to Gideon. "Your backpack is all you need, right?" Gideon nodded. Traveler turned to Dumakleiza. "And you?"

Duma looked down at the sacks of gold in her hand. Traveler had insisted that she leave her weapons behind in case she was caught and ultimately jailed for possessing them. In addition to the lighter clothes, not having her swords made her feel vulnerable and naked. She sighed at the treasure and slowly nodded, forcing herself to trust the alien bossing her around.

"Yes, I have Coobs and my treasure. I have all that is needed to be complete."

Traveler rolled his eyes. "Good. It's time to go." He watched Duma smiling nervously. He was a little hesitant, worried she may have a violently adverse reaction to light travel. "Now, normally I prefer people experience being lit without providing a detailed briefing prior to. It ruins the raw reaction to the first exposure. However, since light travel is many millennia beyond Cul's technology, I don't want it to, uh, scare you."

Duma swallowed some nerves and nodded. "What is it like?"

"Gideon, you've jumped twice now. How would you describe it?"

Gideon smiled. "Oh, it's not that scary. It's rather fun, actually." He waved his hand. "You see bright light, go comatose, fly into the stars, and then come to feeling a little numb on a new world. It's relatively painless and really cool to just suddenly be on another planet." His eyes lit up as he grew more excited for their upcoming jump. "And once the numbness fades, your body actually feels better than you've ever felt before. You know, pretty typical day."

"This truly sounds like a magical experience."

Gideon nodded. "I'm sure you'll like it." He turned to Traveler. "My only regret leaving here is that you still haven't allowed me the magical experience of flying with Cooby."

Dumakleiza looked down at Cooby cooing up at her. "He may ride your back, he may like you, but I am the only one he flies with."

"Talking you into changing your mind is a new life goal."

Duma smiled. "No world is ready for one monkey riding another through the sky."

"Ha! Okay, now I like her." Traveler looked up, smiling as he went to read the forecast between worlds. "Oh," he marveled. "We're in for a rare treat." He turned his eyes down and blinked his right eye a few times before looking back up.

"What?" Gideon cocked his head to the side. "Not sure if I trust your excitement yet," he half-sarcastically admitted. "Everything okay?"

"Yes, more than." Traveler's smile was replaced by intrigue. "We are privileged to witness something unique to worlds like Cul."

"Unique to medieval worlds?"

"No, to worlds with multiple moons," Traveler clarified. "Behold, syzygy."

"Syzygy?" Gideon asked. "Now, that's a sci-fi word if I've ever heard one." He held up his hand, shielding his eyes from the sun as he followed Traveler's gaze. His jaw dropped a little, a smile curling up the sides of his mouth as he saw two moons creeping in toward Cul's sun. They were encroaching from opposite sides, one marginally larger than the other, and their shadows were already noticeable as they promised to blot out the light.

Duma, too, looked up, curious what in her familiar sky had the abnormal men so rapt. As soon as she realized what was happening, her heart sped up and she gasped. She dropped to her knees and bowed, hands and arms outstretched as she began rattling off a muttered prayer. Cooby crawled around, sniffing her face and barking at her strange behavior.

"That's intense." Gideon squinted, trying not to blink as he watched All of Yagūl's isle begin dimming in the shared shadow.

Gideon brought his eyes down, knowing the brightness would soon be blinding. "A dual lunar eclipse?" he asked, wishing he could stare directly at it. "Is that a thing?"

"Sure," Traveler said. "I don't know what the frequency of lunar eclipses is here on Cul but they're likely much more common due to eight orbiting moons." He stared at the approaching phenomenon. "However, I venture the assumption that two moons simultaneously eclipsing is a rarity—even here."

"Won't they collide or something?" Gideon asked.

"No," Traveler chuckled. He narrowed his eyes, getting a reading beyond what his naked eyes could see. "There looks to be—about seventy miles between the paths of their orbital circumferences. They're merely aligning by perspective."

Gideon nodded with a smirk. "Damn it, I should've guessed that one."

"No, it's a fair concern."

"Okay, next stupid question: Not that we can look, but if we did, would it be any different than a normal lunar eclipse?"

"I don't think so," Traveler said. "I've never seen one before, but I'll let you know as it happens."

Gideon looked up at Traveler, still staring skyward. "Wait. Can you look directly at it? Without burning your eyes out of your skull?"

"Optical implants," Traveler answered. "My natural eyes can withstand the blinding light no better than yours."

"Dude," Gideon whined. "Do you have any for us? I wanna watch, too."

Traveler shook his head. "My superiors deem translators the only necessary introductory tools for aliens of less-advanced worlds."

"Not fair," Gideon pouted before looking at Dumakleiza. "Duma, you okay down there?"

Dumakleiza didn't hear him as she desperately prayed under her breath too softly for either man to understand.

Traveler glanced at her and smirked before returning his eyes to the sky. "Likely a primitive superstition. Most worlds fear the wrath of their first deity: their sun, during the majority of their first phase. It's common."

"It is not the sun that I worship in holy fear," Dumakleiza said. "It is the shadow of Grim. As was taught to me by my parents and their parents before them, when Grim walks closest to Cul, we bathe in his mighty shadow."

"There is only one shadow maker I fear," Traveler ambiguously said, an inexplicable concern lacing his voice.

Duma noticed he was still staring upward. "Grim's glory glows too brightly for the eyes of the living. Should you not bow in his presence, he will take your sight with him while you still breathe. You will walk blind in this life until he claims the rest of your body."

Gideon smiled as the island grew darker. "That's a way cooler superstition than worshipping the sun."

"It is not a superstition, Sir Gideon," Duma hastily clarified. "My mother was blind the entirety of my life, as she was foolish enough to stare at Grim early in hers. Her humbled testimony proves my faith more than a superstition."

Traveler grinned. "Gideon, she's your slave project. You get to handle this."

"Pet project." Gideon flexed his jaw, not wanting to undermine Duma's beliefs with science. "Duma, I believe in God, too. I have my doubts and my frustrations with him, but I believe there's a divine creator out there somewhere—but—" He paused. "It wasn't a deity that blinded your mother."

Duma scoffed. "Even *if* I entertained your blasphemy, what do you believe blinded my mother?" Gideon could see her hands inch toward the knives no longer on her hips. She grunted in frustration. "Your science?"

"Yes," Gideon said matter-of-factly.

Duma shook her head. "Non-believers will find any excuse to deny the face of Grim, even as he currently stares down upon us."

"More likely his butt since he's mooning us," Gideon muttered under his breath, giggling at the joke he couldn't help.

"Speak up," Duma demanded. "What words did you speak in secret?"

"Nothing. Nothing." Gideon focused. "When your moons are directly between Cul and your sun, it creates what's called an eclipse. They're too bright for humans to look at—that much you are correct about. They will blind you. However, Spaceman here has some scientific doohickeys in his eyes that will allow him to stare at it unscathed."

"Duma," Traveler spoke up as Yagūl's isle darkened to the dimness of a setting sun, "do you worship your moons? Surely, you can see the eclipsing moons before they reach your sun. Do you believe them to be Grim?"

"Of course not," Duma scoffed. "I am no fool. I know what moons are." She understood their confusion but was struggling to word her argument most effectively. She stared at Traveler. "Who do you believe puts the moon between the sun and Cul?"

"Okay." Gideon nodded. "Welcome to the current debate between evolutionism and creationism on my world. We understand that science can explain all living things and how they operate but believers argue that someone had to set everything in motion—a creator of all things, if you will."

Duma tentatively took her glare from Gideon to Traveler. "Can you conclude an answer, Diviner?"

"Not definitively," Traveler confessed. "There is no evidence confirming a god unless you claim that all of existence is the proof—as so many do. And there is no evidence disproving the existence of a supreme being unless you claim that our self-sustaining, evolutionary lives are the proof—as so many do."

"Precisely," Duma agreed. "We may not be capable of seeing his beauty in this life, but as the moons cross between us, could that not be the stage on which he steps to closer visit us?"

Traveler shrugged, growing weary of arguing medieval beliefs. "I don't know, Dumakleiza. If there is a creator that resides in another dimension of existence, there's no denying the possibility of when, where, or how they visit us."

Duma nodded proudly. "I claim no ability to see him in the flesh. But I can feel his guidance. I can hear his voice."

For a moment, Traveler's stalwart poise flustered. "I don't like formless voices. They, uh, scare me."

"As it should," Duma snarled.

"What?" Gideon asked, curious about Traveler's faltering confidence. "What do you mean?"

Traveler cleared his throat. "Nothing. Just—nothing. Keep your eyes down. The eclipse is nearly full."

Gideon shook like an excitable puppy as he forced his eyes toward the ground. "What's it look like? Spare no detail."

Traveler smiled in awe as even he bared witness to something new. "It's really quite stunning. The moons are not perfectly aligned but they're close. I can see shimmering outlines of both. It looks like glowing golden rings within one another—surrounded by the blackness of the sky."

Duma covered her dragon eye and squinted up at Traveler with her other. "You really——" She paused, in awe of his ability to stare directly at the blinding light. "If your science allows you to see Grim's splendor and maintain your sanity and your sight, I long for the other miracles it will provide me beyond the stars." She pet Cooby's head next to her. "Greatness awaits us, Coobs."

"Beyond the stars, indeed," Traveler dubiously commented before bringing his eyes down. The island brightened as both moons continued on their separate journeys, allowing the sun to begin peeking through once more. "Don't look up yet, but we can start getting ready to go."

Gideon grinned curiously. "What would happen if you used the light of an eclipse to jump? Would it make any difference?"

"Yes. Quite." Traveler's eyes widened at the risky idea. "Eclipses focus light similarly to one of your magnifying glasses but not into lasers. Essentially, the elasticity is intensified in the focused light and difficult to wield. It would be very easy to shoot too far or fall too short. Plus, during the brief passing of the moon, the amplified tension is in a constant state of flux, so even if I could accurately harness it, the window is challengingly brief. Multitudes of calculations in the literal blink of an eye. Almost as impossible to harness as lightning."

"That's a fun problem to have," Gideon said as he walked over and offered Duma a hand up.

"I can stand on my own without being carried," Duma stiffly said as she got to her feet. She looked to Traveler. "Do your eyes not suffer in the slightest?"

"Not at all." Traveler looked back up and blinked his right eye a few times. He smiled and then turned to Gideon and Duma. "Are you both ready?"

Gideon smiled and turned to him. "Have you given her a translator implant yet?"

"Oh, no, I haven't." Traveler glanced at Duma tentatively as she returned a puzzled look.

"My what?" she asked as the island returned to the normal glow of daytime.

"It's a—" Traveler sighed. "—a, uh, scientific implant, er…a tiny machine I will put into your ear that helps you understand the foreign tongues of every world we go to." He sighed again. "But it stings pretty badly."

Duma raised an eyebrow. "Do you sincerely question my ability to tolerate pain?" She leaned forward and brushed her long black hair away from her ears. "Give me this machine you speak of." Her brazen confidence made Gideon eager to see how she'd handle the sting.

Traveler refrained from scrunching his lips in protest as he fished around in one of his many pockets for the translation tube. He pulled it out and took a deep breath before holding the foreign-looking chrome out toward Dumakleiza's steady eyes. She didn't budge. He took a second deep breath and placed its tip near her right ear. Again, she held still. Traveler slowly nodded, giving himself a quick pep talk before sliding it in. He hit the button. *Zing!*

"Yuh!" Duma's outburst was quickly followed by a reactive fist. Her right hook caught Traveler across the jaw. He stumbled back and fell onto his butt as Duma cupped her ear, waiting for the unfamiliar, electric sting to go away. Tears welled in her eyes. "Holy spirit! Is that what you say, Sir Gideon? That stings like nothing I've ever felt!"

Gideon tried to stifle a laugh as Cooby leapt onto Traveler before he could get up. The protective creature began clobbering Traveler, little balled up fists wildly slamming down on him as Cooby shrilly screamed and barked. Traveler kept trying to bring his arms up to protect himself, but there were too many monkey hands for him to deflect them all. Gideon couldn't help it anymore. He laughed loudly and pointed.

Dumakleiza opened her eyes and mouth as wide as she could to help her throbbing inner ear relax. She wiped her tears and shook her head before looking down at Cooby pummeling Traveler.

"Coobs!" Her voice was shaking. Cooby immediately snarled and crawled backward off Traveler, who quickly scooted back, waving away fists that were no longer coming.

"Holy spirit, indeed, Ms. Duma," Gideon playfully jabbed as he forced his laughter away. "Everyone okay?"

"I'm fine," Traveler grunted, trying to slow his pulse. His pride, on the other hand, was not fine.

Duma continued rubbing her ear. "I apologize. I have felt pain, but that was oddly foreign."

"It's fine," Traveler repeated himself. "I was attacked by monkeys on the Isle of Beasts, you shot me with an arrow, why not end my visit to

Cul with a beating by you and your pet?" His humiliated sarcasm held nothing back.

The left side of Gideon's mouth perked up. "You were attacked by the monkeys?"

Traveler waved his question away. "It doesn't matter. Are you both ready to go?"

Gideon eagerly nodded and gripped his backpack tighter as he walked over to Traveler. Duma breathed slowly as her subsiding pain was replaced by nerves. Up until that moment, the idea of traveling through the stars to a new world excited her. But as the departure quickly fell upon them, she grew nervous. She took Cooby's hand, and they both tentatively walked over to Traveler's other side. Traveler brushed some dirt off his clothes and looked at the three beings on either side of him. He breathed out the last of his frustration and cleared his head.

"I need contact with your skin for us all to travel together." At his instruction, Gideon reached out and grabbed his right wrist, smiling in readiness. Duma, still holding Cooby's paw, put her free hand firmly on the back of Traveler's neck. He winced a little, visibly scared of her violent reflexes. He didn't want to give off any obvious signs of fear but her hand being near his throat gave him a whole new list of phobias.

Once everyone was touching him, Traveler looked up and squinted into the bright sky, holding his hand out as he calculated the details of their journey. He closed his fingers into a fist and continued staring into space.

Dumakleiza closed her eyes, squeezing them tightly as she whispered under her breath, "Grim, I pray this journey is not a fool's endeavor." Her words poured out as her heart raced in her chest. "Watch over us that we may live to slay your foes another day. Keep our bodies from harm, that we may be glorified in many bloody battles to come." Gideon stared in peculiar fascination as she continued. "I pray we find you walking among the heavens as we venture through their magnificence, but should we not, guide us and show us the way, that we may find you where you reside." She took a deep breath. "So, let it be made true."

Gideon nodded. "In Jesus' name, amen, girl."

Duma opened her eyes and shot him a glance. "What?"

"My version of what you said."

Traveler smirked as he stared upward, waiting for the right moment. "I can't believe I'm recruiting a medieval spiritual warrior. Calling that an open-minded decision is an understatement."

"Not the person you had in mind," Gideon said with a sly smile. "Strange that we stumbled upon a strangely qualified spiritual leader— as if led to her by our hearts and not our minds."

"Shut up." Traveler grinned. "Bury your poetry somewhere in your backpack."

Duma shot a nervous glance between the two men. "Diviner, Sir Gideon, what happens when we have completed the mission of finding the man of science we seek?"

"Well—" Gideon looked expectantly at Traveler. "At that point, we'd better be off to see what this ominous fourth phase is all about."

The mere mentioning of the fourth phase made Traveler visibly tense. "*If* we find the Thamioshling scientist—and *if* we all survive—then and only then."

Gideon nodded excitedly. "Then we'll be ready."

Traveler brought his eyes down, alarmed, all of his previous delight replaced by something disturbing. "Even then—even if we make it to the fourth phase, I don't believe we'll ever be ready."

Dumakleiza scoffed as she joined Traveler looking up into the heavens. "You need not believe. I possess enough belief to protect your doubt."

Then, before they could say anything else, Traveler opened his fist, and everything went white.

21

The catatonic numbness faded away, along with the blinding white. The refreshing cold wind Gideon had felt the first two jumps passed faster as a new sensation came over him. Something was different this time. It felt like someone was sitting on his shoulders or lying over his entire body. As his eyes came to and the blurriness cleared, he realized no one was on top of him. His body was being crushed by nothing.

"Ugh," he groaned and shook his head, which immediately felt different, too. It was like he was shaking his head in slow motion, as if each movement was being dragged through heavy mud. "What is —"

Then it came rushing in, along with his other senses. Traveler had warned them that the planet had overpowering gravity, and he hadn't been lying. Gideon's head was pounding, even though the light travel had just healed his body. As he tried to get control, his ears cleared and he heard the uncomfortable groans of Traveler, Dumakleiza, and Cooby. All three of them were experiencing the same pain. Even Traveler was struggling in Thamiosh's unforgiving environment.

Dumakleiza was the first to attempt forcing herself up to her feet. She gritted her teeth and looked around, her jaw suddenly dropping from the gravity. She collapsed on her stomach and surrendered, taking in their surroundings.

They were in the middle of a fancy town square or some kind of city. It had small shops within the bases of taller buildings all around. Pristine skyscrapers stretched toward the cloudless sky on every side of them, brightly shining into the air. Thamiosh's sun reflected off their thousands of windows like invasive flashes. Duma's eyes peeled open as she took the unfamiliarity in. Everything was clean, orderly, and neat. It was unlike anything on Cul. There were no castles, no dirt, no trees, no nature at all other than potted plants strategically placed about the public. Everything was steel and paint, pavement and cement, posters and advertisements, whirs of motors and machinery pining away, voices of people in multitudes of conversations all around them. Dumakleiza's barren emptiness of Castle Yagūl was gone, along with her solitude. She'd spent her entire life wary of a single person invading her home, and suddenly she was inundated by a city's population.

In the brightness, she managed to slip a couple fingers into a pocket and withdraw her eyepatch. It took most of her strength to drag the heavier-than-normal string up her body and painfully fasten it around her aching left eye. There was no fog to protect her sensitive vision.

Gideon smiled as he looked at the somewhat familiar sight from his back. It reminded him a lot of Earth, except there were no cars rushing about. Instead, as his head continued clearing, he saw people walking through the middle of the streets and looking down at them, judging and sneering. The formally dressed natives of Thamiosh stared at them like freak show abnormalities. They were dressed the same way, so that wasn't why they were staring. Perhaps it was because the four of them were struggling to stand. They were probably coming off as drunkards sobering up.

Then Gideon looked closer at the people walking by. Of course. It immediately made sense. The people of Thamiosh were all shaped like massive dwarves, heads twice the size of his. They all looked to be no taller than five feet, some even about four feet tall, with short necks built thick and sturdy. Their bodies were broad, shoulders spanning three-or-more feet across, the men and the women alike. Even the children Gideon saw looked to be at least one and a half times as broad as him. Their heads weren't as egg-shaped as earthlings.' They were more circular with powerful jawlines.

Gideon momentarily forgot about the ache that gravity was putting on his muscles and joints. All the well-dressed, gorilla-like people were fascinatingly alien. They were definitely not what he was expecting, and that made them all the more exciting and intriguing. He wondered why not even one of them had offered to help them up.

Then, from his position on his back, Gideon barely noticed as a few people rushed by them on what he assumed were rollerblades or skates since he couldn't see their feet. They were going fast, but it looked like they just *whooshed* down the street with quick whirring sounds.

"Huh." Gideon squinted, trying to see where they went, but they were already gone.

Cooby groaned and growled, frustrated with his inability to move freely. He was a nimble creature with regularly quick twitch reactions and movements. The difficulty was making him antsy and irritable. He pawed at Duma, slowly dragging his heavy body over to her. She winced and grabbed his paw, interweaving with his clawed fingers.

Traveler, being the tallest and thinnest, was having the most trouble moving. He blinked rapidly and looked around, trying to get his senses to adjust. He rolled his head around and turned, making sure the others had all made it. He ground his teeth, utilizing all the strength he had to move his arm, flopping it over onto the cement's hard surface. He pushed a little harder and managed to point down one of the streets.

"He's that way." Talking was exhausting.

Gideon moved his jaw around, trying to stretch his already sore muscles. "How do you know…where he is?" He scooted a few inches toward Traveler, and though he couldn't stand, he was still grateful for the back brace.

Traveler took a heavy breath as he tried to push himself up to his knees. "It's where his laboratory is." He failed, collapsing back down.

"Does this—" Gideon tired at just speaking. "—get any easier? Is getting up even doable?" He wondered how the people of Thamiosh had managed to erect skyscrapers with such murderous gravity. He could only assume that their steel was thicker, stronger, and denser. Everything on Thamiosh probably was.

Traveler slowly shook his head. "Your mind will accept it...and your body will adapt as much as it can. But, no, it definitely doesn't get easier. Our bodies were not...intended to undergo such stress and pressure. By my calculations, our bones...muscles...joints...will break and tear if we spend more...than a couple days here."

Duma stared upward through her one determined eye. "It will make us...stronger if we view it as a challenge and not...an obstacle."

Traveler rolled his eyes, though the optimism was welcomed.

Gideon glanced at her. "Want some...protein with that pump, bro?"

Duma twitched. "What?" She looked around at the people scowling at them. "Why do they...glare at us with such disdain?"

Traveler grunted an exhale. "The people of Thamiosh...are not tolerant or hospitable...they don't even like their own kind most of...the time. Hence...the majority of the planet is...poor, oppressed, and detested by the Conurbation Supreme."

Duma squinted at Traveler as she watched a few more brutish people scoff at them and walk by. "You brought us to a world you...clearly deem hostile...searching for a man of magic, er, *science*, believing that he will join our cause? And that you...can convince him to do so in...less than two days?"

Gideon thought about it. "Yeah, what's the plan here?" His question rabbit trailed through his own mind, quickly reminding him that his shoulder was healed. He closed his eyes, trying to contain the instant darkness that began spreading through his mind. He didn't have the strength or tools to cut it there.

"I have only heard rumors," Traveler said. "But the officials of the Conurbation Supreme will likely...see us as disfigured from birth defects, due...to our weaker bodies. I've heard that this scientist is their first response to...those with bodies similar to ours. There are many born on this planet...who are not equipped for the gravity... so they often perish. The harshness of this planet leaves the majority of the population...disfigured, injured, broken in some way or another. The Conurbation banishes all who aren't... 'supreme' out into Thamiosh, the rest of the planet." He tried to clear his throat. "The man we come for is...known for experimenting on them...to try to improve upon physical flaws and imperfections... to improve abnormalities. So, the plan...is to get taken to him...since we can't walk there on our own."

Gideon's eyes widened. "A mad scientist? You're serving us on a silver platter to...a mad scientist in a city that hates...abnormal people like us?"

Dumakleiza immediately longed for her weapons. "I, too, feel this plan is ill-omened."

"It doesn't matter what kind of man he is," Traveler said. "I've heard he's brilliant...and I have no doubt that telling a scientist...about worlds beyond...will inspire curiosity."

Gideon took a deep breath, trying to get his lungs to fully inflate. "What if he's more Dr. Frankenstein than Albert Einstein?"

"Huh?" Dumakleiza asked.

"A dark wizard," Gideon growled.

Traveler shot him a sharp glance. "What is wrong with you?" He realized it was the shoulder. Then, before he could respond further, a loud, shallow voice barked from somewhere unseen. They looked up to see some men in uniforms walking toward them with foreign firearms drawn. The group was obviously police of the Conurbation Supreme. While the regular citizens were walking around with black and white outfits similar to those the four of them arrived with, the cumbersome officers were decorated with silver medals and badges. The man in charge, an even thicker officer with a bulldog jaw and short, black hair, pointed down at them.

"Get them on the gurneys. Highness Trollop will want to see the banished before they're dealt with." The other officers squatted down and grabbed Gideon, Traveler, Duma, and Cooby off the ground like wet towels. They groaned in helpless discomfort. With a few heavy grunts, the hulky officers *thwapped* them onto some gurneys. They even sounded like gorillas with how heavily they exhaled. As soon as they had the four of them off the ground, the same order barking captain pointed. "To Trollop."

At the command, the officers leaned over the gurneys. The same whirring sound caught Gideon's attention as he noticed they were moving forward along the street, but he didn't feel any traction or friction beneath him. The table seemed to be gliding forward, and so were the officers holding onto them. Gideon winced as he forced his head to turn and look at the other gurneys. Both they and the officers were hovering, propelled forward by a force he didn't understand. All he could figure without Traveler's explanation was that the foreign looking metallic bases at the bottom of the gurneys were made of up some kind of magnets. The officers' boots had similarly made soles. They glided forward, passing pedestrians at what Gideon assumed to be at least thirty miles per hour. The increasing speed amplified the intensity and shock that his body was already experiencing. As the overpowering inertia turned murderous, his eyes rolled back in his head and everything went black.

It felt like Gideon was only out for a moment before a sharp slap across his cheek roused him. His heavy eyelids shot open. His senses were immediately overwhelmed by bright indoor light and the pungency of perfume clogging his lungs. His eyes slowly adjusted to an ogress face overflowing with long orange hair staring down at him. The dense woman was smiling a large smile with caked-on eyelashes beneath her protruding forehead. Gideon was startled, and his healed shoulder had him disgusted.

He glanced around the room. Gaudy decorations covered the walls. Glittery, glimmering, sparkling everything. It made Gideon want to gag. Clashing senses of style combined bright colors that intensified his headache.

The woman leaned down a little closer, her smile growing. "They're unlike any inferiors I've ever seen," she said with an awkwardly happy voice. "How did they get in?"

Dumakleiza failed to sit up. "Inferiors? How dare you?" She roared as adrenaline surpassed her speaking difficulty. "Who do you think you are to deem us less than you, foul witch?"

Traveler winced as he tried to turn his head toward her. "Dumakleiza, be quiet!" There was an abundance of officers in the room with the woman and he didn't want to cause trouble.

The looming redhead giggled as she daintily pointed a manicured finger at Dumakleiza. "Close that one's lips. I don't like her voice."

"Yes, Highness Trollop." The police captain grunted as he sluggishly pulled out what looked like a taser. He took two brutish steps toward Dumakleiza, placed it against her throat, and clicked. *Bzt!* An electrical pulse zapped through her neck. Dumakleiza went to roar but her vocal chords didn't engage. Gideon shook, desperately wanting to help. Duma's eyebrows lowered in confusion as she tried to yell again. Nothing. She was rendered completely mute. She wanted to liberate herself and slay all of the officers, but she could barely even lift a finger.

"Ah, that's much better. I'm sorry, sweetie." Highness Trollop delicately patted Duma's shaking shoulder with her large hands before smiling the same slighting smile toward the police captain. "Thank you, Captain Diggid. You're such a dear." Her grating voice somehow made the captain grin with bashful appreciation. Trollop wiped her hands on her glistening white dress, removing any filth she could have contracted from touching Dumakleiza's skin.

Gideon watched Duma aching to retaliate. Cooby, too, squalled and screamed, wanting to protect his person. Gideon fumed, his rage consuming him. He fought gravity as hard as he could, trying to sit up. He roared at Trollop as he barely managed to lift his head.

"I'll snap your fat neck, you pig-faced harlot!"

Trollop gasped as she shot him an offended look, tears welling in her eyes. "How could you say that? To *me*? After all I've done for your kind?"

Diggid quickly stepped forward and zapped Gideon in the throat. Gideon was instantly muted as Diggid turned and silenced Cooby, as well. They both pushed and pulled, trying to force any movement, begging themselves to budge, but to no avail. Diggid smiled at their attempts before stepping back in line next to the other officers.

Trollop wiped her offended eyes as she looked down. "So." She playfully clapped. "How did you all break into Supreme? You're too weak to even stand. And what kind of mutated inferior garbage is that?" She giggled as she pointed her long fingernails at Cooby. "And what did you think you would do here? You know there's no one that would harbor your kind in Supreme. You should have stayed where you belong in Thamiosh. Your kind is better there. Happier." Her voice was irritatingly chipper for such blatant condescension.

Duma squirmed, slowly reaching for where her swords normally were on her hips.

Traveler spoke for them as Gideon violently brooded in forced silence. "We heard you have a scientist in your employ that you allow to help…those like us. We came in hopes we could be granted an audience with him."

Trollop lowered her large eyebrows. "I would never *allow* inferiors into Supreme." She scoffed with a squeal lacing her words. "That would be outlandish and quite—" She stopped and brought a finger to her painted lips, tapping them a couple times. "Do you think maybe he's talk-ing about Timrekka?" She nodded.

Diggid blindly mirrored her nodding. "Yeah, probably."

Trollop sighed and tapped her nails together. "He was always exper-imenting on them. It was grotesque and heart-tearing, really."

Traveler paused at the wording. "Was?" *Deep breath.* "Did he die?"

"Oh, no." Trollop shook her head, annoyed. "He was a cockroach, darling. I couldn't kill him—or reason with him." She giggled and scoffed before brushing her hair back.

Traveler began to panic. "Where is he?"

"I told him to stop trying to fix those that can't be fixed. You can't save those that nature itself deemed deserving of merciful deaths. That's why you're all out there in Thamiosh where you belong. It's kinder, merciful, you see? Supreme isn't for you. Don't you under-stand that?"

Again, Diggid nodded. "Don't you all understand that it's better for you out in Thamiosh? Inferiors belong there."

Traveler was over Trollop's arrogance. "If we could just talk to Tim-rekka, I promise you'll never see us again."

Trollop chuckled and placed her large hand on her stomach. "You've come over the wall in search of someone you could have stayed in Thamiosh to find." She snorted as her giggling got the better of her. "Please, I wouldn't allow his insolence to continue. He insisted on helping the inferiors instead of focusing on everything I told him to—instead of helping those who actually needed his brilliance—so we replaced him. Timrekka is banished to Thamiosh. He can toil away with the hopeless till he dies of inferior infections." She gagged.

Traveler was sensing something off about where the conversation was heading. "I see. How far from Thamiosh are we right now?"

Trollop sighed scornfully as she looked over the four of them. "We're in the capital of Supreme, of course, perfectly centered in this beautiful city. We're safe from your kind, one hundred and sixteen miles from the wall in any direction." She tapped her nails together again. "Makes me wonder how you got so far inside our walls with your—bodies."

"I see." Traveler's mind raced through calculations. "Then we sincerely apologize for breaching your walls. We—" *Deep breath.* "—simply sought Timrekka. Send us back and we'll be on our way."

Trollop shook her head with sadistic sympathy. "You will probably die before you find him. I should probably put you out of your misery now. It'd be the right thing to do—the humane thing for animals like yourselves." She smiled at them lovingly as Diggid nodded along with her plan, drawing his gun.

"At your command, Highness Trollop."

"Do it now. They're making me sad to look at."

Traveler suddenly wished he would have cut Gideon's shoulder as soon as they'd landed. They were in dire need of Gideon's enchanting charisma. Traveler had heard rumors of the dictator's ruthlessness, and her selfishness was only worsened by her inexplicable insanity. He had to think quickly.

"Highness, if I may be so bold: I humbly request you execute us outside, so we don't stain the beauty of the capital walls with our inferior blood."

Trollop gasped and nodded, bringing her hand to her heart. "Oh, that would be an unfortunate blemish." She motioned toward Diggid. "He is so sweet." She pointed at Traveler. "Take them outside and execute them."

22

Supreme's capital building was the tallest skyscraper in the city. It was forty stories high, built to the exact specifications of her highness' demands. She had wanted it to be one hundred stories, but the structure hadn't been able to handle the weight. It overlooked all Supreme as far as the eye could see.

Diamond elevator doors opened on the capital's roof. Captain Diggid led the way as four officers behind him hovered out the gurneys. The bright light of Thamiosh's midday sun stung Duma's dragon eye, even through her eyepatch. She groaned in muzzled frustration, clenching her heavy fists. Powerless and angry, she silently prayed to Grimleck for help.

Cooby was squalling, or at least he was trying to, but he couldn't make any noise, either. His long, clawed hands wiggled, wishing to glide away off the skyscraper. The loyal animal's dark, beady eyes pleaded with Dumakleiza, making her tear up. She felt as much pressure from guilt as she did from Thamiosh's gravity.

Gideon wasn't even paying attention to their predicament. He'd tuned out as soon as they'd been guaranteed executions. He was blinded by lividity. It wasn't their imminent deaths. Something darker threatened to unbury itself. His lips were going pale. His fingers were losing color from clenching.

Diggid grumbled as he unfolded a large tarp, whipping it in the air and laying it on the ground. He groaned and then motioned for the officers to put the inferiors down onto it.

As the cops scooped the four of them into their arms like piles of laundry, Traveler spoke. "Don't worry. None of us will be going into the stars alone. Just remember to hold each other's hands, so we can stick together in the heavens." The cops laughed at Traveler's hope for the afterlife, but Gideon and Dumakleiza got the message.

The officers tossed them onto the tarp with lackadaisical carelessness, the inferiors' limbs smacking the hard surface and heads all but cracking at the impact. The stronger gravity was not kind to their bodies as bruises immediately formed from what would have normally been a little fall.

Without wasting any time, the officers popped the latches to their holsters. Traveler flexed his jaw as he used every ounce of his strength to raise his trembling hand and aim it toward the sky. He peered through the straining gravity, focusing his attention on what only he could see. He squeezed his fingers shut, grabbing hold of something. His other hand was trapped beneath Gideon's torso. He could feel skin-on-skin contact and that was good enough. Duma lay tossed over Gideon's legs, with Cooby right next to her. She grabbed Gideon's ankle with one hand and one of Cooby's paws with her other.

The officers took aim at the dogpile of limp inferiors. After a few deep breaths fueling empty thought, Captain Diggid nodded his wide head.

"Do it."

Duma's prayer went silent as Traveler opened his hand.

In one moment, the officers squeezed their triggers. Muffled *zaps* zipped through the air as electrically charged bullets tore through the roof. All the officers' eyes peeled open as they stared at the empty tarp. There were no bodies, only holes. The inferiors had vanished.

Diggid walked over to the tarp, tapping it with his foot as his mind failed to comprehend what he'd just seen. "Where did they—how did they—" His monotone voice spiked a little as his mind short-circuited.

As he and the other offices puzzled in a dumbfounded stupor, they heard Highness Trollop's bubbly voice in their earpieces.

"Are those poor little sweeties disposed of?"

Diggid slowly reached up and touched his earpiece as his eyes stayed glued to the tarp. "No, they, uh, disappeared."

"They what?" her displeased voice shrieked.

"They, uh, disappeared."

"Then go find them!" Her shrill hysteria screamed into the officers' ears. They winced and reached for their heads, ducking as if she was standing right in front of them. They could hear Trollop burst into tears. "I can't have them infecting Supreme like a disease! I expect better from you, Captain Diggid!" Her voice had a sour sting to it. "What good are you if you're not fulfilling your highness' needs—if you're not doing what's necessary to sustain Supreme's way of life? I may as well throw *you* out into Thamiosh with the other worthless inferiors! Do you not want my love?"

Diggid fervently nodded. "No. No. Yes. I mean, no. I mean—we'll find them." His deep monotone was back. "We'll find them."

Gideon's eyes fluttered as white light once again faded from his vision. He still couldn't move, but at least his muscles, bones, and joints didn't feel smashed like they had just moments prior. He looked around from his back. Traveler, Dumakleiza, and Cooby were around him, all lying on the ground.

They were in the middle of another street, but this one was not as pristine. On either side of the road were worn buildings with fading paint jobs, graffiti, and tattered tapestries with once vibrant colors hanging like forgotten decorations. A few of the buildings looked like they were homes, similar to decrepit apartments Gideon was familiar with in third world countries back on Earth. There were differences, most obvious of which was the height of each floor. Gideon was accustomed to the eight to eleven-foot floors, but these apartment buildings looked to be only six feet per story.

Gideon slowly rolled his head toward Traveler. "Where...are we?"

"Thamiosh." Traveler drew labored breaths. "I used a light travel technique called 'whipping.'" *Deep breath.* "Whipping keeps us in the same planet's atmosphere by...leveraging the light's elasticity within the planet's gravity so we can travel the planet without leaving it. The more gravity...the easier it is to pull off." *Deep breath.* "As you can tell, there's more than enough gravity to work with here." He chuckled painfully.

Gideon rolled his eyes as he held his hand over his smooth left shoulder. "You didn't take the opportunity to...get us off of this awful planet?" His words were thick with contempt as his darkness returned. "They... do...not...want...us...here."

Dumakleiza turned her face from Traveler to Gideon. "Is this not the quest you...pleaded for me to accompany you on?" She was confused by his shift in demeanor. It was his magnetism that drew her interest in in the first place. "You warned me that this journey would not be...without difficulty. Why do you wish to flee before the quest's completion?"

The truth to her words only annoyed Gideon. The longer he went without cutting his shoulder, the more he just wanted to be alone. He was used to being alone, to traveling alone, eating alone, sleeping alone. Only short, first impressions were familiar. Having a growing number of travel companions with evolving dynamics was taking a toll.

Traveler sighed. He was already frustrated with the gravity, Highness Trollop, and the difficulty finding Timrekka. Gideon's dark neediness was only making their situation worse.

"We will look for Timrekka here. If we can't find him soon, we will leave."

Gideon flexed his jaw as his eyebrows lowered. "How the hell do you expect us to find *anything* when we can't...even stand?" His anger spiked his ability to speak. "You *really* don't plan well."

Then, as Traveler was about to respond, some low voices caught their attention. Three people walked up. Traveler, Gideon, and Duma looked to see two stout women, one with pale skin, and the other as dark as night. They had baggy clothes that shared the same worn colors of many of the tapestries. With them, a darker man, no taller than the women, but quite a bit huskier, bulging with muscle reminiscent of a rhinoceros, stood, staring down at the thin people on the ground. He gave them a pitiful look before stepping closer.

"They're not okay," he said with a surprisingly silky voice.

Traveler thought quickly just in case they weren't friendly. "We need to see Timrekka. Do you...know Timrekka?"

"Yeah," the thick man said with a loud, hacking cough. "You lookin' for Rekka from Supreme, right? I know where to find him." With that, he motioned to the two burly females. They stomped over and scooped the four of them off the ground. The same whirring sound buzzed as the massive humans' boots propelled forward, hovering a couple inches above the street. Once again, the combination of intense inertia mixed with the gravity made Gideon pass out.

Again, light accompanied the fading numbness as Gideon slipped back into consciousness. Again, he was lying on a table, but it didn't feel like a gurney.

Gideon blinked as he realized he was indoors with another large head looming over, studying him. He was immediately furious, fearing it was Highness Trollop again. His vision cleared. He saw a new face staring down at him. The new man's ogrish head had long white hair down to his nonexistent neck in thick strands. Wrapped around his wide face were what looked like some kind of bifocal, welding glasses. His magnified eyes studied Gideon behind the thick lenses. He stared him up and down while rubbing his chin and nodding.

Gideon looked from him to their surroundings. They were in what he assumed was an underground room since there were no windows anywhere. The walls were lined with shelves, brimming with books of all sizes, and papers plastered all over the place with handwriting, mathematical equations, drawings, and scribbles. There were desks and tables, all messily covered with numerous trinkets, miscellaneous tools, and parts of all matters of things, most of them colored blue. Gideon couldn't tell if the room was a mess, or a living workspace of methodical disorder. He looked back up at the man reviewing him. They made eye contact and the man jerked back, trembling like a spooked squirrel.

"Oh, you're awake, I thought you'd never wake up, and were just gonna die, flatten, not get up, because you seem sickly and broken." He rattled off words so erratically and quickly that it sounded like he spoke only in run-on sentences.

Traveler looked over at the curious man. "Where are we? We're looking for a man named Timrekka."

"That's me." The white-haired man smiled through his goggles, quickly patting his chest before returning to his hunched position over Gideon.

"Oh good," Traveler said in a strained wave of relief. "We were hoping we would find you sooner than later. We're from—"

"Somewhere far away, right?" Timrekka adjusted his goggles and smiled. "I knew right away you weren't from here, probably another world by my guess; part of why I was banished—not only for helping people which, lemme tell ya, I've always known Trollop Highness to be a dense, daft meat bucket, but damn, the mercilessness of that self-entitled monster—but anyways, I also ruffled too many fists with my theories of life on other worlds, and theories that didn't coincide with her agendas." He took a deep breath as his only means of punctuation. He poked Gideon's arm.

Traveler and Dumakleiza looked at each other. They were struggling to keep up with how fast Timrekka spoke.

"I've always thought there was more out in the universe than just Thamiosh, and here you are, aliens—though *we* are probably the aliens to you, which is fascinating, but I'm just trying to figure out what advanced societies like yourselves used to get here; I've figured that spaceships are impractical, but hey, what do I know? I've never been able to study much of space at all, so I really don't know how it works, where all it is, how it—sorry I talk faster when I'm excited." He beamed with happiness as he looked from one of them to the other, waiting for any kind of confirmation or answers.

Traveler smiled. "How did you manage to figure out that we're from another world?"

"Psh." Timrekka waved the question away. "Infant's play; I've spent my entire life studying the differences of the strong and the weak, and even with everything I've seen, which is everything here on Thamiosh, I've never come across anyone with anatomy like yours; your physiology is completely unlike anyone I've ever seen so, of course, obviously you're not from this world—well, maybe not obvious to everyone else, but you didn't fool me for a millisecond." Again, he smiled while waiting for them to sneak a word in. He scratched his head as his eyes twitched and oscillated between the limp beings.

Dumakleiza stared at Timrekka with her mouth open. "How does one such as yourself—" *Deep breath.* "—manage to even breathe? You speak faster than men I've lit on fire."

Traveler smiled, entertained by the hyperactive scientist. "Sounds like the preceding claims of your brilliance were…well earned. I'd be happy to—" *Inhale.* "—answer all of your questions, but first—" *Gasp.* "—in your scientific studies, specifically with inferiors, is there—" *Deep breath.* "—anything you can do for us?"

"Oh, of course, my apologies; I don't know why I didn't do that first, I'm sorry." Timrekka spun around, quickly walking over to a desk and sliding a drawer open. He fidgeted through what sounded like a mess of random junk. "Aha!" He spun back around with a handful of syringes, all filled with some kind of blue liquid. "These should do the trick, or at least something interesting should happen; let's find out."

Traveler wanted to trust him, but their experiences on Thamiosh weren't very encouraging. "What is that?"

"I call it blue super juice; I'm not a very creative type with names, but I can make just about anything *with* just about anything, you know, breaking everything down to its base components and reorganizing whatnot." He squinted, the magnification making his already monstrous eyes look like giant slits as he slid a thick needle into Traveler's arm. It found its mark in one of his veins. Traveler winced as Timrekka carefully forced the fluid into him. "Hopefully, it makes its way directly into your bloodstream because we don't want it getting anywhere else, because then it would cause—you know what, it'll be fine either way, so don't worry about it." Gideon and Dumakleiza strained themselves, trying to see what was happening from their pinned positions.

Traveler's eyes shot open and his mouth shook. Whatever Timrekka had given him made his entire body tremble. He could feel it coursing through his chest like an electric shock. It quickly flushed through his arms and legs, vibrating his fingers and toes with intense burning.

Dumakleiza's breath quickened. "What devilry is this? This can't be the science you spoke of."

Traveler arched his back and screamed before convulsing and sitting up. He shoved himself off the table and onto his feet. He stormed over to a desk and gripped its corners as he heaved over it, his arduous breathing starting to slow down. Cold sweat broke over his skin. His internal organs, respiratory system, muscles, bones, everything felt like it was swelling and then shrinking, growing and then tightening.

He coughed and shook his hands as the pain subsided. The sweat continued as he focused on breathing. Once he'd regained a little of his composure, he opened his eyes and stood up, blinking hard. Blood red immediately started fading from his eyes, leaving pure whites around his vibrating irises.

"Wow, that was—" He looked down, suddenly realizing he was standing. "How did you——?" He cleared his throat, finding the air much easier to breathe. Each little movement had become manageable. "What was that?" He chuckled. "I was just expecting that maybe you'd have better back braces or something of the sort. Not that you'd—how did you do that?"

Timrekka shrugged with a happy expression. "Oh, you know, muscle-densifier protein compounds, microscopically explosive myo-statin inhibiters, bone-densifying, calcium-infused steroidal micro-fibers, capillary expanders, blood soupers, vegetable minerals, a handful of animal hormones, blue dye just so it'll look blue because I think blue is a beautiful color, and a few of my other concoctions that help 'incapable *inferiors*' withstand the physicality of Thamiosh; it helps them strengthen up, you know—basically my version of a super soldier pick-me-up, though I think with you, it'll just help you function like a normal person would here." He smiled a goofy grin. "How do you like it?"

"It's incredible!" Traveler shouted. He smiled and stretched his jaw around. "Give it to them."

Timrekka gave an enthusiastic nod as he quickly walked toward the tables. "I can't tell you enough how refreshing it is to have someone actually appreciate something I've made; everyone in Supreme, especially Trollop, couldn't understand—let alone appreciate— anything I'd done. She was just always nag, nag, nag, make me look better, never, ever condoning or supporting my innate desire to help the less fortunate, preferring I simply leave them to their fates or her merciless version of kindness through executions."

He sped between the tables as he stuck Gideon, Duma, and Cooby with needles faster than their strained eyes could keep up with. Once all three syringes were plunged and emptied, Timrekka turned back toward Traveler and smiled.

"All right, I have so many questions, like where are you from, how many planets are there exactly and, of course, just based off your anatomies alone, I can tell you're all from three separate planets, confirming my long time theory that each world has different physiology, conditions, and exponentially different variations of humanity; I'm super interested in how you travel from one to the other, and what is it like in space?" Timrekka's speeding words surprised Traveler with their accuracy in subject matter.

Gideon, Dumakleiza, and Cooby groaned and roared as they seized on their tables, convulsing and foaming at the mouths. The blue super juice coursed through their veins, one by one sending them lurching to their feet as they thrashed around the room, knocking things off tables and screaming. Timrekka smiled as he watched, studying their reactions and jotting down mental notes for improving his formula. He even maintained his smile as Cooby broke a few things. He didn't care. All that mattered were the results of his work.

Traveler chuckled. "I'm glad to see them handling it as poorly as I did. It would have been embarrassing to be the only one to have a violent reaction."

Timrekka smiled and nodded. "Definitely much stronger of a reaction than Thamioshlings have to it."

Dumakleiza and Cooby finally caught their breath, coughing and focusing on the ins and outs of their lungs as they stood. Cooby hobbled over to Dumakleiza's legs and cuddled around them, whimpering. Recovering from the blue super juice was painful, and he was scared by the whole ordeal. He whined and pawed at Duma's pant leg. She patted his head, petting him as her pulse slowed.

Gideon swallowed and looked up as he regained composure, staring at the ceiling. A cold sweat beaded on his head, but at least the gravity wasn't beating him down anymore. Once he could move, he wasted no time taking care of what was at the top of his priority list. He couldn't even hear Traveler and Timrekka speaking. Without taking the time to warn anyone, he grabbed what looked like a scalpel off the table next to him and wielded it like a poet's quill, slicing his shoulder with one swift motion. As blood streamed down his arm from the slice, he exhaled heavily and dropped his head. Deep breaths poured from his quivering lips as he felt the darkness leaving.

Dumakleiza's eyes shot open, her attention suddenly distracted from the wonder of standing. All that mattered was Gideon's self-mutilation. She backed away, ushering Cooby behind her legs to shield him. Had the blue super juice driven Gideon mad?

Traveler watched in relief, knowing Gideon would soon return to his normal self, while Timrekka, who hadn't been watching, turned to see what they were all gawking at. He saw the blood streaming down Gideon's arm. He nodded, focusing as he turned to one of his many desks. Without asking any questions, he pulled a couple drawers open and started digging through more junk. Dumakleiza watched with stern eyes as the hefty scientist fiddled around, unfazed. After a few seconds, he stopped.

"There you are." He pulled out what looked to Gideon like a blue hairdryer. He walked over to Gideon's side and stuck his tongue out of the side of his mouth as he flicked a switch, aiming the tool at Gideon's wound. "This might sting a little." He squeezed a trigger and *voosh*! A powerful suction from the machine latched to Gideon's shoulder, enveloping the cut. Timrekka, the tool, and Gideon all vibrated at the whirring. Gideon winced, returning his attention to the land of the living as he looked to see what was going on.

Traveler's eyes were plastered to what Timrekka was doing. It looked like he was making the cut worse. A few seconds of powerful suction later and Timrekka released the trigger. The shaking stopped.

"There you go, all better, as if nothing happened," he said with a chipper voice. "I call this one 'the wound sucker' — once again, not a good title, but it basically administers an overdose of aggressive white blood cells and a regenerative cocktail of microscopic vitamin powder, electric stimuli, and some other inventions of my own, filling open wounds before they have a chance to fester." He pulled the tool away.

Gideon, Traveler, and Duma leaned in to see what had happened. Gideon's left shoulder was perfectly healed as if he'd never cut himself at all. Traveler sighed as Gideon glared at Timrekka. Then, without warning, he reached up with the scalpel and sliced his shoulder again in the same spot.

Timrekka's throat tightened as he slowly stepped backward, keeping his eyes on the new stream of blood. He turned and gave Traveler a silent look of distress that begged to know if he was in danger.

Traveler sighed as he shrugged. "I don't know. It's just something he needs to do every time we go to a new world. I know it's weird, but I promise you that from here on out, as long as we're on Thamiosh, he'll probably end up being your new favorite person. Trust me."

Timrekka slowly nodded. He wasn't satisfied with the answer, but he decided not to debate with the advanced people from other worlds. He cleared his throat, keeping the wound sucker in his hand. If need be, he could use it as a bludgeoning defense. He cleared his throat again and hesitantly looked at Gideon.

"Are you all right?"

Gideon took a deep breath and let it out, nodding as his normal smile finally returned. "Yes, I'm really sorry about that. I know I probably made you uncomfortable but believe me when I say that's the last thing I intended." He took a few more breaths and wiped his shoulder. "I just needed that more than you know." His smile returned in its full glory. "So." His voice perked up. "I really wanna see all of your inventions!" He looked around the room, smiling at the giant mess of brilliance scattered about. It was like an unexplored playground. "Mind giving me a tour?"

23

Timrekka slipped off his lab coat and dropped it, revealing suspender-like shoulder straps and a utility belt around his thick body. They both held numerous little inventions that looked to span the full spectrum of function and purpose. He kept his lips pressed tightly together and his wary eyes on Gideon.

Gideon was perfectly content with his bleeding shoulder. He smiled as he waited to be shown all the bizarre scientist's toys. He was sitting back on the table, hands clasped on his lap, and legs gently swinging back and forth. His attitude was a complete paradigm shift, and only Traveler was able to shrug it off.

Timrekka stared at him for a moment and then shook his nerves away. "Um, most of these I haven't tested on anyone other than my friend, Schlayfe, and, uh, let's see, uh, thirty-eight meeblesks now, of course, but I have high hopes for—"

"What are meeblesks?"

Traveler answered Gideon's question for Timrekka. "Mouse-like creatures. Just larger, and with horns that resemble those of your rams."

"Oh, cool." Gideon brought his head back. "Go on."

Timrekka nodded at Traveler, thanking him for the translation. "Um, this one was one of my firsts." He pulled a marker from his belt. "Basically, just color anything with this and it infuses skin cells with fabricated hair follicles, planting roots if you will, so, yeah, goodbye baldness—however, be careful because it will literally grow hair anywhere; I have a—or I should say, I *had*—a friend, nah, he's still a friend, Schlayfe, who now has to shave his eyelids. We drew on each other while we were intoxicated. I really need to create a cure."

Gideon laughed. "There would be so many hairy dick drawings growing out of people's faces back on Earth. Good thing we don't have that one."

Timrekka looked down, sucking his lips between his teeth in shame. "Yeah, Schlayfe has that on his rear end; we really should never drink together—better yet, I should just never drink, let's be honest, too much of a high-risk factor, but I love plu."

Gideon gave him a curious look, but Traveler had it covered.

"A much denser version of tequila, something *you* specifically should *never* have. I can only imagine the chaos you'd incite."

"Ah." Gideon smiled. "Okay, I'll be good." He leaned in toward Timrekka and whispered. "You'll have to share this plu when my babysitter isn't watching." He pointed a thumb at Traveler and winked.

Timrekka smiled. He slid the marker back into its belted slot and then removed a glass vial containing a flower with blue petals. Gideon cocked his head curiously, trying to guess what the flower could be. Timrekka held it in an outstretched hand and stared at it with reverent caution.

"Never smell this flower out of this case or even stand downwind of someone holding it, because if you breathe its sweet-scented pollen, its chemical makeup will specifically target your bones, eating away at the osteoblasts on their outer layers, literally reversing the process by turning your bones into acidic, suicidal weapons, leading to them dissolving within you until your bloodstream absorbs them like food nutrients."

Gideon, Traveler, and Dumakleiza stared at him with ghastly wide eyes. Gideon cleared his throat in disgusted surprise.

"It removes bones?"

"All of them. It's surprisingly painless actually, but it dissolves every bone in any mammalian body, leaving every other part of the anatomy untouched, so anyone who suffers its power can ultimately and theoretically survive, but without a single bone, no skull, skeleton, teeth, anything."

Gideon blinked a few times, trying not to imagine what that would be like. "Holy spirit. And this flower just friggin' grows on this planet? Like, there's fields of them somewhere?"

"Good greatness, no." Timrekka shook his head as he pocketed the vial. "I invented it, slowly cross-breeding, cross-pollinating plant species, and feeding it a specific mulch I've made over a few years made of experimentation with different animal feces, human feces, and varying chemicals, of course, and I did all this trying to concoct a cure for fedolinaclis, a disease here on Thamiosh that eats away at digestive tracts and the irises of people's eyes, but I accidentally created this little beauty—" He pointed at the vial with the flower. "—that I've come to call Trollop's Petals, because *she* seems to have removed the spine of her entire police force."

"Nice," Gideon chuckled with an approving thumbs-up.

Timrekka smiled sheepishly. "The wound sucker will not help you if you suffer Trollop's Petals." He cleared his throat, hoping that mentioning scars and wounds wouldn't bring any more crazy out of Gideon. "While the wound sucker cauterizes, sutures, and electrically stimulates cell regeneration, I feel like there's something missing, like an element that I'm not thinking of."

"Light," Traveler answered for him.

"Is that it?" Timrekka itched his temple and smiled. "I cannot tell you how refreshing it is to have someone actually understand what I'm talking about and believe in what I'm doing without thinking I'm doing—"

"Witchcraft?" Dumakleiza guessed.

Timrekka giggled. "Exactly, again! Wow, you're clearly a well-rounded, diverse group of aliens; hmm, okay, let me rush through some of these, and then I have a plethora of questions that I cannot wait for you to answer." He pointed at Traveler, who nodded and then motioned for him to continue. Timrekka smiled, adjusting his goggles. "Whew, okay." He pointed to another syringe in his crisscrossing chest straps. "Love potion infused with the pheromones of thirteen of the most sexually aggressive animals on Thamiosh—I'm not sure if it's considered consensual if you inject someone with this because they acquire an insatiable libido that borders on inhuman; they nearly go mad with desire until climax is reached as many times as it takes. So, yeah, I haven't given it to anyone other than a meeblesk that ultimately, um, mated four other meeblesks to death and then continued until its heart gave out and it, too, died——so, not my best invention, but I figure it'll come in handy one day, maybe, probably not, but who knows? I'm keeping it," he said decidedly, his tone challenging anyone to argue.

"Ha!" Gideon shook his head. "Super-powered reverse roofies. Instead of giving someone a date rape drug, you give them a drug that makes *them* a rapist. On one hand, kind of brilliant, and on the other, terrifying." He laughed, avidly entertained.

Timrekka nodded and shrugged. "Like I said, not my best." He pointed down the line on his chest from one item to the next. "Endorphin enhancers and diminishers in pill forms, experimental microbots I'm still working on, meant to increase memory, grappling hook gloves, camouflage powder, a dream maker, and—"

"Whoa. Whoa. Whoa." Gideon waved his hands as he leaned forward, bursting with questions. "What are those last two? You can't just drop names like those without explaining them."

"Agreed," Duma chimed in, trying to understand any of them as she slowly made her way over next to Traveler. To her surprise, he was the one she felt the safest with in the moment.

"Uh, let's see here." Timrekka recounted his last words. "Ah, right, well camo powder, when ingested, triggers adaptability within the pigmentation of the skin by introducing an absorbing, digestive agent so that the skin mimics the colors of whatever it's touching — something I think our military could find very useful, but Trollop Highness just tossed the idea to the garbage, because, you know, helping the military blend into their surroundings more efficiently isn't at all important." He rolled his eyes and grunted before moving on. "And this little dream maker —" He pointed to a metal box the size of a deck of cards with two electrodes connected to it. "—is a clever little device, if I do say so myself, and I absolutely do, that attaches to both sides of someone's temple; they select what kind of dream they want with this little knob here, such as erotic, fantasy, good memory, bad memory, nightmare, zombie, adventure, flying, and a few others, then when they go to sleep, it uses electrical impulses to stimulate specific parts of the unconscious brain to create corresponding dreams, and most of the time it's worked for me."

"Those both sound awesome," Gideon said in amazement. "And they all work?"

Timrekka teetered his head back and forth. "Eh. Like I said before, I've not experimented too much on people, as no one's been super eager to take the place of my meeblesks, though I've definitely made enemies, or at least some grudge holders, of some of the locals who *thought* they could handle the task."

Gideon beamed with eagerness. "Well, I would be happy to be your guinea pig, er… meeblesk for any and all of these. Worst case scenario, you hurt me and Spaceman here —" He motioned to Traveler. "—has to heal me with a light-speed vacation."

Timrekka stared at him in disbelief. "No really, don't toy with me, I'll get my hopes *way* up; do you mean it? I can experiment on you and that's, you're, I mean, you're all right with that?"

Gideon mulled it over for one thousandth of a second. "Yes, of course! Why not?"

Timrekka brought a hand to his mouth, trying to contain his excitement. He squealed, unable to keep it in any longer as he gleefully clapped his broad hands together. Once his palms started turning pink, he calmed down and looked around at all his contraptions.

"Okay, there's no time like the immediate; here, let's just start off simple." He pulled out a small case and opened it, exposing two contact lenses. "These are called chameleon eyes, and I think they have the potential to help with a wide variety of things, but for the life of me, I can't find anyone who will give them a go, so if you're sure you're willing, all you do is put them in your eyes."

Gideon puffed out his lip as he stared at them. He'd worn his fair share of costume contacts for Halloween parties, but his twenty-twenty vision had never medically called for them, and now that light had healed everything over and over, his eyes vision was better than it had ever been before. Dumakleiza watched with a slightly horrified expression as Gideon put them in his eyes. She'd never seen contacts, and placing something *in* one's eyes seemed barbaric, even by her standards. Traveler watched with pure curiosity. Everything Timrekka was showing and demonstrating counted to him as micro-testing to see if he was a good candidate for the fourth phase. So far, he was impressed and a little unsettled by some of Timrekka's brainchildren.

Gideon blinked and moved his jaw around as he adjusted to the thicker than normal contacts. "Huh, okay." He blinked more rapidly. "So, what do they do?" Nothing weird was happening. He looked at Timrekka, waiting for some kind of unusual explanation. Timrekka grabbed two pencils out of his pocket and held one up in each hand for Gideon to look at. Gideon stared at them, still experiencing no abnormality.

Then Timrekka simultaneously tossed one pencil to his left and the other to his right. Gideon's eyes immediately looked in separate directions, both pupils turning to the outer sides of his face. He lurched back as he saw in split-vision.

"What the——?" He blinked a few times and nervously chuckled. His heart was racing. "Okay, um." He tried moving them. Slowly, both pupils began moving around independently. Gideon laughed, enjoying the absurd ability.

His left eye saw Traveler, Duma, and Cooby staring at him with disturbed expressions. Duma was horrified. She scooted back as Cooby mirrored her energy, nervously squawking.

Gideon's right eye was looking at Timrekka, who was smiling at the success. The excitable scientist cleared his throat and adjusted his giant goggles as he leaned in to study Gideon's reaction.

"Each contact severs each eye's optic nerve's connection to the other, freeing every muscle, or rectus, in the eye to move independently as long as the wearer is capable of mental multitasking; I can imagine it takes a lot of focus, though it looks like you're doing a pretty good job."

Gideon concentrated on breathing. "This is absolutely insane." He smiled, taking in the sensory overload. "It feels like I'm playing a two-player game on one screen." His eyes toggled around, starting to move faster as controlling them individually began making a tiny bit of sense. "And I just realized, you said your dream maker has a setting for *zombie* dreams?"

Timrekka nodded. "Oh, of course, those are scary, but every now and then I'm in the mood for a good fright, chased by the living dead; I know most people will probably never select that one, but I love it—I try to find a different melee weapon each time! I think I'd be too scared in real life."

Gideon smiled, looking at the ceiling with one eye and the floor with another. "I'm just surprised that the idea for zombies exists on other worlds. I think it's cool that Earth isn't the only place to have imagined the undead."

Traveler shrugged. "It's actually a popular lore on many planets. When thinking about what scares people, the dead coming back to life is pretty common."

Gideon turned one eye to Traveler. "Seriously? That's really cool."

Traveler nodded, staring at Gideon's left eye with some reserved discomfort. "In fact, did you know that even on your planet, zombies exist?"

The question piqued Gideon's curiosity, momentarily bringing both of his eyes together. "What?" He continued looking around in different directions, nearly causing Dumakleiza to vomit. "It's not that I doubt anything you tell me but what do you mean?"

Traveler nodded again. "Indeed. There's a species of ants and a species of fungi that interact in a strangely fascinating way. The ants walk through this fungus, and small spores from the fungus attach to the ant's skin. Using metabolism and unique mechanics, the spore burrows into the ant's head and takes over, basically killing the ant, and making the zombie-ant-corpse a slave to the fungi's needs. At a certain point, I believe it is when the Earth's sun is either at its highest or lowest, the ant attaches to the main vein of the fungi, its jaws locking onto it permanently. It stays there until it dies, and then the spore tears out of its deceased head, growing a new extension of the original fungi. The new extension then drops new spores to be picked up."

Timrekka's brain was buzzing. "It controls the ants, turning their brains to zombie mush to serve the purpose of the queen, or original plant, growing, spreading, breeding, and perpetuating the species?"

Traveler nodded. "Something like that. Once the ant dies, the fungi keeps its body functioning postmortem in order to serve its purpose for a short while longer. It's one of, honestly, hundreds of thousands of examples of biohacking we've observed in the natural order on every planet. Zombies are real and quite common."

"Hmm, fungus spores. I have to experiment with that." Timrekka scratched his head. "I've done some dabbling with parasites that mimic similar behavior but to no effect, but now I'm really excited to explore spore possibilities, keeping tissue alive postmortem; I have some very promising ideas rolling around in my head thanks to you." He smiled at Gideon.

Gideon chuckled. "You are totally the Doctor Frankenstein of this planet."

Timrekka cocked his head to the side. "Doctor who?"

"I don't see a Tardis anywhere." Gideon laughed while scanning the room. He knew no one would get it so he moved on. "Doctor Frankenstein was a mad scientist, obsessed with reanimating dead tissue by sewing body parts from different corpses together and then bringing the amalgamated freak show to life with a machine powered by lightning."

Timrekka cocked his head to the side. "Why would he use lightning to—" His eyes widened as his hands went to the side of his head. "Why didn't I think of it before? Reanimating dead tissue!" He spun around, clearing one of the desks and grabbing some papers. He snatched up a pencil and started furiously scribbling while mumbling under his breath.

Gideon took the contacts out. He shook his head as his eyes corrected and then placed the lenses back in their case. After adjusting to normalcy, he watched Timrekka, who was completely engrossed in his brainstorming.

"I'm surprised you don't have a hunchbacked assistant," he said as he looked around at the piles of junk and gadgets about the room.

Timrekka cocked his head unsurely. "I've met a few inferiors with hunched backs, but I found it better to correct their deformities and allow them to lead normal lives than to take advantage of their vulnerable handicap."

Duma leaned in next to Traveler's ear and whispered, "Why did Sir Gideon wound himself? A powerful evil left his eyes upon the bloodletting."

Traveler slowly nodded, keeping his eyes on Timrekka and Gideon. "I don't know. I'm hoping it doesn't jeopardize everything. Maybe one day he'll tell us why—what happened to him that made him the way he is."

Dumakleiza wasn't satisfied with the answer. "I shall pray for his sanity and for our safety in his presence." Then her unpatched eye widened as her left hand hung limp at her side, patting her clothing. She looked down, searching for something. After a bit more patting, she froze, eyes rolling back in her head. "The witch took them," she hissed.

Traveler turned to her. "Who took what?"

"Highness Trollop. She took the treasure of Yagūl. She took my holy sacrifice to Grim." Dumakleiza was seething. It felt as though her entire purpose had been stolen from her. Traveler wasn't sure what to say or how to console her since her treasure wasn't anywhere near the top of his priorities.

"I'm sorry, Dumakleiza."

She shook her head and looked at the table Gideon had been hovered in on. "Why did they not take the bag of Sir Gideon?"

Traveler smirked. "Because there's nothing of actual worth in there. It's full of keepsakes and souvenirs. No treasure."

"I will disembowel that witch and then we will see who is inferior."

Traveler nodded. "I don't like this world."

"Well, Timmy," Gideon said. "Any time you want to play show-and-tell, I'll happily be your meeblesk."

"Timmy." Timrekka bunched his lips, pondering the name. "That's an odd shortening; I've had people call me by Rek or Rekka, but never by the first half of my name. That's odd—I think I like it: Timmy, Timmy."

"Really?" Gideon smirked. "What about Tim?"

"Oh, that's a fun one: Tim, Tim, Tim, I like Tim."

"Deal!" Gideon laughed at Timrekka's excitability.

"I need some air," Traveler said, feeling vulnerable in Timrekka's medley of scientific torture devices that he called toys.

"Me too." Gideon grinned. "Well, Tim, shall we?"

Timrekka nodded and led the way, walking out the door as he rolled the name around in his mouth. "Tim, Tim, Tim the scientist, Tim the man of tools, Tim the tool man, Tim the—"

"Oh, my god." Gideon laughed as he followed.

24

Outside, they saw the town in a new light. For the first time on Thamiosh, they weren't pinned on their backs. Being able to stand and move around freely allowed them to see the territory for what it truly was: disheveled, worn down buildings, and decrepit neighborhoods, reminding Gideon of overpopulated shacks in Brazil. He looked around in every direction, trying to see the Conurbation Supreme but it was too far away. Sometimes he forgot they weren't just traveling cities, but entirely new planets.

"Tim, you wanna give us a tour of your city?" Gideon asked. "What are the sights around here?"

"Sure, I can show you arou——"

"Actually——" Traveler interrupted. "Gideon, if you and Dumakleiza want to take a walk around, I would like to talk with Timrekka."

Gideon smirked. "Oh, of course. Getting down to business. I got you."

"No, Diviner," Dumakleiza said. "If it wouldn't offend, I would prefer to stay and learn what is to be said of the stars."

Traveler recognized Dumakleiza's discomfort being alone with Gideon after his self-mutilation. "Fine. Try to keep up."

Gideon was already looking around as he walked away. "Cool if I borrow Cooby? Maybe try coasting off some buildings while you guys talk about grown-up stuff?"

"You will never fly with him. I have told you this," Duma shouted.

Gideon raised his hands and chuckled as he kept walking. "One day, Duma. One day."

Traveler smiled with obvious impatience before turning to Timrekka. "Your reputation truly preceded you. I was told you were brilliant, but I can't even think of a scientific equal, except for maybe on my world."

The topic instantly stole Timrekka's attention. "Where *is* your world, and why did you come to Thamiosh seeking me out of all nineteen billion people here?"

"Holy spirit, there are nineteen billion?" Traveler stopped as he realized what he'd said. He closed his eyes and pinched the bridge of his nose. "Gideon has me saying it now." He shook it off. "You being advanced and intelligent enough to comprehend that we're from other planets really expedites this conversation. We came seeking you—specifically you, because I'm recruiting a team, and that team needs a scientist—a prodigious scientist with an open mind."

Timrekka's eyes lit up. "What are you recruiting for?"

Traveler looked up into the sky. "How far have your people adventured into space?"

"Pfft," Timrekka grumbled. "Space—whatever is out there beyond Thamiosh is something I've been curious about since I was a child, something I've wanted to explore, that I've implored Trollop to fund a group to research, but you know Trollop Highness." He grunted irritably. "She threw all of my theories about space and what is beyond our world into the dump, and anyone who's ever tried to discuss the possibility of going into space has been silenced."

"What?" Traveler shouted. "Nothing? You've never sent a shuttle? An unmanned craft? A crew? Nothing? What about telescopes?"

"I don't know that word."

"You can't be serious. Trollop governs the entire planet, and she won't even—" Traveler growled. He was stunned, and his tone had Dumakleiza all the more curious. She was trying to understand as much of their conversation as she could, but it was difficult. She'd expected it to be, but she refused to be left behind under the pretense of inferior intelligence. Traveler shook his head. "Thamiosh, as advanced as it is, hasn't even begun the third phase? That's embarrassing."

Timrekka perked up. "The third phase of what?"

"Of human exploration!" Traveler yelled, throwing his hands out. "You haven't even manned a mission to one of your own moons. Every planet at least does that, so long as they have at least one." He counted the phases out on his fingers for Timrekka. "First phase: exploring one's planet until it's mapped out. Second phase: exploring the scientific properties held within one's planet. Third phase: exploring what's beyond one's planet. Space. Fourth phase: exploring what's beyond the ho—" He composed himself. "The fourth phase is a mystery, and its exploration and documentation is what I'm putting the team together for."

Timrekka's eyes were wide with interest. "That sounds incredible, but I have to qualify, right? *Have* I qualified already, have I passed whatever test? I am very interested in participating, though I have to warn you, I'm easily startled and scared, but I'll definitely try to help however I can."

Traveler shrugged and lifted his hands. "I think you're a perfect candidate. You're highly intelligent, brilliant enough to maybe pioneer even Whewliss—my world—into new territory, and you look durable. However, since you haven't even learned about space yet, there's going to be a lot you don't understand."

"I'm a quick learner."

"I don't doubt that." Traveler looked around for Gideon, but he was gone. "As soon as Gideon comes back, say goodbye to any family or friends. Pack anything you can that you need, so long as you can carry it, and I'll take you with us."

Timrekka shook his head, blinking under his magnified eyes. "Oh, I can't leave now; I thought you meant in a few weeks or so, I can't go yet. I promised the Darchangels I would help them create a sustainable power source, so they don't have to keep giving sacrifice payments to Trollop Highness."

Duma stepped closer, intrigued. "Who are the Darchangels? Spirits? The demons of Thamiosh?"

Timrekka smiled. "The gang that prominently runs this territory. They're really quite nice people, that is, unless they cross their rivals, the Dust Wranglers, who I think are nice people, too, but they maintain a rough reputation."

Traveler looked around at the worn-down area's poor condition. "What kind of sacrifice payments are they paying Trollop? And what kind of energy source are you trying to create?"

"Trollop has hundreds of planes going at all times, filled with officers that visit each territory, and they collect a life tax that covers all basic necessities, such as running water, electricity, gas, and also keeps the fangs at bay, or as truth would explain it, prevents executions to bury any suggestion of rebellion."

Traveler shook his head. "She's really quite the monster. How long has she been in charge?"

Duma stepped up. "It's a royal bloodline, is it not?" Timrekka nodded. Duma scoffed understandingly. "It is the same on my world of Cul. Her family has ruled in tyranny for generations, and will continue to do so, so long as no rebellion ends her oppressive reign."

"Oh, I've tried explaining that," Timrekka said in frustration. "I've tried telling the Darchangels that if they put their differences with the other gangs aside, they could rally up and outnumber the Conurbation Supreme one thousand to one, but their stubborn division makes them weak."

Traveler brainstormed. "You're trying to create a self-sustaining energy source, so they won't have to pay Trollop for energy. But how will that help them? Wouldn't she execute them when she realizes they're trying to replace their need of her?"

Timrekka sighed. "One problem at a time. They already have plenty of weaponry—I mean, they're gangs, but it pales in comparison to the arsenal that a single Supreme police plane carries on board; after all, I invented most of the firearms and body armor they use, and I'm good at what I do, so I'm not sure how to solve everything, but I'll think of something." He cleared his throat. "Once I've successfully left the Darchangels better off than I found them and they're safe from Trollop, I would be enthusiastically delighted to be your mission's scientist, as long as you're willing to wait for me, of course."

Traveler racked his brain for any shortcuts shy of kidnapping Timrekka that he could use. Nothing was coming to mind. He nodded through his impatience. "I'll see how I can help. You're a rarity, and likely invaluable, so I'm willing to assist you in that if it means you'll join us."

Dumakleiza read the moment as an acceptable time to interrupt. "I do not intend to be rude, Timrekka of Thamiosh, but could I bother you for something to eat for Cooby and myself? Back on my home, I cooked everything on my own; usually fish. I can do so here as well if need be, but I am unfamiliar with what animals you possess that I may——" She covered Cooby's ears. "——kill and cook. I assume Sir Gideon and the Diviner hunger, as well."

"Oh, of course." Timrekka shoved two of his sausage-sized fingers between his lips and whistled.

Traveler and Dumakleiza turned to see a horde of burly children come running out of their homes and into the street. They laughed and ran to Timrekka. As they swarmed him, he skittishly patted their massive heads.

"These are my assistants. They've been helping me with my project; their parents are far too alarmed of me, so they send their little minions to be my little minions, brave children." He looked up before jerking his head back down. "Ah, yes, would you all do our guests a favor and get them some food? They've traveled a long way and have only experienced the hospitality of the Supreme—I think we can show them better here."

A couple of the kids spat on the ground at the mention of Supreme.

"Oh, we are much better hosts," a large version of a little girl belted out before lumbering off.

"I'll get my mom to make something." A beast of a boy smiled out his words and then ran home with heaving thuds.

"My dad's burning some burgers right now." All the kids ran off in different directions like scavenger animals, collecting for the group.

Dumakleiza cocked her head to the side. "What are burgers?"

Traveler smiled. "One of the best things that nearly every planet at the end of the second phase inevitably invents. It's a guaranteed satisfied stomach. I promise you it'll be one of the best things you've ever eaten." He looked up through the sky. "The food I *really* can't wait to introduce you all to is on Whewliss."

"Not since my parents has food been prepared for me." Dumakleiza's mouth watered just thinking about eating. "Thank you, Timrekka of Thamiosh. Your hospitality is honorable."

"Oh please." Timrekka waved her graciousness away before pausing and staring at her for a moment. "I hope I don't offend you with this question, but I love studying anatomy and physiology and experimenting on bettering everything I touch, so, if I may, what happened to your eye?" He pointed at her eyepatch.

"Oh." Dumakleiza reached up and flipped the patch up onto her forehead. She squinted at the daylight stinging her dragon eye. "It is not injured. However, the light of day causes much discomfort."

Timrekka groaned excitedly. "What is that?"

"A dragon eye. A gift from Grim."

Timrekka stared deep into Dumakleiza's purple iris. "Is that what you call it?" He held her eyelid open to get a closer look, studying the intricate lines and lightning patterns of vibrant purples, blues, and neon pinks. "I've seen eyes like this in some of our nocturnal animals—feared by most—but I think they are all the more beautiful in their rareness; would you be opposed to me studying it?"

Dumakleiza held still, wary of even flinching in the scientist's grasp. "I would be interested in what you would find, so yes, you have my permission. However, I warn you, should you injure my eye in any way, I will plunge my fist through your giant skull and rip *your* eyes out."

25

After a heavy meal of foreign meats, dense breads, difficult-to-chew fruits, and some dry vegetables, Traveler disappeared with a pen and paper to brainstorm. He was determined to solve Timrekka's problems and expedite their departure. Timrekka followed to help, and to barrage him with compiling questions.

With the scientific minds gone, Gideon, Dumakleiza, and Cooby were left alone in a house full of Darchangels, all of whom were staring at them unsurely. All the kids that had been so eager to join them for dinner had scampered off to play in the night streets. Dumakleiza and Cooby silently stared back at those glaring them up and down, while Gideon blissfully snacked on a few more burger bites.

"You know, at first I wasn't sure about the tanginess of these patties, but—" He chewed the mouthful. "—it's kinda growing on me." He gulped. "What kind of animal do you guys make it out of? Cow? Do you have cows? Large bovines? With horns?" He held his index fingers on top of his head like horns.

One of the smaller women around the table shook her head with a snarl. "The hell's wrong with you? Course we got cows. Dunno what you're injectin' though. Cows ain't got horns." She scoffed. "You're thinkin' of dingzels. Cows has the *one* horn, ya' dim rear." She pointed one finger off the center of her forehead like a unicorn. The tattooed, shaved sides of the woman's thick head roughly complemented her black hair spiking out.

Gideon smiled. "Of course. That's what I meant. Dingzels."

"But," Dumakleiza quietly murmured to herself. "Cows do not have *any* horns. They have spikes running down their backs." Though she was beginning to understand that animals evolved differently per planet, it was a struggle to digest.

The woman slowly cocked her head to the side, studying the new-comers' strange appearances. "So, where ya' from?" She wiggled the bullring in her nose, licking it out of habit.

Dumakleiza had absolutely no idea how to answer, so she deflected the question to Gideon.

Gideon shrugged and swallowed the last bite. "We only met a few days ago." He nodded toward Dumakleiza. "She's from Cul, and I'm from America. Name's Gideon, by the way. What's yours?"

"Hmm." The woman stared, studying him as all the other Darchangels vicariously interrogated through her. "Odd name for a place. So, you're a what? An Americite? Americish? American?"

"A Badass," Gideon answered with a smile, unaffected by the room full of silent brutes.

"And what do they call people from Cul?" The woman nodded toward Dumakleiza.

Dumakleiza stared back. "Yagūlamite."

"Badass. Yagūlamite." The woman mulled over the words with a bubbly voice. "Not very menacing, but you are tiny. Everyone calls me Kailuna."

"Yeah, we're travel sized." Gideon smiled and scooted his plate forward before leaning back and groaning. "Gah, I'm full. It's very nice to meet you, Kailuna. Pretty name." He yawned and then shook it off. "What are the rest of your names?" None of the staring faces budged. Gideon's unwavering smile waited a few seconds as he looked around.

"So, we got a small taste of Supreme." There were immediate grunts and muttered fantasies of bloodshed. Gideon nodded. "Yeah, they weren't the *most* hospitable people I've ever met." He cleared his throat and swallowed. "We haven't actually heard about Trollop in America, so I don't know the whole lowdown. What's her deal?"

Kailuna took a breath as the room grew more tense. "She'd look better with two to the body and a few hundred to the head. Or better yet, a lot to the whole body, too. What else ya wanna know?"

Dumakleiza cracked a smile. "I share your opinion of the foul witch. She stole my family's holy treasure."

Kailuna flung her hands up. "She steals everything. That's life."

Gideon grinned. "Well, you all don't seem so bad to me. Why's she hate you so much?"

"That's just how it is," Kailuna remarked. "She was breastfed some dingzelshit about being a preordained crown. Just like her mother was before her, and her mother before her, and so on. Just the way things is. How they always been."

Gideon puffed out his bottom lip. "Lame sauce."

Kailuna motioned around the cluttered table. "Use whichever sauce you wanna." She motioned to Cooby wrapped tightly around Dumakleiza's back. "What's that wiggly thing?" He was nonchalantly sniffing the air and chewing on burger. His beady little eyes moved from one person to the next, trying to get a read on the overwhelming number of giant dwarves.

Dumakleiza reached up and caressed the underside of his chin. "He's a tanion."

The thickest man in the room cleared his throat. "What's a tanion? Where'd you get'm?"

"He's been mine since he was a pup. I got him off a ship that invaded my isle of Yagūl."

"Where the hell's that?" Kailuna stared at Cooby. "I like his little face." Her tone softened as she admired him.

Dumakleiza stared off to the left. "It's my, uh—" She tried to remember how they were wording things on this planet. "My, um…gang…territory?" All attention was on Cooby, so her wobbly words went unnoticed. A couple of the other quiet hoodlums smiled. Cooby was looking from one to the next, taking in all the new scents and studying their strange faces. His nose wiggled as his tongue flickered through the air, distracting the scowls.

Kailuna squealed, undone by his cuteness. "Oh, my goodness."

Gideon seized the moment. "So, what do you all do for fun around here? Rap battles? Dance offs? Art? Make grills for your teeth? Walk your pit bulls on chains?"

One of the larger men stepped forward, leaning over the table. He allowed his presence to be felt more than seen as he stared at Gideon through cold eyes. Gorilla-sized fists led up to arms the width of logs. His pitch-black skin hid most of his expression, and the sheer breadth of his frame blotted out the ceiling light. Gideon couldn't get over how menacing the natives' jawlines were. It was obvious that the intention was to stare down at Gideon but being shorter, the man's stature was eye-level with sitting Gideon.

"M'name's Grezzik, chief Darchangel," the man growled. "I let you in m'house, let you eat m'food, all in the comp'ny of m'people." He waited. "A token of our 'preciation for what Timrekka done for us. At's it." His deep voice all but bared fangs.

Gideon smiled and patted his stomach. "Oh, and the food was delicious. Thank you for th—"

"But we ain't 'bout to just treat ya' like Darchangels, toss back drinks, laugh'n and glid'n together." The monster of a man cleared his throat. "Ya' spent time in the Conurbation and none of ya' group was executed." He puffed out his giant bottom lip. "I ain't trust that. I ain't trust you. I respect Rekka, he vouched for ya, and at's all that's keeping you un-shot." The energy in the room thickened as the other Darchangels' postures agreed.

Dumakleiza slowed her breathing and eyeballed a knife nearest her on the table. She didn't want to engage such a brutish group of what looked like trolls, but they were getting aggravated and she wasn't going to stand around helplessly if they attacked.

Gideon maintained eye contact with Grezzik, sucking his teeth as he studied the thick man's stone expression. "Hadn't thought about it that way. I suppose I wouldn't trust us either." He paused and assessed. "So, how do we go about mending that? This part of the world is all about trust, territory, and protecting what's yours. I respect that. Being a Badass has its benefits, but how would I go about becoming a Darchangel?"

Grezzik laughed. "Ya' wanna change y'loyalty? Don't like bein' a Badass? Or jus' don't like bein' a Badass in Darchangel territ'ry?" He leaned forward, his intimidating size looming closer to Gideon.

Gideon didn't flinch other than raising a challenging eyebrow. "You're probably right. Maybe the Darchangels wouldn't be a good fit for a Badass. Probably not safe to add a carnivore to a herd of grazers." He returned the glare, unwilling to be the first to back down.

Dumakleiza shot him a shushing glare. She was ready to grab the knife, and Cooby could feel her energy. The tanion gripped her neck tighter, ready to mimic whatever action she took.

Grezzik's eyebrows lowered. "Ya' treadin' thick ice, American. Ya' mouth won't run s'freely four feet unda ground."

Gideon smiled. "Gah, that's so cool. You only bury people four feet under? Because of the gravity and density of Thamiosh's soil, I'll bet."

"What ya' talkin' about?"

Gideon shook off his fascination. "Nothing. Nothing. Sorry. Back to aggressive negotiations." He cleared his throat and switched to a stern expression, though his playfulness was hard to hide. "So, how does one go about getting initiated?"

Kailuna smirked. "I like him."

Dumakleiza shot her a protective scowl. She brought her head back and looked down, unsure why she'd reacted in such a way.

Grezzik slowly turned his eyes from Gideon to Kailuna and whispered. "I don't even understand what he's sayin'." He turned back to Gideon, his gruff tone a little unsure. "Ya' know how initiations work. Comm'n knowledge all through Thamiosh, ya boob." Gideon shrugged helplessly. Grezzik huffed. "Ya' move to a new territ'ry, ya' put on their colors, 'at's it. It's how y'move through differ'nt territ'ries and avoid trouble. Keep ya' head down, wear the clothes, and be on ya' way."

"Really? That's it?" Gideon asked, a little disappointed with the lackluster response. He'd expected something violently reckless, his specialty.

Kailuna scoffed. "It's pretty basic stuff. It's like you don't know the world you live in." A few Darchangels chuckled.

Gideon smiled. "Back where I come from, a lot of the gangs require initiations, like killing someone, especially someone from a rival gang. Sometimes they required stealing something or painting graffiti somewhere. It gets pretty intense sometimes. Bloods, Crips, Latin Kings—"

Kailuna's eyebrows rose. "Is America one of those slaughter territories we hear about across the Igli?"

"The Igli?"

"The ocean. The Igli Ocean."

Before Gideon or Duma could answer, Grezzik cracked a smile. "I like the way ya' thinks. We should g'rob those fat Dust Wranglers."

Gideon smirked at his liberal use of the word "fat."

Dumakleiza looked away from the knife and raised a finger. "Let us not steal from anyone." They all looked at her. "Rather, why not *unite* with these Wranglers of Dust, form an alliance, and march upon the witch that is Trollop? With gathered forces, her head can be mounted on a pike, and all the territories of Thamiosh can reclaim their liberty."

The Darchangels began laughing as Grezzik smiled, entertained by her speech. "Territ'ries stay out of each otha's business. It's how we survive. B'sides, it'd take lots more than two gangs to ova'throw Supreme. Y'two really live in a blind dream where y'come from, don't ya?"

Gideon shrugged as a thought crossed his mind. "Let's go talk to them. I'll go. Are they the next territory?" He pointed in different directions. "Which way?"

Grezzik gave an amused laugh. "What? You wanna g'talk to the Dust Wranglers?" He laughed harder. "Their chief, Hangman, he'll string ya' up s'fast y'fancy tongue won' do nothin' but get bit off as y'neck breaks." He scratched his massive jaw. "'e's smart enough to stay away from 'ere, but if ya' tread through the Wrangler territ'ry, you'll eitha' be shot dead by bandits, o' Hangman's outlaws will drag y'ass to him."

Gideon's smile instantly grew. "Futuristic gangster-cowboys living like the Wild West? Ha! Well, that settles it. I'm going. I can't miss the chance to see that." He slammed his fist on the table and jumped to his feet.

Kailuna shook her head. "Grezzik's right, Badass. Hangman will kill you. His name's Hangman for a reason."

Gideon lifted an eyebrow. "What would you do if I brought this Hangman guy back here willing to start uniting gangs in order to form a rebellion against the Conurbation?" He stared Grezzik, who smiled and shook his head.

"You do that'n I'll name ya' new chief of the Darchangels, give ya' m'favorite gun'n kiss ya' on th'mouth." He scoffed as the other Darchangels laughed. Grezzik popped his neck and shook his head. "Won't 'appen, though. Hangman won't b'lieve anythin' you say 'bout a rebellion, but feel free t'stretch y'own neck." He stepped back and held out his hand toward the door.

"Challenge accepted." Gideon adjusted his shirt and smiled. "How do I get there?"

Dumakleiza immediately jumped to her feet with Cooby on her back. "You are not going on any quest without us."

Kailuna grinned at them. "Ooh, I see you. I wonder what a Badass and Yagūlamite child would look like."

Duma shot her a sharp glare.

"Oh, of course," Gideon said, skipping over the comment. "Wouldn't go to crazy cowboy land without my pirate princess and the Coobster."

Grezzik looked Gideon dead in the eye, trying to figure out if he was driven or insane. "Dust Wrangler territ'ry is a three-hour bootride, 'r two days on foot."

Dumakleiza squinted. "What is a bootride?"

Gideon smiled. "Those hover boots?"

Grezzik cocked his massive head. "Badasses and Yagūlamites don't even know what gravity boots are?" He scratched his chin. "Y'confuse the hell outta me. Ever'one's heard of gravity boots. Hmm." He shook his head. "They're boots that deflect gravity, or magnetism or some shit. Idunno. But you wear'm'n travel by leanin' forward. They come with gloves'n y'steer by tiltin' with them. They also come with a shirt of simil'r material to prevent you from fallin.' It's cool shit. Can't b'lieve you haven't heard of'm. It's like not knowin' how t'read." The Darchangels chuckled. "Get you some o' those'n you'll be there by mornin'. Just head through the mountains."

Kailuna jumped in and addressed Gideon. "What do you use for transportation?"

Dumakleiza looked to Gideon to see how he'd answer. She had no idea how to deal with interplanetary secrecy and still answer the locals' questions.

Gideon thought about how to respond. "Cars. Large, motorized vehicles a bit bigger than a cow, er…dingzel. Metal bodies." His animated hands failed to paint a convincing mental picture.

"Huh. Sounds clunky and dangerous," Kailuna concluded. "Bout as dangerous what the Dust Wranglers ride. Gravity boots are graceful."

"That's awesome." Gideon's eyebrows rose. "Do you have any I can borrow?"

"Hell, no." Grezzik and the other Darchangels laughed. "Get your own. Can't take m'boots to your death, ya boob. I'll never get'm back."

"If only the witch hadn't stolen my sack," Dumakleiza despaired. "I would be willing to trade holy treasure for these tools of retribution."

Kailuna piped in, "You can take mine." She walked out of the dining room, toward the entryway. She reemerged with large boots like those Gideon had seen on the police's feet. She held them toward Dumakleiza and smiled. Duma hesitantly reached out and grabbed them, studying the heavy footwear. Kailuna's smirk remained. "They should fit ya. I got tiny feet."

Dumakleiza marveled at the seemingly magical footwear. "Still twice the size of mine."

Grezzik brought his hands up. "What're you doin'? They're gon' get themselves killed'n you're just throwin' your boots away with'm."

"Why not?" Kailuna shrugged. "They're tryin' to help. No one else is. Boots are a small price to pay if they succeed. And even if they don't—" She shrugged again, nearly hissing at Grezzik.

Grezzik shook his head. "Anyone else wanna donate their transp'rtation to a suicide mission?" All the other Darchangels shook their heads. They'd worked hard to earn enough to buy their gravity boots, many of them still making payments to Supreme. There was no way they were just going to throw them away for charity.

Gideon nodded and looked on the ground next to him. "Well, I don't have any money, so I can't buy any. Let's see if maybe I have something worth trading."

Grezzik laughed again, his deep voice getting more comfortable with Gideon's personality. "Ya' ain't gonna have nothin' worth as much as a good pair o' boots."

"Hey now." Gideon smiled as he grabbed his bag off the floor. "Don't judge a book by its cover." His words made the Darchangels quiet down and lean in to see what he was rummaging for.

"Books," Grezzik said lowly. "Now, if you 'ad a book, that'd change y'colors in my eyes."

Gideon looked back up at them, intrigued. "How's that?"

Kailuna kept her eyes on Gideon's backpack. "I dunno how things are in America, but we don't get many new stories here in Darchangel territory. We done read everything Supreme gave us so many times that they ain't worth readin' anymore." She nodded toward the backpack. "So, if you got a *new* book in there —"

"If you got a new book in there," Grezzik took over. "Then you can have all th'boots y'want."

Gideon scoffed in disbelief, "Well, if this isn't fate, I don't know what is—especially with *which* book I have." He opened his old backpack and reached in, quickly fishing around for one of the larger items. He pulled out a novel and smiled. "This is *West Side Story*. Strangely fitting, actually. It's about love between two members of rival gangs."

Grezzik's eyes shot open, his guard dropping. "How many boots d'ya want f'r 'em? Do y'have any otha' books?" All the Darchangels crowded around Gideon, leaning over him with newfound admiration. They murmured amongst themselves about how excited they were to have Kailuna read to them.

Gideon chuckled, "Just one pair, so both Duma and I can make the journey. Um." He reached back into his backpack. "I have one more, too. It's called *The Time Machine*. It's a classic about —"

"I'll take it," Grezzik spat out. "What do you want f'r it?"

"Uh." Gideon looked to Dumakleiza to see if she could think of anything.

"Weapons," Duma blurted out. "And new cloaks for the journey."

"Sold." Gideon waved his hand. "Weapons for her, and jackets for both of us."

"No weapons. But jackets I'm good with givin'," Grezzik barely said, staring at the priceless books. One of the other Darchangels handed Gideon some gravity boots while also keeping his eyes on the books. The room was hypnotized by them.

Gideon smiled and took the boots. He and Dumakleiza reached down and pulled pairs of gloves and shirts made of strange material out of them. All the accessories were darkly colored, with a texture that was both silky and hard, obviously sewn together with some sort of metallic string or something. After putting the roomy clothes on, they slipped their feet into the boots. They were loose but they would work. As they moved their hands and feet around inside the Darchangels' gifts, Kailuna grabbed *West Side Story*. She opened it and looked inside the first page. She furrowed her brows and flipped through the pages.

"I can't read anything in here. What words is this written in?"

"Ah, yes," Gideon said as he fidgeted in the boots. "When Traveler and Timrekka come back, have them assist you with that. Traveler has translation tools, and Timrekka is a genius, so yeah."

He hoped he was right. Otherwise, the Darchangels would likely shoot and kill them for misleading the deal. Luckily, the Darchangels were too excited about their new stories to let the minor setback faze them.

Gideon puffed out his bottom lip and nodded at Dumakleiza. They both slowly stood, prepared to fall during the first attempt. To their sensory surprise, once they were upright, the boots levitated a few inches above the floor.

"Cool," Gideon said as Dumakleiza's eyes widened. Balancing wasn't hard, but it still scared her. She looked from them up to Gideon.

"Is this still science or has witchcraft possessed us?"

Gideon laughed. "Still science." He stepped forward, curious what would happen. "Whoa." His feet glided above the floor with ease. There was a light whirring as they hovered in such a practical way that it almost felt like ice skates. Gideon smiled at the boots and then glanced back at the Darchangels. They were crowding Kailuna, who had a death grip on *West Side Story*. "Jackets?"

Grezzik motioned over his shoulder without looking up. "Closet by th'door. Take what y'want."

Gideon nodded and motioned for Dumakleiza to follow him with Cooby still wrapped around her. "All right, you all have fun with those books." He skated forward, hovering over the floor. Duma rigidly followed.

"This is magical. Grim, protect us."

Gideon nodded in agreement. "Magical, yes. But still science. Just so there's no misunderstandings." He opened a brown closet door by the front entrance. Inside were many different jackets, all black, ranging from hoodies to alien-textured coats. As he leafed through, trying to find a good one for each of them, he looked out a window into the night. "You ready to go meet some Wild West scofflaws?"

Dumakleiza lowered her brow. "What?"

"Gangster-cowboys." Gideon could barely contain his excitement. "I wish we had horses." With that, he opened the front door with a couple large jackets in tow. "Let's go see if we can start a rebellion." He glanced back into the house toward the Darchangels, who were obsessing over their gifts too much to pay any attention to them. "May death not find— eh, none of you are listening." He chuckled to himself. With that, he saluted and headed out, followed closely by Duma and Cooby. Their movements were wobbly and uncoordinated, but they were both too stubborn to give up. Awkward legs and waving arms had them fighting for balance and stability like newborn giraffes.

26

In the morning, Traveler, Timrekka, and his reluctant assistant, Schlayfe, returned with arms full of drawings and blueprints. The early air was quite warm on the larger planet, making Traveler sweat while Timrekka and Schlayfe shivered in what they thought was brisk.

Schlayfe led the way, walking up to Grezzik's dilapidated front door and pounding his relatively small fist on it. It only took a couple knocks before the door was whipped open by an overzealous Grezzik.

"Yo, Rekka'n mista Traveler. Mornin'," he said swiftly. "Come on in. The Badass said y'could help translate a book f'r us?"

"Whoa, slow down. The Badass?"

"Gideon. The talk'tive fella."

"Of course." Traveler furrowed his brow and extended a piece of paper. "This is a list of things and parts I'll need in order to help Timrekka build your people a self-sustaining energy source."

"Can ya' translate the book 'r not?" Grezzik asked.

Traveler sighed and hung his head for a moment. "Let me guess. He gave you a book out of his backpack that's in a language you don't know, and he told you I could fix that?"

"'at's exactly right." Grezzik nodded. "So, come translate it."

Traveler tapped the paper he'd handed Grezzik. "First, get me these."

Grezzik stepped closer and crumpled the paper, tossing the balled-up list up at Traveler's face.

"Translate th'book 'n we'll get ya' what y'want," he growled through his flexed jaw. "'n never tell me what t'do again, 'nless y'tired of havin' teeth." He pointed his thick finger straight up at Traveler's face. "Y'feel my truth?"

Traveler sighed, annoyed with everything. "That'll take me time. Go get the items I've requested and I'll be able to work on the more pressing matter of giving you independence from Highness Trollop. By the time you get back, I'll have something worked out for the book."

Grezzik narrowed his eyes and leaned up at Traveler. "Pick th'paper up'n it's a deal."

Before Traveler could do anything, Schlayfe quickly squatted down and grabbed it for him. "Here ya' go." He unfolded it and handed it to Timrekka, who timidly dipped his head before giving it to Grezzik.

Grezzik leaned in an inch away from Traveler's chest, eyes glaring up. "If Kailuna can't read th'book by th'time we get back, you'll need a list of body parts t'find instead of these things." He grunted and walked inside.

"And please send Gideon and Dumakleiza out here," Traveler requested as he looked over some other blueprints.

"They gone," Grezzik responded as he paused in the doorway.

"What?" Traveler looked up. "Gone where?"

"To hunt down Hangman in Wrangler territ'ry. Plannin' on startin' a revolution but they'll prob'ly be dead b'noon." He walked into the house. "A shame. I was just startin' to like'm, too."

Timrekka gasped.

As Grezzik disappeared inside, Traveler turned to the scientist. "What is he talking about?" He waited as Timrekka's eyes darted around behind his bifocals. The prolonged seconds only increased Traveler's concerns. For all he knew, Gideon had gotten both him and Dumakleiza killed. Traveler repeated himself, taking a firm step toward Timrekka. "Timrekka. What's Wrangler territory?"

Timrekka nodded, rapidly gathering his thoughts. "The Dust Wranglers are a gang the next territory over; they're very aggressive and hate outsiders, not unlike every other gang, but they have a nasty reputation for hanging foreigners, hence their head's name, Hangman." He cleared his throat as he saw Traveler's stress levels rising. "They're always riding around in packs of pippos, wielding incendiary pistols, very dangerous, shooting first and asking questions never; Gideon and Dumakleiza are not safe there—probably dead."

Traveler reached up and put his hands over his eyes as his cheeks turned red. "Dammit, Gideon." He wiped his hand down his face. "All right, let's go get them." He snarled and shook his head. "No. Never mind. We don't have time. We're not going after them. I can't always watch over Gideon." He turned to Timrekka. "Stay on task. Let's get a translator in place for this book. It'll be easy between the two of us. Then, once the Darchangels have retrieved everything we need, we'll get the power source built." Another deep breath and audible exhale fumed from his mouth. "Hopefully by that time, we'll know if Gideon and Dumakleiza are alive. Either way, once it's built, we're leaving."

"Okay," Timrekka said, wanting only to obey and avoid Traveler's wrath. "Just tell me how to help and I'll do whatever you need."

Traveler heavily exhaled, needing to focus on something else. "Timrekka, you're brilliant, genius even. I'm surprised you don't create more weapons because, no offense, but many of your inventions seem like they're torture devices."

Timrekka shrugged. "I know a lot of them backfire with somewhat unfortunate side effects, but no, I don't ever want to make weapons. Not again. Not after seeing how they get abused by power, and besides, if ever I *was* to torture anyone, I know exactly how I'd do it, and it'd be much simpler."

"Oh?" Traveler's interest was piqued. "How's that?"

"Easy, I'd sedate my target, and while they were unconscious, I'd squeeze a strong adhesive into their urethra, and then I'd squeeze their penis shut, and once they woke up, they'd have an IV in their arm, forcing fluid into their system with no way out. You know, simple."

Traveler stared at him with horrified eyes. "That is one of the scariest things I've ever heard. You've thought about this?"

Timrekka shrugged again. "No, just thought of it as an answer to your thoughts."

Traveler blinked a few times with a dead stare. "You are officially the second scariest person I've ever heard of. Remind me to never upset you."

Timrekka looked at him curiously. "Who's the first?"

"A story for another time. But, for now, let's get started on that translator."

"Yes sir." Timrekka smiled, eager to invent something with his new friend. He adjusted his goggles and walked inside. "Is there anything else you need me to grab first?"

Traveler followed him into the house with his hands defensively in the air. "I was going to say glue, but you've made me afraid of adhesives."

27

Coming to a gentle stop was proving to be the only difficult part of operating the gravity boots. Otherwise, momentum, rapidity, and steering were simple matters of leaning and adjusting the hands. It was becoming an enjoyable and effective means of transportation.

They zipped over snaking roads between the mountains. All through the night, the low glow of neglected streetlamps had guided their way through the darkness; the whirring from their magnetic friction and the wind passing by serenading their journey. They'd been passed by many Thamioshlings who'd gotten irritated by the slow inexperience.

Morning light from Thamiosh's sun slowly unveiled their new surroundings. They both tilted back enough to slow down so they could take in the rolling hills. Thamiosh's versions of mountains were only a couple hundred feet high, miniature in comparison to those Gideon and Dumakleiza were familiar with on Earth and Cul. However, what had them so captivated were the dense trees tightly bunched together. The trunks were colossally thick. Gideon smiled at what may as well have just been gigantic mushrooms with their short stature, broad trunks, and looming branches.

Dumakleiza was wide eyed. "The trees on this world resemble huts I built back on Cul. I feel as though chopping one down for the sake of firewood would be grueling. Though it would keep the flames stoked for days to come. A worthwhile task," she concluded with a nod.

Gideon chuckled, "If there are any lumberjacks here on Thamiosh, I'll bet they're the toughest sons of bitches ever. Three-hundred-pound, flannel-wearing, hulk dwarves chopping down *those* trees? Forget about it."

Dumakleiza stared at Gideon, studying him while his attention remained on the trees. "Why are we here, Sir Gideon?"

"What do you mean?"

"I mean, why do we seek out people with whom we have no association? Why do you desire to mend the broken parts of a world to which we have no allegiance? Especially now that the Diviner has found Timrekka? You set us upon a quest impertinent to our larger mission." Her voiced curiosities made Gideon smile, which only gave her more questions. "I simply do not understand why you enjoy risking your life for the Darchangels."

Gideon slowed even more until they both came to a complete stop. He looked up at Thamiosh's sun and let his smile fade. Deep breaths were proving difficult. He closed his eyes and absorbed the warmth into his thick beard. It felt good. Thamiosh had already been such a quick-paced world that he hadn't taken the time to step back and just enjoy breathing as he so often did. At least on Cul when he'd been bait, he'd been allowed the opportunity to take it all in. The memory made him smile. He opened his eyes to look at Dumakleiza.

"Because asserting oneself into a situation without invitation is the scariest decision for most people."

Duma narrowed her eyes. "You do this to overcome fear?"

"No." Gideon chuckled. "I do it because, what most people don't realize is, sure it's scary, but it's the best way to live."

Dumakleiza squinted at him. "Explain that."

"Well." Gideon tried to decide what route to take. "The only guaranteed thing in life is death, right?" Dumakleiza nodded, not seeing the picture he was trying to paint. Gideon breathed in the mountain air. "We're all going to die—something none of us can escape. Though it seems Traveler is helping us postpone it a bit longer. But most people exist in their worlds, avoiding conflict, avoiding resolution, avoiding everything. Not living before they die. Usually, the only way people will get involved in anything is if they're forced—even with fun stuff." He cleared his throat. "Stepping outside of our comfort zones is something that most people will do anything—make any excuse—to not do." He shook his head. "It's not until after they're forced to participate in life that they realize it's where they were meant to be all along. Life isn't about hiding, avoiding, playing it safe, waiting, or making excuses. Life is about participating, making mistakes, developing relationships, and risking it all."

He took a moment to smell the scents of alien trees, wildflowers, and whatever else was in the air.

"Look at us right now. We're riding *gravity boots*." He looked at his gloves and metallic shirt. "Through a mountain pass on a foreign planet. And you—you are from a world thousands of years away from this technology. This is crazy for *me*. I can't even imagine how much this is for you." He marveled. "You wouldn't be here if you hadn't proactively volunteered for this. You chose to come along before you were even invited. And as a result, correct me if I'm wrong, but I'm guessing you're feeling pretty alive right now."

The edges of Duma's mouth began curving up. "Your love for life is contagious, Sir Gideon." Her smile grew as she lowered her defenses. "This is certainly the greatest adventure I have embarked upon, and yes, I truly never have felt such freedom in my life. I believe I have already seen more of this world than I ever did of my own."

Gideon smiled. "It was a giant leap of faith—a gamble really, and we've already almost died just from the atmosphere and, you know, execution." He chuckled. "But, even with those experiences, do you regret your decision to come along?"

Dumakleiza's smile maintained. "I do not. Not even after the threats of demise. In fact, I would venture to claim that danger sweetens the taste of this mysterious quest."

"Exactly." Gideon's expression reflected understanding. "Miss Duma, I do believe you're beginning to catch the same madness that others claim I have in spades."

Dumakleiza lifted her chin with a stern expression. "I am seeing the truth of you, and you are not mad. You are brilliant—in a mad way, I admit. You live life as a fire that seems impossible to douse. Your words are true. To hide from life is mad." She turned and looked down where they were heading. "And we venture now to find the Wranglers of Dust because you find no question that begs strong enough of reason not to?"

"Because I live a life of *why not*. So, you know, why not?" He shrugged. "And I'm lucky enough to have a pirate princess along for the ride." He winked at her. "And because, I mean, who doesn't want to meet advanced Wild West cowboys?" He laughed and fired a couple finger guns into the air while mouthing *bangs*.

Dumakleiza's eyes burned with passion as she stared toward their destiny. "Sir Gideon, though we may venture to our deaths, I feel no regret in the decision to join this crusade. Let us ignite a rebellion against the witch Trollop until the flames of injustice engulf all of Thamiosh, and freedom is claimed through blood."

Gideon chuckled. "God, the way you talk is so badass. Sexy, really. Can you just narrate my life for me?"

Dumakleiza was momentarily withdrawn as she glanced back at him. "What do these words mean?"

"Nothing." Gideon shook his head. "Shall we?" He motioned forward.

Dumakleiza smirked. "You wish *me* to lead our way?"

"Just trying to be chivalrous."

Dumakleiza laughed. "I do not know how it is on your world, Sir Gideon, but on Cul, chivalry has but scraps about the treatment of women. Its true purpose is battle etiquette. Thusly, by that truth, your ignorance on the matter actually claims that you wish me to take the helm of our venture, only that you may engage me from behind."

"Wow," Gideon chuckled. "I took that in a way that I'm guessing you didn't intend." He smiled and raised his hands defensively as Duma shot him another confused look. "You know what? I think I'll go first." He chuckled and tilted forward, using his hands to propel him down the road.

Dumakleiza smiled. "I'll have you trained as of yet, Sir Gideon." She tilted forward and followed as Cooby continued his deep sleep, hands clasped around her.

Together, they whirred past trees and mountains, flying up over knolls and down through valleys. It wasn't much longer until they crested a mountainous hill and stopped in the middle of the road at its summit. It was the last mountain of its range, and down below, they saw Dust Wrangler territory. Similar to the ghetto where the Darchangels resided, the territory spanning out at the base of the mountain range appeared well-built but worn and bedraggled. The highest structure they could see was only two stories. Every building looked to be made of wood, prob-ably from the surrounding trees. It was a smaller territory, looking to only be a few square miles from atop the mountain, which further re-minded Gideon of old Western towns.

Dumakleiza voiced both of their thoughts as they gazed downward. "This place has such potential for beauty. If only they were free of the fat witch." She stared fondly at a lake on the far end. It reminded her of home, seeing a large body of water sparkling in the distance.

Gideon smiled. "It really does look like the Wild West. Oh god, I hope they have a saloon."

"A what?"

"Uh." Gideon tried to think of the medieval equivalent. "Um, a tavern?"

"I believed you to venture here for rebellion against Supreme, not for drunkenness."

Gideon laughed. "Oh, I'm not wanting to get trashed or anything. I get very manipulative when I'm intoxicated. I once convinced a group of Dubaian sheiks to turn on each other with a few lies about betrayal and infidelity. I don't remember much of it because I was blackout with the ninety-proof coursing through my veins, but I was told that one of them had the others abducted and beaten." He winced. "My bad. Apparently, I stole one of their Lamborghinis for a joyride, totaled it *and* a Bugatti, and narrowly avoided the authorities by convincing a group of women to hide me because I was both a sultan's son and an eligible bachelor. The story gets awkward after that, but the point is that me drunk equals trouble. It's not good." He puffed his lip out. "Although I would like to try the plu that Timrekka was talking about. Sounds interesting." He smiled at Dumakleiza glaring. She didn't understand most of what he was talking about, but she got the general idea: Stab Gideon if he tried to consume alcohol.

Gideon shrugged it off. "I just wanna go to an actual Western saloon. It's the social watering hole in an old Western town. I mean, as long as it's that similar. If we're lucky, maybe we'll see a brawl." His voice grew excited as Dumakleiza shot him a confused look. "Chances are, someone there will be able to point us in the direction of Hangman."

They reached the outskirts of Wrangler territory and immediately felt out of place. Approaching, they saw the locals walking through the streets. To Gideon's disappointment, they weren't dressed like cowboys from the eighteen-hundreds, but there were subtle similarities. The stocky Thamioshlings wore thick outfits made of some kind of animal's hide. Layers upon layers reminded Gideon of cowboys, but their hats were different. Tight, leathery caps extended down to the bridges of their noses, with slits for their eyes. The tops were similar to cowboy hats, with pinches and creases evident. However, there were no fronts to the brims. Next to the eye slots, the edges widened, wrapping around the back.

"All right." Gideon smiled. "Let's just stroll into town like normal folks."

Dumakleiza had immediate doubts about their lack of a plan. "Our bodies are covered in the cloaks of the Darchangels. As the nemeses of the Wranglers of Dust, we are likely to be spotted and engaged as hostiles."

"Yes, we will. And be quickly brought to Hangman. We unfortunately don't have time to dillydally, which sucks, because I'd love to spend some time here. We'll have to skip the foreplay."

"Your tongue is odd, Sir Gideon."

Gideon chuckled. "A more fitting comment than you know." He looked around, studying Wrangler territory. "All right, I don't see gravity boots on any of them. Probably best if we take ours off."

Dumakleiza nodded. "Agreed."

They knelt and unlaced their boots, slowly stepping out of them and back onto solid ground. It was still strange to see the boots hovering a few inches above the road. After removing their other Darchangel garments, they hid the boots in some bushes.

"Alrighty," Gideon said. "Let's giddyup and go."

"Wait a moment," Duma cautioned with a hand up.

"What's wrong? Do you see something?" Gideon looked around.

"No," Duma said with a calming tone. "I simply wish to bless our quest with divine guidance."

It took a second, but Gideon understood. He hoped it wouldn't leave them too vulnerable, but he was excited to hear the Yagūlamite's prayer.

"Oh, mighty Grim," Dumakleiza spoke loud and confident, as if her god was standing there with them. "Protect us and honor our cause with good favor. Direct the words of Sir Gideon, that he may sooth the flames of prejudice between the Wranglers of Dust and the Darchangels. Validated, in your eyes, may we rise up, united against the true enemy, witch Trollop." She instinctively patted her hips for the knives that weren't there. "And should our venture turn violent, I pray you provide me weapons, that I may smite our enemies in your name." With that, she gave a satisfied grin and looked up. "So, may it come to pass." Cooby barked in agreement.

"Amen," Gideon said with a thumbs-up.

They started forward on foot, wearing only the clothing Traveler had provided them. As they walked down the first couple blocks, they looked around at the numerous small businesses. There were food vendors, ranging from fresh produce to cooked meats and baked goods, and clothing shops with hand-sewn items. A couple shops were dedicated metalsmiths with varying weapons and accessories hung around the walls, and then some second-hand electronics stores.

Gideon raised an eyebrow. "It's strange seeing a world older and more advanced than my own being oppressed. Seriously, it's to the point of seeming a couple hundred years behind mine in technological status."

Dumakleiza looked around. "Your world of Earth holds more science than Thamiosh?" It was difficult for her to comprehend.

Gideon tilted his head back and forth as he shrugged. "Yes and no. Supreme is more advanced looking. Didn't really get to see much of it, so maybe, maybe not, but the rest of Thamiosh is held back." He smiled at the shops they were passing. "Out of the three places we've seen here, I'd call this territory home if I were to stay. I like the old Western style. This town is very cozy and neat. Needs a little elbow grease but I like a good fixer upper."

"What concern is it now if you have grease upon your elbows?"

"No, I—"

"Mama?" A little voice drew their attention to the side of the road ahead, where a woman was walking with her two children. A little girl in a faded dress was pointing at them. It still confused Gideon and Dumakleiza to see such burly children. The young girl looked from her mother back to them. "Mama, what are they?" The woman's eyes widened as she brought her head back.

Dumakleiza leaned into Gideon's ear while keeping her eye on them. "That is not a good omen."

Gideon went to put his hands up and alleviate the woman's concerns, but it was too late.

"Darchangels!" The woman's deep version of a shrill voice echoed through the air. Gideon and Dumakleiza were sure the whole territory could hear her. Cooby bared his teeth at the woman.

Gideon shrugged at Duma. "Well, cat's out of the bag. May as well keep going."

Dumakleiza looked around, confused. "What cat? And of what importance is it in this moment?"

Gideon smiled and started walking forward to where the family had run off. Dumakleiza hesitantly followed. She would have had no problem walking into the gates of hell if she had her swords and bow but being without any melee weapons had her skittish. Her eye darted around the rooftops and down alleyways as they strode, watching the fleeing townsfolk. The vacating streets were unnerving. It meant something else was coming, and it bothered her that Gideon was so casual about it.

Heavy galloping caught their attention. The storming feet sounded more like anvils than hooves. There was no way it was horses. Gideon and Dumakleiza stopped, waiting to see what was coming as the stampeding thunder grew closer.

A group of Dust Wranglers spun around a building down the street, whooping and hollering atop gargantuan creatures. The obese animals were difficult to recognize at first glance as kicked-up dust blurred the stampeding herd. Gideon's mouth widened in amazement as he realized what they were: giant, short-haired hippopotamuses. Their backs reached at least five feet and their plump stomachs were even thicker than he was familiar with. Earthy brown and plum fur blanketed their bodies, from massive snouts to tailless hindquarters. Colossal mouths gaped and huffed as they ran, giving preview to long tusks.

"Wh—what manner of beasts are those?" Dumakleiza stammered.

"Hippos," Gideon said in disbelief. "They're riding hippos."

The Dust Wranglers yanked back on the reins just before Gideon and Dumakleiza were trampled. The giant creatures came to a halt, screeching hooves into the dirt and heavily panting steamy breaths. There was no aggression in their faces, just docile expressions of obedience, completely uninterested in the visitors.

The men atop the hippos stared down through their eye-slits, cracking the beginnings of smiles, like confident predators ready to toy with prey.

None of them spoke.

Gideon took the opportunity to aim the situation in their favor. "We come in peace." He couldn't help himself. "We have no weapons or anything. We're here to talk to Hangman on behalf of Grezzik."

There was no response. The Dust Wranglers clearly wanted them to feel lesser and submissive. It was having an adverse effect on Dumakleiza, as she mentally prepared for a fight. Gideon, on the other hand, took the silence as an opportunity to voice some growing curiosities.

"What are your animals called? Hippos?" He wanted to walk up and pet the large beasts. "They're beautiful. Really sheen coats." He stared at the motionless men. "Are they difficult to ride? I think I'd have to do the splits to get my legs around one of those suckers."

One of the Dust Wranglers scoffed in amusement. The others joined in, laughing, and neither Gideon nor Dumakleiza knew why. The rider pulled a strange gun from a holster and pointed it at them. The foot-long pistol was cumbersome in design, looking to be made of something similar to steel, but with a glowing orange chamber.

"Is that a weapon?" Dumakleiza asked.

"Yes, it sure is," Gideon calmly answered. They stood still with their hands in the air, Cooby snarling from Dumakleiza's back.

The other Dust Wranglers pulled guns and aimed down, one of them blowing a kiss to Dumakleiza. The first man motioned with his pistol for them to walk. He was going to lead them somewhere and was uninterested in a debate.

Other townsfolk watched from around buildings, obviously feeling safer knowing that the two invaders were at gunpoint.

Gideon smiled. "Hangman this way?" He pointed toward the center of the town. After no response, he nodded and then started walking. Dumakleiza stayed by his side as they brought their hands down. The Dust Wranglers waited. Gideon smiled and waved to the people they were passing. After watching a moment, the Dust Wranglers kicked spurs into the hippos and followed.

28

Traveler oversaw the Darchangel children helping build his mysterious energy source. They were assembling it in Grezzik's basement because Traveler had insisted it be kept in a room void of windows or any other natural light. The unexplained instruction only fueled Timrekka's curiosity but answers had to wait. Traveler's list of items included rounded sheets of two-way mirror, large metal beams, and a plethora of electric cords and connectors. The odd list had everyone helping trying to guess what the finished product would be. The two-way mirror was the only difficult item to procure, requiring some quick inventing by Timrekka to even manage it at all. From what Timrekka could see, it seemed like they were making a giant light bulb. The foundation was coming together, and it simply looked like a metal frame. The fascinating part of the structure was the two-way mirror being fused together at the edges to form a sphere, precisely six feet in diameter, from floor to ceiling.

The basement was inundated with sounds of machines, some of which were cutting glass, others soldering, welding, and hammering as the children toiled away. Grezzik's house was a mess, supplies and discarded remainders scattered about. They'd barely just begun a few hours earlier, and it was already almost done. Even Traveler was surprised with how smoothly construction was going with willing kids as his assistants. To be fair, the children of this world were stronger than the adults of others.

Upstairs, Kailuna sat in a chair in Grezzik's living room with as many Darchangels as could pack around her. Many more stood out of sight but within earshot. Kailuna had a pair of clunky reading glasses, compliments of Traveler. He and Timrekka had brainstormed, designed, and fabricated them after reverse-engineering translator implants. During their time together, Traveler had preemptively given Timrekka the light shot and implanted a translator in his ear. With some quick ingenuity, the glasses displayed translated languages on the lenses, pulled from Traveler's people's database back on Whewliss. They weren't perfect, as they hadn't had time to do much testing, but the overall invention was functional. Slow but functional.

Kailuna flipped through the pages of *West Side Story*, marveling at the translating technology. She wasn't reading as much as simply enjoying watching the glasses work. Every page she turned took a few seconds before the lenses would display translations in real time. Kailuna was eager to escape her reality and explore this foreign tale.

The group of Darchangels impatiently whined, urging her to begin. Grezzik coughed without any subtlety.

"C'm'on, jus' start it already."

"Sorry. It's really cool," Kailuna said as she closed the book so she could read the cover first. "She cleared her throat. "*West Side Story*, a novelization by Irving Shulman. What a strange name. Must be another Badass." There were some enthusiastic comments whispered as the Darchangels packed in tighter. Kailuna flipped open the cover and began.

Downstairs, Timrekka approached Traveler and peered around him at the blueprints.

"I still don't understand how it works—you said this is one of the power sources on your planet, right, or did I misunderstand, and it's something new you've invented yourself?"

"Huh?" Traveler peeled his eyes away and glanced at Timrekka before looking back down. "Uh, it's a simplified version of one of our primary power sources back on Whewliss. It functions as a glass ball, trapping light within it with the mirrors. From there, the perpetually spinning light reflects as long as the glass remains intact, causing continuous flow. This creates a harvestable energy that acts the same as a gear would in a stream, or a wind turbine. From there, the Darchangels will simply harness the collected energy and manipulate it to create electricity. A self-sustaining energy source, and liberation from Trollop." He lifted his hands as if it was as easily done. "And by my calculations, this should be enough to power all of Darchangel territory. Maybe even more, depending on how much, umm, light we put into it."

Timrekka slowly nodded as it began making sense. "How do you trap light inside it? Doesn't light stop once the source stops emitting, or how does that work?"

Traveler took a deep breath and held it before shrugging the question away. "It'll be easier to explain when we get to my world."

"Okay, what's it called?"

"A Winkloh Star."

"Winkloh Star? That's peculiar, not what I was expecting; why is it called that?"

"It was invented by a man named Eevan VanWinkloh, and it has the power of a hyper-miniaturized star."

"How fascinating. I look forward to seeing more advanced worlds than Thamiosh; I want to see what else has been invented."

"Indeed," Traveler said solemnly. "So, as we get closer to our departure from Thamiosh, I want to make sure that there's nothing else we need to tie up here. I need to make sure that you recruits have only the future in mind. None of us can afford to be put in jeopardy by one of our members aching for home or haunted by loose ends. Do you have any family, friends, unfinished business, or anything else that needs taken care of before we go?"

For the first time since they'd met, Traveler watched Timrekka's energetic eyes dull. He looked off and cleared his throat before looking back.

"No, I don't have any fa—mmmm—" He ground his teeth together and aggressively scratched his head as if there was an itch he couldn't satisfy. "I don't really have any fami—mmmm—" Again, he scratched, looking around at anything but Traveler. "My uh, my, um—" His words bottlenecked in his throat, and the only ones that made it out were transforming into gibberish. It was odd to see him in such a state. Regurgitating rehearsed positivity was proving difficult, and Traveler could see straight through it.

"What happened to them?" He put the papers down, giving Timrekka his undivided attention. Timrekka just looked farther away as he fought the question. Traveler had a dark hunch. "Was it Trollop?" The words made Timrekka's shoulders tighten.

"They were a distraction from my work, that's what Trollop told me, and maybe they were—" Timrekka's normally breathless rambling was broken. "I *have* gotten more done since they were 'removed,' so maybe it was for the best." His eyes started blinking like a short-circuiting light as tears unevenly welled. "I, uh." He forced some hoarse words. "I'll be ready to go as soon as this is done, and I have no additional business that needs tending to, so I would be happy to focus all of my energies into the future."

Traveler studied Timrekka. "You've mentioned grievances with Supreme and Trollop before, but nothing of this." He tried to think of a gentle way to word what his gut was telling him. "I'm a busy, goal-oriented person, and as such, have lost all subtly and ability to beat around the tree, as Gideon's people would say." He looked at Timrekka's avoiding glare. "Did Trollop have your family executed?" Timrekka gave no response. "To remove distractions? So, you could focus on her agendas, uninterrupted? Undistracted?"

No response.

All the machining sounds felt distant as Traveler finally began to understand Timrekka, seeing why he was the way he was.

"You should find someone else for your mission," Timrekka whispered as he deflated. "I'm a coward. My family would still be alive if I had fought back."

"You'd be dead if you fought back."

Timrekka couldn't think of an argument. "That'd be better than knowing I did nothing—that I idly stood by, afraid, weak."

"Okay," Traveler demandingly pushed. "Feed me a scenario in which you fighting back would have been successful. Tell me about your combative training that would have paid off, and your escape plan that would have saved your family's lives." Timrekka stared down, his tear-stricken eyes darting around, but his lips squeezed shut. Traveler nodded. "I'm blunt but I mean what I say, Timrekka. Yes, you were a coward. You could have died in a futile attempt to save your family. But you didn't. You're here. Are you going to wallow or are you going to learn from your mistakes?"

"The task is my therapy, my medicine, my cure, the only path salvation might exist down." Timrekka shifted his energy back toward the task. "Once this Winkloh Star is built and functioning, where are we going next?" He returned to crazed inventor with the simple flip of switch.

Traveler took a second, debating trying to unpack more of Timrekka's emotional baggage. "Well." He cleared his throat. "We will depart for the world of Borroke, where your test awaits."

"My test?"

"Yes. My superiors require that I subject all recruited candidates to a continuous series of tests in order to ensure they are capable of surviving the unknown exploration ahead."

Timrekka slowly nodded as the brightness returned to his eyes. "Gideon and Dumakleiza have begun their testing?"

"Yes," Traveler said. "Gideon is from a world called Earth. It's slightly less and more advanced than Thamiosh. As our resident adventurer, he was tested by being left all alone in the company of a violent people called Vaquilemen on a planet called Cul, a world about a millennium less advanced than what he's used to. The test was to survive their hostility in order to prove he's prepared for unexpected encounters with unknown and potentially aggressive cultures."

"How'd he survive?"

"I don't know all the details, but by the time I arrived to see whether or not he had, he'd earned his way into their military rankings. They were all but carrying him on their shoulders and praising his name. I'd literally left him with nothing but the clothes on his back. But using his unique charisma, he got them to love him just like that." He snapped his fingers. "His persuasive rhetoric and likeableness verge on apocryphal at times. He's something else."

Timrekka nodded with raised eyebrows. "First impressions agree with that statement; even after he startled me with his self-mutilations, he's proven impossible not to like, so I really hope he survives his encounter with the Dust Wranglers, because I wanna go on this adventure with him there."

"Oh, I wouldn't be surprised if he finds a way," Traveler commented as the conversation reminded him of how annoyed he was with Gideon.

"And what was Dumakleiza's test?"

"Oh, she is from the same world I tested Gideon on."

"Cul?"

Traveler nodded. "That's where we found her. So, she's approximately one thousand years less advanced than he is, and even more so in comparison to Thamioshlings."

"Really?" Timrekka was becoming even more intrigued. "And *her* test?"

"Simply being here." Traveler scoffed at the purity of it. "Her test is handling more advanced worlds without losing her sanity. Her people perceive technological advancements as witchcraft, magic, or miracles by gods. Her mind will either open to accept everything new as education, or she'll reject it and retaliate with primitive naïveté. She's already shown indications of either outcome being possible." He glanced down at the blueprints and pondered his next move. "And, um, as our resident spiritual leader, she has to be prepared to explore the spiritual possibilities in the fourth phase. If prayer proves to be a necessity for the team's survival, she will be the one to implement it."

"What do you mean 'if it proves to be a necessity?' What are your beliefs, and where exactly are we going? For someone who claims to never beat around the tree, you seem to dance around the overall goal of this mission." Timrekka brought his head back at his own unleashed outburst. "I'm sorry, that was overstepping myself a bit, and I apologize; I just meant that—"

"It's okay." Traveler smiled and raised his hand. "You don't have anything to apologize for. You wouldn't be a good candidate for our scientific recruit if you didn't demand answers."

Timrekka tilted his head back and forth. "As a scientist, I also know all too well that if I demand answers too earnestly, it'll often times blow up in my face—literally, and I don't want to overstep my bounds and make myself ineligible."

Traveler looked at the children working around them. He was impressed with how well they focused and followed directions, building away with minimal supervision. For a moment, his mind flickered around the regret that he had no way to pay them for their labor until he remembered that everything he was doing was to help them. He nodded, satisfied with the realization. He looked around, double checking that everything was being properly constructed, and then turned back at Timrekka.

"For the most part, I've told the three of you all that I know about the four phases of human exploration."

"But you really haven't told us anything about the fourth," Timrekka said, once again wincing at his outburst. He put a hand over his mouth and scratched his head with the other.

Traveler chuckled. "I'm not trying to hide anything from any of you. But there is an order to understanding what is to come. There are layers of introduction so your minds can fully digest and comprehend each step of what you don't yet understand. You, Gideon, and Dumakleiza have all proved intelligent enough to see the truth." His eyes stared through the floor as his mind wandered somewhere darker. "The truth is that the fourth phase scares me. It scares everyone who knows about it." He cleared his throat. "If that's any indication—" His eyes disappeared further through the floor, unsure of where he was going with that statement. "I understand everything that has been discovered, invented, and explored. I've studied all that is, and I have access to the largest database of information that I know of in existence." He took a deep breath. "This team is barely assembled, and yet it is the furthest I've personally ever made it. The other recruiters and I have made many attempts but have all lost people along the way." His eyes circled a spot on the blueprints in front of him as he recalled. "Romnesh was killed by the Cratiels, Bupei was eaten by one of the Membra's Niffs after trying to ride it, which I distinctly remember them warning him about. Saalgia thought she was smarter than me and tampered with her translator, which caused it to malfunction and got her in trouble with the Honixlets. She's serving a life sentence in one of their black honey penitentiaries. And after what she said, I can't really blame them."

He grabbed a glass of water from the table and drank before continuing.

"Recruits get killed frequently, and thusly, I've had to restart over and over and over. If we're being honest, it's made me question all of this."

"What do you mean?"

Traveler sighed. "People I've grown to care about die in the name of a cause that no one understands. No one knows what the fourth phase is, and recruits die in the name of its exploration. All to see what's beyond the horizon."

Timrekka understood. "In that mindset, what would have happened if early man went to venture beyond the horizon, but stopped after the first few failures and deaths? Sure, it would have been safer for them and their loved ones, but it would have limited them and their realities to their singular body of land, and eventually that's all their legacy would have been, all that my entire planet's legacy would have been." He twiddled his thumbs as he recognized Traveler hiding behind a veil of silence. "Please forgive me if I'm overstepping myself here, but I'm guessing that it's more than guilt that haunts you, and don't get me wrong, I'm sure there's plenty of guilt to——" He cleared his throat. "Sorry, that was insensitive, but my point is that while I'm sure you have ghosts of those that you've lost, you'd had to have overcome those depressions if you're still recruiting. I'm guessing it's something else."

Traveler slowly nodded. "You three recruits seem to be able to see through me as if I were perfectly transparent." He took a deep breath. "I suppose, after a while, I start expecting recruits to die, and I begin getting comfortable in that guarantee because it means I won't have to be the one to explore the fourth phase. One of my competitors will do it before I manage to keep a team alive long enough." He looked up at Timrekka. "But something is telling me that the three of you won't be so easily killed." His eyes widened. "Which is a good thing, of course." He shook his head, realizing how poorly he'd worded himself. "But it means that if we stay the course, we'll be stepping into the unknown, where *no one* has ever been before."

Timrekka nodded, unable to dim the glimmer of excitement twinkling in his eyes. "And that doesn't thrill you?"

"It terrifies me," Traveler admitted. "It terrifies me more than literally anything."

Timrekka smiled as goose bumps flew down his spine. "I can't wait to see what kinds of scientific properties exist within this fourth phase; the possibilities alone will be worth the trip."

Traveler slowly nodded, trying to pull his mind from the fear it was slipping into. "We will all be tested."

Timrekka patted Traveler on the back. "Well, I'll leave you to it then, and if you all need any help from me, let me know, but otherwise, there are a few things I want to work on before we head out." With that, he looked around at the construction going on, smiled, and walked to the staircase. He left the basement and headed to his lab. As he scurried off, Traveler could hear him mumbling something about Gideon and reanimated corpses.

29

Gideon and Dumakleiza approached a wooden building with heavy swinging doors at its front. They stopped and stared at it. Even with the bright sun shining down, the building all but snarled at them. The windows were boarded up, and just from quick glances, they could see that all the women and children were steering clear of it. Only the men riding the beasts behind them were comfortable walking up to its front doors.

Gideon smiled and leaned in next to Dumakleiza. "I don't mean to sound overly optimistic, but this is looking very similar to a saloon. Fingers crossed." He winked.

Cooby held tight to Dumakleiza and stared behind them, snarling at the men who had led them there. Dumakleiza was tense, but her expression displayed nothing more than a stern stare ahead. She was a warrior and was prepared to leap into action. In fact, she hungered for it. She hadn't tasted the sweetness of bloodshed since the Vaquilemen.

One of the men riding barked down from his hippo, "Get inside!"

Gideon stepped forward, long, confident strides with arms swinging. "Thanks for the escort, fellas!" He waved backward as Dumakleiza hesitantly walked behind him, her uncovered eye glancing back in case of an ambush. Gideon stepped up to the heavy wooden doors and grinned. "Let's go meet Captain Hangman. I see a comic book in the making."

Dumakleiza didn't understand what he was saying, and she didn't care. "Do not hesitate, Sir Gideon. Do not fear the hanging man, for Grim guides me."

Gideon gave her a confident nod. "Yes, ma'am."

With that, he pushed the doors open. They creaked and groaned as he entered the tavern. It was much dimmer inside, with low lit bulbs on the ceiling. The yellow glow created a murky ambiance within the sinister edifice. The immediate scent was unmistakable: beer, whiskey, pent up aggression, and visible smoke. The smell clung to their clothes and skin like sickness. They were going to carry it for days if they managed to make it out. They could almost feel a secondhand drunkenness creeping up in their throats merely by breathing.

Murmuring voices gruffly muttered to each other in the cloudy darkness.

Before Gideon's pupils could fully adjust, Dumakleiza lifted the eyepatch from her dragon eye and closed her other. The darkness was instantly lit. She flexed her jaw as Cooby silently held onto her, nuzzling into her neck for safety. Gideon was able to make out silhouettes of a bar, tables, and an abundance of burly men sitting around the room. He assumed they were staring at them, but he couldn't quite tell. Only faint yellow outlines gave them any shape. Gideon smiled.

"Totally a saloon."

Dumakleiza, on the other hand, saw everything. She did a quick head count. There were eighteen men inside, all staring at them through eye slits like predators. She looked behind them. The men that had led them to the saloon were off their beasts and blocking the doorway. She turned back, taking in as much of their surroundings as she could. Her instincts guided her eye to every holstered gun she'd just learned about. Every man was armed with the magical weapons. Her muscles tensed.

A little hope glimmered within her as she noticed knives mixed among the silverware on the tables. They looked like dull knives used for dinnerware, but they'd suffice if need be. There were larger knives tucked into some of the Dust Wranglers' pants. If she could get her hands on four, she felt confident that her and Cooby could hold their own long enough to get away.

One of their escorts step forward. "Two Darchangel twigs lookin' for Hangman. Said they here on behalf of Grezzik. I trust'm." His blatant sarcasm made some of the men snicker while others unbuckled their holsters.

Gideon seized the opportunity. "Grezzik wants to dismiss all prior rivalry. He wants to join forces and start a rebellion against Trollop."

"Oh, I'm sure he does, "an even grainier voice said from a dark corner. Gideon turned and peered, trying to see who was talking. "Ironic. I was about to march over to Grezzik's home and see if he wanted to go dancing after nightfall. Maybe I could be his king, he could be my queen, and we could devour Supreme's police force with our love." The men in the saloon laughed as they got to their feet. The voice kept its gravelly cool. "Hangman, at your service."

Dumakleiza took a deep breath, trying to remain calm for the sake of diplomacy. "It is as Sir Gideon says. Grezzik of the Darchangel territory truly wishes for peace. It is a truce for the sake of an uprising."

More laughter.

"You don't talk like Darchangels," Hangman said. "Where are you really from? Supreme?" he growled.

"We truly are here on behalf of Grezzik. I assure you," Dumakleiza said before realizing her way of speaking was betraying them. She lowered her head a little, hoping Gideon would take the reins. He did without hesitation.

"Grezzik wants to meet with you and discuss an alliance."

Before Gideon or Dumakleiza could say anything else, a sharp whipping sound flung through the air. Dumakleiza dove and rolled onto the ground, narrowly avoiding a lasso. Another flung rope wrapped around Gideon's belly, immediately cinching tight. A quick yank made him grunt as he was dragged away.

Dumakleiza rolled as Cooby scrambled to follow her through the murky room. She snatched two butter knives and ripped a larger blade from a man's belt. Without waiting for anyone else to make the first move, she leapt to her feet, slicing up the legs of men on either side of her. They yelped and fell as Dumakleiza jerked around, tossing one of the knives to Cooby. It bounced along the hardwood, landing at his feet. He snagged it off the floor and began flailing the blade around wildly, screaming and barking.

Most of the men's laughter continued. The commotion was nothing more than a daily brawl. They all gathered around the wild woman and her pet, circling her with amused grins. Dumakleiza and Cooby stood in the center, daring any of them to engage. The two men Duma had felled struggled to get to their feet as some of the others laughed at them. Dumakleiza looked around for Gideon but she couldn't see him behind the wall of stocky dwarves.

"We got ourselves a lively bunch!" Hangman's voice came from behind. "Shoot'r if you're scared, boys. I'm sure none of ya can take a little girl in a knife fight anyways." His patronizing was received like a punch to their chests. All the men immediately holstered their guns, grinning and withdrawing knives. Dumakleiza glared at them, coiling in preparation.

One of the men stepped into the circle, tossing his knife between his hands. Dumakleiza held perfectly still while Cooby growled. The group surrounding them jeered and yelled, encouraging the action to begin. It only riled Cooby more, making him swing his knife more frantically.

The man lunged forward, plunging his blade at Dumakleiza's throat. She ducked with trained reflexes, spinning under his arm, trapping his wrist in her armpit and slamming her elbow into his jaw. With the same motion, she whipped around and swung the knife at his neck. The man grunted with wide eyes and lurched back just enough to catch the blade across his cheek. He fell to the ground with blood trailing behind him.

The others laughed at his inability before another stepped into the circle.

"She put you in your place, Jebbadain!" The new man laughed before blowing a kiss to Dumakleiza. "Let me try a dance with her." He spat on the floor and lunged forward. He faked a swing with the knife, anticipating Dumakleiza's counterattack. As she went to duck under his blade, he smashed his left boot into the small of her back. Dumakleiza roared and fell forward into the onlooking men around her. They caught her and threw her back in, laughing as she stumbled.

Her opponent stopped her mid-stride with a right hook to her face. Dumakleiza staggered backward again, trying to gain her bearings as her head throbbed. She'd been hit many, many times but the sheer force of a sucker punch on Thamiosh redefined power. She stepped past Cooby and snatched him off the bar floor. With one motion, she spun around and threw the screaming tanion straight at the man's head. He managed to block three of Cooby's rabid paws, but the remaining three found their mark. Cooby landed on his chest like a spider, quickly jabbing his body with the dull butter knife. The man went to grab Cooby off his face but was stopped by Dumakleiza driving her foot up between his legs.

He squealed and fell to the ground as Cooby leapt for Duma, only to be caught by a lasso. It barely registered in Dumakleiza's mind before another flung around her, cinched tight and dragged her back.

"That was getting embarrassing," Hangman yelled as the men tackled Dumakleiza and Cooby. "She's a third your size, but her and her weird little monkey put two of you down like sickly dingzels."

The Wranglers hung their heads as they bound them; the beaten tending their embarrassing wounds.

"Release me, you putrid scum!" Dumakleiza thrashed against the thick ropes. "A gaggle of men fear a woman and her tanion! If I had my Yagūlamite swords, you would all lay cut in twain at my feet! Cowards! Cowards! Cow—"

Crunch! The man whose face she'd sliced open smashed his fist into her jaw. As soon as her rattled head turned back up to face him, another

Wrangler wrapped a gag around her head, filling her mouth with dry cloth. She screamed but her rage was muffled.

Once they were completely immobilized, Gideon was dragged out next to them. He, too, had been bound and gagged, and he couldn't help wondering if this was going to happen on every world Traveler brought him to. It made him chuckle a little thinking about what Sir Tereth would say if he could see him tied up again.

"They're more difficult to keep quiet than bleeding pippos." Hangman walked into the dim lighting, allowing them to catch their first glimpse of him. He was a relatively leaner Thamioshling, clad in dirty and worn leather pants, a thick trench coat, and a black helmeting hat with blood red lenses. He was chewing something they couldn't see, and he was obviously pleased having them at his mercy. He blew in their faces, stinging their nostrils with thick gusts of alcohol and meat. "As if I didn't already see through you, you threaten us with *swords*, of all weapons?" he sneered, "I know for a truth that Darchangels trust their guns more than their own eyes. They wouldn't touch a blade for any purpose other than to shave their ugly faces. Supreme has made tiny spies with no knowledge of who they impersonate. But why are you here?" He looked them over and chuckled. "And how *are* you both so thin and alive? You look like still-born pippo pups."

Gideon and Dumakleiza mumbled beneath their binds.

Hangman shook his head. "Coming here under this, er, strange and unconvincing disguise, claiming that Grezzik of all people wishes to join forces?" He gave a small belly laugh. "You're outside your minds to think that feces would fly." He leaned in and grabbed a handful of Gideon's hair, craning his head back. "I'm insulted you think I'd believe such a trick." He took the rope ends he was holding and tossed them up. Only Dumakleiza saw them fly over a wide beam in the rafters and back down to Hangman. "Your necks are strangely long. He held a fat finger up. "Let's see just how long they can get."

With that, he pulled. Cooby helplessly watched as Gideon and Dumakleiza were ripped into the air. They squirmed and kicked around, struggling to breathe, their arms immobile at their sides. Cooby squalled and thrashed but couldn't get away.

Hangman watched with a blend of amusement and disgust. "We pay Trollop's abysmal tax, and yet she still sends spies here under false pretenses?" He let his words sink in as Gideon and Dumakleiza began turning purple, spit bubbling at their lips. "I'm about one horse piss deception from that witch away from actually seeking Grezzik out and really starting a rebellion." He handed the ropes to two of his men to hold taut. "Too bad neither of you will be there to see Supreme fall when the day does come. You chose the wrong territory to try your tricks on, twigs."

As they began blacking out, a loud roaring descended from outside the saloon. It sounded to Gideon like a large plane or helicopter. It made the whole building vibrate as it grew louder and closer. The men in the bar grunted at the inconvenience.

Hangman yelled through the loud whirring, "Take them down and keep them quiet!" He turned and walked out of the saloon.

The others lowered Gideon and Dumakleiza, catching their limp bodies as they fell. They dragged them back behind the bar and piled them next to Cooby as they gasped for air. The gags and bounds remained in their mouths and around their arms. Gideon and Dumakleiza took deep, inhales through their noses, their eyes rolling around as consciousness came fluttering back. They couldn't see anything beyond the bar, let alone outside of the tavern, but they listened as best they could.

The blaring engine quieted to a dull hum. Gideon and Dumakleiza could see guns drawn as Wranglers crouched behind tables and chairs. The tension in the saloon had shifted in what appeared to be a worse direction.

"I'm looking for four fugitives of Supreme." Captain Diggid's voice was unmistakable with its deep, monotonous snore. "Two men, a woman, and, a, some sort of—monkey." He sounded embarrassed of his task.

"You managed to lose *four* fugitives?" Hangman could be heard mocking him. "And one was an animal? Some police force you got there, Diggid. Way to keep the peace." There was a moment of silence that they assumed was a stare down after the comment.

"I'm also going to need your payment to Trollop for this eighth," Diggid said with sour pleasure.

"We done paid her highness three weeks ago," Hangman growled back. "You best get the record straight there, *Captain*."

"You will pay her highness today or you'll be behind in payment." Diggid's tone sounded like he was poking a wound with a stick. "Unless you'd rather see what happens when you don't repay Trollop highness' generosity. You know how much fun I can have with one plane." It sounded like he was smiling. "Don't make me bring more, Hangman."

"You sure have a full scrotum with your planes," Hangman sneered. "Too bad it's never just you and me having these little talks. Then you'd hear me better when I say I already done paid, and you wouldn't be stupid enough to argue."

"Greedy swine!" a shrill woman's voice yelled from somewhere outside, followed by some quick footsteps. *Zap!* There were some gasps, and then a heavy thud. A scream sent a few pairs of feet running away.

"Now, unless you want to join her in the dirt," Diggid barked. "I'd recommend you collect what's owed and have it ready."

"You rotten pieces of—" Hangman bit his tongue. Everyone in the saloon could only guess it was because of a gun aimed at his face.

"I'm going to the Darchangels to check for the fugitives," Diggid said. "When we're done, we're coming back here to collect. Be ready or we'll just fly over and—you can figure out the rest."

The anger in Hangman's heavy breathing was so loud that it could be heard from inside. "What exactly did these fugitives do?" he fumed through clenched teeth.

"They broke into Supreme, where your kind doesn't belong," Diggid spat out dully. "And snubbed their executions."

"You don't say." Hangman's words shook. "I'd like to find them, too."

Diggid could be heard holstering and buckling his gun. "If you find them, Trollop has promised to pardon two payments owed."

"Oh, you misunderstand," Hangman growled back. "If I find them, I'm shaking their hands and giving them a mug of my finest plu."

Silence.

"You have two hours to gather what's owed," Diggid said through tight teeth. "If it's not here when I return, every single Wrangler will pay," he growled. "Dust Wrangler. Stupid name for a place."

With that, the engines roared back up until the noise became deafening. It wasn't long until they could be heard ascending into the sky. The disappearing ship still had the other Dust Wranglers jumpy, their guns remaining up and aimed for any straggling officers that might wander inside.

Hangman walked back into the saloon with a powerful hit to one of the doors. It opened and cracked against the wall. His rage seemed to make the other Wranglers even jumpier than the Supreme intrusion.

"Turn up the lights," he barked as he marched over to the bar. At his command, someone immediately flicked a switch, brightening the tavern. Gideon and Dumakleiza closed their eyes. Hangman's fist slammed the countertop.

After holstering his gun, the barkeep grabbed a glass and filled it with what looked like brown syrup from a black bottle. He placed the glass on the counter and slid it to Hangman. Hangman emptied it without looking at it. He snarled, seething at the bitterness as he licked his teeth.

An impatient man with a bushy mustache spoke up from one of the tables. "What're we gonna do? We done paid the tax three weeks ago, j—just like ya said."

Another joined in, "We *have* the fugitives. Let's just hand'm over. We'd get two payments removed. That's pretty good deal, if y'ask me."

"Yeah," a third said. "But they're looking for four, and we only have three. And you know Supreme. If we only give'm three, they'll find a way to punish us even more for an incomplete offering."

Another nodded. "I'd say an obvious answer is to get them to give up their fourth's whereabouts, hunt him down like a coyat, and then turn them all in together." The comment made Gideon and Dumakleiza worry for Traveler. Supreme's police were heading his way and they had no way of warning him. Gideon longed for a cellphone as the debate continued.

"Yeah, that's not a bad idea. String'm back up until they tell us where their fourth is."

"Quiet!" Hangman finally yelled. "I'm thinkin'." He downed a sixth glass and then wiped a dirty sleeve across his mouth. He cleared his throat. "Drag that talkative fella out here."

Some large hands reached down and grabbed Gideon. They planted his bound feet directly in front of Hangman. Gideon stared at him in silence, waiting to see what would happen. He couldn't talk or move so he relaxed and waited. He hoped he got to be the deciding factor with the fence that Hangman was teetering on. That was a role he thoroughly enjoyed.

Hangman took a deep breath, studying Gideon over in a new light after the police intrusion. After another shot, he removed Gideon's gag. Gideon licked his lips and cleared his throat, trying to shake the flavor.

"Did Grezzik really send you?" Hangman demanded. "Don't lie to me or I'll gut you while you hang." He leaned in close to Gideon's face. "You have till the bottom of this bottle to convince us. If we don't like your side of things, you're going back in the air."

Gideon nodded and furled his brow. "For sure. For sure. Hook me up with a glass of whatever you're drinking to wash that rag's gnarly taste out of my mouth and then I'd be happy to."

Hangman smiled. He stared at Gideon, intrigued with his carefree energy while being threatened. He motioned for the bartender's bottle.

"Doesn't look like your body can handle plu, but I'm willing to risk it."

30

Many Darchangels gathered around the finished Winkloh Star. They still didn't understand what it was, but the prospect of being free from Trollop's tyranny had them eager to see what it was capable of. The children were carrying the trash and scrap parts out, piling them on Grezzik's lawn.

Traveler double-checked everything to make sure it was where it needed to be. Timrekka followed him like a shadow, curious about every mechanical working. While they went over the details, making minor adjustments, the Darchangels watched and exchanged guesses.

After prolonged deliberation, Traveler looked up at everyone and gave a professional smile. "Okay, I think it's ready. Go get some food and rest, and I'll take it from here. Your Winkloh Star should be functioning soon."

Many of the Darchangels and their children nodded through tired eyes and took off to their homes. A few lingered behind, hoping to catch an early glimpse. The giant lightbulb contraption was unlike anything they'd ever seen, and Traveler seemed completely confident that it would provide enough power.

Around and around the device, Traveler tweaked chords and knocked on the glass to ensure structural integrity. The lingering Darchangels began growing bored and ultimately left.

Timrekka twiddled his thumbs. "Is there anything else I can do to help right now?" His scientific mind felt paled compared to whatever Traveler was up to, and he wanted to learn.

Traveler shook his head, distracted. "No." He glanced up at Timrekka and then back down. "I've never built one of these before, but by my understanding of how they work, this should be rather accurate. It's a crude version of those on my world but it's impressive for a lesser developed people throwing it together with scraps." He nodded, not considering the offensiveness of his comment.

Timrekka peered around at the blueprints and gave a small smile. "I just like that they're called *blue*prints; kinda makes me feel like our whole meeting was meant to be, like the stars literally aligned."

Traveler sighed at the comment and began to chuckle. "Of all the signs that could point to such a conclusion, it's the word blue?"

Timrekka nodded. "Sure, I mean, it's the insignificant things in life that tend to prove the most significant in the end, no?"

"Sure, sometimes." Traveler blew some air through tight lips as he stared up at the Winkloh Star. "Timrekka, you're a logical man. A student of science."

Timrekka slowly nodded. "I strive to be, but you are, too—probably even more so with everything you know that I don't."

"Yes, yes, of course," Traveler quickly said. "So, I'm curious about your thoughts."

"Concerning what?"

"Concerning what comes next. After we die, what do you believe comes next?" He sounded like a child needing post-nightmare reassurance.

"Uh, I'm not really sure, if we're being honest, and I don't really like to think about it because I don't have any absolute proof, and as a person who's lived in research and study, I don't pursue anything that I don't have tangible evidence for, so, I guess we'll see." He shrugged.

"Mhm. Mhm." Traveler nodded, clearly unsatisfied with the answer. "But, what do you think happens to us?"

"Uh, okay, well, um." Timrekka tried to scramble an answer together. "I don't know what I believe when it comes to that, so let's break it down scientifically. I think the best I'll be able to do is begin with the fundamental law that nothing ever disappears: energy and matter are only transferred or transformed." He tilted his head. "Things that burn don't disappear, they just become ash and eventually something else; tissue that dies is absorbed by the ground and feeds plant life; nothing comes from nothing, everything comes from what something that was before, simply transformed, so all that matter does is become other matter, whether it's on a molecular level or on a larger scale. Life is transformation."

Traveler nodded while staring intently. "That is our understanding of matter, yes. That much makes sense. But what happens to us? The age-old question. What happens to who we are? Our consciousness. Our souls, if you will."

"Okay, okay, okay, um." Timrekka tightened his lips and puzzled. "Thinking along the same lines, I theorize that whatever consciousness scientifically is, or however our souls can be quantified, when we die, that 'matter' is either transferred back into the planet, or perhaps recycled into new life, new humans, babies maybe." He tilted his head back and forth. "Maybe it restarts with every life, maybe consciousness is all one eternal thing, and yours and mine and everyone else's is just one network of consciousness that gets passed down and restarted every time one person dies and another is born."

"Okay." Traveler thought about it. "And what about at the end of a planet's existence? When its sun dies and the whole planet turns to barren stone, eventually falling apart or colliding with another celestial body and exploding?" Traveler's questioning didn't sound like a test, but earnest curiosity. "What happens when that inevitability occurs? Do you believe that our unified consciousness just floats around aimlessly through space, waiting to just...transform into something else? Or would a planetary explosion split the consciousness and divide us?"

Timrekka shrugged defensively. "I—I—I don't know, but you're the advanced alien who knows more than me, so it's a bit disconcerting to have you asking me what I think, unless this is a test."

Traveler shook his head and walked over to the Winkloh Star, inspecting it further as he spoke. "What if there *is* a spirit realm? What if amidst all the insanity and absurdity of the religious fanatics, they're actually onto something? What if this entire life, regardless of belief, location, or even planet, is only one plane of existence? Just one page in an eternally flipping book."

"Well, if that is true, then what if it's not the first step, as they all believe, but what if it's much further along? What if this universe is one we're born into after dying in another, and what if the multiverse or multiple dimensions theory is true and we die in one only to be born into another?"

"A large topic." Traveler appeared to be glancing over the Winkloh Star to distract himself from whatever was bothering him. "Any one of those are good hypothetical what-if questions worth discussing. I guess I'm just more or less curious, as a scientist, what do you think about whether or not there is a god—a man in the sky."

"*You're* the only man I've ever seen come from the sky." Timrekka secured a loose bolt as he thought about it. "The only times that a creator has ever made sense to me is when I myself have created something." He scratched behind his ear. "If I were to create life, intelligent beings, capable of free thought, free will, and put them on a location I also built, and left them to their own devices while I watched from afar to study them, I imagine they'd come up with the same controversial theories about me, whether or not I existed, and that their scientific properties were evidence of my intelligence, or that every scientific discovery only further suggested that I don't exist and that chance created them. I dunno, it's an odd concept, but ultimately, if there is a god out there somewhere who created us, I theorize that he's studying us, otherwise, why wouldn't he walk among us to be worshipped?" He cleared his throat. "If god exists, I believe he's an experimental creator, satisfied with testing us like meeblesks, so there is no right or wrong, only conclusions drawn from one test to better apply to another."

Traveler stared through the Winkloh Star. "I've visited many anthills, and no matter what shape of hill, size of the ants, or tools they use, they all wonder the same thing."

"What's that?"

"If one day they'll look up and see someone holding a lens to destroy them all."

Timrekka glanced up at the ceiling with a cockeyed expression. "That's uncomfortable."

"Yes, but as you said, I can understand the person holding the lens. Makes sense sometimes." Traveler cleared his throat. "I've traveled the stars, and everywhere I've been, I've seen overwhelming evidence of creative and intelligent design, and yet, no actual proof of the creator. Evidence but no proof. No fingerprint. No signature."

"So." Timrekka happily turned the tide. "What do *you* think happens to our consciousness postmortem?"

The question made Traveler pause. "I believe that that saying 'light at the end of the tunnel' is accurate. Not just because of the loss of vision as death occurs, but I believe that the tunnel continues beyond that. I believe there's a dark tunnel that takes us, uh, somewhere else."

"What kind of tunnel?"

"I'm not sure exactly." He tightened a screw and flexed his jaw. "And I have no clue what is on the other side, but it scares me."

"Hold on." Timrekka smelled a clue. "Are you talking about an actual —"

A loud buzz interrupted him, vibrating Grezzik's house. Traveler and Timrekka looked at the ceiling as it grew louder, making everything in the basement rattle. Timrekka's eyes shot open. He held a finger up to his lips, shushing Traveler and ducking down a little.

Timrekka listened as the Supreme ship landed. It caused an uproar amidst the Darchangels upstairs. Heavy footsteps pounded outside as

Grezzik grumbled something difficult to understand about the interruption of *West Side Story*.

The ship powered down in the street a ways down the road. Darchangels gathered around it while keeping their distance. They weren't scared or angry as much as irritated by the imposition.

Police spilled from the ship, barking for everyone to stay back and waving guns around. Diggid was the last one out, squinting in the bright daylight as he grunted and belched his way forward. He took some heavy breaths and looked around at the amassing Darchangels.

"Where's Grazzisk?" His annunciation made some of the Darchangels chuckle. Diggid scowled. "Where is he?"

"Yo! Dickhead! I'm right here y'bulldog boob."

Diggid growled as he watched Grezzik emerge from the other Darchangels. "It's Diggid. *Captain* Diggid."

Grezzik shrugged while sauntering forward. "You gonn' mess up m'-name, I figure it's only polite t'mess up yours." He smiled. "What ya want *Captain*?"

Diggid glared at Grezzik and drew his gun, keeping it at his side. "I'm looking for four fugitives from Highness Trollop. Two skinny men, one skinny woman, and a, uh, monkey."

Grezzik held it together for a moment and then started laughing deep belly laughs. "You got permission to use Supreme fuel t'scour Thamiosh looking f'r a monkey?"

Diggid glared with embarrassment. "Trollop demanded it."

More Darchangels showed up as Grezzik laughed harder. "Oh, that's even better." He stopped abruptly, giving a concerned look. "Did y'bring fruit? Gonn' be tough trackin' down a monkey with no fruit." His comment even made some of the Supreme police crack smiles, which they quickly hid from Diggid.

"I dunno," another Darchangel joined in. "I think monkeys can find their own kind, no problem. You know, the smell."

Diggid flexed his jaw and looked around. He'd been to twelve territories and gotten nothing but insubordination and mockery for his hunt.
He was loyal to Trollop, obsessively so, but even he was beginning to
think they were wasting manpower and resources. He was about to wave
the officers back up into the ship when something caught his eye. He
took a step forward and pointed at Grezzik's front yard.

"What's all that?"

Grezzik glanced over his shoulder. "What's what?"

Diggid marched forward, closely followed by his officers. He stopped
a few feet shy of Grezzik's property and stared, not at the house, but at
the mountain of scraps heaped on the lawn. He motioned up and down
at the garbage pile.

"What's that?"

Grezzik scoffed, "Trash. Look around ya. This whole territ'ry's trash.
What's it t'you?" He chuckled. "Poor monkey dunno what 'ghetto' mean?"

Diggid skipped over Grezzik's derision, keeping his eyes on the heap.
"What are you building?"

Grezzik shrugged. "Remodelin'. Wanna help?"

The Supreme officers glanced at each other, unsure of why Diggid
cared about garbage. They were ready to leave Darchangel territory. It
was unkempt and depressing.

Diggid looked closer. "Doesn't look like any remodeling I've ever
seen." He paused, silently gloating at his sleuthing prowess. "Where
is he?"

"Where's who?"

"Timrekka. I know he's here. I'd recognize his messy handiwork anywhere."

There was subtle restlessness as the Darchangels inched their hands
toward their weapons. They were hoping Grezzik would be able to talk
the police into leaving, but Diggid seemed convinced of Timrekka's in-
volvement. The Supreme police were no longer confused, and their guns
were up and aimed.

Grezzik shrugged and rolled his eyes. "He's the one gots you emotional? Yeah, he was here, but 'e aint no mo'. B'sides, thought he was banished, not a fugitive."

"Where is he?" Diggid held his pistol up, aiming it directly between Grezzik's eyes. Grezzik's eyebrows lowered as he stared over the barrel at Diggid.

"Ya didn't bring enough men for threats, Dickhead."

Diggid cracked a smile and nodded. "You're right." He reached up and hit a small button on his earpiece. His grin maintained as four more ships descended from the clouds.

Grezzik looked up and slumped at the overpowering force from Supreme.

Diggid cleared his throat. "Now, let's try this again. Where is Timrekka?"

The descending ships hovered a ways above the streets, blowing wind and dust through the crowd. More Darchangels amassed to see what Supreme wanted this time. The ships stayed where they were, awaiting Diggid's word. Large barrels aimed out of the side doors, more than capable of overpowering the territory's handguns.

Over the resounding roar, Grezzik glared at Diggid and yelled, "I told you he's not—"

"I'm right here!" Timrekka caught everyone's attention as he emerged from Grezzik's house. He'd hid for as long as he could, but it wasn't hard to predict where things were heading. He wasn't willing to let any Darchangels endanger themselves on his behalf. He walked into the street with his hands raised.

Diggid grinned at Grezzik. "Well, look at that. He *is* here." He turned and looked at his officers. "The fugitives came looking for him. Search that house."

Timrekka timidly looked at Diggid. "Who are you looking for? I thought I was banished. Can't you just leave me alone now?"

Diggid ignored him, keeping his eyes on Grezzik's home as the other officers walked past them and went inside. The ship's engines were all anyone could hear as they tensely waited. All the Darchangels stared at the front door, worried, knowing Traveler was inside. They were all too familiar with public executions.

Sure enough, moments later, Traveler was marched out through the front door. Five officers escorted him with guns aimed at his back. They ushered him forward with the promise of a quick death if he resisted. His expression didn't suggest any fear or concern, just frustration with being interrupted. He was already behind schedule. Being threatened with a second execution was irritating. Without even acknowledging Timrekka or the Darchangels, he looked up at the sky beyond Supreme's police ships. He held a hand out while being marched, ready to inexplicably vanish if things got worse. It would be a shame to lose Gideon, Dumakleiza, and Timrekka, but there wouldn't be any venturing into the fourth phase for any of them if he got killed.

31

"Where are the others?" Diggid asked his officers.

They shook their heads. "He was alone."

Diggid grunted labored breaths before pressing his earpiece. "Highness Trollop, we have one of them."

Trollop immediately screeched back, "Oh, thank heavens! Those poor things." Her excited clapping was audible.

Diggid slowly nodded. "What should I do with him?"

"Put the poor thing down. For his sake."

"Yes, highness."

"And find the others," her shrill voice shouted.

Diggid nodded and brought his hand down. "Execute that one." He pointed at Traveler. "And then we need to search for the rest of them," he said as if it was his idea.

Traveler rolled his eyes. "There's not an inch of leeway on that leash, is there?" He scoffed, trying to buy time while he searched the stars for an escape route. "You're not so much a captain, as much as a sycophant."

Diggid stopped himself mid-lunge. "I'm the captain, inferior." He looked at his officers. "Put him down."

They nodded as the officer closest to Traveler kicked him behind the leg, forcing him to his knees. Traveler winced as he maintained his stare into the sky. He wasn't seeing anything guaranteed, and he needed to hurry. It was coming down to a couple gambles.

A loud rattle of bullets riddling metal drew everyone's attention to the sky. They all looked up to see one of the Supreme ships' underside speckled with holes. Smoke billowed out like a hemorrhaging wound. Everyone looked around, trying to figure out who had fired as the ship swerved through the air. Alarms sounded, as it nosedived with red lights flashing. The other ships steered out of the way, narrowly avoiding a collision.

"Who did that?" Diggid demanded, lurching back. The other officers aimed their guns around.

Black smoke spilled out as the ship spiraled toward the ground. The Supreme officers inside leapt out, blindly flailing down. Their screams were short lived as the ground broke more than just their falls. Everyone beneath moved to avoid the splatting. There was immediate screaming from snapped ankles, broken arms, and other injuries.

The ship continued spinning without a pilot to try to maneuver through the smoke. It flopped over and over midair as it caught flames and careened down behind some homes the next street over. The loud explosion made everyone jump as blazing smoke erupted into the sky.

Diggid froze at the devastation. His officers panicked, trying to help their fallen to their feet. The mounted guns from the remaining Supreme planes were searching for a target from the sky. They were trigger-happy, eager to rain bullets, but it wasn't been the Darchangels that had fired.

The flash of chaos distracted Traveler from where he was looking. He let go of the light. Everything went silent.

Two long lassos flung out from behind a brick home, each snatching an officer around the waist. With one powerful yank, they were snapped back. The two unsuspecting cops yelped as they were dragged away. Diggid jerked around, appalled by whatever was happening.

Grezzik smiled as he realized Gideon had won their bet.

"Now! Get'm boys!" Hangman screamed out from behind the house. Everyone turned. The police aimed in his direction, only to hear a sudden outcry of whooping from behind them. Guns turned all over as Dust Wranglers galloped in on pippos, tearing around the streets.

One of the Wranglers rode past some Darchangels and fired his incendiary pistol. *Zzzzap!* An officer stumbled backward as he was whipped around, staring in disbelief at his left arm. It fizzled black and fell apart like ash in the breeze. There was no blood as the combustible blast instantly cauterized, and the blood evaporated. He couldn't manage a scream as he went into shock and fell.

Zap! Zzzap! Zap! Electric blasts zipped through the air. Officer after officer fell from ships, while a few others dove out of the way.

Diggid's lazy eyes shot open. "F—f—fire! Fire!"

The police panicked, aiming and firing at every 'inferior' they could see. Wranglers and Darchangels began dropping as the entire crowd panicked. Kailuna ducked and retreated into Grezzik's home, shielding the children as the three forces collided, bullets tearing through the air.

Grezzik took the opportunity to uppercut the unwary captain. He caught Diggid in the jaw and snagged the pistol out of his hand. Diggid snapped into focus and swung back. He narrowly missed as Grezzik ducked, but he managed to smack his stolen gun down to the dirt. With the revolver unavailable, both men began swinging.

The Supreme ships rained fire down from the sky, loud *booms* echoing through Darchangel territory. Most bullets dug deep holes into the dirt, while many found their marks in fleeing flesh. Darchangels and Wranglers were mowed down as they ran, pinned into the ground and shredded apart. Loud screams, gunshots, and blasts susurrated into a maelstrom of violent thunder.

Traveler couldn't help but smile as he peeked out and saw a winged creature appear on one of the rooftops, silhouetted against the midday sun. He recognized Dumakleiza diving off with Cooby on her back. Dumakleiza was armed with two knives, along with one in each of Cooby's spread paws. The tanion's familiar squall made a few of the officers stop and stare. Before they could process whatever they were seeing, Dumakleiza and Cooby had landed on their feet and swung into action.

A quick jab, spin, and four flailing blades dropped two officers to their backs. A third panicked and raised a gun right next to Dumakleiza's face just as one of Cooby's knives stabbed into the side of the head. Dumakleiza gave a proud nod.

"Good boy." She turned and flung another officer's opened throat through the air. "Grim, bring forth as many trolls as need be slain."

Cooby flailed, following her charge, reveling in her fury.

Timrekka hid next to Traveler, holding onto the bush branches, wishing they could stop bullets. Both men spun to see Hangman burst into view. With one hand, the Dust Wrangler chief unloaded his incendiary, tearing through officers and walls while he whooped and laughed. *Zap!* *Zap! Zap! Zap!* He turned and ripped a lasso from his hip, thrusting it forward with an underhand fling. The rope wrapped around a distracted officer. It went snug as Hangman yanked the man off his feet.

A loud voice followed behind him. "Not looking so *Supreme*...anymore!" Gideon stumbled out. He staggered and smiled with the bottle of plu in hand. "How can I help?" He slurred aimlessly, his eyes wandering as though he had the chameleon contacts in.

Timrekka ducked with bullets spraying overhead. "Is he drinking plu? *Now?*" Screaming and gunshots drowned his words out as Traveler wondered the same thing.

"He is. He's drunk. Look at him!" Traveler scooted to the side as an ashen officer fell dead and disintegrated where he'd been. "How did he manage to get the Dust Wranglers here, drunk?"

Timrekka shrugged. "They're *all* probably drunk, as well." He gawked at the battle around them. "I could use a drink, too." He screamed a high-pitched yell and ducked.

An officer saw Gideon wandering into the blood-soaked street. "I see one of the fugitives!" he yelled.

Trollop came over his earpiece. "Stop making me wait! Execute them!"

The officer nodded and ran forward, randomly ducking beneath the barrage of fire.

Gideon peered through blurry eyes at the dense, short man charging him. "Hey!" He hiccupped and quickly swung the bottle. *Smash!* The glass exploded over the officer's head, rendering him unconscious. He fell limply to the dirt. Gideon chuckled and nodded. "Sleep w—well." He staggered a little and went to take another drink. Nothing came out of the bottle. Gideon squinted at the broken bottom and dropped his shoulders.

He looked at the surrounding havoc. Darchangels and Dust Wranglers were fist-to-fist against an army of Supreme officers. Pippos galloped about, spooked by the gunshots and shouting, trampling people and he even saw one chomp an officer's leg clean off. Gideon smiled through fuzzy eyes and started laughing at the ocean of short, thick men and women. Within the drunkenness of his mind, he couldn't help giggling. "I'm a *giant*."

Hangman rolled his eyes at Gideon staggering toward him with exaggerated steps. The thin man had clearly slipped the restraints Hangman had used to keep him tied to a tree. Hangman sniggered as he took a few quick steps and punched Gideon square in the face. *Whack!* Gideon's eyes fluttered as he fell over.

"Stay there, twig," Hangman laughed and then turned to reengage.

More and more officers dropped out of the ships. They slid down cables, firing at the rebels. Bullets caught Darchangels and Dust Wranglers alike, many children among the fallen. The body count from both sides was filling the street with opened corpses.

Dumakleiza dove off another rooftop. She and Cooby cut down two of the descending officers as they coasted into the battle. Cooby barked, basking in the action as Dumakleiza wiped blood from her face. The gravity didn't allow them to coast as long or far as it did back on Cul, but they still had the advantage of aerial maneuvers. Dumakleiza growled as they hit the ground and resumed slashing.

Grezzik and Diggid continued trading punches, both of their faces bruising red and blue. Diggid ducked under one of Grezzik's swings and spun to return one of his own. Before he could land it, a loud *zap* shot through his foot.

He grunted and looked down. There was a sizzling hole straight through his boot. He winced as both he and Grezzik looked up to see Kailuna walking toward him holding a smoking pistol. There was no fear in her, though she was frustrated by missing Diggid's head.

Diggid grunted and spun, jabbing Grezzik in the throat. *Gich!*

Grezzik's eyes shot open. He couldn't breathe. Before he could bring his hands up to hold himself, *zap, zap, zap!* Diggid pulled a reserve pistol from his boot and unloaded into Grezzik's chest. The Darchangel chief went limp and collapsed.

"Grezzik!" Kailuna screamed in horror, her eyes reddening with tears she fired. *Zap! Zap! Zap!* A bullet caught Diggid in the shoulder as he dove away. With a cumbersome roll, he dodged her other shots and snagged his other pistol off the ground. He scrambled to his feet, taking another shot to the thigh.

"Die, you bastard!" Kailuna screamed.

Diggid spun and fired.

Kailuna stumbled backward and stopped. She looked down to see a smoke pouring from a hole in the upper-right side of her chest. She blinked a few times and dropped.

"Kailuna," Timrekka whispered. His eyes peeled open, his mouth trembling. He wasn't a fighter but seeing the closest things he had to friends slaughtered around him had him wishing he was. He felt like a useless coward. He could barely hear Traveler urging him to follow to somewhere safer.

Diggid turned and stared at the mess of blood and bodies. There were plenty of dead Darchangels, Dust Wranglers, and pippos strewn about, and that was a gratifying sight, but there were just as many officers lying next to them. Those remaining were outnumbered, and he wasn't willing to lose everything over a monkey.

He awkwardly galumphed toward one of the ship cables and yelled, "Retreat! Retreat to the ships!" He took some deep breaths, hurdling dead bodies and avoiding live ones. "To Supreme!"

At his command, the remaining officers turned and ran for the cables. They'd been anxiously awaiting the order. One tripped and fell, but none of the others helped him as they desperately fled. Another was caught by a flying noose around the neck. It ripped back, snapping his vertebrae with a vicious yank.

The Darchangels and Dust Wranglers chased after them, firing and throwing whatever they could. A few more officers fell.

As soon as Diggid reached one of the cables, he shouted, "Take off! *Now!*"

Most of the remaining police managed to grab hold of the retracting cables as the ships turned and started toward Supreme. A few weren't quick enough. As they flew away, Diggid stared back with sweat pouring down his face, watching as some of his men were swarmed.

Traveler and Timrekka stayed hidden until the Supreme ships became nothing more than a low hum in the distance. It didn't take long until the only sounds were those of heavy breathing and groaning from the injured bodies strewn about the streets. The battle had begun quickly, escalated out of nowhere, and ended abruptly. They all knew the Supreme ships would return in greater numbers and then they'd be slaughtered.

Timrekka was in shock. The people he was trying so desperately to help were either dead or injured. It wasn't a ghost town, but with the silence, the eerie sense of loss was the same. He walked through the street, trembling as he looked around. He blinked in disbelief at familiar faces lying motionless before him. He opened and closed his hands, trying to get some feeling to return.

Schlayfe walked up to Timrekka and shoved him in the chest. "Where were you?" Timrekka stumbled back, his eyes glued to one of the children's dead faces. Schlayfe shoved him again. "You were hiding! We needed you. You invent weapons. You *have* weapons. You could have helped, but you only help Supreme! You allowed the guns you built to destroy us! Look at all this!"

Timrekka blinked again and looked up, unable to think or speak. "I—" He shook his head. Schlayfe was right. He could have used some of his lethal inventions. He could have gotten involved. Maybe he could have even kept Grezzik alive. He shook his head again. Everything was a blur, and he couldn't process it. All he could do was stare at the dead as Schlayfe continued yelling at him. He gradually looked up. "I'm not—" He scratched his head and scrunched his eyebrows, still trying to process what he was surrounded by. "I'm sorry."

32

Dumakleiza was the only one enlivened by the battle. She scratched Cooby's panting chin and looked around with unsatisfied blood-lust. The sunlight stung her dragon eye, but she reveled in the pain. In that moment, the heat of battle ran savagely through her veins. It had been too long since she'd killed with divine purpose. She spat on one a dead officer and tucked her knives into her belt. Cooby cooed in her ear and held his weapons out for her to take, just as she had taught him.

"You fought bravely, my Coobs."

Cooby chirped and licked her face. He looked around for a water source.

"You are quite the skinny li'l fighter, ma'am," Hangman remarked as he approached her, holstering his pistol and reeling in his rope. "I'm impressed. And by your warrior monkey, as well."

"He's a tanion," Dumakleiza snapped back, struggling to turn off her killing switch.

Hangman smiled and nodded. "Course he is." He cleared his throat and finished putting his lasso away. "Well, figured I should apologize for gettin' ya hanged and pay my compliments. You two flyin' things are a force to be reckoned with. Some of my men can certainly testify."

Dumakleiza glared at him. "We were no equal to your flying ropes."

Hangman puffed his lip out and shrugged. "Well, to be fair, you were outmanned, and I engaged ya from the dark where ya couldn't even see me. I wouldn't say that was a fair fight."

"I could see you," Duma corrected.

Hangman dismissed the impossible with a grin. "Course ya could."

Traveler stepped up next to them and looked at Dumakleiza. She stared back through crazy eyes, recognizing his frustration. It wasn't hard to see his eagerness to leave all of Thamiosh behind. Traveler took a deep breath and blew it out, trying to focus as he turned to Hangman.

"Hangman, I'm assuming?"

Hangman nodded. "Yep." He looked Traveler up and down and smirked with his gravelly voice. "I assume you're the last one they're lookin' for?"

"Indeed." Traveler nodded. "Grezzik swore you wouldn't come. How did Gideon convince you?"

Dumakleiza tilted her head. "What makes you believe it wasn't I who convinced the Wranglers of Dust to come to your aid?"

Traveler stared at her before aiming the question back at Hangman. Hangman glanced in sleeping Gideon's direction before turning back.

"It all happened really fast, as I recollect."

Traveler nodded. "I'm assuming he told you a story, gave you something from his backpack that somehow altered your life. And now you trust him wholeheartedly. Something similar to that narrative?"

Hangman and Dumakleiza looked at one another before turning to Traveler. Hangman cleared his throat while fondling the rabbit foot in his pocket that Gideon had given him.

"I wouldn't say *wholeheartedly*."

"But, I'm right, aren't I?"

"How did you know that?"

Traveler shrugged. "It's what he does—something he's managed everywhere we've gone."

Dumakleiza nodded. "It was good fortune that Sir Gideon was there. Without him, I fear the Wranglers of Dust and I would have fought until only one remained."

Hangman scoffed a chuckle before looking at Traveler. "Just from first impression, it does seem as though he makes his way as freely as water."

"Nearly everywhere we've been, he manages to make friends of even the most dangerous people."

"Except Supreme, apparently." Hangman motioned in the direction the ships had flown. "Trollop wants his head. She wants all of your heads. Not that that's much of an odd thing, I reckon."

Dumakleiza followed his gaze and clenched her fists. "If they are to return with more men in those flying demons of metal, we must rally as many warriors as we can to our cause."

"You talk odd," Hangman commented as he checked his gun's condition. "But, yes, we better regroup 'cuz that's exactly what they're doing back at Supreme. When they return, and I promise ya they will, they're going to finish your executions. Ours, as well."

Traveler thought for a second and then nodded to himself. "You two work on that. I've got to go get the Winkloh Star working." With that, he turned and walked away.

Hangman looked to Dumakleiza. "He doesn't seem to care about your wellbeing. Nor his for that matter. You skinnies are an interesting breed."

"I imagine he does appear foreign to you," Dumakleiza said as she watched Traveler walking off. "After all, he is a diviner of sorts."

"A diviner?"

"A sorcerer."

Hangman smiled. "Course he is." He courteously tipped his helmeted head. "Well, I best be helpin' with the regrouping. No time to bury the dead just yet."

Dumakleiza headed after him as he walked away. "And educate me in the ways of guns?"

Hangman chuckled, "Yeah, I'll teach ya how t'shoot. Come on."

Traveler walked over a few bodies with his eyes locked on Timrekka. He weaved around some grieving people and made his way over to him. Timrekka was crouched down, his eyes fixated on Grezzik's body. He was despondent, mumbling a moaning whine as he examined the bullet wound.

"I need access to your lab," Traveler said, wasting no time.

Timrekka nodded as if dismissing the demand as he stared at Grezzik's corpse. "Do you believe it's possible to bring him back? Gideon spoke of that Frankenstein doctor reanimating the dead, and Grezzik didn't deserve this; none of them did, and I've been working so hard to provide them a better life, so maybe if I bring him back to my lab now I can save him."

Traveler sighed and shook his head. "Yes, there are ways of bringing the dead back to life, but only shortly after their demise, and only if certain body parts are still intact. Resurrection has fragile rules." He exhaled out of pity and impatience. "But the structural integrity of Grezzik's vital organs have been blown apart. I'm afraid he's staying dead. I'm sorry, Timrekka." He felt bad rushing the grieving process, but they didn't have much time. "But I need access to your lab, and if you by any chance have a tranquilizer dart gun, that would be extremely helpful."

The request caught Timrekka off guard. "I have something of the sort, what do you need that for?"

Traveler blinked as he thought of a quick answer. "In case there are any problems or interruptions while I finish the Winkloh Star. I need to get it done tonight, and if there are any lingering Supreme police lurking around, I'd prefer to put them down without any more bloodshed."

Timrekka stared for a moment and then slowly nodded. "What you're looking for is in the box second from the bottom in the far-left corner."

Traveler gave a quick nod and then walked away. He had to get everything done much faster than he was comfortable with. He was ready to be done with the miniscule problems of the young planet and refocus on his primary mission. Just one more test. Then he could finally concentrate on the fourth phase.

Timrekka stayed squatted, staring at Grezzik's body. His mind numbly ran through numerous ideas and theories. There had to be a way to replicate Gideon's tale of reanimated tissue. The possibility intoxicated him.

"Oh, of course." He stood up, realizing Gideon was still unconscious from *his* intoxication. He hurried over to where Hangman had knocked him out. As he reached Gideon, he pulled a square, three-inch box from his utility belt. Timrekka reverently opened the grey container like a surgical instrument.

Gideon was flat on his back, snoring with the broken bottle still in his hand.

Timrekka grinned, grateful for the distraction. "You had too much, and I wish I had, too." He grabbed Gideon's arm and gently turned him onto his side. Gideon gurgled. Timrekka lifted Gideon's shirt, exposing his lower back. Gideon's snoring stopped, which hadn't been Timrekka's goal, but it was a nice bonus. Timrekka took the tin box and pulled an equally grey sponge out of it. He held it to the center of Gideon's lower back and pressed in. He waited patiently before pulling the sponge away. It was heavier and dripping. He coolly held it away and rang it out. Dark liquid poured to the dirt until the dripping stopped. "Oh wow, that's strong, no wonder you're so far gone." The plu smell made Timrekka's eyes flutter. He held the sponge to Gideon's lower back again and pressed, calmly repeated the process eight more times until there was practically no more plu being wrung out. Timrekka squeezed the sponge one last time and then put it away.

A few quick breaths and Timrekka's urgency got the better of him. He rolled his eyes and flipped Gideon back onto his back. Gideon hadn't responded to the draining yet. Timrekka reached forward with his large hand and *thwapped* Gideon on the chest.

"What?" Gideon lurched up, his eyes shooting open. He blinked and shivered as he came to in a hurry. He felt surprisingly alert. "Oh my God, I'm thirsty." He looked around, seeing Timrekka squatting in front of him with a confusing expression. "What's wrong?" Gideon looked around. "Oh." He gulped as he processed the body-ridden street. "What happened?"

"You and Miss Dumakleiza got the Dust Wranglers here, and they saved Traveler's life and probably mine as well, but it started a big fight, and they killed a lot of Darchangels and Dust Wranglers, including Grezzik." His words fell out like weights. "Captain Diggid got away, and he'll be back soon with a superior force." He cleared his throat. "Hangman had to knock you out because you were belligerent, but I purged your body of the remaining plu with my booze sponge, which basically draws alcohol through sweat glands and pores, so you can place it on the small of the back or in your armpit or your—"

"Where's Traveler?" Gideon interrupted. He needed a moment to process what Timrekka was saying. He closed his eyes. "I'm sorry." He looked up at the pain on Timrekka's face. "Are you all right?"

Timrekka's head hung heavily, his eyes dead at the bottom of his goggles. "I've never seen anyone killed before. I heard Trollop sentence many people to executions, even my family, but I never witnessed it, because I was always kept in my lab, and I've seen many dead bodies—studied them, dissected them, even experimented on them—but it's different seeing the life disappear. They're just suddenly not a person anymore."

Gideon knew there wasn't anything he could do that would mend what was broken inside of Timrekka. "I'm sorry, Tim. I know there's nothing to say, but if there's anything I can do for you, just let me know." He took a deep breath as he looked around at the carnage. "I've experienced it before, and it's—there aren't words."

Timrekka's eyes threatened to shatter. "What happened to you?"

"I, uh—" Gideon looked up at the sky for a moment. "I tried my hand at being a missionary. You know, bringing religion and supplies to a third-world country. It was one of my first travels."

"On a third world?"

"Uh, bad wording on my part. A poorer, less-fortunate place on Earth."

"Back on your planet?"

"Yeah." Gideon nodded. "I spent a lot of time in a village in the Amazon. Basically, a large jungle back on Earth. I was there nineteen days, providing medicine, getting sick and shitting my brains out, teaching simple education, spending time with the locals." He cleared his throat, fighting past his thirst. "I got pretty close to some of the children. They brought me under their wing and taught me how they hunted in the jungle, and included me in their version of football." He glanced at Timrekka. "Just a game. Anyways, one of the kids, Ana, told me a ghost story around a fire one night. Their people believed that there was a jungle spirit that came whenever someone died. Da Rahz Sik was the spirit's name, though they affectionately called him SikSik. They described him as a tall, slender shadow with long fingers, long hair, and faceless; the typical superstition monster. Whenever someone died, SikSik supposedly came to collect their soul, and take it into the jungle, where he would return the person's energy to nature. It was how they believed they lived forever. Their soul would be returned to nature by a demon of the Amazon. SikSik." Saying the name brought a hallowed reverence over Gideon. "I couldn't tell if it was supposed to be a sacred spiritual belief or a horror story, but the way Ana told it, it was poetry." Gideon ached at the memory. "Sometimes there's more beauty in an archaic belief, just because of the purity in it."

"What happened?"

Gideon puffed his lip out. "Well, one night I woke up to gunfire. A lot of it." He shook his head. "Rebels upriver had raided the village to take the supplies we'd brought. I ran out of my hut to try and help, but one of them cracked me over the head. Pretty much like what happened to me here. Except I wasn't drunk, and I was still conscious enough to see hell unfolding around me. They burned the huts." He took a deep breath and held it for a moment. "I watched them kill most of the villagers and all of my group. I saw Ana's vibrantly hazel eyes go dark." He stared off into the distance for a moment. "And it could have been the crack over the head, but once the rebels had left, and I was left there surrounded by the dead, surrounded by the silence of their faces, I swear I saw a tall, slender shadow in the fire's light—lurking through the bodies." Gideon stared further into nothingness as the memory vividly played before him. "Perhaps it was SikSik. Perhaps it was nothing. But I could feel the dead around me. I helplessly witnessed the final ballet of their ghosts."

Timrekka stared into Gideon's eyes. "How do you process it?" He didn't want to look around. He didn't want to look at the dead as his tears fell.

Gideon slumped. "Everyone deals with it in their own way. I choose to grieve the dead by celebrating all life. There are many people that I've lost. Especially my——" He cleared his throat. "It's just part of the deal. My vengeance is to live so fully that my death will be welcomed." He knew Timrekka needed more but he wasn't sure that he wanted to give it. After a deep breath, his voice softened. "One of the hardest lessons that I've had to learn is to forgive myself. It's cliché but cliché things are cliché for a reason." Another deep breath. "If you cling to guilt for someone's death—a death that you didn't cause—you dishonor their memory by smothering it in darkness. And you burden yourself with a weight that nothing but forgiveness can heal."

More tears escaped from under Timrekka's goggles. He looked at Gideon, unsure of what to say. "Was the——was the missionary trip how you injured your shoulder?"

Gideon looked down at his shoulder and shook his head. "No. But it is where I got one of my favorite items in my bag." He finally smiled. "The night of the slaughter, before everything happened, the villagers had a little feast. Part of it was an insanely delightful dessert made of mashed beans that grew around their river. I finished my portion so fast, I forgot to savor the flavor. There wasn't enough for seconds." He smiled bigger. "Ana insisted that I take the rest of hers, and after a heated debate, she won. She explained that the beans were really quite bitter when eaten alone, but the dessert was her favorite, simply because of the transformation the flavor went through. She loved that something so bad could be turned into something so good." He calmly sighed. "The morning after the slaughter, the rest of us buried the dead. Afterward, I collected some of the beans and put them in a small sack. I keep them with me to remind me that death is bitter, but I can turn the memories into something—better."

Timrekka's tears flowed freely. "I'd like to see them."

Gideon reached out and rubbed Timrekka's arm. "Of course. They're yours now."

Timrekka shook his head. "No, they're not."

"I insist. I believe mementos have a purpose to serve before they're passed on to whomever needs them next." Gideon's words hit Timrekka exactly how they were supposed to. "Now, where's Traveler?"

Timrekka brought his hand up and wiped under his goggles. "He—he's at my lab, working on the Winkloh Star, and Miss Dumakleiza is—" They turned and saw Hangman showing Dumakleiza and Cooby how to handle guns. Timrekka grinned sheepishly. "Apparently, they're learning how to shoot. Is it safe for Cooby to hold that?"

Gideon thought for a moment. "Can you get me, like, a gallon of water? And then, between your science and me being your guinea pig, er, meeblesk, let's see what we can come up with before Supreme returns."

Timrekka smiled and nodded fervently. "Okay, I like that idea." He immediately felt more optimistic. "Gideon, I don't know how but you somehow make me believe that it was okay that I survived."

33

The next morning came without any surprise from Supreme. The lackluster night *was* the surprise. A few of the Darchangels and Dust Wranglers had cleared the streets of bodies, bringing their fallen onto nearby lawns. They knew it wouldn't be wise to wear themselves out digging graves just yet, but they could at least get them off the road.

The dead police were piled on an empty lot. A few votes had demanded that they be burnt or at least displayed as a warning. The majority had voted against further mutilation, focusing their efforts on the living.

Messengers had gone to the nearest territories to share what had happened and hopefully rally them. There was no telling if they would be killed for intruding on the wrong colors, but the cause was worth the risk.

With no one feeling much like speaking, the streets had gone quiet.

Kailuna was recovering from her chest shot, wrapped in blood-soaked gauze and rags. She was reading more *West Side Story* to the children and the injured, all propped up around her bedside.

A loud scream rang out from somewhere in the distance. Everyone outside turned and looked as one of the Wrangler emissaries came galloping in on his pippo.

"They're gone! They're gone! They're all gone!"

The yelling startled everyone, making them reach for their guns. They saw it was one of their own and lowered their weapons.

"What is he talking about?"

"Who's gone? The other territories?"

"Do we need our guns right now? I left mine in my house. I'll go get them."

"Wait. What's going on *now*?"

The rider sped around a corner toward where everyone was gathering. "Great news!" The pippo came to a stop next to a large trough of water on the side of the road. It went for a drink, but the Wrangler didn't slow down at all, leaping from its back and running. "Trollop is gone! Diggid, too! And a bunch of the police, apparently!"

Hangman stepped out in front. "Slow down. What are you saying? Diggid is on his way here?"

"No, he's gone, apparently. All gone." The exasperated rider jogged up to Hangman and put both hands on his shoulders. "News is spreading faster than Trollop's legs. All of Supreme's ships are in Supreme, but Trollop is nowhere to be found." He shrugged with a giant smile on his face.

"What?" Hangman blinked, dumbfounded. "Gone where?"

"I don't know! Ha!" He wiped his mouth. "Just gone. Apparently, the rest of the police are scouring Supreme, looking for them. But they're gone, or kidnapped, or if we're lucky, dead." He happily shrugged again. "They apparently don't get about us anymore. Their focus is aimed internally."

Murmurs exploded throughout the crowd.

"Do you think she's dead?"

"Oh, we've never been that lucky."

"Who would have killed her?"

"Who *could* have killed her?"

"Did someone sneak onto their plane yesterday and infiltrate Supreme?"

"Maybe. Who's missing?" People started looking around, doing a headcount.

"No, that's impossible. Even if someone did, how would one person do that? They'd be killed before they could get near her."

As the discussions grew, Timrekka and Gideon walked up. They were both wearing utility belts, packed full of what looked like small water balloons. As usual, the balloons were all blue. They made their way through the crowd until they were next to Hangman.

Timrekka looked around. "What's going on?"

The rider happily repeated himself. "Trollop and Diggid are gone. Supreme is losing its brain trying to find them, but they've either been taken or killed."

"Or," Gideon interjected. "Are they plotting? You know, deceiving you by convincing you that they're out of the picture so that we all lower our guards?"

Timrekka shook his head as his eyes sparkled. "No, deception is not within their repertoire, or anything clever for that matter. I'm not trying to get my desires too high, but this sounds promising."

"So, wait," Gideon deliberated. "Then what do we do now?"

Hangman smiled. "We take Supreme, twig—while they're confused and leaderless." All the Thamioshlings broke into an uproar of cheers. Having the element of surprise over Supreme was a delicacy that had only ever dangled in violent fantasies. Hangman hushed them and looked around. "Send more emissaries out. Tonight, we take Supreme and put an end to Trollop's reign!" Deafening praises broke out as many of the gathered riders dispersed to get their pippos or gravity boots. They weren't Darchangels and Gut Wranglers, they were united Thamioshlings.

Traveler emerged from Grezzik's house. He looked around at the excitement and grinned. His eyes had large bags under them. He'd worked all night and his hands showed it. It was a feeling he didn't get often, being as he was usually bathed in light, but it was strangely rewarding to ache. He walked out, trying to avoid getting run over by the madhouse of rebellion. It didn't take long to spot Gideon and Dumakleiza standing a head above everyone else.

"Gideon! Dumakleiza! Timrekka!" The three of them turned to see Traveler motioning them over.

Gideon smiled. "Did you hear what's going on?"

"Yes." Traveler looked around and puffed out his bottom lip. "Apparently Trollop's gone missing—something like that?"

"Yeah," Gideon said with a hesitant smile. "Odd."

"Indeed. It's a lucky morning." Traveler's words were quick as he turned to Timrekka. "The Winkloh Star is functioning. Would you'd like to come see it?"

Timrekka nodded, distracted by the morning's news but he was curious. "Uh, yes, I would."

Traveler smiled. "Great. Follow me."

Dumakleiza paused. "I will see this Star of Winkloh later, for I must accompany the Wranglers of Dust on their quest."

Traveler shook his head. "No. We're leaving after, so you need to be here."

"But." Dumakleiza begged. "What of the attack on Supreme?"

"That is the business of the Thamioshlings. We have much larger matters to tend to."

"But these matters *are* big."

"No, they're not."

Dumakleiza carried Cooby after Traveler. She slumped, desperately disappointed.

As they walked, Traveler glanced at the orbs around Timrekka's and Gideon's belts. "What are those?"

"Oh." Gideon smiled. "Timrekka and I spent a few hours making little bombs out of his flower, Trollop's petal. We throw these, *poof*, boneless police. Cool, huh?"

Traveler uncomfortably glared at them and gulped. "You two shouldn't be friends."

✳

They walked down into the basement and immediately covered their eyes. All the lights were off, but the massive glass sphere was glowing like the sun. It emitted a low hum so subtle that they almost couldn't hear it. They squinted, peering through tight fingers at the Winkloh Star. Dumakleiza had her dragon eye completely shut with a hand pressing over it. Cooby yapped and buried his face in Dumakleiza's neck.

Traveler nodded, quite impressed with his work. "I'm rather happy with how well it's functioning. This is my first attempt at a Winkloh Star. They are meticulous masterpieces back on Whewliss."

Dumakleiza's uncovered eye began adjusting as she stared in amazement. "This is the work of the heavens." Her jaw hung open as she looked around to see if everyone else was as mesmerized.

Timrekka studied the mechanics of it. Bright eyed and inspired, he reached forward, watching the light break between his glowing fingers.

"It feels like I can almost see the light moving inside of it."

"Yeah," Gideon said as he smiled through slits. "It's like the light is alive."

Dumakleiza couldn't pick her jaw up. "And this contraption of time to come is capable of powering all of this territory?"

"Yes." Traveler nodded. "Maybe even some of Dust Wrangler territory. Not likely, but it might be able to generate enough if more light is added to it."

Gideon glanced down as something didn't make sense. "Wait." He looked to Traveler. "What do you mean by——"

"Oh!" Traveler shouted. "I almost forgot." He pointed at the ground next to the Winkloh Star. "I found that while I was installing the base-conductor."

They looked where he was pointing and saw a sack. In the blinding light, it was difficult to understand its familiarity. Dumakleiza lurched as she recognized it.

"The treasure of Yagūl!" She rushed forward and picked it up, ripping it open. Sure enough, it was all there. In the blinding brilliance, her treasure glistened like an explosion of pure whiteness and rainbow. The golden items shone like mirrors, making the grungy basement glow. All the trash piles and random boxes in the room's corners suddenly looked like priceless objects bathed in the cornucopia of light. Dumakleiza teared up as she held the sack. "Where did you find this?"

Traveler nodded nonchalantly toward a pile of metal and glass scraps. "Around there. I guess Trollop didn't take it after all."

"Hmm." Timrekka smirked as he looked around. "That's officially the first accusation that she's not actually guilty of, but I don't remember seeing it anywhere in here, and I don't know how I missed it."

Gideon smiled at the recovered treasure and the Winkloh Star. "There have been some solid moments during this adventure that have taken my breath away."

Dumakleiza looked from her treasure to him. "Was there such a time on Cul that took away your breath?"

"Many." Gideon nodded. "Mostly when I stood on a legendary island, having flaming arrows fired at me by a flying pirate princess."

Timrekka looked to him. "What?"

Dumakleiza tried to conceal a small smile. "It was I who took away your breath?"

"Holy spirit, yes." Gideon chuckled. "That was one of the single most captivating moments of my entire life."

Traveler smiled. "And you've barely seen anything so far." He felt like Gideon, wanting to share secrets that he'd sworn oaths not to.

"Oh, I'm sure." Gideon's smile grew as he realized that it was almost time to go explore a new world. "Each planet is so fascinating with its different cultures, traditions—landscapes. I can't wait to learn about more of them. Holidays, histories. There's just so much to experience. I don't think I'll ever be satisfied, and that's a good thing." Traveler and

Dumakleiza nodded while Timrekka's mind grew anxious. Gideon stared at the Winkloh Star. "And the different rates of development are spellbinding."

Dumakleiza turned to him fearfully. "*Spell*binding?"

Gideon chuckled. "Uh, magical, er, I meant mesmerizing. Fascinating. Let's stick with fascinating."

Dumakleiza slowly nodded. "Not magic."

"No. Not magic."

"Just wait," Traveler beamed.

Gideon tilted his head. "One of the things about Thamiosh that really blows my mind is you said that they're only a little more advanced than Earth. But I feel like in many aspects, they're way behind us. But in other areas, they're weirdly ahead of us."

Traveler nodded. "Once technological advances begin the inevitable upward slope, they increase exponentially. For example, on your world, Earth, there were some people whose short, one-hundred-year lives began in the epoch where horse-drawn buggies were the primary method for transportation and died after a time where Earthlings had begun their third phase, traveling to your moon. In less than one century, Earth advanced from horses to spaceships."

Gideon pondered the fact. "That's pretty nuts. I'd never thought about that."

Traveler raised his eyebrows. "It won't be long until Whewliss will send an emissary to Earth after you discover light travel for yourselves and introduce you to LOLA."

They all looked to Traveler, asking in unison. "LOLA?"

"Laws Of Light Act. Since the discovery of light travel, there have, of course, been some planets and people who have invaded, committed crimes on other worlds, or waged wars against other planets. In response, the world leaders of many planets met and set agreed upon laws to oversee all interplanetary light travel."

"Makes sense."

"So, now, whenever a new planet discovers light, they're kindly and firmly introduced to the legalities they must follow if they wish to partake in light travel between worlds."

Gideon nodded. "Gotta keep the peace, yo." He smiled. "I wonder how many years it'll take us to get from the moon to that."

Traveler stared into the light of the Winkloh Star. "I find it very lazy that Earthlings simply named their moon 'moon.'" He chuckled. "Even the uninhabited planets in your solar system have names for their moons, but not Earth. 'What should we name our moon? Oh, I know: moon.' Well done, Earth, planet whose name literally translates to 'dirt.' Well done." The other three smiled, enjoying Traveler's rarely seen sarcasm. "You even named your sun *the* sun. Rather pretentious, Earthlings. As if yours is the original and every other solar system's sun is lesser."

Gideon stroked his beard and laughed. "I love days we light jump. You get so sassy, Spaceman."

Traveler laughed. "I'm not serious. It's somewhat of an initiation joke." He stifled his amusement. "Nearly every habitable world does the same thing when they believe themselves to be alone in the universe. They all call their sun *the* sun and their moon *the* moon. Typically, once a world discovers that they are one of many, they give their celestial bodies more personalized names. I'm sure Earth will do the same when their time comes."

"Huh," Gideon said with a smile. "That's fun."

Dumakleiza secured her treasure sack to her hip as she stepped up next to Traveler. "To what manner of world does our quest lead us next?"

"Actually," Traveler said. "It's a world less advanced than Cul. It's called Borroke."

Dumakleiza smiled. "Less advanced than Cul? So, I shall be the more intelligent being than the men of this world of Borroke?"

"Yes, you will. They still believe their planet is flat."

"Is it not?" Dumakleiza asked. "Of what shape is their world?"

Traveler stared through the Winkloh Star, his mind seemingly having to reboot. "Duma all worlds—all worlds are spheres. Including yours."

Duma looked at him, trying to decipher whether or not he was joking. "How is Cul not flat?"

Traveler had to refrain from lashing out at Gideon for convincing him to recruit Dumakleiza. He had no prejudice against lesser evolved intelligence, but he'd never had one as underdeveloped as Dumakleiza on his fourth phase team. "There are zero flat planets in the universe. The only flat——" He composed himself. "They're all spheres."

Gideon laughed at Traveler's frustration. "So, what kind of clothes do you have for us this time around?"

Traveler pointed at the ceiling. "They should be expanded by now. They're up in Grezzik's living room."

Upstairs, the garments were laid out on the floor, and Gideon, Dumakleiza, and Timrekka were studying their peculiarity. Traveler stood back, smiling as he watched them. The clothing was made of large animal pelts crudely sewn together, but they were unlike any species of animal any of them were familiar with. The long-haired skins were bushy, many inches thick, with a brown so vibrant, they almost appeared red.

Gideon squatted down and ran his fingers through it. "Oh, wow." It felt like soft porcupine quills. Somehow, there was a comfort to their rigidity. "That's incredible. I want to lie in a bed of it. What kind of critter is this from?"

Traveler shrugged. "I don't know. I've never been there. A fellow recruiter gave them to me to use should I ever travel to Borroke."

"Have many of your people been there?"

"Just the one recruiter. Her recruit was killed there, and she narrowly managed a jump before the Vulgairs got her, as well."

"The Vulgairs?" Dumakleiza asked.

"They're the tribe we'll be nearest on Borroke."

"Are they dangerous?" Dumakleiza half-wanted the answer to be yes, and half for it to be no.

"They're certainly not the most dangerous we know of, but they dole out death as comfortably as they breathe." Traveler looked at her. "They'd like you, though. They think of women as holy."

"Oh, is that true?" Dumakleiza smirked.

"And what am I supposed to do on this planet?" Timrekka asked. "It sounds like a dangerous location for a test, so what do I need to do while we're there?" He brushed his white hair back over his ears while shuffling his feet.

"Simple," Traveler said with a quick shrug. "Assist me in documenting an undocumented planet." He ran his fingers through one of the wild fur pelts. "Each new world has unique scientific properties. There are distinctive minerals, elements, wildlife, ecosystems. Everything is always slightly different than any other planet." He looked up at Timrekka. "So, your test, as the scientific recruit for the journey to come, is to do what you do best: Study the world, document it and, of course, experiment as much as you want." Timrekka's eyes sparkled. Traveler held a finger up. "Just, obviously, don't try to introduce the indigenous to advanced technology. Especially the Vulgairs. They're quite barbaric."

Gideon smiled. "I'm excited to meet them."

"Oh, no, no, no, no, no." Traveler looked at him sternly. "This isn't a social visit. We're going for the planet. Our sole purpose is testing Timrekka."

"You remember my rule, don't you?" Gideon responded with firm sass.

"I remember just fine," Traveler snapped. "You're just going to have to make an exception. We've had enough danger and gotten quite lucky so far. Leave the people of this world alone." He brought his head back.

"In fact, we need to remember to make sure you cut your shoulder immediately when we arrive. I don't want *any* possibility of you upsetting any indigenous if we do stumble across them."

Timrekka quickly nodded. "Agreed." He didn't want to deal with any hostility anywhere, ever.

Gideon's smile didn't waver. "This is going to be a fun one. I can tell already."

"No, it's not." Traveler suddenly regretted planning their next jump to Borroke. "No fun will be had. You're allowed zero fun on this planet."

Gideon leaned forward and quickly kissed Traveler on the cheek. "Spaceman, you're adorable when you're scared." With that, he stood up and grinned at all of them. "Shall we?"

Dumakleiza was infected by Gideon's smile. "I, for one, revel in Sir Gideon's temper before his blood release. It is the nearest he ventures toward being a warrior."

"An incompetent warrior," Gideon added with a finger in the air.

Traveler took a deep breath and held it behind closed eyes before letting it go. "You three are a dangerous combination."

Gideon nodded. "The spice of life."

They gathered on the vacant street in front of Grezzik's house, dressed in the animal skins. The coats covered their entire fronts and backs, long quills bursting outward. Gideon slung his backpack over his new clothes, and that was all he needed to feel ready. Timrekka had his lab coat underneath his coat, with more than a handful of portable inventions tucked into as many spots as he could fit. Dumakleiza had four knives tucked away within hers, and her bag of treasure was secured so she wouldn't lose it a second time. Cooby held on extra tight to her back. He loved the long fur. It was so much more nuzzlable than Dumakleiza's thin, human skin. He cooed and cuddled, rubbing his face on it over and over. They were all ready to go.

Traveler stood with his hand closed in the air as he stared into the sky. He'd been standing still for a few minutes, waiting for the forecast to be perfect. Timrekka's heart was racing. He was trying to stay calm, but what they were about to do was overwhelming him with delight. Traveler double-checked that they were all connected through touch and then nodded.

"I'm done with this world." With that, he opened his hand.

34

As the numbing light faded away, Gideon felt coldness grip his skin like shrink wrap. It felt like he was trying to breathe above water after being submerged for too long. Adjusting took a moment but he easily recognized the lighter gravity, a much-welcomed sensation. He blinked a few more times and then looked around, immediately grateful for the thick animal coat keeping him warm.

They were in a winter wilderness. More than a foot of untouched white snow covered everything. Traveler had landed them in the middle of a clearing surrounded by massive pine trees. The looming forest was eerily silent as nothing moved. Even the air seemed to be frozen in place. All Gideon could hear was his own steaming breath as he stared into the darkness of the snowy wood. They'd arrived just as Borroke's sun was setting, which only made their surroundings more nameless.

"Well, looks like we've made it to Narnia." His quiet comment echoed over the ice wonderland. He turned around to see how the others had fared. "How we doing?" He saw Traveler and Dumakleiza brushing snow off their animal coats, still recovering from the jump. Cooby batted at his nose, sniffing and licking puffs of snow. Gideon was just relieved that they were standing without the gravitational obstacles of Thamiosh. He looked around. "Where's Timrekka?"

Traveler and Dumakleiza stopped brushing themselves off and looked around. Gideon was there, Traveler was there, Dumakleiza was there, and Cooby was there. They turned and searched their surroundings. Timrekka wasn't there.

Gideon squinted suspiciously. "Did you send him somewhere else? You know, like you did with me for my test?"

Traveler shook his head, distress growing behind his eyes. "No." He began scanning frantically.

Dumakleiza was confused. "Where is he then? Did he not leave his world with us?"

"He did. I know he did," Traveler said as his pulse started racing. "Do you see any tracks anywhere? Maybe he recovered quicker than we did and went somewhere. He's probably fidgeting with something he found."

Gideon and Dumakleiza checked the snow around them. It was pristinely untouched, sparkling in the fading twilight. No one had been there since the snow had fallen, not even a woodland creature. The snowy landscape showed no signs of life in any direction.

"I see nothing," Dumakleiza said.

"He wasn't —" Gideon didn't want to say it. "—shadowed, was he?"

Traveler clenched his jaw at the mere mentioning of the possibility. "No, I checked the forecast. We had clear passage." He looked up at the sky. Thick, grey clouds covered Borroke like a heavy blanket with limited breaks in between. It was through one of those partings between the clouds that he'd shot them in order to land safely. Traveler took a deep breath. He didn't want to look into space to see what answers he'd find. All signs pointed to a disheartening conclusion. He blew a steaming breath out and squeezed his fists as he searched the heavens.

Gideon watched him as patiently as he could. Each passing second made him worry more. Did Timrekka maybe land somewhere else on the planet, and they'd just have to hunt him down before the indigenous did? Could he have actually been shadowed? What would happen next if he had? All his questions bottlenecked in his throat as he stared at Traveler.

Dumakleiza scooped Cooby up and held him close to keep them both warm. She prayed under her breath as a bad feeling gripped her.

"I ask, powerful Grimleck, if it is within your divine plot, spare the life of Timrekka of Thamiosh, for he is a good man. If your will is for his life to continue on our quest, I will find gratefulness within that verdict. But, should his life be yours to claim this day, I will find peace within your decision." It had been a long time since she'd felt sadness at someone's death rather than reveling in it.

Traveler held a shaking fist against his lips as he looked down and closed his eyes. He let out a few deep breaths, trying to get control of his pulse. He flexed and unflexed his jaw, his mind burning.

"There was a meteor shower that passed through our course." Painful inhale. Heavy exhale. "Timrekka was shadowed." Traveler's excruciating cocktail of shock and frustration was visible as he steamed in the cold.

Gideon's eyes widened as he looked from Traveler, up to the sky, and then back down. The news felt colder than his feet. He'd been with Timrekka on Thamiosh what felt like only minutes earlier. He couldn't actually be dead, could he? Gideon looked at Traveler.

"Something you couldn't see in the forecast?"

Traveler closed his eyes and ground his teeth together. "It's difficult to see, but I should have. I've never shadowed anyone." He turned, discouraged, staring through the dark forest around them. "Ah!" He kicked some snow as his yell echoed away. He was filled with so much self-loathing that he didn't feel the impact as he fell to his knees.

Dumakleiza stared around at the shadowy forest as it darkened in the fading light. Behind the tree line was blackness, holding secret the unknown things that resided within its untouched wilderness. Each new world held different creatures, and the unknown filled her with concern. She motioned for Cooby to climb onto her back as her hands readied. If need be, she had the Dust Wrangler knives. She turned toward Traveler, hesitant to interrupt his gloomy ire. "Should we perhaps travel with light to a safer world?" Even on her planet, she was accustomed to having the protective walls of castle Yagūl at night. She didn't like the vulnerability of being out in the open.

Traveler barely glanced up before his eyes fell back to the ground. "Borroke's sun is setting and the clouds are closing together. We don't have any light to jump with." He realized he was forgetting to breathe as depression dragged him down. "We need to find shelter tonight. We'll jump in the morning."

Gideon looked around at the quiet world. "Where are we going to go?"

"I'm not sure yet. I'll figure that out tomorrow. We need to—find a new scientist." He got to his feet. After all the work he'd done on Thamiosh. After all the labor to build the Winkloh Star. After risking his life. He groaned. One little mistake had rendered all his efforts worthless. "Let's just go find shelter for the night."

"After the healing light, I feel no sleepiness," Dumakleiza commented.

Traveler slumped. "I'm going to sleep."

"Okay," Gideon said, his irritability kicking in after the light jump. The addition of a new friend being killed only worsened his new-world gloom. "At least he died knowing he succeeded in helping Thamiosh."

Dumakleiza's eyebrows hung low. "I truly admired Timrekka of Thamiosh. It is a loss that he has become as shadow. Though he is a beautiful addition to the stars."

Traveler turned to Gideon like he was going to say something and then dropped his hands to his sides. "And I asked Timrekka to bring a scalpel for your shoulder, but now that he's not here, I guess, I don't know. Find something to cut yourself with so you'll be helpful. It's already dark enough here. Don't make it worse."

Dumakleiza pulled one of the knives from her waistband. "You can use this, Sir Gideon." His self-mutilation still made her defensive, but Gideon being of sound mind was more important than her reservations.

Gideon reached up and held his left shoulder, feeling the perfectly healed skin. He immediately felt rage rising in his throat. Before he focused on anything else, he had to feed his inner demons. He took the knife, giving a small, grateful nod. Without waiting, he brought it up and sliced his shoulder from top to bottom. Blood immediately streamed down his arm and started dripping into the snow. Dumakleiza glared, still confused. Gideon cleaned the knife on his coat and handed it back. He wiped his shoulder with more of the long animal fur, firmly holding it to slow the bleeding as he felt his positivity returning.

"Thank you." He felt better, but there was still the heavy shock at Timrekka's death. Gideon thought about it for a moment and then looked at Traveler, who seemed crippled. "*What if* he's still alive?"

Traveler barely managed a scoff. "How could he possibly have survived being shadowed in space, Gideon?"

Gideon shrugged. "I don't know. I guess I was just wishing there was a way. I've already seen some miracles on this journey so far. It doesn't seem too far outside the realm of possibility."

"Well, it is," Traveler responded flatly, his eyes still on the ground.

Dumakleiza thought for a moment. "*What if* Grimleck decides to return Timrekka to us?"

Traveler ignored the question. "We need to find shelter. It's almost night." He wasn't in the mood. There was too much guilt on his shoulders. In fact, Gideon and Dumakleiza's attempts at cheering him up with irrational questions were beginning to piss him off.

Dumakleiza looked around. "Where shall we find shelter?"

Gideon turned to her. "This world seems most similar to yours. Kinda makes you the expert. Where do you think?"

"I—" She looked around again. "I do not know. I was raised in Castle Yagūl."

"Then I'll spearhead some construction," Gideon said, exaggerating a neck pop. He smiled. "I believe the best course of action would be to build an igloo. Right here in the clearing would probably be best. No fire though. Just in case we draw attention. Don't want to spook any natives or animals. We'll stay warm with the trapped body heat, and hopefully Traveler brought enough dried food pouches that we can use melted snow to expand them. It should be good enough to tide us over till morning."

"Good plan," Traveler said with forced gumption. He didn't want to waste time. "Our strength appears to be normal here, so Timrekka's blue super juice must have worn off during the jump." He sighed, disappointed to have lost the boost. "Let's get piling snow and dig it out."

Dumakleiza looked at the forest one last time as the sun set. Something twinkled in the darkness. Somewhere in the distance, small, bright reflections caught the last of the day's light. Dumakleiza squinted, trying to see better with her dragon eye, but whatever the small flickers were, they were too far away. She couldn't tell if it was just snow in the woods, sparkling in the final twilight, or if there were eyes watching them from afar. Either way, she was on edge.

"Let us build quickly."

35

The next morning, Dumakleiza woke with a start. Her heart raced before her eyes even opened. Something was wrong. She could sense it. She sat up in the dugout igloo and looked around. Gideon, Traveler, and Cooby were gone. Maybe they were outside? No, something certainly felt wrong.

A violent throbbing pulsed in the back of her head. Dumakleiza ground her jaw as she reached around to touch what felt like an injury. She winced, feeling a tender lump. Someone had clubbed her over the head in her sleep. She couldn't remember any of it. If she'd been alerted and woken beforehand, she had no memory of it. She lurched forward and crawled out of the small snow cave.

Bright light from the morning sun shone off the surrounding snow so brightly that Dumakleiza had to cover her dragon eye. She scurried until she could stand and then leapt to her feet. It only took one quick scan to find the answer she was looking for. There were two sets of footprints in the snow. They looked to be larger than those of normal men, and about twice the size of hers. Next to them were a few sets of animal prints. Dumakleiza racked her mind for familiarities, trying to assess what kind of beast could have left them. They looked like wolf prints but were larger than the human prints next to them. Curious.

Dumakleiza held her head again, the bright morning sun worsening the ache. She couldn't figure out why whoever took the others had left her. To her understanding, especially on a primitive world, wouldn't a woman be taken first? She saw random red stains in the snow alongside the tracks heading away.

"Grim, where is my Coobs?" Someone had bled as they were taken. Perhaps it was Gideon's shoulder? Not that that answer would bring her much comfort, but it was better than new injuries.

Dumakleiza flexed her jaw and gripped her knives. She looked up at the forest where the prints led. It was about a thousand paces away. The already piercing blue of her right eye glowed like crystal with the snow's reflected light. She couldn't see much in the shadowy wood, but whoever had taken Gideon and Traveler had also taken her Cooby. That fact alone left her no choice but to go after them. If those responsible hurt her tanion, they were already dead in her mind.

She took off running alongside the tracks. The instant her feet launched forward, her eyes widened. She leapt much farther than anticipated. Her entire body felt light, as if her weight had suddenly been cut in half. Each landed foot was about half a stride longer than she was used to. She felt faster and stronger, which was extra surprising in the snow. As she struggled to understand, she continued running faster. The warrior princess may have been on a vengeful hunt, but she couldn't help smiling at the empowering phenomenon. Something in her less-advanced mind knew that it had to do with this new world's science or something along those lines, but she couldn't help wondering if maybe the kidnappers had put a spell on her. It felt too incredible to be real. The questions were quickly tossed aside as she took advantage of the sensation and focused. She buckled down and crossed the clearing before she'd even reached full speed. She didn't slow down at all as she burst through the tree line and into the forest.

The blinding snow was instantly gone, swallowed up by the heavy darkness of the woods. Dumakleiza slowed down and closed her right eye so she could focus on what her dragon eye saw. It took a moment, but she was able to see everything. Inside the foreboding woods was a peculiar strangeness. There was no snow. Dumakleiza looked up. The trees' branches and leaves were so tall and thick that they'd gathered and trapped the snow atop them, forming a thick ceiling of ice.

She looked back down. Beneath was a dark, coniferous domain, thick with plant life. Bushes and massive tree trunks were blanketed by pine needles. Dumakleiza was reinvigorated as she noticed that the thick floor of dirt showed the same footprints and paw indentations. She didn't see anything else but more forest for as far as her dragon eye could see. She took a couple deep breaths and continued her hunt.

"Cooby and Sir Gideon, do not fear, for I shall tear open those who took you." She brought her head back, immediately feeling guilty for not thinking of Traveler as well. "And the diviner, of course. I come for your sake, as well. Grim, keep lit my path." She ran forward, bounding over bushes, felled trees, boulders, and slipping on loose ground. Again, her movements felt effortless. It was as though her energy hadn't waned in the slightest. Trees passed by like blurs as she struggled to keep her eyes focused on the tracks. A cold breeze whispered in her ears as she sped up. Aside from what she was creating, there was no airflow in the co-cooned forest. The ceiling of snow kept everything beneath preserved in a kingdom of silence and statue trees.

A low growl caught Dumakleiza's ear. She came to a stop and ripped the knives from her waistband before the dust settled around her feet. She slowed her breathing and honed in on the noise in the blackness around her. She couldn't see any signs of life, but she knew it was there. Another guttural growl. It was so deep that she felt it vibrating in her bones. It sounded large, and the crunching needles from its footsteps, heavy. Whatever it was, it was nearby, watching her, following her. Dumakleiza widened her eyes, squeezing the knives tighter as she prepared to turn.

She spun with a violent roar of her own, ready to attack. She stopped, stepping back as her feet threatened to give way. Not thirty paces from her was a wolf—an enormous wolf. Its shoulders were as tall as her, and its head was larger than her torso, lowered with ears tucked. Its glowing eyes shimmered with primal instincts, yellow and green reflecting against her purple. It didn't blink. With bared fangs, it inched forward, growling as it closed in.

Dumakleiza didn't know what to do. The beast was larger than any bear she'd ever seen, but as a wolf, she knew it'd be nimbler, more cunning. She didn't have faith in herself to kill it, but by the way it was approaching her, she knew she was going to have to try. Both her and the wolf's breath rose like smoke in the frozen air.

"Grim, if it is my destiny to die here, aid me in bringing at least half of this wolf with me."

Then, before she could charge, a warm light appeared. She had to turn away as it burned her dragon eye. A large man walked into sight from behind some trees with a wooden torch in hand. The light from the small fire illuminated him and the monster wolf he was walking toward. He stood two heads taller than Dumakleiza and had a black beard the length of her hair. Wrapped around his large frame was a thick animal's pelt. His was a dirty shade of white, with dark grey stripes running diagonally across his body.

The man stopped as he approached the wolf, coating them both in a warm yellow glow. He stared at the beast's posture, and then turned to see what it was growling at. Dumakleiza dreaded what was about to happen, but when he saw her, he reacted unexpectedly. The giant man stared for a moment with no expression at all. Then he subtly bowed. Dumakleiza was waiting for him to threaten her, to try and take her, to attack her, to have his way with her, but no horrors happened. The man cleared his throat and smiled. He didn't say anything as he continued over to the wolf. Dumakleiza's presence didn't surprise nor deter him. In fact, it seemed to enliven him.

As soon as he placed his hand on the wolf's back, the beast stopped growling. It lifted its head a little, but kept its shimmering eyes locked on Dumakleiza. The man's curious gaze was also fixated on her. He shushed the beast, running his hands through its bushy fur. After studying Dumakleiza more, he reached up and motioned for her to come to him.

"I no will hurt you, woman of great face." His rich voice teemed with more secrets than the dark wood.

Dumakleiza was completely caught off guard by his nonaggressive demeanor. "By what name did you call me?"

The man motioned for her a second time as the wolf glared. "Come with me, woman. You be fed. You given drink. Great chair waits for you. Games begin when the light leaves." He motioned overhead.

Dumakleiza suddenly understood what Traveler had meant about the people of Borroke being less advanced than the people on Cul. She adjusted her grip on her knives as she studied the man more meticulously. She couldn't see a single weapon on him. It would have made sense in a barbaric world for everyone to be armed, but the intimidating man had nothing on him aside from his clothing and torch. Then again, with a wolf standing taller than her head, he probably didn't need anything other than a command for it to kill any threat. Dumakleiza gulped some hesitance down and spoke.

"I seek my traveling companions. They are a party of two men and a tanion. Have you seen them?" There was no doubt in her mind that the wolf's paws would match the tracks in the snow. She just needed to see if the man was honest, or if he would try to trick her.

The man nodded without hesitation. "They wait behind wall of branches. They make you smile this night. We leave now. Arrive before games. Come." He motioned again.

Dumakleiza wasn't sure what to do with the unusual situation. She took a step forward into the torch's light. As more of her was illuminated, the man got a better look at the animal skin on her back and the knives in her hands. He squinted, curious, and then defensive as Dumakleiza became visible.

"What you hold?"

"What do you mean what do I hold?"

The man repeated himself. "What you hold? Rocks that look like pointed branch. Small rock spear." He pointed at her knives.

Dumakleiza was confused. "Knives. Blades? Have your people no knives in their possession?"

"Knives." The word sounded clunky and awkward coming out of his mouth. "Knives."

Dumakleiza couldn't help cracking a smile. "You truly are a less advanced people than I. I admit, that is a refreshing change. Your world is not flat, but that of a circle," she boasted the information. She stood a little taller, keeping her eyes on the wolf. The wild beast wasn't as aggressively postured, but its glimmering glare hadn't left her. Dumakleiza slowly looked back to the man. He took a step toward her with outstretched hands.

"Give me one knives."

Dumakleiza took a step back. "Excuse me?" Her instincts told her to engage, but she didn't feel threatened.

The man cocked his head to the side impatiently. "Give me one knives."

Dumakleiza shook her head. "Take me to my companions." She kept her voice calm, as not to spook the horse-sized wolf. She wasn't sure what the social protocol was with Borroke's people, but it was better to be safe. Gideon, Traveler, and Cooby were taken, and she was face-to-face with a giant man and a giant wolf. There was no time to be coy. She stood her ground with knives held tight.

The towering man took two lumbering steps over to her and grabbed at her knife.

Dumakleiza lurched backward with wide eyes, quickly slicing the man's hand just enough to warn him. She positioned herself with the blades held out in front of herself, expecting him to retaliate and attack. The man stopped. He didn't flinch or cry out. He just turned his hand and stared at his palm as blood streamed out of the clean slice. Dark crimson dripped into the snow. He cocked his head to watch it. The wolf immediately sniffed the air, feasting on the aroma of fresh blood. It finally turned its gaze from Dumakleiza to its master, hoping for permission to try a bite of whatever was bleeding. The man held his torch closer, wanting to get a better look at the injury. He smiled and looked up at Dumakleiza.

"What are you called?" He seemed even more excited to make her acquaintance than before.

Dumakleiza was completely bewildered. "I am Dumakleiza, last of the Yagūlamites. What is your name?" Her knives were still aimed at him.

"You will be called Blade Maiden," the man said, as if branding her. He wiped his bloody hand across his chest, smearing red into the fur. "I am called Dim Rōk." He gave a happy smile that was barely visible beneath the bushy, unkempt beard. He turned and patted the giant wolf's head. "This is called Muz Hont. She is great wōlf. She is mine." He looked at Dumakleiza proudly. More blood dripped down his fingers, so he wiped his hand across his chest again before motioning for Dumakleiza to come pet his wōlf.

Dumakleiza didn't move. "Where are my friends, Dim Rōk of Borroke?"

Dim Rōk's demeanor maintained. "They are behind wall of branches. Where do I get knives?"

"I, uh——" Dumakleiza was at a loss. "I do not know of where one can be found here on Borroke. Knives must be tempered and made by a blacksmith."

The man nodded, though it was clear he was confused by her answer. "Are knives how you kill great mammōth?" He pointed at her fur coat.

Dumakleiza blinked a few times. "A mammoth? I am wearing the coat of a mammoth?" She glanced down at the thick fur around her body.

Dim Rōk nodded. "It take many Vulgairs to kill mammōth. Many Vulgairs die." He held his hands out with all ten fingers trying to depict how many. He closed and opened them a couple times.

Dumakleiza smiled as an idea crossed her mind. "I was given this coat by one man—one man who killed the mammoth alone."

Dim Rōk brought his head back, hesitant to believe what he was being told. "*One* man kill mammōth?" He held his breath.

Dumakleiza nodded.

Dim Rōk gasped. "I no believe this! Did he use knives?"

Dumakleiza grinned. "I am unsure of what weapon he used." She was beginning to revel in being the higher intelligence.

Dim Rōk looked around the dark forest, suddenly unnerved. "Where is man who kill mammōth with no help?"

Dumakleiza smirked. "You said he is behind a wall of branches." She added a little threat to her tone. "It is not safe to keep him there."

Dim Rōk's eyes widened. "He in Vulgairia? Come now. We go now." He switched to urgency. It was what Dumakleiza intended, but now that it was happening, she wasn't sure what to do next.

"How far away is Vulgairia? How do we get there?"

Dim Rōk patted the giant wōlf. "Muz Hont take us."

Dumakleiza hesitantly looked at the monstrous animal. "Lead the way. I will follow."

"No." Dim Rōk shook his head. "You are slow. Muz Hont is fast. Muz Hont take us." With that, he grabbed two handfuls of the wōlf's long hair, and leapt up, hoisting his massive body onto the beast's back. Muz Hont barely budged at the added weight.

Dumakleiza stared wide-eyed with her knives still held up. She could only imagine how much the large man weighed, and the fact that it didn't even make the wōlf flinch made her more scared of the creature.

Dim Rōk ushered her again. "We go now."

Dumakleiza was having trouble overcoming her fear. "Grim," she prayed under her breath. "Sir Gideon would have the courage. In fact, he would be without fear, and likely upon the beast before invitation. Grant me the same strength." She slowly lowered her knives, taking few steps toward the daunting carnivore.

Dim Rōk held his hand out to help her up. "Come, Blade Maiden."

Dumakleiza tightened her lips and ignored his assistance. She tested her enhanced strength by running and leaping. Sure enough, she managed to jump high enough to land on the wōlf, right behind Dim Rōk. She straddled the wide animal and hesitantly held onto Dim Rōk's coat, keeping the knives in hand.

Dim Rōk slapped the wōlf's neck and roared. "Hyah!"

Muz Hont whined and launched forward. Dumakleiza's eyes shot open as she grabbed on tighter. The giant wōlf tore through the forest so fast that the torch all but blew out. With heavy, growling breaths, the beast ripped around trees and over bushes, carrying their two bodies with absolute ease.

Dumakleiza reached down with one trembling hand at a time to put her knives away. As soon as they were both tucked into her sash, she reached around Dim Rōk's waist and held on, praying she wouldn't be thrown off. Her strong fingers dug into his sides as she prayed he couldn't see how utterly terrified she was.

"Grim, keep me safe! Grim, keep me safe! Grim, keep me safe!" She squeezed her eyes shut.

Dim Rōk chuckled as he leaned forward, instructing the wōlf to run even faster. "Hold strong, Blade Maiden! We have long ride to get to Vulgairia this night."

36

It felt like they had been riding the wōlf all day. Its running rhythm had become numbingly hypnotic, and honestly, Dumakleiza couldn't tell when Borroke's day ended and the night began. The darkness of the forest shed no light, leaving her at the spiraling mercy of mystery.

Every now and then, Dim Rōk would grunt, spit, or kick Muz Hont to get her going faster, but otherwise they rode in silence. Dumakleiza maintained her death grip on Dim Rōk's waist, sure she'd fall off if she let go for a single breath. Her fingers had frozen into clamped icicles. She wasn't sure if she'd even be able to grab her knives if she needed them.

Finally, Dumakleiza saw a glimpse of light in the distance. They were approaching the first break in the igloo forest she'd seen since entering it. No sooner had she caught sight of it did the wolf close the distance and burst through the last trees. The setting light was blinding after the darkness they'd spent hours in. Their only light had been the waning torch, and even that had gone out a ways in.

She looked ahead at where Dim Rōk was taking her. Across another valley, nestled between snow-covered mountains, was a village. It was of decent size, looking to have a few dozen huts, all covered in animal skins, which in turn, were covered in snow. A handful of larger structures were made of felled trees. In the back of the town, built against a mountain side, was one building about half the size of castle Yagūl. She guessed that for their advancement, a building that size was important, and what intrigued her further was that it was the only building with no roof.

As they got closer, she saw many people within the encampment. A quick head count put the visible population around forty to fifty. They were all taller than Dumakleiza was familiar with people being. But after Thamiosh, everyone seemed tall. Between her enhanced strength and the strange first impression with Dim Rōk, she wasn't worried about any one-on-one confrontation. However, if she was caught in the middle of a violent multitude, she didn't know how she'd fare. Additionally, there were many more monstrous wolves wandering freely throughout the encampment. Dumakleiza knew her scent was going to be different from the Vulgairs. Standing out was something she didn't want. She prayed that none of the carnivores had eaten Cooby. He'd be nothing more than a snack to them.

From how far out they were, she couldn't differentiate the women from the men, which only made her wonder if there were both in Vulgairia. They were all completely covered in thick animal pelts to keep them warm in the frigid climate. Dumakleiza couldn't stop wondering why Dim Rōk had referred to her as "woman of great face." Was Traveler right? Did it mean the bearded giant was attracted to her, that he respected her? Did it barbarically mean he wanted her head on a pike as a trophy? Was he going to try to wed her? She shook her head. She needed to focus. She continued studying the Vulgairs as they approached the town. The most troubling problem was that she didn't see Cooby, Gideon, or Traveler anywhere.

Muz Hont slowed down as they approached the outskirts of Vulgairia. A few men gave acknowledging waves and nods as they rode in. Dim Rōk waved back. He grunted and readjusted his position as they came to a slow trot. Dumakleiza could feel the giant man's body relax in his hometown. She winced, finally feeling the bouncing bruises on her butt from the wōlf's spine.

"Blade Maiden, we are here." Dim Rōk sounded excited, clearly expecting her to be in awe of the settlement's majesty.

Dumakleiza looked around through defensive eyes. Everyone was staring at her. It seemed as though no matter where they went, she was always a pariah. On Thamiosh, she was one of the tallest people, and on Borroke, she was the shortest. She was beginning to long for a world where the people were similarly sized so she wouldn't feel so out of place.

As she glanced around, she finally saw a couple of women sitting together under a tent. They were dressed the same as the men. Heavy animal coats draped around their heads and bodies. The only clear difference was the lack of big, bushy beards. Aside from the facial hair, it was difficult to tell any of them apart. And once again, Dumakleiza was confused by the lack of any weapons. She remembered Dim Rōk referencing wooden spears, so she knew they at least had those somewhere. But there were no swords, knives, axes, or shields. She didn't know what to make of it. It was easier to deal with the strangeness of new worlds and new peoples with Traveler there to guide her, and Gideon to make her feel comfortable, but without them, the experience was troubling.

As Dim Rōk led them farther into Vulgairia, two wōlves sat up and sniffed the air, licking their lips at the new scent. Dumakleiza watched them cautiously. They began growling as their mangy necks stiffened. A couple barking commands by their owners did little to deter them from snarling at her. Dumakleiza felt comfortable enough riding to let go of Dim Rōk and place her hands back over her knives.

She waited before looking away from the restrained beasts to see where they were headed. Muz Hont was panting as the tired beast carried them toward one of the larger huts. Dumakleiza wasn't sure what to make of it. She hesitantly leaned in to Dim Rōk's back.

"Where are you taking me?"

"I take you to Eyrayor Ash Vizla."

Dumakleiza racked her mind for references. "You will take me to what? What is that?"

"He is eyrayor of Vulgairia," Dim Rōk said plainly. "He is called Ash Vizla."

Dumakleiza nodded, trying to prepare herself for whatever was about to happen. "What is an eyrayor? Is it a manner of king? Your leader?"

Dim Rōk nodded. "Ash Vizla is eyrayor of Vulgairia."

"Does he have my friends in his hut with him?"

Dim Rōk grinned as Muz Hont stopped in front of a large hut. "Do not be afraid, Blade Maiden. Eyrayor will have much happy for you."

Muz Hont walked over to a carved-out stump that was filled with icy water. The large wōlf lay down in front of it, dipping her massive head in. Water spilled all around it as she took big gulps to quench the long run. Water splashed over her face as Dim Rōk took the incentive to kick his leg over her back and step off. He brushed a layer of ice off his beard that he'd acquired during the ride. It had set deep into the hair and coated his eyebrows. After a few headshakes, he turned to help Dumakleiza dismount, but she was already standing behind him with her hands on the hilts of her knives.

Dumakleiza still wasn't sure what to make of Dim Rōk's lack of response to her threats. He didn't seem to have any concern at all about the knives. Instead, he gave the same smile behind his beard and then motioned to the hut. Dumakleiza nervously stepped toward the front flap. Many Vulgairs watched her. They wanted see what would happen, and it made Dumakleiza more nervous than she already was. She flexed her jaw and kept walking. If it would help save Cooby and her traveling companions, then the danger would be worth it.

Dim Rōk trod ahead and pulled the hide-curtain aside so she could walk through. The courteous gesture added to her uncertainty as she stepped inside. She took in the warmer ambiance of the midsized hut. The multi-pelt roof was about two of her high, and doing a decent job keeping snow out. In the middle of the dirt floor was a fireplace made of stones. It kept the hut warm as smoke filtered through the holes and gaps in the roof. To the left of the fireplace was a large pile of leaves. It was spread wide, with a few animal furs covering it. Dumakleiza assumed it to be a bed. She prayed under her breath that it was not the reason for her being led there. Luckily, she had her knives, but she would have felt much safer with Cooby on her back. To her right, against the far end, was a table made of logs and smaller branches, and that's where she saw him.

Sitting behind the table, staring at her while he shoved carved meat into his face, sat a tall man with long, dirty blonde hair. The ripe aroma of wild game became palpable as Dumakleiza evaluated him. The man's eyes looked as hungry as his stomach seemed to be. He examined her with a violent excitement as meaty juices dripped down his hairless face. Dumakleiza stared at him, expressionless. Every other man she'd seen had a full beard. This man only had one layer of animal pelts covering half of his torso, lightly slung over his right shoulder. Similar to the rest of the Vulgairs she'd seen, he didn't appear to have an intimidating amount of muscle on him, but he was massive in frame. Dumakleiza felt unsafe. She knew the history of at least her own world, and women never fared well in these situations. She didn't want to imagine how women were treated with the Vulgairs. She had to take control of the situation before anything happened. She cleared her throat.

"Ash Vizla of the Vulgairs, I am —"

"*Eyrayor* Ash Vizla," the man corrected as he gulped down some half-chewed meat. He pointed at the smoothness of his jaw. "You not recognize face of great woman?"

Dumakleiza squinted, confused by the comment. "Apologies. Eyrayor Ash Vizla, I wish to see my —"

"You are real woman of *great* face," Ash Vizla remarked as he smeared his forearm across his mouth. "Where is your home?" The fire crackled and popped, flaring up and brightening the room.

Dim Rōk stepped closer from behind her. "I find her at hunt one day that way." He pointed off in the forest's direction. "She say she belong to bad eyrayor."

Ash Vizla slowly nodded and stroked his smooth chin before Dumakleiza in the fire's light. "What your people called?"

Dumakleiza oscillated, ensuring she was ready no matter where anyone moved. "I am Dumakleiza, last of the Yagūlamites."

Ash Vizla smiled. "Your words make my mouth full." He brushed them away. "Tonight, your eyrayor go to ground in great circle of Vulgairia. Tonight you become Vulgair." He smiled and opened his arms as if welcoming her to the family.

Dumakleiza glanced over her shoulder at Dim Rōk, who was nodding with reassuring approval. She turned and watched as Ash Vizla stood, towering above her from behind the table. Both men dwarfed her, making her want to engage or run.

"I request an audience with my companions."

Ash Vizla laughed in amusement. "Why you want that? They behind wall of branches. No good place to speak to bad eyrayor."

Dumakleiza wasn't in the mood for a debate. She slowly withdrew two knives from her waist and held them out for both men to see. She lowered her eyebrows.

"I will not ask again. Take me to see my Cooby, Sir Gideon, and the Diviner."

Ash Vizla leaned forward and looked at the knives. "What do you hold? Fangs of wōlf?"

"She has knives!" Dim Rōk exclaimed, pointing with his bloodied hand.

"What are knives?" Ash Vizla couldn't take his eyes off them.

Dumakleiza seized the opportunity. "They are mighty weapons, and if you do not allow me to —"

"I show you," Dim Rōk interrupted her. He stepped back, opened the hut's front flap, leaned out, and bellowed. "Sawm Ket!" Dumakleiza watched Dim Rōk motioning for someone. He held the flap open as another formidable man stepped inside. The new man looked around at them and then turned to Dim Rōk.

"What you bring me for?"

Dim Rōk grabbed the man's shoulder and smiled. "Wait." He turned to Dumakleiza and held out his other hand. "Give me one knives." After Dumakleiza's expected headshake, Dim Rōk persisted. "I will give back."

Dumakleiza didn't know why, but she decided to trust Gideon's advice and take a leap of faith. "Do not make me engage, for I will not refrain from removing your tongue through your throat." She slowly extended a knife to him. As she did, Ash Vizla leaned forward over the table, eager to see what would happen.

Dim Rōk took it and smiled at her. "Many thanks."

Sawm Ket was instantly captivated by the blade reflecting the fire's light. "What do you hold?"

Dim Rōk held it out. "Knives." He looked at Ash Vizla. "Eyrayor, watch knives." With that, he turned and plunged the blade hilt deep into Sawm Ket's chest. Dumakleiza's eyes shot open as Sawm Ket grunted. He gurgled something and then fell to the ground, dead. Dim Rōk turned around and held the blood-covered knife up for Ash Vizla to see. "It go in like air." He nodded gratefully toward Dumakleiza as he wiped the knife on his cloak and then handed it back to her. Dumakleiza silently took it and smiled, trying to stay calm.

Ash Vizla clapped a couple times. "I very like knives! Give me one knives."

Dim Rōk smiled, happy to share his excitement with his superior. "We all must have one knives." He shoved Sawm Ket's body to the side of the tent.

"Yes," Ash Vizla said. "Give us knives."

Dumakleiza thought for a moment. "I will give you *one* knife if you take me to my friends." She had more knives tucked away, so the trade wasn't overly risky.

Ash Vizla didn't hesitate. "I agree. We take you to wall of branches now."

Ash Vizla and Dim Rōk led Dumakleiza into the large roofless structure. It appeared to be a small coliseum, thirty paces across by Dumakleiza's guess. Its tall walls were held together with logs and crude attempts at rope. The structure was three quarters of a complete circle, with the last quarter made up of the mountain it was built against. Dumakleiza looked around at the spectacle. Seats were dug out of the cliff, presumably by smashing other rocks against it. Many more seats were set up around the outer walls, made of logs and boulders. Dumakleiza saw a few scattered stains of deep red randomly strewn around the snow-covered arena. There was a low growl echoing throughout the shadows. Dumakleiza turned and saw four wōlves tied against support beams. The beasts stared at her, licking their lips and whining. She had a feeling that she knew what happened to the dead in the coliseum.

"Where are my friends?"

Ash Vizla pointed toward the rocky cliff face. Dumakleiza followed his finger and noticed a wooden door at the base. It looked to be made of thick branches tied together, propped against a small cave with more boulders pinning it in place. Dumakleiza understood what was going on. She exhaled and offered one of her knives to Ash Vizla.

"Many thanks." He took it and stepped back, staring at it, worshipping the priceless item. He looked back at her and motioned to the wooden door. "Go talk to friends. Do not free them or wōlves eat you."

Dumakleiza took a slow breath and nodded. She turned and walked away from Ash Vizla. She crossed the empty arena, reminding herself with every step that they hadn't invented bows and arrows yet. She felt like one was going to pierce through her at any moment. She looked up at the tall mountain looming overhead. It was the tallest mountain she'd ever seen, much taller than castle Yagūl, and it towered over the hills they'd sped through on Thamiosh.

"Grim, please let them be alive," she prayed under her breath as she reached the wooden door. She squatted down next to it and peered through the closely bound branches. It was difficult to see anything in the blackness of the cave. "Cooby? Sir Gideon? Diviner?"

"Duma!" Gideon's cheerful voice said before his face became visible. "What brings you to this lovely place?" As Gideon spoke, Cooby squalled from within the cave. With a few pitter-pattering footsteps, a small monkey paw stretched through an opening in the branches.

Dumakleiza grabbed onto it and leaned in against the freezing wood. "Cooby!" She closed her eyes and smiled, kissing Cooby's small fingers and rubbing them to keep him warm. "Are you okay, Coobs?" He let out more squalling and cooing at her touch. Dumakleiza felt a combination of relief and rage. As she held his paw, she peered inside. "Sir Gideon, are you all right? Is the Diviner with you?"

"Yeah, he's here."

"I'm here," Traveler said deadpan.

"He's grumpy," Gideon said under his breath. "How'd you enjoy *your* abduction? This was my third since meeting Spaceman."

Dumakleiza was able to make out their shapes with her dragon eye. "I do not understand this place. They are barbaric and strange."

Traveler sighed. "Since Timrekka isn't here to study the world and the people, I've been doing it in his stead. What I've been able to gather so far is that they're primitive enough to do everything by hand."

"Yes," Dumakleiza blurted out. "They believed my knives to be more wondrous than anything they'd bared witness to before. I traded one in order to have an audience with you."

"Great," Traveler scoffed. "They have a knife now." He coughed in the cold. "Anyway, they revere women and treat them like precious jewels. They keep them safe, practically worshipping them. However, they still keep them under the men's rule. They revere them so much that only the ruler, or eyrayor, is allowed the honor of removing all hair from his face in order to closer resemble a woman. It's a unique hierarchical dynamic, though I'm under the impression that they 'shave' by yanking out all their beards straight down to the roots—once again, by hand."

Dumakleiza nodded. "That answers a few of my questions."

"Yup!" Gideon chuckled. "However, that's what got us in trouble, apparently."

"What?"

"Well, Spaceman here has a face as smooth as a baby's butt, so Eyrayor Ash Vizla believes him to be a rival eyrayor from another tribe, or something like that. We apparently landed on their land, and that's not allowed by other eyrayors. I would have been overlooked since I have a beard, but since I'm with Traveler, I'm guilty by association and have to fight alongside him since I'm clearly under Eyrayor Traveler's command."

Traveler coughed again. "It's too bad Timrekka's not here."

"How do you mean?" Dumakleiza asked.

"Well, have you felt the difference in strength you possess here on Borroke?"

"Yes," Dumakleiza blurted out, hoping Traveler would explain. "I do not tire when I run, and I leap like a wild beast."

"Exactly," Traveler responded. "Borroke is a smaller world with weaker gravity. We are stronger, faster, denser, and genetically more powerful than the people of this world. So, imagine if Timrekka had survived. By my best guess, he'd be able to punch straight through these branches and barely feel the impact. He'd likely be able to jump almost as high as the walls of the arena."

Gideon's smile was barely visible in the darkness. "He'd be a superhero if he was here."

Dumakleiza nodded. "Even if he were here and freed you, the wōlves would eat him."

"Unlikely," Traveler said. "His skin would be very difficult to tear through. They could do it, sure, but it would take hours of relentless clawing and biting. He would have been able to kill all of them single-handedly."

"And he wasn't even a fighter," Gideon added. "Imagine if Hangman was here."

The concept astounded Dumakleiza, but she felt a little insulted. "I, too, could kill each Vulgair single-handedly. I will do so if you believe it the wisest course of action."

"No. No. No." Traveler shot her down. "The wolves *would* kill you."

"Then what do we do?"

"I don't know." Traveler's moroseness was only getting worse.

Gideon took over. "Duma, you just go stay safe and alive. They won't kill you. You're a woman, you're hot, and you're a warrior. You should be fine. I'll see if I can talk them into letting us go instead of making us fight. They seem like reasonable people."

Traveler blinked his eyes, dumbfounded. "I am determined to find the screw that's loose in your head and weld it in place."

"You think there's only one?" Gideon asked. "You're adorable."

Dim Rōk stepped up and grabbed Dumakleiza by the shoulder, pulling her backward. "Enough talk, Blade Maiden. You come, prepare with other women now."

Dumakleiza held Cooby's hand until Dim Rōk forcibly separated them. "I do not wish to leave my friends at this time." She stumbled backward until she regained her footing and faced Dim Rōk. "Leave me here." She swatted his hand away.

Dim Rōk was caught off guard by Dumakleiza's strength. "You bathe with Vulgair women. Be ready for night." With that, he grabbed her shoulder again and walked away, leading her out of the arena. Dumakleiza wanted to fight back, but she knew Traveler was right. She would be able to slaughter her fair share of Vulgairs, but the wolves would tear her apart before she could really accomplish anything. She bit her tongue and went along for her bath.

37

Traveler sat against a rocky wall with his head tilted back and eyes closed. His breathing grew shallower as failure consumed his mind. He wasn't trying to escape. He didn't care.

Gideon, on the other hand, sat with his forehead leaned against the wooden gate, peering out as best he could into the empty arena. Cooby was latched firmly onto his back, squeezing onto him for warmth. The freezing tanion cooed and shivered, making its little jaw tremble in Gideon's ear. Ghostly whispers crept through the branches, foretelling their doom. Gideon's mind wandered as he tried to predict what the night had in store. He turned and looked back into the cave's darkness.

"What do you think is gonna happen?"

Traveler took a loud breath, as if speaking required warming up first. "I don't know."

Gideon nodded, recognizing Traveler's depression. "I wish I had Duma's eye. It'd be nice to be able to see better in here."

Traveler sighed a couple times before saying anything. "On Whewliss, you could."

Gideon brought his head forward. "You have dragon eyes on Whewliss?"

"No," Traveler sighed. "We have implants."

"Right. Your optical implants. Tell me more."

"May as well." Traveler heavily sighed again. "I'm sure you've recognized on Earth how as technology advances, it comes in smaller, more compact sizes."

Gideon nodded until he realized that Traveler couldn't see him. "Yes." He smiled at himself.

"Well, Whewliss' technology has advanced and shrunk to the point of implanted enhancements." He tapped his ear in the blackness. "Just like the translator you have."

"And your optical implant. Got it."

"I have many implants. However, abiding by LOLA, the only implants we're able to activate on pre-lit worlds are our light cells, optical, and translators. We're only allowed to communicate with younger worlds and escape if need be. No harm can be done with more advanced technologies."

"Huh." Gideon thought about it. "I guess that makes sense." He shrugged. "So, Duma giving them a knife is technically against the law?"

Traveler nodded in the darkness. "Yes. If we survive, you can report me for allowing her to break LOLA, and I'll be reprimanded and punished."

Gideon grinned and shook his head. "Damn, I was just curious, drama queen. Your criminal activity is a secret I'll keep, Spaceman." He scratched Cooby's chin the way he'd seem Dumakleiza do it. "So, since you're so hopeless right now, why don't you break the law and activate your enhancements to get us out of here? Or do you have any that could do that?"

Traveler sighed. "Every other enhancement is confined to Whewliss' atmosphere. Lord Coyzle's command. Strict guidelines have been set in place by LOLA that only activate enhancements on Whewliss and lit planets."

"Lord? Is that what you call your leader, or have you guys discovered a tangible god somehow?"

Traveler chuckled condescendingly. "Ignorance isn't becoming on you, Gideon. You're smarter than that. We call our planet's leader a lord.

We were once divided like Earth, separated into different continents with different presidents, kings, emperors, and whatnot. They feuded amongst themselves and fought for small scraps of the world, but the Universal Liberation War united us as a planet, and now we have one anointed lord. He is supported and advised by a council made of different factions on Whewliss."

Gideon smiled in the darkness. "I have so many curiosities about your world. I want to learn about everything you've discovered, created, invented, explored. Tell me about this Universal Liberation War. I'm *really* interested in that history lesson. What could unite an entire planet? Was it an invasion?"

Traveler couldn't see Gideon's large, excited smile, but he knew it was there. "Yes. I'm not at liberty to divulge the entire history, though, as it could lead to knowledge of abilities certain worlds' peoples are not ready for. If we survive, there is an entire Hall on Whewliss dedicated to the ULW. I have a feeling our lord will want to take you on a tour."

"Come on, man," Gideon playfully groaned. "We're stuck playing the weirdest game of seven minutes in heaven ever. What else are we gonna do? Get to third base? I won't tell anyone you told me universal secrets." Gideon winked in the blackness again. "By the way, I winked. You probably didn't see it, but it was a very convincing wink. Trust me."

Traveler shook his head. "I've already broken enough LOLA getting us this far, and I shadowed Timrekka." He tensed, torturing himself. "I'm not breaking any more laws or endangering anyone else."

"What all laws did you break?"

Traveler waved the question away. "I was so close to assembling the first completed team—so close. I can't believe it's just fizzling apart."

Gideon nodded as Cooby licked his face. "I know Timrekka's death sucks, and I understand the guilt. Believe me, I do." He waited a second. "However, I also know it really wasn't your fault. It was an innocent mistake."

"Yeah?" Traveler's tone dismissed everything Gideon was trying to say. "You got some personal testimony and weird toy in your backpack to help me feel better?"

Gideon puffed out his bottom lip and nodded. "I can think of three or four off the top of my head that would serve that purpose well enough. However, rather than give you something, I'd want you to give me something."

Traveler turned toward Gideon in the dark. "You want something from me? Now? Really?" He sounded annoyed.

"Yes, sir."

Traveler was confused. "What?"

"Your reasons for why you're here."

Traveler scoffed, and Gideon could hear his head knock back against the wall. "Be more specific."

"Okay." Gideon cleared his throat, adjusting his seated position to better face Traveler. "You come from the most advanced planet there is, right?"

"Currently."

"Okay. I'm assuming that means you *chose* to go out into the universe to recruit people, yes?"

"I was selected. But, yes, I chose to accept the job when it was offered."

"How were you selected?"

"Uh." Traveler had an entire lifetime of answers bottlenecking in his throat as he considered where to begin. "That's a little harder to explain." He organized his thoughts as best he could. "One thing we're seeing is true of almost every world is a decline in social behavior as technology advances. I noticed Earth was getting close to it when I was there." He leaned forward, placing his elbows on crossed legs. "Basically, the more fascinating and high-tech the gadgets and advancements of a world become, the less involved with each other the people become in turn. They lose interest in what matters. They lose interest in what they can do with each other and find simple comfort in exploring what they can do alone. It happens to each world." He thought for a moment. "When Whewliss' technology sent us through our social decline, the worst of it lasted for nearly a century. Social activity minimized. We only interacted with each other when absolutely necessary. For the most part, everyone worked from their home. We rarely went outside. Even activities such as concerts, city events, parties, or even going to lunch with a friend became cumbersome and forgotten." He chuckled at the embarrassing history.

Gideon shook his head. "That doesn't even make sense."

Traveler gave a slight nod. "As a result, Whewliss became a highly intelligent planet with a worldwide population of shut-ins." He cleared his throat. "I wish the Vulgairs had left us some water." He coughed a couple more times, unable to get his throat to settle. "Anyway, the longer we locked ourselves away, the more fearful we became—of everything. We became scared of talking to each other, of the world around us, and certainly of everything we'd already started exploring beyond our world. It sounds silly and childish, I know, but we're seeing it true with the most advanced worlds we find. The more closed off and antisocial people become, and the more technologically advanced we evolve—the more fearful creatures we regress into."

Gideon nodded. "Makes sense. On Earth, our social networking is slowly shutting us off from each other. I can see it getting worse all the time. Supposed to connect us, but it's really disconnecting us. That's why I really never carried a phone for the most part."

"Exactly. Anyway, things stayed like that for long enough that it just became the way of the world. It was normal. Children born into it—it's all they knew. I was part of such a generation, knowing nothing but technology. I was raised as an only child in an antisocial household, by eremitic parents, in a society where no one spoke to each other unless it was through technology."

"That's crazy." Gideon thought about it. "So, you didn't even have any friends growing up?"

"No, I did. But, once again, we really only spoke through our devices. We'd only see each other in person if we had to, and in those cases, we'd avoid contact. We rarely left our homes. It's all I knew. It's all any of us knew. It was normal." Traveler shrugged. "It wasn't until the Universal Liberation War that everything changed, but that's a story I can't tell you the details of."

Gideon raised his hands and slapped them back down. "Dude, you're killin' me over here."

Traveler held an unseen finger up. "But, after the war was over and we were saved, we realized that that safety wasn't guaranteed. We realized that, as a planet, we needed to be aware of others that existed beyond Whewliss so we could better prepare for the future. Thus, the journey to find, observe, and study every inhabited planet began, no matter their developmental level."

"Okay." Gideon's tone smiled in the darkness. "That's really cool. Keep going."

Traveler readjusted himself as his legs started cramping. "Whewliss' lord, council, and military designed a highly extensive and intricate training program for light travel. The program was called Lighted Leap Learning, or 3L for short."

Gideon thought for a moment. "I'm assuming that was a difficult adjustment for Whewlisslings, Whewtians—Whewlissese? Whatever you call your people, being as you'd all become such antisocial creatures."

"Whewlights, and good job. You're reading ahead." Traveler nodded. "Out of a worldwide population of three and a half billion human beings, only nine-hundred and seventy-four people volunteered for the program. Less than a fraction of a percent of our entire world was interested in exploring the universe. The rest of us were too scared to even step out of our homes. Only nine-hundred and seventy-four."

Gideon nodded. "You were one of them."

"Yes. I don't know why I volunteered. The idea terrified me just as it did everyone else. I guess I just felt I had something to prove. I don't know to whom. Maybe just to myself. I didn't want to be lost to the embarrassing part of Whewliss' history." Traveler coughed. "So, one day I just decided to go on my own all the way to the council and volunteer in person. At that point, that was the scariest thing I'd ever done, and I knew that what was to come would be even worse." He smiled fondly at the memory. "The next day, I began my 3L training."

"Wow." Gideon nodded with an impressed smile. "And that was the twenty-eight years' worth of schooling you went through you were telling me about."

"Close." Traveler finally cracked a grin that immediately went away. "It was only twenty of them."

"Oh?"

"I was an observer. That was my title. As observers, our instruction was to blend in with every world and to remain incognito throughout each observational trip. Even if we got stuck somewhere, it was illegal to divulge information about our world, our people, or the fact that there *are* other worlds and other peoples. We were under strict instruction to learn but not interfere, ask questions but not get involved. We were to stay in the shadows, document, and report back to Whewliss. That's it."

"Okay, I mean, that all makes sense." Gideon thought about it. "I like that your people are avid learners but aren't interested in colonizing other worlds or trying to invade and rule them."

"Yeah." Traveler slowly nodded as he stared through the darkness with wide eyes. "We've seen what that can do…"

Gideon motioned for Traveler to continue as he played with one of Cooby's ears. Nothing happened. He smiled at himself, realizing again that Traveler couldn't see anything he was doing.

"Go on."

Traveler shook his head for a moment. "Where was I?"

"You were told to just observe and report."

"Right. Well, that went on for eleven of my people's years. Whewliss developed and built an entire city dedicated to 3L missions. All our brightest minds and best resources went into it. There was practically no protest since, planet wide, Whewlights wanted to feel safe in the universe again. Within the city of EBOO, an acronym for 'Everything Beyond Our Own', we have our forecasting center that processes every iota of data collected by our satellites aimed in every direction away from Whewliss. Additionally, it also processes the exponentially higher amount of data reported back from each of us observing."

"So cool." Gideon smiled. "So, if we survive, do we get to go to EBOO?"

"Oh, it is where we are going if we survive."

"Badass." Gideon patted Cooby's head as the cold and tired tanion started drifting off to sleep against his warm back. "So, what happened after those first eleven years?"

"Well." Traveler tilted his head as he chose his wording carefully. "We made a discovery." It wasn't hard to tell where his words were trailing off to.

"Ohh!" Gideon bounced on his butt, shaking Cooby back awake. Cooby was not pleased, but Gideon couldn't help himself. "The fourth phase!"

Traveler nodded. "Yes, the fourth phase."

"Do I get an Easter egg peak at what the fourth phase is? Just you and me. In a cave. Telling stories. Bonding. It's the perfect bro date." Gideon scooted closer to Traveler as he begged.

Traveler cracked a full smile and continued. "So, after the discovery of the fourth phase, our lord realized something had to be done."

Gideon slumped backward, pouting at the cave's ceiling. "You *suck*."

"The fourth phase was a complete mystery. In order to understand it, we had to explore it." Traveler paused. "Out of all three and a half billion people, its discovery was only shared with the workers at EBOO. It was deemed too delicate in its mystery to be shared with the public, and therefore was classified above top secret. That being said, its exploration was offered to us observers, as we were the most adventurous and brave of all Whewlights. Not a single volunteer stepped forward. Not a single one. Everyone, including myself, was, and still is, not only scared, but terrified of the fourth phase. So, in the end, the fourth phase is still, to this day, untouched by mankind."

"Damn. I can't tell you how much I want to know what it is."

Traveler shrugged. "I know. So do I. Hopefully we will find out."

Gideon rolled his eyes. "So, basically, no one is willing to take a boat to the horizon and see what lies beyond. No one is brave enough to leave the guaranteed comfort of the shore for the unknown."

"Exactly." Traveler got his story back on track. "Our council suggested to our lord that they select the best observers and train them further. Train them for, uh, something else."

Gideon started laughing under his breath., "Your scaredy-cat people trained recruiters to find people like me from planets that weren't born into fear, to be your guinea pigs that you can send into fourth phase for you."

Traveler nodded. "Basically."

"You guys are ridiculous." Gideon tilted back, leaning on his hands. "A lot to think about." He looked in Traveler's direction. "So, how many of you got recruited to recruit?"

"The job was offered to all observers. Twelve of us accepted."

Gideon chuckled. "The twelve disciples sent out as fishers of men."

Traveler scoffed a smile. "A slight perversion of the intended meaning, I believe."

Gideon grinned and nodded. "You guys really are scared of talking to people, aren't you?"

Traveler nodded. "That's an understatement." He cleared his throat as he yearned for water. "Eight Whewlight years of social education later, nine of us passed our testing and were sent out."

Gideon held his hand up. "What did you learn about?"

Traveler sighed. "I know, it's pathetic, but it was necessary. We were taught how to interact with other people by our own people, who were as equally bad at social interaction as we were. Most of our lessons came from our history—how we were before the social decline. It's rather embarrassing, knowing how we used to be."

"I can imagine."

"If you would have met me in my youth, before going through all of 3L, before the ULW, you wouldn't have recognized me. I was scared of everything, everyone. I'm still striving for improvement every day."

"Wait." Gideon scooted closer again. "So, on that Neanderthal planet you took me to for the Roaring Valley, I remember you saying that you were being tested, too. That's why you jumped with me."

Traveler nodded. "Yes."

"Was that a required part of your training or were you testing yourself?"

"I—" Traveler's voice sounded more vulnerable than he wanted to let on. "I just, uh, I would like to be the first person from Whewliss to brave the fourth phase. Yes, I want to provide a recruited team, but—— yeah." He dipped his head, embarrassed.

Gideon slowly nodded as a giant smile grew from ear to ear. "Well, now." He scooted closer. "*Now* things are getting spicy. I thought you weren't coming with us?"

"I'm not," Traveler snapped back. "Not unless I can overcome my fear of it. Our mission is to recruit a team so that the lord and council can brief that team on their mission and then send them into the fourth phase. That's it. My job will be completed when I deliver you to them. That's all any of us recruiters are striving for." He cleared his throat. "But I want to prove that we can be brave, too."

Gideon nodded with a genuinely admiring smile. "I'm impressed, Spaceman."

"That's secretly part of why I recruited you," Traveler admitted. "I'm hoping some of your fearlessness will rub off on me over time."

Gideon tilted his head. "Eh, I'm not so sure how much you wanna be like me, but I'll happily help you step out of your comfort zone."

"Oh, that I've learned more times than I would have liked to already." They both laughed a little. Traveler sighed. "I hate you."

"Ha! Why?"

"Because you were right."

"Oh? About what?"

"Reminding me why I'm doing this." Traveler took a deep breath, allowing his chest to fill. "Losing Timrekka made me feel like a failure. It has been rotting within me, but you reminded me why I'm doing this. Every adventure has setbacks, not that I want to dismiss his death as simply as that, but it's something I must overcome. Thank you. I'm impressed, Gideon."

"Always happy to be of service."

Traveler raised a finger. "Okay, I opened up a bit to you. You may as well tell me about the shoulder while we're in here."

The comment made Gideon lock up. He wanted to avoid that conversation as long as he could. He thought for a moment, considering how to escape, to change the topic. The cave was silent. Then, as he took a breath to talk, a yellow glow broke through the branch gate.

Gideon sighed. "Saved by the bell." They both crawled forward and peered through the cracks to see what was happening. It was difficult to make out, but after some adjusting, they saw Vulgairs carrying torches into the arena. Both of their hearts started racing. Gideon glanced in Traveler's direction. "Any ideas on how to get out of this one? Any knowledge on their people?"

Traveler shook his head. "We don't know much about them." His pulse leapt from zero to one hundred. "Can you think of anything in your bag that would magically help us?"

Gideon racked his brain. "I'll work on that."

"Please do. I really want to get you to Whewliss. I think we have a chance at being the first to explore the fourth phase. I really do."

Gideon smiled at him. "Me, too. We're going to find a way to survive this, we're going to find a new scientist, and we're going to be the first.

And you know what?" He placed a hand on Traveler's shoulder. "You're going with us."

38

The Vulgairs grunted and groaned as they struggled to roll the
heavy stones aside. Yellow light from their torches shone brightly
through the cracks. They hoisted the door away and tossed it. Light
flooded the cave, exposing Gideon, Traveler, and Cooby. The three cap-
tives covered their eyes as they adjusted.

"You come out now," a Vulgair insisted.

Another ushered them forward with demanding gestures. "Come,
bad Eyrayor."

Traveler and Gideon looked at each other and took a deep breath as
they got up. Cooby stayed latched onto Gideon's back, hissing at the
burly strangers. The cold made it difficult to stretch their soreness away.

Gideon shrugged. "Let's go play." He smiled at the towering Vulgairs
glaring down at him. "Lead the way, gentlemen." One stared at him
through bushy eyebrows and adamantly pointed into the arena. Gideon
nodded. "Concise directions, sir." He walked forward with pep in his
step. Traveler took a moment to reminisce further into his reasons for
continuing, and then followed.

Once again, the evening was upon them and the fading sun was hidden by cloud cover. Gideon and Traveler looked around the packed
arena. Every man, woman, and child of Vulgairia was in attendance,

watching them enter with hungry eyes. Torches burned around the perimeter, creating the ambiance of an ill-omened séance or sacrifice. The Vulgairs were discussing their keenness for broken bones and disembowelment, but with much smaller words.

Gideon turned to Traveler as they stopped in the center. "I don't suppose your education involved futuristic combat or self-defense?"

Traveler shook his head and looked around. "I took some self-defense classes. They were a mandatory portion of my post 3L training."

"Oh, good. That will be helpful."

"I failed them all."

"What?" Gideon couldn't help smiling and then laughing at him.

"The general in charge of our training let it slide because we didn't have enough volunteers not to. He had to make the best of who he was given." Traveler shrugged. "I'm not a fighter. Not going to pretend to be. However, tonight I don't have a choice." He looked at Gideon with a fading sliver of hope. "How about you? Any training?"

"Pretty much the same story," Gideon said. "Tried and true, but none of it stuck. I'm more of a hugger."

Traveler racked his mind. "The only advantage we have going for us then is our physicality. Our cells are stronger and denser. We can take a hit better here, and we can deliver one better, as well. So, hopefully that will be enough."

Gideon looked around at the bearded monsters of human beings. "Yeah, hopefully. That, and the fact that we're, like, way, super-duper smarter than them. So, let's just put our bigger brains to work."

Traveler rolled his eyes. "I'll get right on that." He looked around at their lack of weapons. "Let's just attack them with our brains."

"That's the spirit," Gideon said with a confident punch to the arm.

Some commotion directed their attention up. There was a balcony above the arena's entrance, clearly designed for the Eyrayor, as it had better seating and a ceiling made of animal pelts. The enclosed balcony's back curtain parted as six women walked through. They looked cleaner and certainly better groomed, which just meant that they *were* groomed. While all the other women had matted hair hanging aimlessly around their faces, the six had their hair brushed back behind their shoulders. Their animal skins had been beaten clean to give off a better sheen in the fire's light.

Traveler smiled. "Look." He pointed. "On the left."

Gideon followed his gaze and then gave an amused smile. "My, my, my, her eyebrows look more furrowed than the barbarians' foreheads."

They both gawked at Dumakleiza, the sixth woman sitting on the end, visibly irritable. Her braids had been undone so she could be presented in the same fashion as the others. The other five women were vain in their display, basking in the crowd's adoration, excited for what was to come. Dumakleiza was the only one who visibly loathed the attention.

Traveler leaned close to Gideon. "We're the ones who are going to fight for our lives, but she looks unhappier."

Gideon nodded. "Poor Yagūlamite princess being treated like a Vulgair princess. Princess life be hard, yo."

Dumakleiza looked down from the balcony. Her eyes immediately locked onto Cooby, refusing to give up his death grip around Gideon's back. She wanted to make sure he was okay, but she was worried about what would happen if she called to him. The Vulgairs might kill him just for sport if he crawled through their legs. She knew she wouldn't survive witnessing his death. She kept her mouth shut and waited.

The curtain parted again as Eyrayor Ash Vizla entered. He stopped and looked around at his women, admiring how well they'd been bathed and groomed. Their presentation pleased him, and he was proud to return the favor. He stroked his own smooth face with the back of his hand, boasting that it matched theirs. Gideon and Traveler smirked as all the Vulgairs gasped at his feminine beauty. He stepped forward and leaned over the balcony. He held his arms out and closed his eyes, humming a flat note. As he did, his five women joined in, matching his pitch and humming a low tone. It didn't take long for everyone in the arena to do the same. Deep, vibrational hums susurrated throughout the coliseum, slowly growing louder.

Traveler's pulse quickened. "That's eerie."

Gideon smiled as he listened to the buzzing. "That's so cool. They sound like monks."

Eyrayor Ash Vizla raised his hands higher and yelled, "Vulgairs!" The crowd's humming immediately stopped, replaced with crude yelling. Gideon and Traveler watched as many of them leapt up and down out of their seats, shaking fists and screaming. Cooby bared his fangs and growled as he tucked his head into Gideon's neck. Eyrayor Ash Vizla waved his hands up and down, encouraging his people to yell louder. He bathed in their cries, closing his eyes again. He waited and then opened his palms. "Vulgairs!" He waved for them to quiet down. The barbarians barked out a few more threats and then obeyed.

Gideon puffed out his bottom lip. "Well, at least *these* cavemen aren't trying to rape me."

Traveler scoffed hopelessly. "No, this is much better."

Eyrayor Ash Vizla cleared his throat as the arena finally became quiet. "Vulgairs! Look down at bad Eyrayor."

The crowd exploded with promises of dismemberment and death.

Gideon looked at him. "You're so popular."

Eyrayor Ash Vizla ushered for enough quiet to hear his words. "He try take Vulgairia!"

More yelling and booing ensued.

Traveler stepped forward and raised his hands, "That is not why we are here! I apologize for trespassing! We will leave!" His argument was swallowed up by the rioting onslaught.

Gideon turned and shushed him. "Dude, you're interrupting the Eyrayor while he's talking. Rude much?" He slugged Traveler in the shoulder. "Just kidding. But, there's slim pickin's on defense lawyers here."

"You're not helping," Traveler said.

Gideon shrugged again. "They can't hear us. We can say anything we want." He cupped his hands around his mouth. "Eyrayor Ash Vizla is the prettiest woman I see!"

The crowd went quiet just in time for Gideon's outburst to be heard. Everyone stopped and stared at him. Ash Vizla waited with a puzzled expression and then smiled.

Traveler blinked a few times. "What did you just do?"

"Uh, helped?"

Ash Vizla pointed at Gideon. "This man says he like my great woman face. I spare him!"

Traveler slowly shook his head. "Are. You. Kidding. Me?"

There was silence as the Vulgairs mulled the idea over. They looked at each other and murmured amongst themselves. A few of them nodded and then cheered. Ash Vizla smiled, looking to the women on either side of him.

"Women choose."

The five women deliberated, staring down their noses at Gideon. His compliment to their Eyrayor's face made them legally have to consider sparing his life. One of them nodded.

"I like him."

Her comment incited a response from a second woman. "He is small, but I like him also."

Dumakleiza nodded fervently. "Yes! Yes, of course, spare Sir Gideon!" Her energy helped urge the other three to agree. Dumakleiza's voice instantly caught Cooby's attention. He looked up at her and went to leap from Gideon's back, but Gideon caught him mid-jump and held him close.

"Whoa, buddy. Stay here." He scratched Cooby's back. "They wanna stomp your grapes into wine."

Ash Vizla smiled bigger. "I let him go." He motioned for Gideon to come up and join him in the balcony. "You are now Vulgair. Come!"

Gideon chuckled. "Well, that was easy." He glanced at Traveler and then looked up at Ash Vizla. "Spare my friend and we will both become

Vulgair. We came to honor you, Ash Vizla. My friend wants you to be *his* Eyrayor!"

Traveler nodded, deciding to go with it. "Yes, it's true. The beauty of your womanly face is far greater than that of my own."

The arena fell silent. They all looked at each other, unsure of what was happening. Even Ash Vizla didn't know what to make of it. Bathing in the compliments was an unexpected pleasure, especially from rival Eyrayor. After a couple strokes of his smooth face, he turned and looked at the six women.

"You choose."

"Spare them," Dumakleiza immediately blurted out as she nodded. "I like them. I trust them."

Another woman jeered and shook her head. "Yes, she trust them. She same as them. I no trust."

The other four shook their heads.

"Bad Eyrayor trick you. Make you like him. Kill you in sleep."

Another agreed, "Yes. They trick us."

One of the women spat over the balcony. "They must die."

The counsel struck Ash Vizla between the eyes. He stood taller and glared down. "I almost believe you like my face. Your tricks not work. Tonight you die!" His decision brought back the eruption of booing and cries for blood.

Dumakleiza raised her hands. "Why? What's wrong with you?" Then, suddenly, an idea struck her. "Oh!" She reached under her animal cloak and fished around. She found what she was looking for and pulled out a handful of gold from her treasure sack. "Ash Vizla, Eyrayor of the Vulgairs, I humbly offer you my treasure of Yagūl for the lives of these two men."

Ash Vizla glanced at the gold and simpered, studying the foreign objects. "What I do with shiny rocks?"

Dumakleiza brought her head back, confused by his lack of interest. "It—it's gold. Holy treasure. It will make you rich."

Ash Vizla squinted. "What is 'rich'?" As Dumakleiza's jaw hung open, Ash Vizla turned back to face Gideon and Traveler. "Who want kill them for our women of great face?"

The uproar grew louder as many men leapt to their feet. Gideon and Traveler scooted together and watched as more and more stood up. Each of the volunteers eagerly looked to the balcony to see if they'd be selected. The weaponless warriors all had clenched fists, ready to bludgeon, snap, and pummel.

Different parts of the crowd cheered for different men, rooting for certain volunteers to be selected. The five honored women stepped forward and leaned over the balcony, each pointing at their nominated executioner. More cheering broke out as five lucky men yelled with raised fists. They were honored to kill for the great smooth faces. Amidst more excitable screams, they made their way down to the snow-covered arena, huffing and puffing in showering cheers.

Ash Vizla noticed Dumakleiza not participating. "You must choose man." He pointed out into the crowd.

Dumakleiza shook her head. "I will not add to the condemnation of my friends." She was tempted to slit his throat but wasn't sure if the outcome would be any better.

Ash Vizla pointed more adamantly. "You choose one man or other women each choose two."

Dumakleiza flexed her jaw shut. She glared at Ash Vizla and begrudgingly looked over the men vying for her attention. She swallowed her distaste and looked for the smallest, weakest looking Vulgair that she thought even Gideon might stand a chance against. It was difficult, as almost all of them were giants. Finally, she saw one man whose right arm had obviously been bitten off by something. She smiled and pointed at him. The man rejoiced, leaping up and down before making his way to join the others.

Gideon and Traveler sized up the six men as they stepped onto the snow. They surrounded their victims with hungry eyes, walking to the sounds of the chanting crowd. Cooby recognized the imminent danger and switched to the offensive. He readjusted, wrapping himself around Gideon's back the same way he did with Dumakleiza. The vicious tanion growled, wishing he was in the air, cutting them down from above.

Gideon stared at the large men as they walked toward them. "So." He looked at Traveler. "Do you want the big one, the bigger one, the hairy one, or one of the other three big, hairy ones?" Traveler didn't respond. He was trying to be brave, but fear had a death grip on his spine. Gideon nodded. "Got it. I'll just get'm all." He took a step forward and held his hands up in surrender. "Last chance. We don't want to fight." His words did nothing to stop the bloodthirsty cries. Gideon shrugged and glanced back. "Well, Spaceman, here's to hoping you're right about us being stronger." He widened his eyes and gave a loud karate howl as he struck an inexperienced martial art pose. "Let's dance!" He roared and pushed off his heels, running as hard as he could at the man directly in front of him. The cheering became deafening as the action began. Gideon wound back, ready to swing, but the man lurched forward and punched Gideon square in the chest. *Oomph!*

"Sir Gideon!" Dumakleiza cried out as Gideon and Cooby flew backward and tumbled across the snow. They slid to a stop by Traveler's feet. Gideon groaned, bringing his hands to his chest as Cooby yelped and let go of him.

"Well," Gideon coughed. "If that was supposed to hurt less on this planet, then I'd hate to feel it —" He coughed again. "—somewhere else." He reached up and brushed some bloody snow from his face.

Cooby squalled and got to his feet, stumbling as he tried to gain his bearings. Traveler reached down and took Gideon's hand, yanking him up. They both looked at the Vulgairs almost upon them as Gideon tried to catch his breath.

Dumakleiza withdrew her knives as she watched with burning eyes. She'd had enough waiting for a peaceful solution on the sidelines. It was time to kill as many of the Vulgairs as she could. If she was going to die, it was going to be fighting with her tanion on her back. She jumped to her feet to leap down, but she paused.

A loud, smashing sound caught her attention. It came from outside the arena, in another part of Vulgairia. It was loud enough to stop everything in an instant. All the screaming Vulgairs went silent as they turned to see. Even the six executioners stopped.

Another loud crash made some of them jump. It sounded like one of their huts was being smashed by something too large to be human—perhaps a mammoth. Everyone waited tensely, frozen in dread of whatever monster was demolishing their huts.

After some brash rustling in what sounded like a pile of broken wood, a loud grunt echoed out from beyond the arena's walls—a man's grunt. Even Gideon and Traveler looked at each other with a loss for words. The jarring cry turned into what sounded like an excited scream soaring through the air above them. Everyone looked up into the night sky as their hearts jumped into their throats. Something was coming, and whatever it was sounded like a creature of nightmarish size. It grew louder and closer, descending down on them from the darkness above. Everyone in the arena scrambled away, trying to back up from wherever it was going to land.

The yellow light from the arena's torches gave minimal warning as the mysterious beast came rocketing in from the sky. Everyone screamed and jumped back as it hurtled down into the coliseum. *Crash!* A giant pile of snow exploded into the air, shrouding whatever had landed in a white cloud. The torches all but went out from the sudden wind. Everyone stared with peeled eyes to see what sort of monster could fly with such devastation. Even Gideon, with his endless lust for adventure, backed away cautiously.

Finally, the snow settled, and everyone stared with terrified gawking. Crouching in the center of a small snow crater, stood a thick, grizzly looking man. He was short in stature, with long white hair standing on end like porcupine quills. Nobody moved. The mysterious man stood up and looked around through thick goggles.

"Oh good, there you are! I didn't know if I was going to find you."

Traveler's jaw dropped. His legs all but gave out.

Gideon's eyes shot open with an enormous smile. "Holy Spirit! Timrekka!"

Traveler couldn't believe what he was seeing. "H-h-how did y-you… you're alive?"

39

The Vulgairs were stunned in place, staring, not sure what to do. Timrekka was much smaller than they thought he was going to be after the destruction they'd heard him wreaking. He was even smaller than the two men they were eager to kill, but they couldn't deny the terror he'd instilled within them. The snow crater he stood in was at least a foot deep into the ground. They instinctively wanted to charge and attack him but none of them moved. None of them wanted to be the first to see what else he was capable of. Everyone and everything stood still.

The only person who accepted the explanation as simple was Dumakleiza. "Thank you, Grim," she prayed quietly.

Traveler was more frozen in disbelief than he was the cold. "How did you—" He couldn't guess a single explanation. His mind came up completely blank. Timrekka's survival was impossible. "You're dead."

Timrekka looked at him with a big smile. "Look." He reached up and touched his hair, standing on end. "Look what Borroke's gravity does to my hair! Ha!" It was sticking straight out with wire-like rigidity.

Gideon chuckled. "You're a fully mad scientist now. But, more importantly, this world has turned you into a freakin' superhero!"

The Vulgairs stared in petrified silence.

"I know!" Timrekka smiled bigger. "I've been breaking everything I've touched, not on purpose, of course, but I bent a tree in half." He giggled in amusement. "I'll have to learn to control my strength, but the fascinating thing is I can jump *really* far! I was never much of an athlete on Thamiosh, but here, I—"

"Timrekka!" Traveler waved his hands, stealing his attention. "How'd you survive being shadowed?"

"Oh." Timrekka focused. "That." He cleared his throat and adjusted his goggles as he pulled an empty syringe out from under his animal skin coat. "I call this 'reanimate'; it's my attempt at recreating what Gideon was talking about with his planet's Mr. Frankenstein, you know, the doctor. I took a small portion of the light shot you gave me and broke down its chemical makeup." He coughed a little and brushed some snow off himself. "I spliced some DNA I had from a jellyfish we have on Thamiosh that has been observed to be immortal, because whenever it's in danger or about to die, it reverts its cells back to infancy, and, in one form or another, can live seemingly forever, it's the only creature we know of that doesn't have to die." He adjusted his goggles again. "I spliced its DNA with the base components of the light shot, since you claimed that light heals for the purpose of purity, so I figured there had to be a way to capitalize on both and merge them to create a cure for death, or at least reanimate dead tissue, and I then added a chemical defibrillator that we use on Thamiosh, intended to resuscitate heart attack victims by intravenously injecting an electrical current that jolts the heart." Timrekka thought for a moment as everyone else stared at him. "I worked on that whenever I wasn't helping you with the Winkloh Star, put it all into this syringe, and was planning on saving it in case we found ourselves in any mortal danger." He looked around. "Not that this seems all that far off."

Traveler slowly shook his head. "But, how did you survive being shadowed in space?"

Timrekka cleared his throat again. "Well, everything went white, and then out of nowhere, I woke up floating in darkness on a giant rock, and

I couldn't breathe, although I got the faintest scent of burnt meat or brimstone, but I immediately lost feeling in all of my extremities, so I acted fast while my tongue bubbled—it felt like it was boiling—so I grabbed my reanimate and injected myself, because I wasn't really sure what other options I had, and I was panicking. I've never not been able to breathe before; it's awful, because apparently there's no oxygen in space, but you probably already knew that." He shook his head at the memory. "The strange thing is, rather than my intended use for reanimate, I'm theorizing that what happened when I injected myself was the chemical defibrillator electrically triggered the active components of the light shot, which activated *my* cells, and, if I'm guessing correctly, since I was still in the wake of your light jump, I was immediately dragged along the same course, like slipping into a river, and everything went white, and then, the next thing I knew, I was lying face down in the middle of a snowy clearing, surrounded by trees; I think I was next to where you four made camp." He took a deep breath. "Some sort of igloo, I believe. I recognized the footprints and, of course, Cooby's were a giveaway, so I followed them. There wasn't much snow back on Thamiosh, so this has all been colder than I'm accustomed to, however, my density insolates me against it."

Traveler couldn't close his mouth. "Bu—but that's impossible."

Gideon nodded in simple acceptance. "That's the most gangster thing I've ever heard." He stepped forward and socked Timrekka in the arm, immediately retracting his fist as it throbbed. "You survived being lost in space." He clapped in profound admiration. "But, if you were only on the meteor for less than a minute, then why didn't we see you before the Vulgairs took us? We were there all night."

Timrekka shrugged. "Again, only guessing here, but for starters, I don't have much knowledge on the light shot aside from what I studied under my microscope, so I could have just not used it correctly after breaking it down, thusly slowing my jump, or it could be as simple as having minimal light elasticity since I was just being dragged by the very end of your jump, but like I said, those are just my hypotheses, and I'm meddling with science I don't fully understand yet, but I'll figure it out."

Traveler blinked over and over, trying to process it. "You survived being shadowed." Just saying it out loud felt like make-believe.

Gideon smiled at him. "Guess that answers a bunch of what-if questions for ya, doesn't it, Spaceman?"

"I suppose I did survive being shadowed," Timrekka said as he finally relaxed enough to let the realization sink in. "That's pretty exciting, and I'm really quite happy about this new look." He reached up and touched his hair again. "I've never reinvented myself before." He smiled. "Anyways, I'm relieved I found you guys, but what is going on here? Everything looks bad."

Gideon followed his gaze, looking at the bewildered bruits. "Oh, they were just about to execute us because they think we're a rival clan. Just a typical day in barbarian wonderland."

Timrekka lowered his brow. "We just left a fight with Supreme, and when I finally find you, you're already involved with another one?" He looked at the blind bloodlust in the Vulgairs' eyes. "Does this happen everywhere you go?"

Gideon smiled and then looked up at Ash Vizla. "Eyrayor! You see what strength we have!" He patted Timrekka on the back. "We want no more hostility. Tell your men to back down. Let us leave, and no one will get hurt. We will go peacefully, and you guys can go back to inventing the wheel."

Ash Vizla thought for a moment, still trying to process the man half his size leaping down from the sky. Would the intruder be easy to kill, or was he sent from the great sky above? The ruffled Eyrayor turned and looked at the equally baffled women. They were huddled together. Only Dumakleiza was leaning over the balcony, smiling down at Timrekka's arrival.

As Ash Vizla waited for their council, one frightened woman managed to take her eyes off Timrekka and look up at him. "He evil ghost from dark trees around Vulgairia." She trembled "He called by bad Eyrayor. Kill evil magic, or it kill us." Her fearful words made perfect sense to Ash Vizla. He nodded as the woman loudly reaffirmed her desperation. "Kill them. Kill them now."

Dumakleiza shook her head. "It is not of magic that Timrekka arrives. It is of science." She took pride in knowing the truth to a fear she once shared. "Do not fear him. Rather, try to learn from him. I understand the fear of the unknown science they possess." She was beginning to relish the idea of helping the less advanced.

Another woman pointed out a calamitous fact that everyone else seemed to be overlooking. "Demon from sky also have smooth face of great woman. *Two* Eyrayor invade Vulgairia!"

Ash Vizla looked down through fearful eyes. "Vulgairs!" His previously confident yell stammered. "All men who kill false Eyrayors get, uh, smooth face of woman, and, uh, two women in their bed this night!"

The offer was unprecedented, and it made the entire arena buzz with consideration. Never had any Vulgair even had the nerve to request such a thing, lest their head be bashed in by rocks. The unheard-of honor was so great that it brought attention away from Timrekka for a moment. They hesitantly looked up at their Eyrayor, making sure they'd understood correctly. Expecting a woman's face when it wasn't truly offered would be a death sentence.

Ash Vizla urgently nodded. "You hear my words. Who go in arena and kill them get smooth face of great woman!"

They didn't need to be told a third time. Motivated energy brought new life to their bodies as every Vulgair man stood. Their lust for power, blood, and a womanly face made them overlook Timrekka's entrance.

"Now!" Ash Vizla demanded with furious terror. All the men yelled and climbed down toward the arena. Dozens spilled onto the ground like a hungry stampede.

Timrekka stepped backward. "W—w—wait." He looked over at Traveler and Gideon. "They're going to kill us for a womanly face?"

Traveler nodded. "I'll explain later." He grabbed Gideon and pulled him and Cooby behind Timrekka.

Timrekka's eyes opened wider as no one stood between him and the onslaught of Vulgairs. "Where are you going?" He waved his sweaty hands in front of himself, trying to ward off the violent barbarians. "I can't protect you, I'm not a warrior, I'm not a fighter."

"Today you are!" Traveler shouted. "You are the only one who can stand against *all* of them."

Traveler and Gideon couldn't do anything to keep Timrekka forward as he backed away, forcing them toward the cave. More and more Vulgairs swarmed the arena, closing in, their confidence rising in larger numbers. Timrekka only stopped and looked up at them when they reached the rock of the cliff face. He squealed at the surprising impact. The Vulgairs encircled their victims, only about ten feet away. Timrekka gulped. He couldn't speak. He couldn't move.

One exceptionally large Vulgair at the front of the group, laughed. "I no afraid of tiny man." He ran forward and swung his enormous fist. Timrekka closed his eyes and winced, defensively raising his hands. *Whack!* The man's punch landed directly against the side of Timrekka's face, barely budging him.

Timrekka scowled. "Ow!" Then his eyes shot open as he realized it hadn't actually hurt. He watched as the Vulgair man retracted his fist and screamed in pain.

"Fight back!" Traveler yelled.

Timrekka had never thrown a punch, and he wasn't sure how. He panicked and spun with closed eyes, flinging what seemed to him like a dainty backhand into the man's stomach. *Thwack!* The man flew back, smashing through the men behind him like paper bowling pins. A pile of them collided into the opposite wall of the arena. The surrounding Vulgairs screamed.

Timrekka narrowly opened one eye and peeked. He looked down at his hand. He'd barely felt the impact, but when he looked back up, there was a hole through the army of men, where at least ten lay injured.

"Huh." He smiled. "That didn't even hurt."

He didn't have time to revel as the violence only inspired more Vulgairs to attack. A handful of them roared and charged. Their combined war cries made Timrekka whimper and cower. He spun to aimlessly backhand again, but with a smidgen more confidence. He closed his fist right before it shattered one of the charging men's thighs. *Whack! Whack! Whack! Whack!* It tore through them, smashing a hip, ribcage, and head. The men flew back like a tidal wave of broken bones, soaring over the others before smacking against the back wall.

"Grim imbues you with his righteous fury, Timrekka of Thamiosh!" Dumakleiza jumped, shaking her fists as she cheered. Ash Vizla stared down, helplessly gripping the balcony. He didn't know how to process what he was seeing. He trembled in terror as Dumakleiza continued. "You are a mighty warrior!" Her cries caught Cooby's attention. He hadn't stopped shuddering behind Gideon since they'd been knocked to the ground. His nose perked up. All the commotion was more than he could handle. He whimpered and leapt off Gideon, disappearing through the crowd of Vulgairs, determined to find Duma. All the men were too focused on Timrekka to even notice Cooby running between their forest of legs.

Timrekka looked up to see that he'd barely put a dent in how many Vulgairs were still coming at him. The reward of a woman's face was apparently worth the risk of death. Timrekka didn't know what else to do, so he reached under his coat and pulled out one of the orbs of Trollop's petals. Without aiming, he heaved it at the closest Vulgairs.

Gideon's eyes peeled as it flew through the air. "Oh shit."

Poof! The orb exploded into a blue cloud against a Vulgair's chest and shrouded three others. They coughed, waving the blue dust away from their faces as they inhaled it. Traveler, Gideon, and Timrekka watched with dreadful anticipation. The men's eyes suddenly shot open in internal agony. They screamed and keeled over, coughing, gagging, and seizing. One by one, they collapsed to the ground, seemingly melting into formless piles of skin-covered muscle. The men around them backed away.

They stared in shock at the gurgling, crumpling piles of flesh wobbling beneath pelts. They randomly flexed with erratic twitches, but with dissolving bone structure, the movement was disgustingly unnatural.

The four melting men were still alive, but without skeletons, their throats would likely fold closed, and their internal organs were vulnerable. Their eyes looked around in shock. The other men could hear them fighting for breath, only able to wiggle a little. Strange sounds blurted through their lips as they tried to form words.

Ash Vizla panicked. "Send wōlves! Send wōlves!" The command was an instant relief to the rest of the Vulgairs in the arena as they backed away, clearing a path for the wōlves to save them. A few Vulgairs untied the giant beasts from the outer walls. They spoke commands to kill into the predators' ears. It had the desired effect. The beasts growled and barked at their liberation before glaring hungrily at Timrekka. A couple of the carnivores crept forward with bared fangs. One wōlf ran toward him with tucked ears and furled lips.

Timrekka shook his hands defensively. "What *are* those things?!"

Dumakleiza lurched forward. "Timrekka, do not kill it!" She tapped her forehead. "Hit it here. But not too hard."

Timrekka fretfully followed her advice. He yelped and brought his fist down on the leaping wolf's head. *Clunk!* He peered through one eye to see it unconscious on the ground.

Cooby scurried up to the balcony. As soon as he reached his paw over, Dumakleiza scooped him up and squeezed him, nearly strangling the tanion.

"Coobs!" She smiled into in his beady eyes. He squealed, licking Dumakleiza's face and pawing at her chest. She gave Cooby a quick kiss on his nose and then tossed him around to her back. There was no time to waste on their reunion. Cooby latched on as Dumakleiza positioned herself to leap. She looked down to see another wōlf stalking Timrekka through the fleeing crowd. Dumakleiza narrowed her eyes and dove off the balcony.

She swooped down, coasting through the air and slicing a blade across the beast's front leg before kicking both of her feet into a Vulgair's chest. The giant wōlf growled and spun to face Dumakleiza as she landed. Timrekka caught the Vulgair she'd kicked. Both men screamed at each other, the Vulgair out of bloodthirst and Timrekka out of fear. Timrekka tried to toss the man into the air just to get him away, but the Vulgair screamed as he soared over the arena walls and out over Vulgairia.

Timrekka winced. "Oops." He turned to see another one riding a wōlf at him. He screamed and threw up his arm just as the beast bore down on him. Its fang-ridden mouth clamped over his wrist and immediately thrashed with hungry growls. Timrekka yelped. His skin was strong enough to keep most of its teeth at bay, but the canines were beginning to pierce through. He freaked and felt around his utility straps. He grabbed the first thing he found: Attract Attack, the love potion syringe. He snagged it and plunged the needle deep into the wōlf's neck. It yelped and immediately retracted its jaws. It shook so violently from what it had been stuck with that it threw the Vulgair man from its back, tossing him into a somersault on the ground. Before either could regain composure, the wōlf's eyes dilated. Its ears perked up and it began huffing aggressively as something strange took over its body. Then, without warning, it charged the Vulgair man. He recognized the lustful look in the beast's posture and scrambled to run.

"Oh." Timrekka watched. "Maybe I shouldn't have done that." He shook the sting from his arm.

Ash Vizla stared down at the remainder of his men and wōlves. He didn't want to lose them all and be the Eyrayor of no one. He threw his arms out.

"Vulgairs!" Everyone turned to listen. "I make wrong choice! I send you to fight men from sky! We no win against warriors of song and dream!" He looked at the huddled group of strangers and cleared his throat. "We make sacrifice to them and live! No more fight!" He nodded, confident in deciding without the honored women's council. "We shave his face." He pointed at Gideon. "And give them each *three* women in bed this night!"

It took a moment as the Vulgairs considered surrender. Submission went against their nature, but after witnessing Timrekka's strength, it was an easy decision. One by one they started nodding. Then uproars of celebratory agreement susurrated throughout the arena.

"Wow," Gideon chuckled. "Fickle."

He and the others hesitantly smiled at each other. Timrekka wasn't sure what to make of what was happening. The Vulgairs were the largest people he'd ever seen, and even with his superior strength, they were intimidating. He slowly lowered his fists, more than ready to stop using them.

Even the wōlves recognized the paradigm shift in the arena's energy. They stopped stalking Timrekka and looked to their handlers for instruction. The Vulgairs responsible for the beasts knew they could no longer feed the intruders to their pets, but the animals still had to eat. They redirected their hunger to the mounds of boneless men. The instruction was well received as the wōlves turned and leapt at the fleshy piles, whose dreadful screams were quickly silenced by ravenous fangs.

Dumakleiza turned to Traveler and Gideon. "I am glad Timrekka survived his shadow among the heavens." She smiled, still gripping the bloody knives.

Traveler nodded and whispered to Gideon. "Are you going to tell him that Frankenstein is a fictitious character?"

Gideon chuckled. "Oh, hell no. I think I'm going to tell him about the legendary brown note next and see what his crazy brain creates from that."

40

The Vulgairs unified in a group effort to transform the arena from an execution chamber to a hall for celebration. The dead bodies had been removed for wōlf consumption outside. Those with crippling injuries had been stabbed to death by Dim Rōk and his new knife before being added to the pile of pet food. Many of the wōlves had eaten so voraciously that they'd gone into food comas almost immediately after. Inside the arena, large logs had been assembled to serve as tables, while other Vulgairs stacked piles of wood in the center to cook over.

Kills from previous days' hunts had been carved into sizable chunks for roasting over the fire. The Vulgairs were in awe of how well Dumakleiza's knives served to slice portions. Gamy aromas steamed through the air, making stomachs rumble. A few children sat against an outer wall, rhythmically hitting logs with sticks and humming ancestral songs for entertainment. Every Vulgair man, woman, and child was in attendance, eagerly meeting the strangers and congratulating them on their godlike victory. The festivities had taken a drastic turn for the better, and everyone was hungry.

Of the aliens, Dumakleiza felt most at home in Vulgairia. She had been given a giant wōlf, previously belonging to one of the slain. Cooby was firmly latched around her back, sleeping after the stressful day. Dumakleiza continued whispering reassuring adoration to the resting tanion as she rode the wōlf around the arena, talking to adoring Vulgairs from atop its back. The wōlf had immediately taken a liking to her, as she hadn't stopped petting and scratching under its fur. Her smaller, stronger hands managed to massage deeper into its thick skin. The beast had a belly full of boneless flesh and couldn't be happier to just wander.

Ash Vizla walked up behind Gideon and slapped him on the back. "You are called Gid——*eon?*"

Gideon turned and smiled. "Yes, sir. And you are the famous Eyrayor Ash Vizla." He extended his hand. Ash Vizla looked at it and squinted. He reached out and swatted it away. He stared at Gideon, wondering if it was the appropriate response. Gideon chuckled and offered it again. "You grab it and shake it. Like this." He took Ash Vizla's hand and shook it.

Ash Vizla smiled and nodded. "Strange. I like this shaking." He continued shaking Gideon's hand as he spoke. "You are brave. You stand and roar against all Vulgairia when we come kill you." He kept shaking.

Gideon smiled as a Vulgair woman walked by and roughly caressed the back of his hair. "Thank you." His eyes lingered on the woman's come-hither expression before turning back to Ash Vizla. "I would prefer to learn about Vulgairs than to fight them."

Ash Vizla retracted his hand as he considered Gideon's words. "Why are *you* no eyrayor? You are more eyrayor than he." He pointed off to Traveler, who was swarmed by talkative Vulgairs. Gideon snickered at Traveler's obvious antisocial discomfort. "Oh, I'm no leader. I'm more of a lone wolf, really. I prefer following him. He's a good guy. And actually, a good leader, though he'll never admit it." Gideon had to make sure he didn't accidentally say anything that would lead to a misunderstanding. The Vulgairs wouldn't have any trouble resorting back to violence.

Ash Vizla slowly nodded. "You *are* wōlf." His expression turned sincere. "You will be called 'The Wōlf.'" He immediately offered his hand to shake again.

Gideon smiled and shook it a second time. "Rock on. I like it."

Ash Vizla retracted his hand to stroke the smoothness of his face as he studied Gideon more. "I make promise. I keep promise. I now make you smooth face of great woman."

Gideon brought his hand up and caressed his beard. He ran his fingers through it, remembering how much time it had taken to reach its rich volume, and all the stories he'd experienced throughout its growth.

"I don't know. I'm pretty fond of the beard. We've been through a lot together."

Ash Vizla shook his head. "No. You are better than man with hair. You are The *Wǒlf.*" He reached forward and grabbed a fistful of Gideon's beard.

"Whoa there. What are you doing?" Gideon quickly leaned forward to ease the tension ripping at his face.

Ash Vizla shrugged as if the answer should be obvious. "I pull hair out. Make your face smooth like great woman."

Gideon immediately grabbed Ash Vizla's wrist and nervously laughed. "Oh, no, no, no." Gideon's carefree, yes-man mentality ended at all his facial hair being simultaneously ripped out.

Ash Vizla was confused. "It is only way to make face of great woman."

"No, there is another way." Dumakleiza's confident voice redirected their attention up. Her ride panted, spilling hot breath into the two men's faces. Gideon stared at the enormous fangs lazily swaying with blood-scented exhales.

Ash Vizla greeted Dumakleiza with a humble nod as he maintained his grip on Gideon's beard. "Blade Maiden." He wasn't sure what her comment had meant. "What you mean there is other way?"

Dumakleiza looked down at him patronizingly. "What is my name, Ash Vizla, Eyrayor of Vulgairia? What is the name by which your people call me?"

"Blade Maiden," Ash Vizla repeated himself, unsure of why she hadn't understood it the first time.

"Exactly," she said. "And if it is of such great importance to you that Sir Gideon —"

"The Wōlf," Ash Vizla corrected her, admittedly excited to share the title.

"Oh?" She smiled at Gideon, who was still waiting for Ash Vizla to release his beard. "You have received a Vulgair title, as well?" Her eye sparkled. "Well, if it is of such great importance to you that The Wōlf have his face shaved, then I shall do it with my blades, for I am the Maiden of Blades."

"Your blades can make man face smooth like great woman?" The concept puzzled Ash Vizla. Her knives only made sense for stabbing.

Dumakleiza nodded. "Yes, and they shall cause no pain. I shaved my father's face since I was a small child. I am quite skilled in the art."

Gideon nodded as best he could in Ash Vizla's stinging grip. "If the beard's gotta go, I'd much prefer Blade Maiden's way. I mean, she is a woman after all, right?" He hoped his argument was well-founded in Vulgair logic. "We should trust her."

Ash Vizla nodded and leaned in close to Gideon's face with a stern expression. "You will be Eyrayor. Good Eyrayor always hear advice from great woman." The life advice was received. Gideon nodded as Ash Vizla stared deep into his eyes, pointing up to Dumakleiza. "If she want use blades on you face, make you Eyrayor, you trust she know best." With that, he released Gideon's beard and smiled proudly.

Gideon moved his jaw around, brushing his beard out with his fingers. "Sounds like good advice, dad." He sighed, wanting to postpone what was apparently inevitable. It went against his nature to avoid change, but the beard was a close friend. There were so many stories he wanted to tell them from the journey of its growth. He wanted to share a tale of when he'd passed through Afghanistan, and how it had kept him concealed. And, of course, there was the time he'd plucked a few hairs out to fasten a makeshift fishing string when he was starving in Guyana. He sighed. He knew that the stories would be lost on the Vulgairs. "Well, Blade Maiden." He glanced up. "I guess it's time to shave this sucker. Haven't seen my baby face in a while." He continued running his fingers through it.

Ash Vizla cocked his head to the side. "Face of *baby?*"

"Uh, I mean I haven't seen my face of great woman in many moon." Gideon grinned. He'd already mourned the beard internally. He processed things quicker than most and was ready for the next adventure—the beardless adventure.

Dumakleiza gave an approving nod. "Well, shall we go, that I may shave you?" The beast beneath her bowed and slumped with each tired breath.

Gideon puffed his chest up with newfound enthusiasm. "Yes, ma'am! Let's give me a face of a great woman."

Dumakleiza looked at Ash Vizla. "Eyrayor, where do you keep water? It is needed to shave The Wōlf's face."

Ash Vizla smiled and walked away. "My tent have water. Come. I want to watch."

Traveler made his way through the loudly chatting Vulgairs, trying to find Timrekka. Everywhere he stepped, he was stopped and congratulated with firm pats to the back, shoulders, or face. Every Vulgair was eager to meet him. He kept smiling and saying thank you as he fought the anxiety of being smothered by fetid barbarians. He was more uncomfortable than when they were chanting for his death.

Finally, he saw Timrekka sitting at a log table, arm-wrestling a line of Vulgair men and women. Timrekka was giggling nervously in the firelight as three men pushed against his hand, straining and groaning with fierce determination to bring the short man down. Timrekka's forearm and wrist barely budged with the giants' full might. He could feel the force but holding them was surprisingly easy. It was as if they weighed nothing more than a toddler. Finally, as he laughed beneath his spiky white hair, he slammed his fist down, tossing them back. The table splintered a bit beneath the impact as they crashed backward, rolling on the dirt with sprained arms. The surrounding spectators clapped and cheered as the line moved forward so a few more of them could get injured by Timrekka. Each of the fallen competitors got to their feet, holding their hurt arms and smiling at the fire of competition. It was as if their wounds meant nothing. Timrekka readjusted in his seat with edgy energy, realizing he was in for a long night of entertaining the crowd. He couldn't tell if it made him uneasy or if he was beginning to enjoy himself.

Traveler smiled at the spectacle. He pushed through a few more Vulgairs and made his way up next to Timrekka's side. He stood with arms crossed, observing the next bout of arm-wrestlers.

"Looks like you've acquired some admirers."

Timrekka smiled, keeping the new competitors at bay while he looked up at Traveler. "You wouldn't believe how effortless this is. It's like I have no limit, and it makes me want to experiment with every element Borroke has, because I'm sure I could create some fantastical inventions from their base elements and resources."

Traveler nodded with his arms still crossed. "I have no doubt." He watched as a couple more Vulgairs lined up to help push the woman arm-wrestling Timrekka. "I need to ask you something."

"Okay."

"How are you feeling after being shadowed?"

"Rejuvenated actually," Timrekka responded without missing a beat. His competition grunted and jeered as they pulled against his curled fingers.

Traveler blinked, still in disbelief. "That had to be a trialing shock. You're the first to ever survive it." He tilted his head to study the Thamioshling. "Are you sure there's nothing you want to discuss or vent after enduring a near-death experience?"

Timrekka's eyes fluttered as he slammed his fist down, tossing more Vulgairs to the side like dolls. "It all happened so fast, and I only had time to react, and it didn't hit me until I'd landed on Borroke and started searching for you all, and then at some point I realized that I'd almost died and that everything would have been over, my whole life, everything I've made, my short legacy, it would have all ended in one abrupt moment flying through the great void of space." He adjusted as more Vulgairs made their way to the table to challenge him. "When I finally found your tracks, there was blood, and I assumed you were dead, and I was scared, but after having some time to process all of that information, I decided that after being shadowed, I wasn't going to be afraid anymore, that if I found you all and I needed to help in order for us to survive, that I actually would. It's a way of thinking I've never been able to do before; I've always just been in hiding, never brave or helpful in dangerous situations, willing to fight to help my friends. I guess I've never really had friends, real friends."

Traveler nodded with a small smile. "I believe that's something we're all constantly striving to better within ourselves. Eventually, each person faces a danger so great that their courage fails. That's when they find out what they're truly capable of. That's one thing that I'm realizing that I'm grateful for." He smiled and stared at the clamoring Vulgairs. "Gideon has helped remind me that this whole journey is a test of *my* courage."

Timrekka nodded. "I don't want to cower and die the next time I'm in danger which, apparently, is expected if I'm to accompany you." He smiled at his own change of heart. "Though I'm curious if there's any danger that would make *Gideon's* courage fail."

Traveler raised his eyebrows. "Maybe we'll find out one day. But if there is something that would scare him, I'm not sure if any of the rest of us could survive it. You wouldn't believe some of the things that man has done just in the short time I've known him." He shook his head and laughed. "Yeah, I don't want to know what it would take to scare him."

"I don't either. I'm still scared, even with my enhanced strength on this world." Timrekka's eyes shot open as he looked out at the Vulgairs, hoping they didn't understand what he'd said. Luckily, they were all too enthralled with the competition to pay any attention to their conversation. He looked back to Traveler. "By the way, I think I broke my little toe with my first high leap, or maybe I just jammed it, but I'm rather positive I broke it, because it took me a couple jumps to figure out how to land, because I've never been athletic so, suddenly, being the strongest person on a world required some adjusting but, anyways, all I have to do is light jump and it'll heal, right?"

Traveler shook his head. "We have to set it first, or it'll heal in a permanently broken position. Light heals the body on the cellular level. It doesn't repair alignment or placement of body parts. But it's going to be nearly impossible to set it here."

"Why? Oh."

"I should also mention that you need to maintain a regular regiment of exercise on any world smaller than Thamiosh. If you don't, your musculature and bones will slowly deteriorate."

"Good to know," Timrekka made a mental note. "Maybe the Vulgairs can help set my toe, because they're large people."

"Eh." Traveler looked around at the savage behemoths. "I don't know. Setting a broken toe would probably be the most complex surgical procedure they've ever attempted. I'm not sure if they'd understand why we're not just executing you like they do with the wounded. Helping mend an injury may not even make sense to them."

"What help?" Dim Rōk's deep voice startled Traveler.

Traveler spun around. "What?"

"Vulgairs help. What you need help do?"

Traveler couldn't help giving the less advanced being a condescending smile. "Setting a broken toe. Timrekka," he pointed, "is injured, and we have to fix it so he can heal properly."

Dim Rōk nodded as he blankly stared back. "I not understand, but we help Eyrayor from sky."

Timrekka smiled as he won another arm-wrestling match.

"Oh, this should be interesting," Traveler said with a slight chuckle. He looked at the surrounding Vulgairs who were waiting to see what was going on. "Okay, here's what we're going to do…"

※

Gideon, Dumakleiza, and Ash Vizla returned to the arena's festivities. Once inside, they took pause, staring curiously at the bizarre spectacle ahead. Timrekka was lying on the log table with his right leg elevated, and the Vulgairs were holding two men sideways in the air. One of the horizontal barbarians had a firm grip on Timrekka's pinky toe, while the second squeezed over his hands like a vice. Everyone involved was amused by the hilarity of their ludicrous task, while the others cheered them on as though it were battle.

Ash Vizla cocked his head to the side. "What they do? They fight again?"

Timrekka winced as he squeezed the log's end for the pain. It splintered beneath his grip as he rapidly took deep breaths.

Traveler smiled. He raised his hand and whipped it down. "Now!" At his command, the group pulled the two men holding Timrekka's toe as hard as they could. They all went taut, straining and heaving against Timrekka's obstinate foot. Groans and aimless insults assisted until finally, *pop!*

Timrekka yelled as pain subsided into relief.

The two Vulgairs dropped to the snowy ground as the crowd erupted in primitive screams of success. They'd done it. They'd done the impossible: They'd set a little toe. They cheered as back slaps were shared all around. Even Traveler threw a fist in the air as he joined in the bonding cries. He couldn't help feeling a strange sense of comradery.

Ash Vizla smiled and yelled with them even though he wasn't sure what was happening. He led Gideon and Dumakleiza through the party, trying to reach the other sky people. The crowd grew quiet as they began noticing Gideon's feminine face. They ogled Gideon with approval and nods. A few of the women gasped and moaned, along with a couple of the men. Finally, they stepped into the fire's light near the center, and the dark mystery of Gideon's shaved face was illuminated. Everyone stared. Dumakleiza had used her blades expertly, shaving Gideon's beard as closely as she could. There were only two nicks where blood had already stopped streaming. To everyone's pleasant surprise, Gideon had a sturdy jaw line that had been kept secret beneath the bushiness. His skin was smooth and even, glowing in the fire's light.

Traveler puffed out his bottom lip with a slow nod. "I'm impressed. Good job, Dumakleiza."

"Yeah?" Gideon reached up and caressed his smoothness. "It's weirding me out a bit. Do I look twelve?"

"Honestly," Traveler reassured him. "It looks good. You've looked like a homeless barbarian since I met you, and it wasn't until we met *real* barbarians that you shaved. Fitting for you, I suppose." He chuckled. "You pull off face of great woman better than I thought you would."

Ash Vizla grabbed Gideon's shoulders from behind. "See! The Wōlf have smooth face of great woman! His beauty is great!" His yelling caused an eruption of responsive shouts, and Gideon was instantly pushed forward by hard pats to his back and shoulders. Ash Vizla ushered for quiet as he smiled, knowing his next announcement would bring even louder cries. He held out his hands. "And I keep promise. Each victor take three Vulgair women to bed this night." As expected, more cheering. "Three for other Eyrayor! Three for Sky Beast! Three for The Wōlf!"

Gideon laughed. "This ought to be interesting."

Timrekka's eyes shot open. "No, no, no, no, I can't do that."

Gideon looked at him. "What? You don't want three giant women for one night? It's an honor that they *want* to bestow upon us. They might even be offended if we say no, and by *they*, I mean the women." He looked around to see wild excitement in the females' eyes. "Why not enjoy this crazy night on an impossible adventure? We're all single here. You're not cheating on anyone. Well, death, you did cheat death. You slut." He winked.

Timrekka blinked as he looked at the hungry eyes ready to seduce him. "My wife. I know she's dead, but I would still feel guilty. I just don't want to."

Gideon nodded understandingly. "Fair enough, my friend. I respect that answer. Besides…" He smiled bigger. "…wouldn't want you tearing any of them in half like a wishbone." He winked and turned to Traveler. "Guess tonight's celebrations are for you and me, Spaceman."

"Oh, no. I'm sleeping alone tonight," Traveler quickly said with obvious nerves. "You can enjoy all of the spoils."

Gideon playfully tilted his head to the side. "Not interested or not your orientation?"

"No, I, uh," Traveler stammered as he quickly fumbled some words together. "I just don't want to risk contracting anything." He nodded, satisfied with his answer.

"Come on." Gideon smiled. "Those ladies put the 'std' in 'stud.' All they're missing is 'u.'" He chuckled, seeing straight through the excuse. "Seriously, though. God forbid you catch anything that's instantly healed with our next jump." He could see how uncomfortable Traveler was. Traveler couldn't formulate a good argument, and he knew it. Gideon nodded. "Listen, Spaceman, don't do anything you don't wanna do, but just remember, part of that whole *becoming brave* thing you're trying to do is, well, saying yes to the things you *want* to try — not just the dangerous things that could kill you. Live a little." He winked.

Ash Vizla turned a joyful face to his people. "All women who want join them in bed this night, come forward." The instruction made Traveler and Timrekka's pulses race. They were in a position they'd never imagined they'd find themselves in. Ash Vizla's words were immediately responded to by thirteen Vulgair women emerging from the crowd. There wasn't much variation in features, as they all had strong Vulgair appearances, and they were visibly eager to help reward the sky people. Ash Vizla smiled at Gideon. "The Wōlf choose first."

Gideon chuckled. "When in Rome." He shrugged as he looked from one aroused woman to the next. They all looked like they either wanted to lick his skin off or eat him. Either way, he was looking forward to being the entree. "Uh." The crowd grew restless as they waited to see which lucky three would be chosen. It was a momentous night. Whichever women got to share beds with sky people would forever have songs sung about them. Gideon clicked his tongue and selected the three he believed looked least capable of tearing his arms off. He found two of them surprisingly attractive for Vulgairs, though they still weren't anywhere near his taste. He thought they might even be solid fives or sixes by Earth standards. The three women gasped elatedly and ran up next to Gideon, immediately holding onto his arms and caressing his smooth face. Gideon laughed at the towering womenfolk. "Well, hello there. I love that Amazon offers overnight packages."

Ash Vizla slapped his hands together. "You have made choice. You go to bed now."

The three females smiled as they pulled Gideon to exit the arena.

Without warning, Dumakleiza leapt in front of them and smashed her fist into the jaw of the woman in front. The Vulgair immediately went limp and crumpled to the ground, unconscious and snoring. Most of the Vulgairs laughed at was they assumed was mere festivity. Traveler and Timrekka, however, jumped and brought their heads back. Dumakleiza stood in Gideon's path, breathing heavily. Her annoyed frustration was palpable as she glared at the other two women with baffled impatience. Her jaw flexed and released as her pulse sped up.

"Sir Gideon is *mine*," she snarled, reaching forward and tearing the surprised Gideon out of the women's large hands. Gideon stumbled to her side as her grip gave him no other choice. He had no idea what was going on. The other women stepped away with raised hands, joining everyone else in wide-eyed surprise.

Dumakleiza had no idea what she was doing or why she was doing it, but she knew if anyone was taking Gideon to bed, it was going to be her. Something was making her feel crazy, something new and inexplicable within her. She didn't like it, but at the same time, she reveled in its intoxication. She wanted control. It was new. She couldn't explain what had taken over her, or why she cared so much. In fact, she didn't even remember wanting to punch the first woman in the face. It had just happened. She took a few deep breaths and looked at the other two women again as she maintained her death grip on Gideon's wrist. She couldn't help how she was feeling or what she was wanting but whatever it was, she was taking it.

"You." She pointed at who she thought to be the prettier of the two. "Come here," she demanded. The woman hesitantly stepped forward, worried that she was going to get bludgeoned, as well. Dumakleiza pulled Cooby from around her with her free hand, gently but firmly shoving the tanion toward Timrekka. "Timrekka of Thamiosh, take great care of Cooby. I shall return for him at first light."

"Uh" was all Timrekka managed. He was afraid to disobey Dumakleiza in her scarily passionate state. Even Cooby could feel her energy, so he didn't fight to stay with her. He crawled up to Timrekka and climbed onto his back, staring at Dumakleiza with some confused chirping.

"Thank you," Dumakleiza all but growled. She turned and grabbed the tentative woman's wrist, taking full control of her. Once she had both Gideon and the woman in tow, she walked them toward the exit without looking back. Gideon glanced over his shoulder at Traveler, who shrugged at him helplessly.

"Holy Spirit." Traveler couldn't tell if Gideon looked scared or excited, but one thing was for sure: His night was about to get much more interesting. Dumakleiza led them out of the arena and out of sight.

Timrekka slowly leaned over to Traveler as their eyes lingered on the vacant doorway. "I thought she was a religious woman, isn't something like—" He tried to keep his voice down. "—*that* kind of off limits or something?"

Traveler shrugged as he whispered back. "I have no idea. Every religion of every world is different. Many revere group sex as holy. I just didn't know Dumakleiza was sexually—anything, I guess. Makes sense, of course, but I just imagine her killing people all day every day." He couldn't help smiling a little. "But I'm not going to question the morals of a jealously violent medieval princess."

Timrekka nodded. "Probably wise, so, um." He wasn't sure where he was going with his comment. "Are we, uh, going to start, um, exploring and documenting Borroke tomorrow, you know, as my test?" Their whispered conversation went over the Vulgairs' tall heads as everyone's eyes remained on the doorway.

Traveler scoffed. "Your test? Are you serious? You survived being shadowed. You survived one of the things that my people fear most. You don't need a test. You need to teach us. You exceeded my expectations and created something that will save the lives of countless to come. Your testing is done." He smiled. "Tomorrow we leave for Whewliss." His answer made Timrekka's eyes widen and sparkle with excitement. "And then——" He paused, shivering as what he was about to say scared him. "—the fourth phase."

Ash Vizla smiled as he finally turned back around. "What great night!" He looked down at the unconscious woman, laughing at her and then turning to Traveler. "Eyrayor, you choose three now."

Traveler nervously looked from Timrekka to the remaining women vying for his loins. "That is, as long as we survive tonight." The women were pulling at their animal coats to give him a preview of the night to come.

Timrekka's palms were sweating. "Are you actually going to do this?"

Traveler tried not to let his nerves show. "To quote Gideon: Why not?"

41

The next morning, smoke was still rising from the coliseum. Fresh, white snow blanketed the town's slumber, painting a picture of non-violent serenity. Most of the men had left before first light to begin the day's hunt. They'd ridden their wōlves off into the darkness of the igloo forest, wooden spears in tow. Only a few warriors stayed behind to ensure protection for the hallowed women and the hallowed eyrayor.

It didn't take long for the rest of the Vulgairs to start coming out of their homes. The sounds of kids playing forced the new day through their thinly walled tents.

Every morning started the same way. It was time to begin preparing wood for that night's fire, cleaning the animal skin coats by beating them, tearing previously hunted animals apart by hand and stone, so a meal could be prepared for the hunters' return. Vulgairia was awake.

Eyrayor Ash Vizla walked out of his tent, stretching his arms and staring at the morning sun. He was followed by Dim Rōk and two women, who all appeared rested and satisfied from a full night of celebrating in Ash Vizla's bed.

Timrekka was the first of the sky people to emerge. He stepped out with bright eyes behind thick goggles. Cooby was still sleeping on his back, an arm wrapped around his forehead, snoring in his ear. Timrekka's white hair stuck out every which way as he yawned and looked around. He felt surprisingly warm in the nippy air thanks to his body's density—especially after a restful, sexless night.

"Sky Beast is awake!" Dim Rōk eagerly shouted. "Sky Beast, eat with us."

Timrekka looked to see a pile of berries and burnt meat on a massive stump in front of the four of them. They all looked happy to see him. After having a night to marinate in the memory of everything that had happened, every Vulgair had come to deify Timrekka. He had done things that none of them had ever even imagined possible in their primitive dreams. It was easy to see how keen Ash Vizla was to share his breakfast with the god, Sky Beast.

Timrekka smiled. He adjusted his goggles as he walked over. As soon as he sat down on one of the logs, a few of the other women saw, and rushed over with more food to offer the deity.

"Oh, thank you very much," Timrekka said as he graciously took some of the berries and studied them up close. "So peculiar that you have berries that grow in this winter. I'm curious what their ideal conditions are; how many months of the year does it snow here?"

Ash Vizla chuckled, "You talk fast, Sky Beast."

Timrekka tossed some berries in his mouth. "Sky Beast?"

"Sky Beast," Ash Vizla said as Dim Rōk nodded. "You fly down from black sky. You kill like long-tooth cat." He held two fingers by his mouth to mimic a sabretooth tiger.

"Oh." Timrekka perked up at the understanding. "I've never had a tough nickname before, only demeaning ones, like goggle face, brain bitch—but, Sky Beast." He thought about it and smiled while eating more berries. "I like that." He chewed. "These are surprisingly good, a little sour, but good, due, I assume to how pure and unpolluted your atmosphere is; how long are your winters?"

Ash Vizla shrugged and motioned to the two women. "They know best."

One of the women took the cue. "Snow most time. Sky fire—" She pointed up at their sun. "—sometime bring green. More food then. More hunt. No clothes." Her answer made Ash Vizla smirk friskily and bite at her in the air.

Timrekka nodded, realizing it was the best answer he was going to get. "What kind of animal is that from?" He pointed at the steaming meat.

"Deer," Dim Rōk said. "Two morning ago, I go hunt. Muz Hont kill deer."

"Mmm." Timrekka tentatively ate some. "It's—good." He swallowed.

Ash Vizla stared at him curiously. "Sky Beast, you are god? That why you no take women in your bed? Even women of great face not worthy of god bed?"

"No, I—"

"Sky Beast," Dim Rōk interrupted. "Blade Maiden tell of you kill mammōth alone. Tell me how."

Timrekka nervously looked around. "She said I did what?"

"Kill mammōth. No help. Tell me great story."

Ash Vizla's eyes widened. "Yes, tell us story how you kill mammōth. With hand?" He held up a fist, recalling how devastating Timrekka's punches were the previous night.

Timrekka was confused. "I didn't kill any—"

"Yes," Dim Rōk insisted. "Blade Maiden say man who give her mammōth skin kill mammōth with no other man. Must be you."

"But I didn't give her the coat. Traveler did, or, I mean—" He looked over as Traveler conveniently exited his tent. "My Eyrayor did—whatever you say."

"He?" Ash Vizla exclaimed in disbelief.

They looked over to see Traveler dragging his feet as he walked out. His normally kempt hair was a mess, sticking all over as if he'd been thrashed around in a storm. He had visible claw marks on his neck and arms, and his eyes were barely open, dark rings drooping around them. His expression, however, looked blissfully content.

Ash Vizla stared in awe. "How *he* kill mammōth? Look like three women almost kill him."

Timrekka couldn't help laughing at Traveler's frazzled appearance. "Trave—Eyrayor, would you like to join us for some breakfast?"

The instant Traveler saw the food, his jaw trembled, drool spilling out. Before he could take a single step toward them, the three women he'd slept with exited the tent behind him, each slapping him hard on the back as they passed. They looked more than happy with their night. Traveler coughed at the hits and tried to compose himself. He prided himself on always being collected and distinguished. He brushed his hair back and wiped his hands down his face on his way over.

"Did you enjoy the rewards?" Timrekka giggled at Traveler's wounds.

Traveler couldn't help grinning. "What's for breakfast?"

"Deer, Eyrayor," Dim Rōk answered to quickly get it out of the way. "How you kill mammōth alone?"

"What?" Traveler asked through tired eyes.

"You know," Timrekka tried to help. "The mammoth coats you gave all of us from the mammōth you clearly killed in order to get it, which Dumakleiza told them you killed without assistance, so tell them the story of how, because they're quite amazed and curious, and scary."

Traveler maintained his confused squint as he piled a fistful of meat into his mouth. His eyes rolled back at the savory flavor. His famished, beaten, and drained body needed as much sustenance as it could get. He chewed and swallowed, one cheek still full.

"This is mammoth fur?" He asked, looking down at it." I mean, of course it is. Right. Of course." He swallowed more and groaned. "Um, I—" He tried to think quickly, but he wasn't good at elaborate improvisation. He looked around and smiled as he saw Gideon, Dumakleiza, and the Vulgair woman coming out from their tent. He nodded toward them. "Gideon did it." And with the simple evasive maneuver, he returned to stuffing his face.

Everyone turned. Gideon was all smiles and vigor, staring at the frozen world through bright eyes. Dumakleiza had a timid grin on her face, her hands swinging by her sides as she all but skipped. Only the Vulgair woman looked tired.

Ash Vizla and Dim Rōk nodded as the answer became clear. "The Wōlf." The obvious answer made complete sense to Ash Vizla. He waved them down.

"The Wōlf! Blade Maiden! Come. Eat."

They didn't have to be told twice. Gideon and Dumakleiza's stomachs growled at what their eyes were already devouring. They walked over, waving good morning to a few Vulgairs along the way.

The instant Gideon's butt touched the log seat, Dim Rōk demanded the question. "The Wōlf, tell me story how you kill mammōth, no help." His eyes pleaded for Gideon to actually answer. He was growing tired of everyone avoiding the epic tale.

Gideon chuckled, "Tell you what?"

"Blade Maiden told them you killed the mammoth, whose coats we wear." Traveler filled in the gaps for him. "She told them of how you killed it by yourself, apparently. Tell them how that happened. You remember."

Dumakleiza smiled and nodded with a twinkle in her eye. "It was quite valiant. He managed the hunt against all odds."

Gideon looked Traveler up and down, recognizing the hilarious overabundance of sex written all over him. "My dear Spaceman." He giggled and pointed like an unashamed child. "It was good for you. Was it good for me?"

"Shut up," Traveler said, embarrassed but smiling. "Focus on the story about whatever you did that's mind-blowing."

Gideon smirked and nodded as he tossed a few berries in his mouth. "Of course." He winked at Duma and then turned to Dim Rōk and Ash Vizla. "Well." He chewed and swallowed as his animated hands came out to play. "It was about a month or two ago, I believe, and—"

"Month?" Ash Vizla asked.

"Uh, many, many mornings ago," Gideon corrected himself with a stern expression. "Anyways, I was out hunting for my village, and I was tracking a boar through thick bush." His story already had the undivided attention of the surrounding Vulgairs as more came to listen. "So, I'm about to bury my spear in the pig's belly, when, *wham!*" He slammed his fist down on the stump, making a couple Vulgairs snicker with excitement. "A giant wooly mammoth came out of nowhere and squished the boar with its huge foot. *Whamo!*" He was getting invested in his own fabricated story, and it had Ash Vizla's mouth hanging open.

"What happen?" a Vulgair woman blurted out, bringing her hand over her heart.

"Well." Gideon quickly thought about a good answer. "The mammoth went to gore me, swinging its enormous tusks right at my body." He jumped to his feet, momentarily losing himself in the fake memory. "I leapt out of the way, just missing its deadly attack. The beast's tusk got lodged into a tree behind me." More Vulgairs gathered around as the story grew. "I had to address the elephant in the room, so I thought quickly because it would definitely get me the next time. I took a stone and smashed the end of its tusk, breaking the tip off. The mammoth was free of the tree, but it was angrier than before. So, I yanked the sharp tip out of the bark and rolled under the belly of the monster with the tusk in hand. Before it could swing at me again, I stuck it right in its chest, piercing its heart."

Everyone went silent, waiting in tense anticipation of the next part of the story.

Dim Rōk stared at Gideon with peeled eyes. "That kill mammōth?"

"Oh." Gideon nodded. "Yeah, of course. It died right then and there, and my village ate well for many, many, *many* days."

Ash Vizla threw his hands in the air. "Yes!" The rest of the Vulgairs joined him cheering for the heroic account. "Best tale ever told! We will tell of this to our children. And their children. And their children. And—"

"Oh!" Gideon raised a finger. "In fact—" He leapt up and ran back to his tent, disappearing inside. The Vulgairs quieted down, waiting to see what he was doing. They heard some rustling and rummaging until finally, he reemerged. He trotted back with something in his hands. "This is the tusk tip I used." He held out an authentic tip of an elephant tusk. It was only a few inches long and was so polished, it glowed against the snow. The ivory necklace had a long chain, and it captivated the entire Vulgair village.

Ash Vizla and Dim Rōk stepped closer and stared. Traveler stood to his feet and walked over, as well. He had no idea how Gideon had managed to fabricate an entire story about a foreign planet and somehow also had the perfect trinket to validate the lie. Only Timrekka and Dumakleiza stayed behind as the Vulgairs gathered to see what Gideon was holding.

As the attention diverted, Timrekka took a couple more bites and glanced up at Dumakleiza. As soon as she looked at him, he diverted his eyes back down to the stump. He peeked back up and then down again when he saw her still staring at him.

"Timrekka of Thamiosh, what troubles you?"

Timrekka cracked a small smile. "Oh, nothing troubles me, and I'm sorry if this is offensive, but I'm curious about last night, because it seemed out of character for you, being as you're our spiritual figure and whatnot, so I guess I'm just curious if your religion condones sexual promiscuity? I am sorry if that's too personally invasive or offensive."

Dumakleiza thought for a moment, trying to find her deepest, honest answer. "To be truthful, I do not fully know what possessed me." She peeled Cooby from Timrekka's back, bringing the tired tanion into her arms to coddle. "I suppose this journey holds many new feelings for me." Cooby cooed and pawed at her face. "I spent my entire life in a castle with only my family and my Coobs to keep me company." She chewed some berries. "The only other men I ever came face-to-face with, I killed." Timrekka winced at the comment, but it was simple truth to Dumakleiza.

"Getting to know Sir Gideon, the Diviner, and yourself, Timrekka of Thamiosh, has been the longest I've ever spent with men not of my bloodline." She shrugged as she recalled the rest of his question. "Neither my father nor my mother ever taught me sexual etiquette, nor its morality, as they told me it would never be an opportunity life would present to me. My duty was servitude to my family's castle and to our treasure. Sex was for my brothers to find in the lands beyond in order to continue the Yagūl bloodline. I was assigned to the keep in order to protect it from those who wished to steal our holy treasure and dishonor Grimleck. That is all. That is all that would ever be, I was told. I do not know if last night would be condoned by Grim, or if I should be condemned and punished for my actions, but either way, I truly believe in my heart that Grim would not put such pleasures on this world, or any world, if they were not meant to be explored." She nodded, digesting her epiphany. "I feel no distance from Grim, but only an appreciation of this aspect of his creation which I have finally experienced."

Cooby perked up. The rested tanion yawned and stretched out all six of his hairy arms. He sniffed the air and then climbed down off Dumakleiza. They watched as he scurried a short distance to where Dumakleiza's wōlf was lying down. With its belly still full, it was lazily people watching. Dumakleiza placed her hand over one of her knives, ready to leap if Cooby's instincts were wrong. Cooby climbed up onto the wōlf's back. The carnivore twitched and flipped its head around to see what was on it. As soon as it saw that it was Cooby, its ears perked up in recognition. It panted as they sniffed each other, and then licked its giant tongue up all of Cooby.

Timrekka turned back to Dumakleiza. "What made you decide to give up your home and come on this adventure?"

Dumakleiza bunched her lips as she recalled. "When the bastards that Sir Gideon and the Diviner arrived with attacked castle Yagūl, I killed as many of them as I could, just as I'd always done. I was prepared to kill Sir Gideon and the Traveler—the Diviner—as well, but Cooby approached Sir Gideon as if he were myself." She smiled at the memory. "It was a sign from Grim. It made me wonder if there was more than my father and mother had taught me. I became curious about the rest of Cul, but, lo and behold, Grim presented me an adventure much larger than that of my own world. I believe that I have the opportunity to represent him beyond the confines of my small castle. That is a much greater purpose than the disintegrating defense of a forgotten home where my family was slain. If I am to be honest, I chose adventure over loneliness."

Timrekka nodded. "I understand that, and it definitely makes Traveler much more gravitational; it's not quite running away, it's moving on, on such a big, eye-opening scale, providing illuminating perspective to my problems and pains, allowing me to find, as you so eloquently said, greater purpose."

Dumakleiza smiled. "Yes, that it truly does."

"So, was last night you simply testing the waters, living adventurously, trying new things, experimenting, if you will?"

Dumakleiza shrugged and looked around aimlessly. "I—" She blushed and smiled bigger, all but giggling. "I am not sure what that was. It all happened so quickly. It was as if my body was making decisions without thinking or tactical plotting. It was magical—liberating."

Timrekka blushed. "You've never been infatuated before, have you?"

"I've never been what?"

"Infatuated," Timrekka repeated. "Your feelings for Gideon, whatever led you to do what you did."

"Oh." Dumakleiza earnestly thought about what Gideon meant to her. "Since our first meeting, I have grown quite fond of Sir Gideon. He's the first man whom I've begun to trust since my father and brothers."

Timrekka stared at her with honest curiosity. "Would you say it's developing into love? Do you think maybe you're growing to love Gideon?"

Dumakleiza gave a lost expression. "I have no prior experience with love, and thusly, am unsure of what it is to feel it." She met Timrekka's gaze. "I am protective of Sir Gideon."

"I see, well, it looks like the beginning stages." Timrekka smiled, keeping his head tilted bashfully. "So." His voice sounded nervous again. "Was last night your first time, and if the answer is yes, are you feeling okay?" He very briefly pointed down at her body, worried that he was crossing a line. His nervously kind intentions were well received as Dumakleiza leaned in a little.

"I am in a bit of pain from the night, yes, but pain is no stranger to me. It was the pleasure that still has me spellbound."

Timrekka decided to push his limit further. "You fascinate me, and what really surprised me about you last night was deciding to still bring a Vulgair woman with you two."

Dumakleiza shrugged. "I do not understand the confusion. Both men and women are beautiful, and I have long been curious about the pleasures each holds."

"Huh," Timrekka said timidly.

"But, yes." Dumakleiza opened up a little more. "It is a strange discomfort lingering today."

Timrekka smiled and nodded understandingly. "Well, if you should want, I have a soothing cream that I can give you, which might help with the soreness. You just apply it when you're alone by putting some —"

Gideon's incoming laughter interrupted as he walked back. "No, that's for you to keep," he insisted to Dim Rōk, who was holding the ivory necklace. The large Vulgair nearly burst into tears as he nodded, graciously clutching it to his chest. Everyone around him swarmed to stare at the sacred gift.

As they walked back, Traveler stared askance at Gideon. "So, what's the real story with the tusk?"

"From some cool African natives," Gideon said. "They'd killed some elephant poachers and taken this from one of their necks as a reminder that killing them was justified. After they told me what they did for a hobby, they invited me to join in on one of their, uh, excursions. Of course, I said yes, because who wouldn't wanna help with some Serengeti street justice? We tracked down some poachers, saved a giraffe that I nicknamed Little Foot, and then they gave me the necklace."

Traveler chuckled, "Of course that's what happened." He smiled. "One day you need to just take me on a tour of your backpack."

"Oh, you're going to have to buy me dinner first," Gideon winked. "I only pull items out when it's their time. Can't just pour it out. It would ruin the magic."

Traveler rolled his eyes. "I bet the Vulgairs will sing stories of you for many years to come. They'll probably show that tusk to their children for generations."

Gideon puffed out his bottom lip and nodded. "Yup, that's what they said. It'll serve them better than it would me. But I hope they don't actually try to go hunting with it. It's pretty dull."

They both laughed as they joined Timrekka and Dumakleiza. Traveler peered over his shoulder to make sure that the Vulgairs were still distracted.

"Okay, while they're fawning over Gideon's gift, let's talk." He cleared his throat. "As soon as we have an opportunity, we're leaving for Whewliss." He looked at Timrekka. "How's your toe?"

"Oh." Timrekka glanced down at his foot. "It still hurts, but the bone is back in the proper spot."

"Okay, good."

"But," Dumakleiza interjected, "I believe you have yet to accomplish the intended purpose of studying this world before our departure." She was hesitant to admit that she wasn't ready to leave the world where women were worshipped, and she got a pet wōlf.

Traveler shook his head, completely oblivious to her disappointment. "No, the entire purpose of exploring this world was to test Timrekka's ability as our resident scientist. However," he smiled, "he managed to survive being shadowed. You've all surpassed expectations in unique and unexpected ways. You are without a doubt the most motley assortment I've ever recruited, but maybe that's why we've made it this far. I can only hope that it means whatever deities may exist—" He motioned to Dumakleiza. "—or whatever forces that be—" He nodded toward Timrekka. "—will continue to keep us alive as venture toward unknown horizons."

Gideon smiled as he picked some meat from his teeth. "We'd better find out what this fourth phase is on Whewliss."

Traveler nodded. "As long as my superiors approve you three as a team, they will brief you, though nothing can prepare you."

"Goose bumps," Gideon said, holding his arm out to show. "I mean, there were already goose bumps from the cold, but check out the goose bumps on my goose bumps." He shivered. "I can't wait."

Dumakleiza sighed, staring at Cooby, still playing on the wōlf. "If we must depart, then let it be so." Her chest deflated with disappointment. "Cooby! Return to me." Cooby perked up and obeyed, hopping from the beast's back. Dumakleiza greeted him with some friendly petting to the side of his fuzzy head. "It is time we leave this delightful world of Borroke."

Timrekka looked to Traveler, rubbing his hands together. "What manner of clothing do you have for us for Whewliss? I can't wait to see what we'll be wearing to the most advanced world in the universe."

Traveler raised an eyebrow, enjoying keeping the answer secret. "I won't be giving you any. We're leaving in what we're wearing now."

"Why?" Gideon asked with a sly eye. "You said that with a tone that makes me wonder what tricks you have up your eternally long sleeves."

"I've been waiting for this moment for a long time," Traveler said. "I've worked hard—so hard—and lost many good recruits on my journey to get here. Now that I finally have a team to bring to Whewliss, I'm not going to ruin any of what awaits you by telling you about it before we get there. The wonders that await you—just—you'll—" He smiled, happy knowing that his words fell utterly short.

"All right, Spaceman." Gideon met his eyes with the same level of mysticism.

Dumakleiza took a deep breath. "And you swear on your life and the lives of your ancestors that there is no black magic in what is to come? Only more of science?"

Traveler smiled. "Yes." He chuckled. "Only science. There is no such thing as magic." He leaned in to make sure that only they could hear him. "As soon as the Vulgairs are out of sight, we leave. If there's anything you need to do to get ready, do it now."

Gideon smiled. "I'll be sad to say goodbye, but I'm ready."

"Yes. I have Cooby and my treasure," Dumakleiza said. "Though I wish I could bring the wōlf. Can I bring the wōlf?"

Traveler shook his head.

Timrekka looked around. "I am ready, but I'm definitely going to miss having this strength; I'll have to readjust to being one of the normal people."

Traveler smiled bigger. "Oh, you'll still be stronger than the people of my world. Thamiosh is one of the densest worlds known, so you'll be excessively strong on the majority of planets in our database."

Gideon leaned forward and interrupted with a mischievous smirk. "*What if* we don't wait for the Vulgairs to be out of sight for our jump? What if instead we play on the deification they already have placed upon Timrekka?"

"What do you mean?" Traveler asked, knowing full-well that he wasn't going to like the answer.

"Well, they call him Sky Beast. Why don't we just tell them we're going back to the sky and then take off? They'd totally embrace it and be anxiously awaiting our return."

"But," Dumakleiza immediately interjected, "they would believe us to be gods, and I will not deify myself under such damning falsehood."

"Just clarify that part then." Gideon dismissed her concern with a wave.

Timrekka smiled sheepishly. "It would be kind of fun."

Traveler rolled his eyes and reached up, grabbing the unseen. "I will only do this if you all swear to secrecy. You can't tell my superiors."

Gideon smiled. "Look at you, Spaceman. You're getting ballsy in your adventurousness."

Traveler thought for a moment. "In fact, don't tell them anything about the Winkloh Star, either."

Timrekka didn't like keeping secrets. "Why not?"

"Yes, why do you wish our tongues be clandestine?" Dumakleiza added.

Traveler turned to Gideon. "Or the fact that I joined you in leaping from the cliff in the Roaring Valley."

Gideon smiled. "Would you just like to do the talking when we get there?"

"That would make me much more comfortable, yes."

Gideon nodded and turned to the Vulgairs still studying the ivory. "Hey!" His yell had the desired effect. All the giant natives turned and looked at him. "Vulgairs, Sky Beast must return to the sky now. And we're leaving with him." His words prompted some murmuring as the Vulgairs looked at them with awed admiration. Traveler hoped that the announcement wouldn't trigger any violent backlash from the primitive savages.

Ash Vizla expressed understanding with an eager bow. "Return soon. Tell more stories of great sky people hunts."

Gideon nodded and waved cordially. "You betcha." He smiled with the utmost respect for his newest friends. "May death not find you sleeping!"

Ash Vizla waved. "Bye, Eyrayor of sky people. Bye, The Wōlf. Bye, Blade Maiden. Bye, Sky Beast." The Vulgairs echoed his goodbyes, yelling out of sync. Gideon smiled as him and the others waved back.

"See? They didn't bat an eyelash."

Dumakleiza tightened her lips. "That is what concerns me." She leaned over Gideon's shoulder and yelled, "We are not gods! So, let it be clarified." She sat back down, content with the amendment.

Traveler shook his head with a smirk. "Anything else? We have a clear window coming up in about thirty seconds. And yes, I have been double-checking for meteors." He felt guilty bringing it up.

"Oh! One for each of you." Timrekka handed a syringe to Gideon, Dumakleiza, and Traveler. "In case you get shadowed, just inject it as fast as you can, anywhere you want except your eyes—I wouldn't recommend that, it's painful—and you'll end up wherever the rest have landed."

They each gratefully pocketed them.

Traveler nodded. "Thank you for this. Truly. Thank you." With that, he reached out and grabbed Gideon's hand. "Everyone, hold on." He smiled. "We've are an impossible fruition." He looked at each of them and then into the sky. "We are the first successful fourth phase team, recruited from worlds apart, selected from chaos for a journey beyond the stars. We leave now for Whewliss, where your adventure finally begins. And then—to the fourth phase," he beamed as they grabbed onto each other. "We set sail for the horizon that no human has ever possessed the courage to. Our destiny exists in the darkness of the unknown."

Dumakleiza couldn't help the butterflies as she took Gideon's hand, but she didn't let it show. Their excitement and curiosities were palpable. The Vulgairs waved as they waited for the mythical departure. The idea didn't seem to faze them after witnessing Timrekka's capabilities. It just made sense that they'd leave by ascending into the sky.

Traveler opened his hand, and everything went white.